SEEMS LIKE OLD TIMES

Others

DANCE WITH A GUNFIGHTER - THE
DRAGON'S LADY -

SEEMS LIKE OLD TIMES - THE GHOST OF
SQUIRE HOUSE -

DANGEROUS JOURNEY

SEEMS LIKE OLD TIMES

JOANNE PENCE

QUAIL HILL PUBLISHING

Quail Hill Publishing

PO Box 64

Eagle, ID 83616

Visit our website at www.quailhillpublishing.net

First Quail Hill Publishing E-book: September 2012

First Quail Hill Publishing Print Book: August 2013

Second Quail Hill Publishing Print Book: August 2018

Third Quail Hill Publishing Print Book: January 2021

ISBN: 978-1-949566-28-4

SEEMS LIKE OLD TIMES

ONE

The low-lying redwood and glass buildings of Miwok High stood on the opposite side of the creek. As Lee Reynolds, news anchor on a national cable television network, pulled into the parking lot, she saw that the school was empty, the gates shut. She hadn't been back here since she had left town during the summer following her high school graduation, seventeen years earlier.

She got out of the car. The door slamming shut was like a rifle crack in the quiet. A wooden Japanese-style arced footbridge crossed over the creek to the school buildings, and along its banks weeping willows bowed their branches.

Lee stepped toward the bridge, then stopped. A part of her wanted to hurry away, warned her that being here was playing Russian roulette with her memories. But another, stronger part pushed her closer to the school. She crossed over the rippling waters of the creek.

The air was unnaturally still as if, could she but listen hard enough, she would hear the bustling and laughter of students past and present, hear whispers of secrets shared and promises broken.

A lone bicycle rider cut in front of her, dropped his blue bike off at the bicycle rack, climbed over the cyclone fence surrounding the school, and disappeared between the buildings. Amused, Lee watched his every movement, wondering what could possibly cause a teenage boy to break *into* his school grounds on a Saturday afternoon. Thoughts of burglary and vandalism came to mind because of stories she heard every day living in Manhattan, but she quickly dismissed them. This was Miwok, California, after all, a small rural town forty miles north of San Francisco. The boy had probably forgotten a homework assignment.

She wasn't about to hop a fence. As she turned to leave, her gaze caught the blue bicycle.

Tony Santos had a bike that color....

She shuddered, then slid her hands into the pockets of her linen jacket and began to stroll along the dirt path that circled the outside perimeter of the school.

She glanced back at the bike once more, wistful yet surprised at how sharply her memories had returned. The first time she'd ever seen Tony he was standing beside his bike, right about where the boy left his. Lee had been waiting for her best friend, Cheryl McConnell. She was fifteen, a sophomore, and Tony was the same. He'd been bending over the bicycle rack, working the combination lock. As he yanked the lock and chain off his bike, he noticed her watching him and straightened, allowing the chain to hang against his long legs. Then he smiled.

She shook her head slightly at the memory. He'd burst into her quiet world with all the charged energy and motion of a sonic boom. He had charm. She'd never forget his charm. or his independence. Or his knowledge of the world beyond Miwok. She'd envied that knowledge with all her heart, and had ached to see that world, away from Miwok, away from her widowed mother, and to become a part of it.

She had heard about Tony since the first day he showed up in class, which wasn't surprising in a school of only three hundred students. He was Mexican, and no other Mexican kids went to Miwok High. Most lived inside the town limits on the other side of the valley and went to Drake, an older, far larger school. But Tony Santos' father worked and lived out at the Circle Z Ranch, so he was in Miwok's school district.

The other kids said he was quiet. Maybe he didn't know English, they snickered, and he didn't seem to have any money. They decided his father probably cleaned the stables and that Tony Santos was, in short, a nobody.

How pompous those kids were. And she was one of the worst. How rudely she'd stared at him there, at the school's entrance.

Thin and lanky, he seemed to be all arms, legs and feet. His black hair was straight and shiny, and the forelock that fell as he bent over the bike reached past his eyes. A high, narrow nose flared slightly at the nostrils; deep-set brown eyes peered under arched brows; and a finely shaped mouth curved upward. His skin was a light olive tone, yet shades darker than hers. As her stare continued, his smile faded, and he stared back, his chin arrogantly lifted.

He took a step toward her. The bicycle chain still hung from his fingers. She stiffened. She had heard Mexican kids were always fighting and get- ting into trouble with the law. At his next step she jumped back, ready to run.

He froze, then turned his back to her as he lifted his book bag onto his shoulders. Sliding the bike off the rack, he swung one leg over it in a

smooth, graceful motion, then standing as he ped-
aled he rode right past her through the open gate,
never meeting her gaze. He reached the street and
sped down it.

Tony Santos...

She felt a chill. Ghosts of the past really must
dwell here, she thought. Either that or the weather
was turning cold.

She couldn't believe how far she had walked.
She reached the backside of the school, past the
classrooms and in view of the playing fields. The
grounds were enormous, almost like those of a private college or university. Swathed in lawns they
included a field for football and another for
baseball.

When had she stopped going to baseball games?

The chain-linked backstop, shaped like a giant
bustle, jutted into the sky and drew her toward it.

Her gaze drifted from the pitcher's mound, to
the diamond, the outfield fence, then back to the
stands and the announcer's booth. Something about
a baseball field, even when it was empty, echoed the
crack of a bat, the roaring cheers of a crowd.

She had sat untold hours in the stands watching
Tony. She could almost see him once again looking
slender but strong in his blue and white uniform
standing at home plate, his knees slightly bent,
leaning forward at the waist, elbows out, a powerful

grip on the bat held high over his right shoulder. A royal blue cap with a white "M" on its crown shaded eyes that stared unflinchingly at the pitcher.

She turned to go home. The image faded, but the memory of the boy lingered. She bowed her head, her pulse drumming, not believing that after so many years the remembrance could be so sharp. Or so painful.

TWO

The small, northern California town of Miwok was abuzz with the news that its most famous daughter, TV newscaster Lee Reynolds, was back. People sat on their front porches or walked along the sidewalks and peered hard into any unfamiliar car that passed by, hoping to glimpse the elegant blonde.

The town lay nestled in a valley, separated from the Pacific by the coast range mountains. The May air was crisp, as if the ocean winds had whipped over the mountains to brush away any soot or grime and leave the homes, gardens, businesses and parks clean and sparkling.

This was how Lee remembered Miwok—small,

one and two-story clapboard houses, ringed with land, and a horse or two in a nearby pasture.

On CABN-TV Lee shared the anchor position of the prime-time news program, Evening Newscene, with Rick Archer. She had cut her teeth studying Barbara Walters, Diane Sawyer, and other top women journalists' interviewing techniques. The years of hard work and study were paying off. Her latest contract, plus the chauffeur and car the network sent to pick her up and take her home to her Park Avenue condo each day, proved it. Behind the scenes, she was working to topple Archer. She gave him another year, max.

She would never have returned to Miwok at all except that four months ago her mother, Judith, had passed away from a stroke. Now, the time had come to do the job she'd been putting off ever since: to clear out and sell the house.

Her original plan had been to simply hire someone to go through the place, fix what needed fixing, donate whatever was useful, and throw the rest away. By also hiring a realtor to sell it, she wouldn't have had to set foot outside New York City. Her aunt Miriam, however, had insisted that Lee personally go through her mother's belongings to see if there weren't keepsakes or other things she wanted.

Lee doubted it. She and her mother hadn't had

a civilized conversation since she'd left home at age eighteen. Truth be told, they had never talked much before that, either. The possibility that there was anything in Judith Reynolds's house for Lee other than bad memories was remote to nonexistent. But she loved her aunt. Miriam Dailey was the only person in the world who could still tell her what to do.

Miriam descended the carpeted steps from the guest room to the first floor of her dead sister-in-law's house. Her brother's house, truth be told. But Jack had died so many years before, thirty come next winter, that she'd almost forgotten what it was like when he lived here. When it was a happy home. No, that wasn't right. When Jack was alive, there was nothing happy about his and Judith's marriage.

Miriam had arrived from San Diego two days earlier to freshen up the house a bit before Lisa—or Lee, as her niece insisted on calling herself now—arrived. Also, she wasn't exactly sure what she'd find here, even though immediately after Judith's death, Lee had paid for a cleaning service to shut down the house, throw away all open food containers, garbage, and the like.

Miriam understood well how hard it was for Lee to come back home—and how very necessary. Last night, Miriam had braced herself for Lee's reaction to being here—tears, anger, or sadness. But Lee showed none of that. Whatever she felt walking through the cold, silent house filled with too many memories, she had kept hidden. Claiming jet lag, she soon retired to her old room. Miriam decided not to press her. Lee was the most self-contained person she knew.

This morning, Lee was collected and business-like. Only a too-bright look to her eyes and darkness beneath them gave a hint as to the kind of night she spent. After hours of sorting through her mother's paperwork, insurance forms, bank statements, real estate, and stock certificates, she had to get away for a while, and had taken a drive. Miriam let her go alone. There were times when company wasn't called for.

"Did you have a nice ride, Lisa?" Miriam sang out cheerfully as her foot reached the bottom step.

Lee was standing in the living room by the front windows. The afternoon sun, beaming in through half-open mini-blinds, cast a warm glow on her. Even Miriam was struck by Lee's classic beauty, and how she had learned to enhance it. Her wheat blond hair was streaked with platinum and flax now, and she wore it pulled back from her face in a fancy bun—what Lee called a "chignon." Her hair style reminded Miriam of a young Grace Kelly.

"I was going to surprise you"—Miriam forced a jovial tone—"with a big dinner, but now you're just going to have to help."

Lee turned around so that her aunt could see the iPhone against her ear. She smiled and went on talking.

"New York already?" Miriam mouthed, then rolled her eyes and made her way into the kitchen.

When the phone call ended, Lee headed for the kitchen to find her aunt. She stopped short at the doorway. Everything was eerily familiar, as if she had last been here ten weeks ago, not ten years ago. The green Formica countertops, the white and green striped wallpaper, the antiquated avocado Frigidaire, the matching Magic Chef electric range...all the same, yet somehow smaller, shabbier.

"I'm making some coffee," Miriam said with a pleasant smile. Tall and big-boned, with a nose too long and a mouth too wide, Miriam had lively hazel eyes and dyed red hair that she wore short and spiked. She regularly jogged to keep her weight down and was darkly tanned from spending so much time on the beach or hiking the hills around San Diego. She had a vibrant personality that made those who knew her come, over time, to regard her as nothing less than beautiful. "Want to join me?"

"Sure," Lee replied. Bracing herself, she entered the room.

An odd feeling enveloped her as she watched her aunt retrieve two cups from the cabinet and wash them. The figure in this small kitchen could have been another: her mother seated at the table, smoking, drinking coffee, or staring out the window.

The bitterness the image evoked didn't surprise her, but the nostalgia that came with it did. That wasn't what she was here for.

As Miriam filled a carafe with water and poured it into the Mr. Coffee, Lee found the coffee filters and opened the coffee canister on the counter. "There must be two pounds of coffee in here." She sniffed. "It still smells good. I wonder how old it is?"

"One day. I bought it yesterday," Miriam replied.

"You bought all this for a seven-day visit?"

"I was thinking," Miriam paused, "since it was so hard for you to take some time off work to come here, now that you're finally free, how about staying two weeks instead of one? I know you can get a two-week vacation if you want it."

Lee wasn't about to argue. She knew Miriam would never understand. "I can't stretch my time away anymore than I have." Especially not when special promos were being run for her vacation replacement, the backstabbing Edie Canham.

"Do you feel so badly about being here?" Miriam asked gently. "Is it too much?"

"Well... it is preferable to a root canal," Lee said.

Miriam put mugs on the table, an orange floral one for herself, and a tall blue one on a pedestal for Lee. Her voice, when she spoke, was soft. "Once you sell this house, all your ties to Miwok will be gone. Mine, too. For old times' sake, I think both of us should spend some time getting to know it again."

Lee turned her back on the small kitchen to look out the window at the wild oaks on the hillside. She tucked her hands into the side pockets of her skirt. Thick gold bracelets clanged together as they slid downward onto her wrist.

"My memories of Miwok ended seventeen years ago when I left home. I came back one time since— and learned it was a mistake within ten minutes of walking in the front door. My mother didn't like me, Miriam, and I sure as hell didn't care for her."

"Lisa—"

"Old times for me means nothing but bad memories. Most of which took place right within this very house."

"You hate it so very much?" Miriam asked.

"I'll be ecstatic to see the last of it."

Miriam drew a heavy breath. "I know you're too

old to listen to your aunt anymore, but I'd advise that you give Miwok a chance. It just might surprise you."

Lee's tongue held words of derision and mockery, but with a glance at her aunt, she simply said, "You left it, Miriam."

"We all have reasons for foolish or thoughtless actions when we're young. And with age, we sometimes learn to regret them." She had heard Miriam's reason for leaving many times—that she had gotten tired of the small town, the chill in the night air from the too-close Pacific, and how she longed for the sunshine and city activities of San Diego. Lee had always felt there was more to it than that.

As soon as the coffee was ready, Lee poured them each a cup, then picked up hers. "Excuse me, Miriam, but I've got to make a few more calls now."

"Of course, dear."

As Lee turned to leave the kitchen, she noticed a look of sadness and concern on her aunt's face. She didn't need that. She hadn't asked Miriam to drive all the way up to Miwok to help her go through her mother's things. Lee's step slowed as she neared the lamp table with her cell phone.

Miriam had offered to come here out of kindness and, Lee realized, as a way for the two of them to spend time together once more, just as they had in the past. Lee would never forget that years ago, when she realized she couldn't stay another moment in this house, it was to Miriam she had run. It was Miriam had stood beside her and helped her through the most terrible days of her life.

What would it matter if she remained here a couple of extra days?

She placed her coffee cup on a coaster and picked up the iPhone. They had seen little of each other over the last few years. Ever since "Lisa Marie" became "Lee" Reynolds, television news anchor, her life had become fuller and busier. She was doing everything from reporting on Presidential campaigns to interviewing movie stars, and she loved every bit of it. More than a job or even a career, being a news anchor was her life.

But Miriam was her aunt, her father's sister, and her only living relative. Although Miriam was healthy and vivacious, she was sixty-one, and would start to slow down in time.

Lee tossed the phone aside, picked up the cup and returned to the kitchen. Miriam, her coffee untouched, looked up at her.

"That was rude of me, and I apologize. My phone calls can wait. It'll be fun to cook dinner together like we used to do. You're right that we deserve some time with each other, and we'll have plenty of time tomorrow to do what we've got to with the house."

Miriam nodded in agreement, a secret smile touching her lips.

Lee answered her phone as soon as she saw the caller ID. "Hey."

"Do you miss me?"

Lee smiled. She was in the family room, seated on her mother's blue and red plaid sofa, an oval rag rug at her feet, and in front of her, a coffee table whose top was marked with gouges and stains she'd caused while growing up. In the background, an old favorite classical music station from Berkeley played on the radio. She had been flipping through a *Family Circle* magazine found on the end table, trying to relax enough to go upstairs to bed. Hearing her fiancé's voice was jarring, as if her two carefully separate worlds had suddenly collided. "Bruce! It's two a.m. there. What are you doing still awake? Don't you have to go to work tomorrow?"

"Right now, I'm lying here in bed. Alone. How can I possibly sleep?"

She laughed the bright, musical way her voice coaches had taught, imagining him half-lying, half-sitting in his bed, leaning against the black lacquer headboard as he spoke to her. His chest would be bare, his gossamer-fine honey-blond hair only slightly mussed, perhaps drooping rakishly over his right eyebrow from a side part. Even after knowing him two years, she had yet to discover anything about Bruce Downing less than perfect.

"Lonely, are you?" Lee asked, making her voice low and sultry. "Why not open the front door to your condo? I'm sure there are several women camped in the hallway. They've probably been there from the moment I stepped on the plane to California." She was only half-joking.

He chuckled. "So how are you doing? You've been there a little over twenty-four hours. Bored yet?"

A beat passed before her answer. "It's not bad."

"Now that you've spent a day with your aunt and seen the house again, go back to your old plan. Hire the help you need to empty and sell it and then come home."

"I'm sorry. Miriam is looking forward to us having this time together."

"Lee, you can't let your aunt cause you to waste your vacation. You work too hard for that. Get the hell out of there! I'll meet you somewhere. The Bahamas? A Greek island? Just name it."

She sighed. The thought of lounging on a beach, being waited on hand and foot, was tempting. "It's not that easy, Bruce. As Miriam says, once the house is sold, our ties to Miwok are sev-

ered. She was born here, just like I was. Did I tell
you?"

"How about London, then? Or Paris?"

"Being here a few days isn't so bad."

"Lee, you aren't seriously feeling maudlin over
some piece of real estate, are you? Good God,
woman, you don't have a sentimental bone in your
body and everybody knows it. You never gave a
damn about that place when your mother was alive,
and I don't believe you care about it now. Your
aunt's playing mind games on you. Tell her to get
lost and come home. I miss you. I need you here.
And also, a week from Tuesday, Larry Baldwin's
invited us to join him and his wife for dinner with
the president of Atlas Insurance...."

As Bruce talked about insurance company politics, Lee stopped listening except to make properly
appreciative murmurs now and then. Was she really being maudlin over Miwok? "Maudlin Over
Miwok"—it sounded like a song. She mentally
shrugged. Maybe Bruce was right and she should
leave here as soon as possible.

She forced her concentration back to him and
could all but see his self-satisfied smile as he spoke.
Bruce spent a lot of time being self-satisfied, with
good reason. At age thirty-four, a year her junior, he
was third vice president of one of the world's largest
insurance companies.

"Baldwin gave me the dinner invitation at about six-thirty tonight," he said. "I was still at the office—I suspected he'd be prowling around today—and he came and sat down at my desk. I think I've got him in my hip pocket, Lee. Right where I want him."

"Can he breathe?"

"You think I care?"

"You're bad, Bruce."

"Real bad, and you love me for it! Like I do you. Well, time to say goodnight. Got to be up for Baldwin tomorrow. Try to get back soon, won't you, Lee? You'll definitely be here for the dinner, right? I'm counting on you."

"That's a week and a half away. I'll be there. Wild horses couldn't keep me here that long."

THREE

The next morning Miriam had her heart set on making a round of short visits to the homes of lady friends she hadn't seen in years. "Won't you come along, Lisa?" she had asked at breakfast—eggs and toast for Miriam, and a half-grapefruit for Lee. "Just like when you were a little girl?"

Lee shuddered at the thought. Luckily, she didn't have time. She planned to spend the morning interviewing realtors to market the house.

An hour later, though, she had talked to five answering machines and one live real estate agent whose questions and comments were so off the wall, Lee hung up on him. She hoped that the realtors calling her back made more sense or the place would never get sold. Blowing it up was high on her list of satisfying alternatives.

Since Miriam was still looking hurt by her refusal to the invitation, Lee agreed to join her. Afterward, she planned to sort through her mother's photographs, books, recordings and other belongings for anything she might want to keep. Everything else was going to the Goodwill. Hopefully, by then, she would hear from some realtors she had called.

As she drove Miriam to the familiar homes, she remembered how Mrs. Moore always gave her chocolates, that Mrs. Collins had two enormous, playful dogs, and Mrs. Truax made the best peach ice cream Lee had ever eaten—even to this day. The ladies hardly seemed to have aged at all. As they chatted about old times and even older friends, she remembered what it had been like as a child, warmly welcomed, sitting beside her aunt with goodies in front of her. Five years after Lee's father died, Miriam moved away, and the visits stopped. Judith never visited anyone, and no one came to call.

Listening to the ladies' belated condolences over her mother's death wasn't as dreadful as Lee had feared. She imagined they had been shocked that there was no funeral. Judith had made arrangements in her will for cremation, and Lee had honored it to the letter.

As Miriam arranged to have longer get-togethers with everyone, Lee saw how happy her aunt was to be with her old friends again. Although Lee didn't plan to stay very long—she would fly back to New York Friday morning and have the weekend to rest before returning to work on Monday—there was no reason for Miriam not to remain here a few extra days on her own. She certainly wouldn't lack for company.

Once back home, Lee checked her mother's answering machine. One realtor called back, but a return call only elicited a frustrating message that the agent was gone again. Lee hadn't wanted to give out her personal cell phone number and used the landline at the house.

Miriam stretched out on a recliner in the family room and turned on the television. A show began with familiar words from the deep-toned announcer, "Like sands through the hourglass, so are the days of our lives."

The words, the voice, reminded Lee of years ago when, as a child, if home from school due to illness or vacation, she would watch that soap with her mother. Judith would spend hours in front of the television. When Lee was very young, her mother stayed home, living off of young widow's benefits and insurance money after Jack's death. After the money was all spent, when Lee was about twelve, Judith got a job in a dentist's office. But she never lost her love of television. Lee often thought the sitcoms and dramas were more real to Judith than the life she led. They were certainly livelier.

Lee fought hard against those memories and the bitterness that lurked just beneath the surface. She didn't want to remember those days, didn't want to remember her mother, and how she used to act back then when Lisa Marie was growing up... the days of *her* life. She excused herself and quickly left the room.

She wandered into the living room, a minefield of early American reproductions, from a green and yellow floral high-backed sofa, to frilly armchairs, and country-style wooden or porcelain knickknacks standing on tables or hanging from walls. Despite the number of do-dads, the room looked strangely empty. Then she realized that none of her mother's constant companions were here. None of the *Premier, Variety*, and *Entertainment Weekly* that cluttered the tabletops of her childhood. Or the filled ashtrays. Or the dirty glasses and empty bottles...

Judith had known Hollywood backwards and forwards. She never let Lee forget that she had planned to go to Hollywood to become an actress. But because of an auto accident—the one in which

Lee's father had died—she didn't make it. The accident had killed her husband, shattered her right hip, and left her alone and limping and with chronic pain. Worst of all, it had shattered her dreams.

She tried to transfer those dreams to Lisa Marie, but little Lisa Marie couldn't live up to expectations, no matter how hard she tried, and she had once tried very, very hard.

Lee turned away, rubbing her forehead, forcing her thoughts back to her job, to Bruce, to anything but the past. Her stomach began to churn for no apparent reason, and she went into the kitchen for a swallow of her ulcer medicine. No one knew about the ulcer, not even her fiancé. She learned early on to never show a weakness, never show she wasn't in absolute control. In her line of work, any flaw was an invitation to attack.

She didn't want Miriam to know about it because she didn't want Miriam to think her perfect job and heaven-blessed love life were anything less than ideal. They were ideal, but that didn't make them lacking in stress. She would have felt far less stress if she weren't a perfectionist, but to be one was part of her nature. She prepared for interviews right up until airtime, and even when over, she would often fret that she hadn't dug deep enough, hadn't been insightful enough.

She folded her arms and paced, waiting for the

medicine to work. As she thought of how much Miriam had enjoyed being with her old friends, she remembered that the best friend of her own childhood still lived in Miwok, and although they made occasional phone calls and sent yearly Christmas and birthday cards, they hadn't sat and chatted together for many years.

She phoned Cheryl McConnell, now Stanton, and was told to get her butt right over there....

An hour later, Lee walked toward Cheryl Stanton's house. She had been there once before, ten years earlier, during a horribly mistaken visit home, the last time she'd been to Miwok.

It was a middle-class home—two-story with dormer windows on the top floor, and a jutting two-car attached garage. The front lawn was more beige than green, and low-lying juniper edged both it and the driveway. A basketball hoop hung over the garage door, three bicycles lay on their sides in the driveway, and two badminton rackets and a birdie cluttered the lawn. Parked at the curb was a shiny and aging Astrovan.

As she reached for the bell, the door opened.

"Lisa!" Cheryl rushed out of the house and

threw her arms around her in a tight, smothering hug.

Lee's first reaction was to stiffen, but soon she hugged Cheryl back.

Lee studied the woman her friend had become. Thirty years ago Lisa Marie Reynolds and Cheryl Ann McConnell met on the first day of kindergarten. Cheryl had lived two blocks away, in a town in which little girls could go two blocks—even two miles—from home and not worry. They went from playing with Barbies to sharing secrets about first loves to learning how to dance. They wore each other's clothes and talked by the hour on the phone.

After high school, when Lee went to live with her aunt in San Diego, Cheryl stayed in Miwok and got married. Lee's career took off, the years passed, and their friendship went on hold.

The photos Cheryl had sent over the years were of her children, not of her. She had always battled weight problems when they were in high school and now was past the pleasantly plump stage. She wore navy blue slacks and a blue and red plaid, short-sleeved blouse. The tail of the blouse was worn over the slacks rather than tucked in. Red clip-on earrings were a giveaway that she'd dressed up a bit to see Lee. She'd said she was cleaning house when Lee phoned. No one wore earrings to vacuum.

"It's so good to see you, Cheryl. You look great."

Lee smiled into her friend's eyes. Cheryl's sun-tanned skin was smooth and wrinkle-free, her hair short, straight, and a deep rich brown. She appeared happy and at peace with herself.

"You, too," Cheryl said. "No, on second thought, you look even better. God, I can't believe you're here." Cheryl hooked Lee's arm and led her into the living room.

The sofa and loveseat were a matching blue floral print, with the centers of the seat cushions dark and shiny from use. There were three over-stuffed chairs in the room. They matched nothing else, not even each other. A television set had the place of honor. The last time Lee was here, Cheryl had three small children and looked exhausted. The living room had been wall-to-wall toys, and a big playpen for the baby had stood in the center.

"It's hard to believe how long it's been."

"Me, too. Ten years, at least. You haven't aged a day. And here I thought it was all TV make-up!" Cheryl's frank brown eyes surveyed the dark green jersey dress with a matching jacket, gold jewelry, the immaculate hairdo and the flawless face.

Lee remembered that when she last saw Cheryl, she wasn't yet working in New York, hadn't yet learned how to use the best make-up, to select appropriately tailored clothes, or to find the most suitable hair style that made her stand out from the pack. It was that visit to Miwok, in fact, that led to her decision to pursue her career. "Miwok is a bit off the beaten path."

"Tell me about it!" Cheryl frowned, hanging Lee's jacket in the coat closet off the entry hall. "I need some coffee. Do you still drink it?"

Lee grinned. "More than ever."

Cheryl hurried into the kitchen. "Still use half-and-half?" she called.

"Black. Got to watch my weight."

"Your weight?" Cheryl came back with a tray, set a cup and saucer before them both, and filled the cups with coffee. "I've seen fatter straws."

They both laughed uneasily, then looked at each other, letting the years melt away.

"At least the Christmas cards helped," Cheryl said.

"And that long talk on the phone after my mother died," Lee added.

Cheryl looked surprised.

"That's right. I appreciated your call, Cheryl. It meant more to me than you'll ever know." Lee took a sip of coffee. When Judith was suddenly gone, although condolences poured in from around the world, and Bruce had offered comfort, there was too much that he didn't know and probably never would. But Miriam and Cheryl understood without her having to explain. There was

SEEMS LIKE OLD TIMES

value in that kind of friendship, in those kinds of ties.

"Well, shoot, girl," Cheryl said. "What are friends for?"

Lee's eyes lifted to Cheryl's and the openness she saw there made her unsure whether to laugh or cry. Instead of either, a small, hesitant smile spread over her face. Cheryl returned it, and both smiles broadened. Suddenly, their old affinity sprang up from some long-buried past. She could almost believe they were Lisa and Cheryl again, best friends, sharing secrets and gossip and dreams. They weren't, of course. Yet an odd imbalance, a juxtaposition of the past with the present, swirled about her.

Cheryl led Lee to the kitchen table, poured her a fresh cup of coffee and took a carrot cake with cream cheese frosting out of the refrigerator. Normally, Lee spurned cake of any sort, but after all the calories she'd ingested that morning with Miriam's friends, taking a few more bites of pure sugar couldn't hurt. She'd forgotten how intimately connected food and friendship were in a small town like Miwok.

"So, tell me"—Cheryl cut a big piece of cake and put it on Lee's plate—"how do you like being back? What was that old song about not staying down on the farm after they've seen Paree? This must seem

even worse than a farm. Sometimes, girl, I can't believe I'm still here myself!" She shot Lee a percep-
tive glance. They had once been as close as sisters,
and each had shared the other's dream. Cheryl was
going to be a teacher, and Lisa was going to be a
Pulitzer Prize-winning journalist.

"Yesterday I drove around town. God, but it's
grown!" Lee replied, skirting away from her feelings
about Miwok. "This morning I went visiting with
Miriam." Lee tasted the cake. It was delicious.
Every little pound magnified mercilessly on TV,
though. One more bite for the sake of politeness...

"I remember how well you always spoke of your
aunt. I'm glad she's here with you."

"It makes it easier, in one way. But if she weren't
here, I'd probably have the house cleared out already and be on my way back to New York."

"Maybe she just wants you to relax. How are
you doing, Lisa? I mean, *really* doing? Are you
happy?"

The question surprised Lee. It wasn't the sort of
thing people asked her. How could she *not* be
happy? "I'm doing what I've always wanted. I have
my job, New York, my career..."

"Are you still seeing that insurance fellow?"
Cheryl asked. "Bruce, is it?"

Lee nibbled at the frosting on her fork. "You remember! He's asked me to marry him."

"Lisa! How terrific!"

"We haven't set a date yet, what with my mother's passing, and all."

"Sure. It'll be soon, I guess," Cheryl said.

Lee paused and looked down at her plate. Somehow, half the slice was gone. Resolutely, she put the fork down. "I haven't had time to think about arranging a wedding. It's too much to handle right now."

Cheryl's brows crossed. "Are you sure about him, Lisa?"

How many times had Cheryl said similar words to her in the past? Are you sure, Lisa? Lisa, though, was never sure of anything. She used to spend most of her time trying to do whatever Judith wanted, trying to avoid arguments, and fights, and tears at home. She would worry constantly about what she should or shouldn't do, fretting over far too much for a young girl.

Lee, however, was the opposite. Lee was sure about everything, chillingly sure. "Of course, Cheryl. I'd be a fool to let him get away. He's very handsome. An up-and-coming executive. I couldn't ask for more."

Cheryl shrewdly studied her friend a moment. "Well, that's sure as shootin' good to hear, Lisa. Be practical. That's so like you. The blond, blue-eyed way you've describe Bruce, I imagine him as looking like those smart, rich guys you used to moon over at school. But once they'd pay attention to you, you'd high-tail it right back to Tony Santos. Funny, wasn't it?"

Lee's stomach knotted. She didn't want to think about Tony right now. "Bruce is a big support for me on the news. Some men would hate the hours I have to keep."

"Oh, kid, I am so envious." Cheryl finished her piece of cake. "I look at you on TV at night and I can't help but remember that we had the same start." She put her elbow on the table, chin in hand. "I guess the difference was that when we were little and played house, I always wanted to be the Mommy and you wanted to be Lois Lane."

"Don't get the wrong impression. Bruce is no Superman."

"That doesn't matter. You don't need any Superman. You can take care of yourself. Me, on the other hand, I've got Clark Kent."

"Oh, poor Mark!" Lee laughed softly at Cheryl's rueful grimace.

Cheryl joined her. "Okay, I'm being unfair. Mark's a good man and I love him dearly but sometimes these four walls are really hard to take." She cut herself a thin slice of cake this time.

"What about you, Cheryl?" Lee asked suddenly. "Are you happy?"

"Despite my complaining, you mean?" Cheryl grinned. "I'm happy. Sometimes, now that the kids are older, I think there's more I can be doing."

"You always talked about being a schoolteacher."

"A part of me still wants to."

"You can do it. Go back to school, get your degree."

"I don't think so."

"Why not? What's to stop you?"

"Me." Cheryl smiled at Lee and gave a slight shake of her head. "You're still the same. You always knew you could conquer the world and think everyone else who puts their mind to it can as well. Not everyone is as driven as you are, or willing to work so hard at it. Some of us are content to do only so much."

"I'm not the way," Lee argued.

Cheryl nearly choked on her coffee. "All A's? Miss Perfection? Sometimes it was a bitch even being your friend! But underneath, I knew you were okay. Especially because you were always harder on yourself than anyone else could possibly be."

Lee took a sip of coffee and didn't say a word. She didn't care for the way the conversation had turned.

Cheryl's kitchen was warm and cozy. Sunlight

shone on the yellow-wallpapered walls and everywhere were signs of a family. Pictures, magnets, and
memos covered the refrigerator door, a wall calendar was filled with red notations, the air smelled
of freshly baked cake and good coffee. A mountain
of newspapers was piled by the back door and a
boy's baseball cap dangled precariously on one cabinet door knob.

With a pang, Tony Santos came to mind.

A fleeting thought formed. If she'd stayed in
Miwok she might be living like this, in a warm
family home...Tony's home?

She held the question for the briefest moment,
then let it go. Some questions had no answers.As if
reading her mind, Cheryl suddenly asked, "Have
you seen any of the old gang yet, or talked to any of
them?"

Lee studied her cake. "No. I don't plan to either.
I don't have time. Before I know it, Friday will be
here. I've got to get my mother's house ready to go
on the market. I'll be horribly busy. But I'd like to
hear about Suzanne and Abby. What are they doing
these days?" The two women she mentioned were
part of the foursome they'd been in high school,
though she and Cheryl were the closest of the
friends. She composed her features, a smile fixed
coolly, determinedly on her lips.

Lee felt herself relax as they talked about old

friends—other than Tony Santos—for a couple of hours when Lee checked her wristwatch and realized it was time to get back to help Miriam with dinner. A whole afternoon, wasted. Where had the time gone?

Cheryl walked her to her car. "Why don't we get together for lunch real soon?"

The thought of spending more time with Cheryl was surprisingly welcome. "I'd like that, as long as we can fit it in before Friday."

"Tell you what, we can make it a quick lunch."

Lee laughed. "Sounds perfect."

FOUR

"Would you like to go back to the house now, Miriam?" Lee asked.

"Not at all. I'm so glad we're taking the time for a Sunday drive. This is wonderful." Her aunt's head bobbed like a doll's with a spring neck as she tried not to miss a single house, shop or street sign. "Things haven't changed much, have they, Lisa?" Miriam asked.

"I was thinking the same thing," she said dryly. Visiting Miwok had been like entering a time warp. Presto, it was the fifties again, and the Leave It To Beaver Cleavers lived in the blue-shingled house down on the next block.

"Miwok is comfortable," Miriam said, settling

back against in the passenger seat, her blue eyes sparkling. "Like an old shoe."

"That's one way of putting it." Lee had a closetful of shoes in her Park Avenue condo and promptly discarded any old ones. Perhaps it was a metaphor for her life. All the old shoes were gone, except for Miriam and Cheryl. And she liked it that way.

Miriam rolled down a window. The air smelled of sunshine, earth and fresh-cut lawns. "Ah, Miwok," she sighed. "When did I forget the clean, healthy way the air smells here?"

Bemused, Lee glanced at her hopelessly nostalgic aunt. "I can put on the air-conditioning if you're warm."

"City girl!" Miriam pursed her lips, but a smile hinted at the corners. "Let's stop at the park, Lisa. I'd love to walk through it once again."

Settlers Park was just ahead. If the red town hall with a weathercock on its clock tower was the heart of town, Settlers Park was its soul. A hopelessly corny soul at that, Lee thought.

Gravel crunched and bounced off the Cadillac as she pulled into the parking lot. Stepping out of the car, she smoothed her pale blue Ralph Lauren dress. The high heels of her blue-suede sling-backs wobbled precariously on the stones as she walked toward the paved pathway.

Beside her, Miriam sauntered along in a striped white and yellow loose sheathe and Birkenstock sandals.

In the park, people ignored Miriam, but their heads turned Lee's way with the same quizzical look that so often greeted her. They recognized her, but without a television set framing her face, she seemed much smaller, more human, even vulnerable. Her pale blond fragility belied the steely nature she had developed. From the moment she began working in New York City, Lee made sure she was coifed and dressed to kill, which was the reason she chose to wear her hair pulled back from her face in a severe, elegant chignon instead of the rounded, breezy style most television news anchors and reporters chose. Her every gesture, on and off camera, was performed in a cloud of self-assurance. She wanted to make a statement, and she did.

Now, she smiled at the gawkers with just the correct amount of cool reserve and acknowledgement, and continued walking.

On a wide expanse of lawn, adults sunned themselves or played with Frisbees, small children ran and tumbled, and a couple of dogs chased each other in circles.

Up ahead, a green park bench stood empty under a wide elm. "This is so peaceful. Let's sit awhile," Miriam said.

Lee wanted to remind her aunt that they had just spent ninety minutes sitting, but restrained herself. Back at the house a documentary proposal she'd brought with her awaited her perusal. The CABN-TV news executives were considering producing a piece on life in Moscow over the past two years, and she was eager to read it. She wanted a major role in the project, if it was well conceived. She had a simple axiom for getting ahead—travel everywhere, cover everything, and make yourself a pain in the ass until you get what you want, when you want it. She wouldn't let her annoyance at wasting time in this park make her short with Miriam, however. Her aunt deserved better, and she was feeling guilty for having thrown herself so much into her career that they had spent little time together. Lee wanted to use these days in Miwok to make up, a little at least, for years of neglect.

She was pacing back and forth, in no mood to sit on the dusty, pollen-laden bench, when a little boy walked by carrying a soda and a hotdog.

"Oh, doesn't that look good!" Miriam said. "Are you hungry?"

Even if she were, a hotdog was the last thing she'd eat. The thought of the calories and fat content, let alone what it was made of, was enough to cause her to lose her appetite. "No. Are you?"

"I am thirsty. I'd love some 7-Up. I believe

there's a stand just down that pathway." To Lee's astonishment, Miriam rose stiffly from the bench, and rubbed her knee. She looked like she was in some pain. "Oh my! I must have pulled a muscle or something. Every so often it acts up."

"You stay there," Lee said. "I'll get it for you."

"If you're sure it's not too much trouble?" Miriam asked.

"Don't be silly." Lee watched, concerned, as Miriam slowly sat down again.

"Thanks. Take your time. I'm in no hurry." Miriam already looked quite a bit better.

As Lee followed the curving walk the boy had taken, she heard cheers from beyond a copse of eucalyptus and shrubbery. One of the town's Little League baseball fields was there.

When she was young, she often went to Little League games with Cheryl. Cheryl's three brothers all played. Another cheer rang out. Years ago, she used to go to lots of baseball games. No more, though. There never seemed to be time for such things anymore.

As she neared the field, she saw a group of little boys wearing red caps and jerseys with the name "Bruins" playing against an equally miniature group in blue called the "Bobcats." She bit back a soft chuckle at the sight of the Little Leaguers in their pint-sized uniforms, their bats as tall as they were, and their batting helmets almost covering their eyes. They looked like jar-headed Charlie Browns come to life. But she was sure every one of them dreamed of hitting a home run or pitching a no-hitter. Jackie Robinson, Mickey Mantle, and even Derek Jeter meant a lot more to them than George Washington or Abraham Lincoln, and if given a choice as to who they'd rather be like, the ballplayers would win hands down every time.

A sprinkling of parents sat in the stands, and behind them stood a snack shack. She would buy the sodas there, and maybe Miriam would finally be ready to go back to the house. Lee was curious about that Moscow proposal. She preferred St. Petersburg, but if she had to live two weeks in Moscow to do the special, she'd manage.

The blue pitcher threw the ball to the red batter. It sailed at least five feet over his head. The catcher leaped and still couldn't reach it. "Good eye!" some parent shouted encouragement to the batter and didn't even sound sarcastic. "Way to watch, buddy."

The batter tapped home plate twice with his bat, wriggled his butt, and raised the bat high over his head, ready for the next pitch. A slight smile touched Lee's lips. At Little League games any boy could be a hero for a day, and the meaning of courage was learning to step into the batter's box with your team behind, two outs and a runner on third.

"Full count," the home plate umpire called. "Three and two."

Only two strikes? This pitcher was better than the ones she remembered. They used to walk everyone, including the team mascot.

She reached the snack shack, bought Miriam's 7-Up and a diet Dr. Pepper for herself, then headed back.

The batter had walked—some things never changed—and now stood at first base, looking for a chance to steal. Another boy was at the plate.

She heard the clink of the aluminum bat against the baseball and instinctively looked over her shoulder to see the hit. Everyone was peering upward. "Foul ball!" someone yelled. "Heads up!"

She lifted her head, too, and saw that the ball popped high in the air was now coming down right in her direction.

She quickly took a step back, then another. The ball dropped a few feet in front of her. "I'll get it, lady," a little boy, not in uniform, said as he picked up the ball and tossed it back into play.

"Fine," she answered, checking to see if the soda that sloshed over the cups had landed on her dress.

The dress was spared, but a blob of sticky brown soda flattened the soft suede of one shoe. Terrific.

She raised her eyes. Suddenly, the world screeched to a halt, then careened backwards in time.

Standing inside the baseball field, staring straight at her, was Tony Santos.

The sound of birds, the murmur of the crowd, the heat of the afternoon sun, all dimmed and disappeared. She felt cold, then warm, then a little light-headed.

She blinked. Tony. Of all the people she had known in Miwok, he was the one she most often thought about. The one she had stayed curious about after all these years. The one she dreaded ever facing again.

He had left Miwok years ago, just as she had—just as they both always said they would. Yet, seeing him here seemed so right, so inevitable, even if she wouldn't admit it, she knew she had imagined he would be here.

He wore a red Bruins cap and although it shaded his eyes a little, she could see that they were every bit as big and dark and penetrating as she remembered.

She felt rooted to the spot, and starkly aware of the damp coldness of the sodas in her hands, the smoothness of the silk that skimmed her body, the dull roar in her ears. It was somehow appropriate that even after all these years she should see him in a baseball cap. That was how she remembered him best.

Yes, she remembered Tony.

As much as she hadn't let herself think about him, he was always there, in her subconscious. Tony...and Miwok. Her insides churned as wretched memories shook her—disgust and hatred, heartache and regret.

The loud cheer of the crowd startled her, and Tony turned his head to see the batter get a hit and make it safely to first base. The runner advanced to third. Then Tony turned to face her again. He didn't smile; he made no acknowledgement. The hell of it was, she understood why, and knew she was to blame.

Still, she could have been sixteen once more, seeing Tony waiting for her after school, after his team practice or after her student council meeting. Against her will her heart raced, just as it used to do, and a yearning, as familiar as it was startling, filled her. She had to stop this, but instead her face burned at the sudden awareness she felt, and at the awkwardness.

Somehow her lips curved in her television smile —polite, charming, and not giving anything away. She lifted her hand, Dr. Pepper and all, in greeting.

"Hey, Dad!" a boy shouted, loud enough for the stands to hear. "Dad! Quick, who's in the hole?"

Dad?

Lee stared at the child and her world became a dizzying spiral. Her fingers tightened on the sodas. *Dad...*

Tony looked over at the boy. "What?"

"Who's in the hole?" he yelled again.

"Just a minute." He pulled a rolled-up paper from his back pocket and checked it. His voice seemed a little deeper now. But it was still low, sexy and musical, with a hint of grit. She'd always loved his voice.

As her gaze leaped from father to son, she felt she was coming apart inside. Tony's son was beautiful. He had Tony's black hair and dark eyes. He still had baby fat where Tony was sleek and well-toned, and he had his father's light olive complexion. She steeled herself against the sudden ache deep within her. Tall, dark and handsome—that described the Santos men. That described Tony.

Her gaze turned toward the stands, scanning them as she heard Tony call out to a boy named Jimmy that he was the next batter on deck...scanning them as she wondered which of the women watching the game was Tony's wife.

What had passed between her and Tony happened a long time ago and was best forgotten. She glanced back at him and their eyes met. His burned, and yet, he still didn't acknowledge her, didn't wave, didn't even smile.

She squared her shoulders, turned and walked with deliberate slowness across the park to her aunt.

FIVE

North of Miwok a string of lakes filled the gullies between the coast range mountains to the west and the foothills that edged San Francisco Bay on the east. Along these lakes were small dairy and horse ranches. Among them stood the Circle Z.

Tony and Ben sat in the remodeled kitchen of the farmhouse and ate their way through a bucket of Kentucky Fried Chicken bought after Ben's Little League game. Tony had spent a lot of time and money on the old house, making it warm and inviting for himself and his son. The old-fashioned, spacious kitchen, filled with modern conveniences and appliances, was the room he was especially proud of.

Tony's father, Vic, lived in the cottage that he

and Tony had shared when Vic was first given a job at the Circle Z over nineteen years ago. The cottages for Vic and the foreman, a bunkhouse for the ranch hands, as well as stables for the ranch horses, boarding stables, and the barn, were grouped away from the main house. Tony enjoyed the business of raising prize Arabian stock and of boarding horses, many of whom had been purchased from his own stables, and he spent nearly every day working with his crew.

The chicken was halfway eaten when Vic, as usual, entered through the back door without knocking.

"How'd the game go, Benito?" he asked.

"We won, ten to seven." Ben waved a drumstick in triumph.

"Want to eat, Pa?" Tony asked.

"I don't eat no food I don't recognize. Anyway, I already ate." He opened the refrigerator and took out a bottle of Dos Equis beer. He sat at the table and watched Tony and Ben finish eating. "You wanna come down and play some poker tonight?" he asked Tony.

"I don't think so." Tony picked up the plates, rinsed them off then put them in the dishwasher without saying another word. Ben ran outside to play.

Vic took a sip of his beer as Tony put the left-

overs in the refrigerator and tossed the food wrap-
pings in the trash. "What's wrong?"

Tony froze. "Nothing!" He slammed shut the
under-the-counter cabinet door, then he stopped
and drew in his breath. He had no business being
irritable with his father. It wasn't Vic's fault that he
crackled with nervous energy. He felt like a cat in a
lightning storm, but he didn't know why. Or did he?
He rubbed the back of his neck. "Look, would you
watch Ben for a couple of hours? I think I'll go for a
drive or something."

"You goin' anyplace special?" Vic's question was
pointed, and Tony knew it.

"No." His answer was equally pointed.

Vic shrugged. His once-muscular shoulders had
lost most of their bulk, but kept a sinewy strength.
"So, to go no place special, you can't take Ben with
you?"

Tony turned from the window. "If you don't
want to watch him, you can just say so—"

Vic waved his hand as if brushing Tony's com-
ment aside. "That's not what I said. You think I was
born yesterday?"

Tony's jaw tightened. "What's that supposed to
mean?"

"A friend of mine saw your old girlfriend's aunt
a couple days ago. She told him Lisa was comin'
back and that the two of them was gonna empty out

her mother's house. Get the place ready to sell. Now you're goin' off and won't say where."

"What? Did I say that?" Tony waved his arms as he spoke. "Did I say I won't say where I'm going? Did I?"

"But you didn't say where."

"Jesus Christ, Pa! Maybe I don't know where. What the hell!" He grabbed his sweatshirt and pulled it on. "I'm getting out of here."

"Don't blaspheme, Tony! You gonna go to her house?"

Tony yanked the sweatshirt into place, then put his hands on the top rail of a kitchen chair. "That's the last place I want to go. Anyway, you're wrong about one thing. Lisa's not back. The woman I saw yesterday was no more Lisa than Astroturf is a baseball field."

Vic's mouth wrinkled in disgust. "Still, you wanna go see her."

Tony's irritation swelled. "I don't want to go see her! I didn't expect asking you to watch your own grandson would turn into an inquisition."

"I'll watch Ben, but I gotta be sure you got the brains to stay away from a woman like her, Tony. You gotta stick with nice, simple women. Ones you can tell what makes them happy."

There was a silence, then a low, deep, growly reminder. "I'm not a kid," Tony said, holding his agitation in check. "I don't need your advice. Especially about women."

Vic harrumphed and picked up his beer. "Don't seem to me you done so good without it."

Anger surged, but died almost immediately. In its place came regret. Tony turned to look out the kitchen window. Ben was out there running around imaginary bases, pretending he'd hit a home run, most likely. Somehow, watching Ben always helped bring him back on track.

From the time he'd heard of Judith Reynolds's death, he'd wondered if Lisa might come back here. A part of him wanted to see her, but another part hated the thought. His feelings for her had gone from a boyhood infatuation to black, pure hatred to, finally, just a quiet disappointment that she had taken their affection and closeness and had made it so ugly. He'd thought he'd forgotten all about her— that she was just another pretty face on TV—until he'd heard yesterday that she was coming home.

Many times over the years he had wondered how it would feel to see her again. He wondered what he would say to her, if anything. The way they'd parted, there wasn't much left to say. No, that wasn't true. There was everything to say. Starting with why?

He had avoided watching her on TV as much as possible. It was more than he could tolerate. His memories were too strong to handle the one-dimensional image. The girl he knew was brilliant, ambitious, and surprisingly tough-minded—Lisa was never the sweet little miss she pretended to be—and she was much more vivacious, much more real than the cool, golden, glittery creation who so seriously presented the news each night. He wondered how she would look and sound without the make-up and hairstyle and jewelry and speech lessons that went along with being a television star. Was any of the old Lisa left at all?

Yes, he had definitely wondered what it would be like to face her again. The only problem was that he never suspected it would feel the way it did. Wretched, confusing, scary. She had looked beautiful, so god-damned beautiful it actually had made his chest ache to see her. Even more than before, and Lisa had looked gorgeous from the first day they met, even though she had seemed scared to death of him.

What had she been doing at the park yesterday? Lee Reynolds at a snack shack, for crying out loud, wearing an expensive blue dress that made her glow, that hinted at the familiar gentle curves, the long sexy legs it covered. Seeing her was like a kick in the balls, and he had reacted in kind.

There was no reason she should have had that

effect on him. Not after all these years. Not after half a lifetime.

God, but he felt like an ass for just standing there that way, gaping at her like some star-dazzled groupie, not saying a word, not even waving. She must have thought he was a complete jerk.

Now that he had seen her again, gotten the shock out his system, he would love just five minutes with her, with that new "Lee" Reynolds. Just five minutes to show her how little she mattered to him, to show her how much he had made of his life. How easy it was, now, for *him* to walk away from *her*.

He folded his arms and turned back to Vic. "Don't ever think I still care about her, Pa. You'd be dead wrong. She's no more to me than a bad memory of how ambitious and cold a woman can be."

Vic glanced at his son. Vic's weather-beaten face had been baked hard by the sun, and his black eyes were barely more than thin slits in heavy folds of skin. "This is a small town, Tony. It's easy for you to say those words now, but don't forget them when you have to talk to her, face to face. For your sake, remember how you felt when she left. Then get the hell away from her."

"What do you think? That she's been on my mind all my life? Well, she hasn't!"

Vic folded his arms. "The sooner she gets outta Miwok the sooner I'll like it."

The front doorbell rang. Vic glanced at his son.

"I'm not expecting anyone," Tony said.

"You better go see who it is, then."

Tony strode down the long hallway to the front door, Vic following. Trish Hollingsworth stood at the door, holding a pizza box. She was young and short, with a knockout body. Her auburn hair was styled with thick, brightly shining bangs that met her eyelashes. The sides fell from a center part to just below her ears where they were bluntly cut all the way around and formed a wedge in back. A low cut, tight white dress with a straight skirt that stopped about ten inches above her knees revealed as much as possible without fear of arrest.

"Hi, Tony, Vic," she said as she breezed past them into the house. "I hope I'm not too late. I figured you wouldn't want to cook after your game today."

"Actually, Trish..." Tony still held the doorknob.

She glanced over her shoulder once, then continued toward the kitchen, her back motor in high gear.

Vic watched her go, raised one eyebrow, then looked at Tony, "Now that's a woman easy to understand. Time for me to leave. I'll take Ben down to my place."

"There's no need for that, Pa."

Vic shrugged. "You can always come and get him later." He went outside and called Ben. Tony glanced at the door he was still holding open, then shut it and headed for the kitchen.

Trish had opened the box, plucked a piece of stringy mozzarella off the top of the pizza and was holding it high in the air. With her tongue, she found the end of the cheese string, then slowly lowered it into her mouth. She kept her eyes on Tony as she licked the oily cheese and pizza sauce off her fingertips, one by one.

His stomach clenched. "Thanks for bringing it, Trish. If I'd have known...We already ate, though."

"No problem." She smiled jauntily, and put the box top back in place, opened the refrigerator and tossed it inside. Then she spun toward him, hands on hips. "Cold pizza's great. Especially for break-fast." She lifted her eyebrows suggestively.

The house was silent.

"No. You can take it home."

She stepped close to him and leaned forward until her breasts touched his chest. "But I bought it for you." She pressed closer. "I wanted to give it to you. To fill you." She placed one hand against his stomach, then began to slide it lower.

He stepped back. "No need Trish."

She wrapped her arms around his neck, rocking

her pelvis from side to side against him as she spoke. "You're just angry that I missed your ball game. I'm sorry, Tony."

Trish had a manicure shop in town. Tony found it hard to believe anyone could make a living off the vanity of women about their nails, but she did. A good living, too. She was too young for him—about twenty-three—and outside of bed, they had nothing in common. The sex was good, though.

Against his will he could feel his body reacting to her slow, seductive movements.

"Trish, stop. Just stop." He put his hands on her waist and pushed her away.

But she closed in again. "You don't mean that." She put one hand on his shoulder, the other brazenly against the fly of his jeans. "We'll have our own ball game, Tony," she whispered then giggled. It was an old joke, one he had grown tired of long ago. "You know you like it," she insisted. "You always do."

Why was he fighting her? Just because an old girlfriend was in town? Who did he think he was kidding? Trish wanted him. Lisa never did. Once, Lisa could have had him on a silver platter, but she kicked it aside and left. Her dreams for a career always came first with her, and, he was sure, they still did. The hell with her.

He looked at Trish. He didn't love her, but he

never had pretended to either. She knew exactly where she stood.

But right then, none of that mattered. He walked to the door and opened it. "Let's just say that tonight I have a head ache."

She rolled her eyes and sauntered out the door.

SIX

Cheryl telephoned Lee early the next morning and suggested going to lunch that very day in the Old Town section of Miwok. Lee had planned to go to a shopping mall with Miriam to look for new carpeting and drapery, but was glad for an excuse to put it off longer. Although the place needed sprucing up before it went on the market, the thought of so brazenly redecorating her mother's house bothered her. She could all but see Judith's furious reaction.

Miriam didn't mind the revised plans at all and sounded pleased that Lee and Cheryl had enjoyed each other's company so much.

Lee changed into an ivory and navy Louis Vuitton dress and Rossetti navy pumps, drove over to Cheryl's, and together the two of them went the short distance to Old Town. There, the town of Miwok had been established one hundred fifty years ago as little more than a junction along the railroad line. Many of the original buildings had been restored and were still in use.

The number of new boutiques in the area astonished Lee, but her heart warmed at the sight of Porky's Chili Bar, the Do Drop Inn, the Old Ball and Chain Pool Hall, Amazing Grace Religious Artifacts, Kettleman's Jewelers, and the rickety old Miwok Cinema with gum on every seat and sticky, spilled coke in every aisle.

Each place had been a part of her youth, even though they now stood side-by-side with a modernistic sculpture and jewelry maker, an art gallery, and a French restaurant.

"Let's take a couple of minutes before we go eat." Cheryl grabbed Lee's arm as she turned into the Cantelli Saddle Company. "Gene Cantelli's a friend. I'd like you to meet him."

The small store, filled with tack, and smelling of leather, hay and saddle soap, had the comfortable, rustic feel of an old time livery stable's tack room.

A man stood in the back of the store oiling a beautiful, hand-tooled Western saddle. He appeared to be in his fifties, with curly, steel gray hair, a gray mustache under a generous nose, and sparkling amber eyes.

"Cheryl, hello," he called out as they entered. "This must be the famous friend you told me about." Wiping his hands on a clean cloth, he stepped around the counter and held out his calloused hand as Cheryl made the introductions.

"Hello, Mr. Cantelli," Lee said, returning his sharp-eyed scrutiny with quiet poise. The twinkle in his eye, she decided, had less to do with her fame than with a masculine appreciation.

"The name's Gene. Welcome to the shop."

"Hey, Gene, that's a drop-dead gorgeous saddle," Cheryl said.

"Yeah. Tony bought it. He should be in here any time to pick it up."

Lee's gaze snapped from the saddle to Gene, then quickly to Cheryl who had discovered an intense fascination with mink oil and saddle soap.

"You probably remember Tony Santos," Gene said to Lee. "Him and his old man are good buddies of mine."

"I remember him," she murmured coolly, her suspicions aroused by this turn of conversation. Were these two up to something here?

"I'll bet Lisa, I mean Lee, has never seen the pictures you've got of Tony and Vic," Cheryl said, avoiding Lee's gaze.

"Right there." Gene pointed to a wall filled with framed photographs. "Take your time. Look around." Gene was effusive.

Lee glanced from one to the other. She walked over to the photos and immediately recognized Vic Santos. Lots of photos showed Vic standing beside a horse, holding an award, and several showed him on the ranch, working with the animals. There were pictures of Tony as well at the Circle Z. Lee stepped closer to get a better look. Why had Cheryl wanted her to see these? Soon, though, she found herself smiling at pictures of Tony and his dad to-gether—Tony as usual wearing a baseball cap, and his dad in a big Stetson. That was so like the two of them, ever at odds, but together, nonetheless. Quite the opposite were her and her mother, who had never openly fought, except once.

Interspersed among them were pictures of a young Gene Cantelli at rodeo shows, holding tro-phies, a few of him hanging tight onto a bronco or a bull.

"My goodness," Lee said. "You look great in these rodeo shots."

"I was great," Gene said with a smile, "until my back went out."

She winced. "I'm sorry." She was impressed, though, and it showed. She went back to the photos.

It seemed odd to think of Tony making a purchase in a store like this. She remembered how much he used to complain about having to spend his summers working at the Circle Z with his father. Judging from the pictures, it looked like his father still worked there.

The smells in the saddle shop awakened her memories of the times Tony invited her out to the ranch to "help" him. She fingered some leather reins, remembering. What might have been work for the ranch hands, was pure fun for the two teenagers. At one point in her life—Lee guessed she was thirteen or fourteen—she loved horses more than anything else in the world. Now, she sometimes wondered if she loved anything at all. Other than Miriam. And Bruce, of course.

Since Tony was buying a saddle, could that mean that he, too, now worked on a horse ranch? Maybe on the Circle Z with his father? Lee's heart sank for him. He had such dreams at one time. Dreams of baseball...

She didn't follow baseball. Not at all. Once, she thought she'd heard his name mentioned by a sports announcer on a news show, but it was probably someone else. So many Latin players were in the game, and Santos was a fairly common name.

She faced Gene. "I see you've known the Santos family for years," she said with forced cheerfulness.

Gene grinned. "I met Vic Santos when I was

busting my a, um, backside, on some mustangs in Montana. We became good friends. One day, after I had to give up the rodeo and was on my way to becoming one of those guys who gets drunk and bores everyone with stories about the good ol' days, Vic called me up and said they could use me at the Circle Z and would I come? Would I! I started working with Vic and that scrappy son of his. Tony was off playing baseball most of the year, but then he got a little more horse sense, I guess, since he finally came back to us."

"I see," Lee whispered. Gene's words confirmed her fears about Tony's job. It had probably been too difficult for him to try to make it in baseball and support a family, besides. Minor leaguers, she'd always heard, made a pittance of a salary, and traveled constantly. For those who didn't have the talent or luck to make it to the top, it was a difficult, stress-filled life.

"Tony helped me get this place going," Gene added. "It's doing real well, too."

"I can see why." Lee touched a saddle, feeling the smooth, warm leather. "Your stock is exquisite."

Gene beamed. "That's 'cause I know where to get the best of everything."

Lee smiled. "It's been nice talking to you, Gene, but I guess we should get going. Are you hungry, Cheryl?"

"Well..." Cheryl looked at her watch, then at Gene.

He shrugged.

"I guess so. Will you join us, Gene?"

"No, thanks. About the only thing more boring than to talk about my old school days, is to listen to someone else talk about theirs."

"We promise not one word if you'll come along," Lee said.

Gene's steady gaze seemed to take in her measure. "Thanks, but I'd better wait for Tony to pick up his saddle. Seems he's late, as always."

"We'll see you around, Gene," Cheryl blurted. "Thanks, anyway."

"Nice to meet you," Lee said, shaking Gene's hand. It was all she could do not to let on to these two the transparency of their plan, although they'd surely deny it. But why would they want her and Tony to meet here? He was happily married, wasn't he? And anyway, she was happily engaged.

Lee leaned back against the family room sofa watching a *Bonanza* rerun with Miriam. Lee had never watched the show before, but it had been a big favorite of Miriam's. Apparently, the most dangerous thing in the Old West was to have been a woman and have a Cartwright fall in love with you. Fifty minutes later, you'd be dead.

Falling in love was dangerous, all right. When had she first learned that lesson? Watching her mother's years of regret or, later, with Tony?

Although she had forgotten, over the years, how she used to feel around Tony, she did know she had never been in love like that again with anyone. Maybe that's what people meant when they said there was nothing quite so wonderful, or so miserable, as first love. That summed it up for her. She tried to stop thinking about him. Dwelling on the past caused nothing but misery. She had to think about the future.

At least she found a realtor she liked and could work with. After talking with her on the phone, Lee had checked her references. Earlier that evening, Janet Lettice had come by, and after interviewing her for almost an hour, Lee signed a contract. Now all she had to do was take care of her mother's personal items, pick out paint, new drapes and carpets, and turn everything to the waiting, capable hands of Ms. Lettice. God bless her.

When *Bonanza* ended, Lee called Bruce and chatted a while. He had a lot to say about company intrigue.

She then phoned Melanie James, a good friend who was also the arts director for the station where

Evening Newscene was broadcast. Melanie worked until nine at night, so Lee knew she'd be wide awake. She filled Melanie in on life in Miwok and Melanie gave her the latest gossip from the newsroom.

Forty-year-old Melanie knew how to live the swinging career-girl dream to the hilt. She was currently living with a man named Jim—Lee never did find out his last name—and they split everything equally, even to the point where they divided shelves on the refrigerator between "his" and "hers." When Melanie cooked dinner, it was a meal for one. If Jim got hungry, she'd point to the microwave.

Lee enjoyed Melanie's biting sense of humor— New York, arty and streetwise. At the same time, Melanie threw herself into everything that interested her, men included. There were times Lee wished she were a lot more like Melanie.

But the only thing she ever seemed to have time for was her work.

SEVEN

The next morning Lee tore through the kitchen and pantry, ruthlessly sorting dishes, food and appliances that should be given away, thrown out, or kept.

Last night, she couldn't sleep. Whenever she'd shut her eyes, strange visions would spring into her head. She didn't know what they were, nor did she want to know. Monsters—a child's nightmare world of snakes, dragons and gargoyles. She was too old to be having such dreams. But, too old or not, they scared her. She would wake up, turn over to go back to sleep and the dream would start up again. At six, she gave up on sleep and got out of bed.

Being back in this house had stirred up too many bad memories of Judith. Between her mother and her old high school, no wonder she dreamt about monsters and gargoyles.

She needed to finish the job here and go home. If Miriam wanted to stay on by herself—since she, at least, was enjoying the town—that was fine with Lee. But she'd had enough. She could hardly wait to see Bruce and her friends in New York. New York was home now, and she loved it.

Miriam stepped into the kitchen, long-nosed shears in one hand and gardening gloves in the other. "I'm pruning the rose bushes in the garden. Why don't you come outside? Relax a while, enjoy being here, enjoy the sunshine."

Lee, dressed in chinos, her hair pulled back in a French braid, was in the pantry filling Hefty bags with old food. "An uneven tan might make my skin look blotchy or dirty on TV. I'd better not chance it."

"The world doesn't begin and end with Evening Newscene."

"Mine does."

"Life happens, Lisa. Despite television."

Lee spun around, a box of stale Wheat Chex in her hand. "Miriam, my life *is* television."

"Well, I hear the roses calling. I made some sun tea, so when you want a break, come sit in the shade and have some." Miriam went back to her gardening.

Lee glared after her aunt. She stuffed boxes and sacks of dry foodstuffs into black plastic trash bags. Miriam's constant, obvious attempts to suck her into this Miwok fantasy was nothing short of perverse.

When Miriam had moved away from Miwok years ago, Lee had always assumed that she'd gone because of sad memories of her dead husband and older brother. Time, she guessed, had healed those old wounds.

After a while, she heard Miriam's high, thin voice singing "All I Have To Do is Dream" while she worked in the garden. Although Lee shook her head at the corny old Everly Brothers tune, she heard the happiness in her aunt's voice. Once this visit was over, Miriam would have little reason to return again.

The finality of it struck Lee. Even though she, herself, didn't like Miwok, and never had, she needed to be respectful of Miriam's feelings about the town.

"I'll go find a sun hat then come out to help you," she called, suddenly wanting to join Miriam and share her happy mood.

"Find some gardening gloves, too. There are a lot of weeds out here...in the shade."

"Ah ha! Now the truth comes out." Lee smiled as she headed for her old bedroom on the second floor of the house but stopped as she faced the photographs of her childhood that lined the wall along the staircase, from her toothless baby smile at the bottom landing, to her high school graduation smile at the top.

Her stomach clenched, and the ulcer began to burn. How she hated that wall. Somehow, up to now, she'd avoided a careful look at it. Now, old, ugly memories rushed back. She averted her eyes and climbed the stairs.

In the photos, her clothes were starched, unwrinkled and spotless, her light blond hair curled and adorned with ribbons or barrettes, her big, pale blue eyes clear and sparkling, and her Shirley Temple-round cheeks dimpled in an angelic smile. The pretty little girl in the photos touched nothing, said nothing and troubled no one. This was the perfect daughter Judith wanted. Far different was the flesh and blood, fault-filled and disappointing child she got.

Lee's breath was coming fast as she rushed to her room and flung open the bedroom door. She stopped, stunned, as her mind again flashed to the past and all the times she'd run in here after school to change her clothes before going right back out again.

She pressed her fingertips against her temples. The effects of too much country fresh air and sunshine after years of exhaust fumes and soot in Manhattan must have been bothering her. That, and seeing old friends...seeing Tony, and his son.

She clasped her hands together, trying to stop the way they shook from stress and tension. But then, they often shook when she wasn't on television. Somehow, on TV, her public persona took over. On TV, Lee Reynolds had poise, sophistication, and nerves of iron. Lee was all the things little Lisa Marie Reynolds, from Hicktown, USA, had worked long and hard to become. In Miwok, though, it seemed more of Lisa Marie still existed than she had expected. That was another reason to hurry up and leave.

The bedroom was still decorated in the feminine style Judith had chosen for her when she was fourteen. The walls were covered with pale rose and white floral wallpaper and oval-shaped pictures from Godey's Ladies' Book. A white-eyelet comforter on the bed was piled high with pastel pillows trimmed with lace, ribbons and flounces. Madame Alexander dolls wearing early American costumes lined a shelf. School souvenirs filled a white wicker trunk, and on the top of it was her collection of stuffed animals.

How upset she'd been when Judith redecorated without asking her opinion. She's been into Star Wars and heavy metal, not dolls and frills. Now, with an adult's eye, she could see that the room was pretty. The sad part was that it represented how completely her mother had misunderstood her and had tried to make her into Judith's own image. And when that failed, had tried to strip her down to nothing.

She failed in that as well. Lee had made sure of it.

The realtor had advised that, although the house was in great need of fresh paint, wall-to-wall carpets and new drapery, it should be marketed while still furnished rather than empty, and she had particularly liked this room. Lee did, however, need to get rid of the clutter.

She decided to leave in the house only those belongings that would be donated to charity once the house sold. That way, she wouldn't have to return here again. Knowing the realtor would handle everything else was quite a load off her shoulders.

She walked over to the window seat, put her palms on it and leaned toward the glass pane, looking out at the familiar view. The window faced a cherry plum tree on the front lawn. She used to spend hour upon hour sitting here thinking about school, her friends, her future. Particularly about one friend. She glanced down at the street, and remembered him standing there, waiting for her.

She spun around. She used to have a couple of straw hats—not that she ever wore them when she was young. But she could use them in the garden now. Where were they? She opened her closet door and looked on the top shelf. Not there. Stuffed in the back? On the floor?

She pushed aside her clothes and peered inside. There was a box in the way and she grabbed it and pulled it toward the door. Curious about it, she lifted the flaps and rifled through the contents.

School papers, yearbooks, pictures, an old diary...

Don't look, she warned herself. The diary was dated twenty years ago. She was fifteen at the time. Flipping through the pages quickly, a lot were blank. A most unmemorable year. She was ready to toss it back in the box when the pages fell open to a date in late October. Despite herself, she began to read.

Dear Diary,

I can't believe what happened today! After lunch Cheryl and Suzanne went to comb their hair and I was alone when that new Mexican boy came up to me. The only other time I was around him was when I saw him on his bike and we just stared at each other.

But he walked up to me as if we were friends or something. He said, "You're Lisa Reynolds," like he was telling me something I didn't know.

I said, "Such news."

He said, "I'm Tony Santos."

I said, "I don't talk to strangers." But he hung around. His clothes are bitchin'. Nobody in Miwok dresses so cool, I started to walk away, but I went kind of slow. He walked with me, I thought he'd have an accent, but he doesn't. He said he's from a place in Texas called Armadillo or something.

His father trains horses out at the Circle Z, which is better than what some kids were saying. I asked him about his mother. He said his mother was dead.

It made me think about when Daddy died, and I felt bad for him.

I asked if she died long ago. He said it was the day he was born. I can't imagine dying because of having a baby. That's so terrible.

I think I must have looked strange because he tried to joke about it. He said, "When I was a little kid I never got to sing happy birthday," and he laughed. But I saw a funny look in his eye when he said it. He stopped laughing, then offered me some Twizzlers. I didn't know what to answer, so I took a piece and gave him back the rest. He has a nice smile. I think I like him.

After school, Cheryl and Suzanne wanted to know every word we said. They said they were appalled that I'd actually talk to somebody like him. It made me feel bad for him. I told them what he said and what I said, but I didn't tell them about his mother. I think he said that just for me to know. I hope he talks to me again sometime.

Lee shut the diary and held it in her hand a long moment. Finally, she dropped it back in the box, and shoved the box to a spot beside the bedroom door. She'd carry it out to the trash when she went downstairs to help Miriam.

That evening, Cheryl got a group of "the girls" together for dinner with Lee.

At that meal, she discovered just how much Miwok had changed for her, and vice versa. As much fun as the dinner had been, it brought home to her how much her life had diverged from that of her friends. At varying times each of them acted stand-offish and shy, at times each seemed to envy her for her success and independence, and at other times, each acted as if she were still Lisa Marie Reynolds, high school classmate. But at no time did any of them, including Cheryl, have any grasp of what it meant to leave Miwok.

The life she lived was a mystery to them, and as a result, so was she. She tried to explain, but her words did no good, and eventually, she gave up trying. When they said goodbye, they hugged each other and promised to get together again soon. They all meant it, Lee felt, as did she, but deep in her heart she suspected that as the euphoria of being with old friends wore off, they'd probably change their minds. There was too much distance—culturally, socially, in life experience—between her and these people from her childhood.

She'd still see Cheryl, but as for the others, they'd probably run out of things to say far too quickly if they tried to get together again. After all, how often can one rehash old times? Once, usually. Twice, rarely.

Strangely, throughout the evening, no one mentioned Tony Santos. Lee wondered if Cheryl had said something to them, because it was so awkward to *not* mention him, that his presence pervaded the dinner.

Late that evening, at her mother's house, feeling lonely and forsaken by her old friends, Lee telephoned Bruce. He didn't answer. She remembered he'd had a dinner engagement planned. It was past midnight in New York and she'd expected him to be home by this time. She left a message on the answering machine that she'd called, then hung up feeling out of sorts, hurt and abandoned. "Where are you, Bruce?" she cried. "For once in my life, I need you!"

EIGHT

Miriam dawdled over breakfast.

"Is anything wrong?" Lee asked.

"Oh, I was just thinking how much I used to enjoy going to San Francisco with Patrick when he was alive. I guess I'll never see it again that way. I don't suppose you'd like to go?"

Lee nearly laughed aloud. She was glad Miriam never wanted to be an actress the way her mother did. Miriam couldn't have made it past melodrama. "This is my last day here. My plane leaves early tomorrow, and I'm not finished yet."

"One day might not be enough time. Why don't you call and change your ticket?"

Lee frowned. "All I have left is to buy the carpeting and drapes. Then I'm done and free to go home. That won't leave time for much else today, though."

"But that means we can't spend the day together in San Francisco. How could you miss seeing the city again?" Miriam was a mixture of hurt relative and a Chamber of Commerce commercial.

"It would be such fun for the two of us to spend the day in the city," Miriam continued. "We could play tourist and hit all the hot spots. Of course, I wouldn't want you to get into trouble at work just because of me..."

Although Lee had told the news director that she wasn't sure how long she'd have to be away, she had fully expected to be finished with Miwok in a few days, and go back to work soon after that. She had a two-week vacation coming and had planned to save the remainder of her vacation time for a later date.

She was quite sure Miriam had understood that her job was not a problem. "I don't know why I didn't simply agree to stay a few extra days when you first suggested it," she said.

"You would have saved me a lot of whining," Miriam agreed with a big smile.

"I knew it!"

"Stay through the weekend. You'll enjoy yourself, I promise."

"Hey, *paisan*, what are you doing?"

Tony, crouching over a disassembled tractor mower engine, looked up to see Gene Cantelli strolling into his workshop. "I'm giving this son of a bitch an overhaul." He reattached the socket wrench and went back to work. "It conked out on us again this morning."

Cantelli put his hands in his pockets and gave a low whistle at the parts scattered over the floor. "I think you should give it last rites."

"It'll be humming soon. Like a babe in arms."

"Or a woman."

Tony frowned then gave a hard yank on a lug that had refused to loosen. "Got it."

"Speaking of women..." Cantelli picked up a rag and rubbing some grease off the exhaust.

"Were we?" Tony bent lower and started working on another lug.

"Your friend Lee's quite the dish. Cheryl Stanton brought her into my shop a couple days ago. Too bad you didn't show up. On TV she looks like a cold bitch, but not in person. I was afraid my teeth would fall out the way my mouth hung open around her."

Wearily, Tony stood, straightened his back, then bent backwards to work the kinks out. He ran his arm over his forehead to wipe away the perspiration. His hands and arms were smudged with grease, and he now had a streak of grease on his forehead. "Yeah, when Vic brought home the new saddle he told me you got the royal visit. I didn't know you had a red carpet to roll out."

"I know Vic doesn't care for her, but I'll tell you, she wasn't that way."

"Well, I wouldn't know. I knew her in high school, that's all." He began putting the sockets he'd used back into their case in the proper order.

"That's not the way Vic or Cheryl tell it."

"Then they're both wrong. I'm sure as hell glad I give you guys something to talk about behind my back!"

"Why are you biting my head off?"

Tony faced him. "What's your problem, Cantelli?"

"My problem?" The older man chortled, and folded his arms across his broad chest as he regarded Tony, a wide, provocative smile spread under his thick mustache. "I'm not the one with something gnawing at my gut. Go see her, talk to her. Here's your chance to get whatever's bothering you out in the open."

"Hell, Gene, it's nothing like that." Tony offered him a bottle of warm Gatorade. When Gene shook it off, he opened it for himself and took a long draught. It took him a moment before he was willing to talk, to try to explain. "Sometimes when you hear about someone, old memories pop into your head. They don't mean anything anymore, but you can't help it. The past's long gone. I don't even know this Lisa, or 'Lee,' Reynolds. The girl I knew died years ago."

"What do you mean?" Gene's smile faded.

He relaxed against a tall workbench filled with tools and parts. "She changed, almost over night. She left town and never came back. Before I knew what happened, Lisa was gone and this Lee character was in her place. Lisa's as good as dead for me. Either way, she doesn't exist."

"Maybe the old Lisa isn't as dead as you think. See her and judge for yourself. She played nonchalant, but I noticed the way she looked at your pictures, and I saw her expression when I mentioned that we were friends."

"It doesn't matter, Gino."

Gene stood in the workshop doorway, eyeing his friend's son, then lit himself a cigarette, letting the smoke billow outdoors. "Are you afraid to see her?"

"Let it go," Tony warned.

"All the years I've known you, I've known there

was something about Lee Reynolds and you—some unfinished business that still bothered you. Now's your chance to get whatever it is over with. Resolve it and put it aside once and for all."

Tony put down his drink, then rubbed his brow. "It's not worth it."

Gene gave him a long look. "Isn't it? I remember listening to you talk to Ben one day after a baseball game. It was a game where he made about four errors, including dropping a pop-fly that let the other team score the winning run. He wanted to quit and never play ball again. You told him he had to go out there and play the next game. That nothing was so bad as running away. Face it, get it over with and go on. You should take your own advice, Tony."

"This is different, Gene. No way—"

"Dad! Where are you?"

Tony looked through the window and saw Ben standing outside the house calling for him. He went to the door to the workshop. "I'm in here, Ben."

Ben came running. "Billy's mother gave me and Josh a ride home. But she got mad and said we were making too much noise—Oh, hi Gene. What're you guys doing?" He walked over to the once-upon-a-time motor. "Uh oh."

Cantelli snickered.

Tony wiped some grease off his fingers with a blackened rag. "I'm fixing it. Don't worry. It'll work."

"But what's Grandpa going to do in the meantime?"

"You keep bugging me and I'll make you ride around with Billy's mother some more."

"Oh, no!"

"Actually," Cantelli said, "I've seen Billy's mother. I wouldn't mind a ride with her myself."

"She's a terrible driver," Ben said.

Gene and Tony glanced at each other. Gene laughed, and Tony picked up a wrench to begin attacking the motor once again.

"I'm going to go see Grandpa," Ben shouted as he bounded out the door.

"See you later, Ben," Gene said as Ben waved and ran off.

"Dinner will be in about an hour," Tony called after him. The two men watched him a moment, each remembering when they had been that young and filled with such energy and enthusiasm.

Gene said, "Speaking of women that you need to deal with..."

"Were we?" Tony cocked a sardonic brow at his friend. It seemed to him that Gene had been doing all the talking.

"Any word from his mother?"

Tony's insides churned sickly at the mention of his ex-wife. "Same old garbage." He tried to sound complacent, but failed.

"And?"

He placed both hands on the motor as if needing it to steady himself. "She thinks I'm going to feel sorry for her, but she's wrong. It's taken her eight years to realize she's a mother. Eight years and a rich husband who can't give her any more kids. The hell with her."

"It's tough. In a way, I do feel sorry for her."

"You don't know her." He slammed the palm of his hand against the motor. "God, I hate what she's doing! Ben deserves to be more than a substitute for what she can't have."

"She still asking for joint custody?"

Tony shut his eyes tight, trying to ward off the nausea that threatened whenever he thought of losing his son. "That's what her lawyer calls it. But they expect Ben to live with her." He yanked a bolt free, and it flew from the wrench across the workshop. "No one's taking Ben away from me, Gene. No one."

Gene nodded, then ground out his cigarette and picked up another wrench to help.

Lee drove straight to the city without bothering to shop for carpets or drapes along the way. Her heart simply wasn't in it. Once she'd given in—in the long run, what did three more days matter?—she found that, like Miriam, she wanted to see the familiar sights.

A few of the spots, like Coit Tower and the Palace of Fine Arts, were places Miriam had gone to with her husband, Patrick Dailey. Patrick had been a black-haired, blue-eyed man of Irish descent. He had flown reconnaissance missions off an aircraft carrier over the Arabian peninsula. Miriam still kept his picture by her bedside, and each night, she'd once admitted to Lee, she still whispered goodnight to him, just as she did when he first went into the service. He'd been shot down and was listed as missing-in-action. As the years passed, and the fear he wasn't ever coming home became a reality, she had become used to being alone. She had thought of remarrying, but every man she met fell short of the one she'd lost. Finally, she'd come to accept that Patrick was the only man she would ever love, and the only one she would ever want to love.

They drove through Chinatown and Fisherman's Wharf in San Francisco, ate an early dinner at an Italian restaurant in North Beach, then went home exhausted but sated. Lee had almost forgotten how beautiful the area was. Now, seeing it again through Miriam's eyes, made it all the lovelier.

About nine o'clock that evening, Miriam had just finished making some tea when the doorbell rang. Lee flipped on the porch light, then opened the door.

Cheryl stood in front of her. "Hi. I hope I'm not interrupting anything."

"Not at all. Come in."

"Actually, I was wondering if you could come out. I just had a huge fight with Mark. I thought I'd stay away from home for a couple of hours so he'll appreciate me better when I go back. Right now, I was heading over to Big Bob's for a hot fudge sundae. I was hoping you could join me. Nothing makes me feel better after a fight than something sweet from Big Bob's."

"Oh...well..." Lee thought Cheryl looked remarkably calm for someone who just had a big fight with her husband. She wondered if Cheryl fought with him often. Maybe that passed for entertainment in Miwok?

"Come on, Lisa. Remember how we used to cry on each other's shoulders? I could use a shoulder right now. I really could."

Cheryl was right. They'd always been there for each other when they were growing up. Anyway, she had nothing better to do tonight. "Why don't you say hi to Miriam while I grab my purse. She's in the family room. I know she'd love to see you again."

Cheryl got them to the restaurant in no time flat. She and Lee sat in Big Bob's parking lot talking of trivial things. Cheryl rambled from one object to another, apparently in no hurry to go inside, and Lee was content to follow her lead, her usual self-restraint standing her in good stead. A jeep pulled into the lot. "We'd better go in," Cheryl said abruptly. "No sense having others ahead of us in line."

Lee looked around at the few cars in the lot. What line? Cheryl's behavior seemed very peculiar. "Sure," she said as they got out of the car. "By the way, I'm not leaving tomorrow after all. Miriam convinced me to stay until Monday."

Cheryl's eyes lit up. "Hey, that makes it even better!"

"What's better?" Lee asked, but Cheryl was walking fast and she had to hurry to catch up.

Just inside the entrance was a large waiting area with benches, cigarette machines, telephones and rest rooms. Cheryl stopped at the cigarette machine.

"I didn't know you smoked," Lee said.

"Only when I'm nervous. Or upset. Like now. The fight with Mark, you know."

"Of course." Lee glanced at the tables beyond the cashier as she waited for Cheryl to find the right change for the machine.

"Oh my, look who's here." Cheryl's voice rang out.

Lee spun around.

Tony Santos stood in front of her, his dark brown eyes intense and questioning as if he were as shocked by the encounter as she. The air squeezed out of her lungs then seemed to rush through her, stronger than before, vibrant and alive.

Her gaze passed over him quickly, absorbing everything that she could. He wore a cream-colored mohair pullover, with drop shoulders and wide, loose sleeves over a yellow oxford shirt. His trousers were brown, as were his loafers. The boy in sweat shirts and denims was gone, and in his place was this handsome man, this stranger.

A husband and a father now.

Her gaze lifted to his and held. She couldn't stop herself from studying his face. His eyes were still the dark, deep pools that carried a hint of the Aztec, his butternut skin smooth except for faint crow's feet at the corners of eyes framed with long, black eyelashes and arched brows. His nose was high, straight and proud, and a few strands of gray brushed the temples of straight black hair, neatly trimmed. He used to be reed thin which made his elbows and knees pronounced; even his feet had seemed too big for him. He'd grown nicely into his body. He was broader and thicker now, but still, everything about his carriage announced the sleek, well-honed strength of an athlete.

Tony felt his mouth go dry as he watched the look of surprise, then pleasure, then caution fill her large, expressive eyes. He could always read her thoughts in those light blue eyes. The remembrance was a bolt from the past.

He took in everything about her in an instant. When he was last with her, she was a lovely eighteen-year-old, but before him now was a mature, beautiful woman. Soft, supple teen-age curves had given way to a womanliness that took his breath away. Even wearing casual slacks and a blouse, she dripped elegance and sophistication so out of place in Big Bob's he would have laughed had she been anyone but Lisa.

He noticed that the freckles on her nose were gone, as was the fullness in her cheeks. Her cheekbones were pronounced now, the skin taut around them, and so smooth and translucent it seemed like fine china. Her mouth was still as kissable as he remembered, the lower lip a little fuller than the upper, giving her a pouty look that belied her untouchable, cool image. He had been the first man to kiss her and he still remembered the taste of her on his lips. He had been the first man to make love to her, and those memories, too, hit him with the force of a hurricane.

He stared, far too long as the pleasure in seeing her again mixed with the aching hurt that he thought had died long ago. Only now, he learned it hadn't.

For no reason she could explain, she stepped closer. She had spent every day since her return to Miwok trying not to think about him, trying not to remember the past. But it had caught up to her. Tony was here. Years had passed, but the intimacy they once shared surrounded them with memories and neither seemed to quite know what to say or do.

"What a surprise!" Gene Cantelli said, a little too forced, a little too loudly. "Why don't we get a table together?" he suggested.

"Sounds great," Cheryl immediately answered. "Excuse me a minute, though. I've got to find the ladies' room."

Gene, too, backed away. "I want to get a newspaper. I'll be right back."

"Gene!" Tony made a move toward him.

"One minute, *paisan*, that's all." Gene tossed the words casually over his shoulder and left, whistling jauntily.

Tony and Lee stood watching their departing friends.

Cheryl and Gene should be horse-whipped for this stunt, Lee thought. With a sigh, she faced Tony.

"Well," she said finally, her voice breathless.

"Hello." With a jerking, too fast motion, she stuck out her hand.

He looked surprised, then gripped it hard, too hard. "Lisa," he answered.

She was aware that his hands were broader now, with a sprinkling of hair on his fingers. They were a man's hands, strong and solid. He was aware that her hands were slimmer than those of the girl he knew and had the creamy softness and perfect nails of a woman who knew the luxury of a pampered life.

They dropped their hands as if burned.

He spoke. "I hope you don't mind Gene saying we should join you." *God, what a dumb thing to say. Right out of the tenth grade.* He put his thumbs in his pockets and rocked back on his heels.

It was a sweetly familiar gesture to Lee. Years ago, Tony had never been one to stand still, and it seemed that characteristic continued. "It's fine," she said, annoyed that she sounded somewhat breathless, and even more annoyed that she *felt* somewhat breathless. What was wrong with her?

She searched his face. His eyes were more wary than when they were young. She wondered what had put the wariness there. After a struggle, she found her voice. "I guess we may as well sit...." What had happened to the smooth, eloquent Lee

Reynolds who had boldly interviewed Presidents and Prime Ministers?

They sat perched on the edge of the foyer bench, both ready to jump up and flee at a moment's notice. The silence grew.

They both began to speak at once, then stopped abruptly, eyeing each other with patent embarrassment and yet amazement to find themselves side by side again. There should have been enough between them to laugh at this; but instead they found there was too much. Still too much.

"You first," Tony said. His voice was like sand, hers smooth as quicksilver.

"All I was going to say was that I'd hoped to get a chance to say hello to you before I left." There was so much she wanted to say, but she didn't know where to begin. She could discuss the news in front of strangers on national television, but she couldn't say "Tell me how your life has been" to one man right beside her, the one man who had once been the world to her.

"I meant to call you as well, to see about coming over to give my condolences...." He leaned forward, legs wide, arms on thighs, his hands clasped. He stared straight ahead.

"You never used to call first."

He froze, his back visibly stiffening, and she cursed the flush heating her face. Why she had said that? Why she had brought up the intimacy of the past? His expression, when he turned to her, was serious, as if he couldn't let himself smile. "I couldn't believe it was you at my son's game on Sunday," he said quietly. "I thought I was dreaming."

Her eyes never left him. Her heart and mind whirled with the force of his presence, and she wanted more than anything to just look at him. To take in everything about him that was the same, and all that was different. Still handsome. Still exciting. *Her Tony.* But he wasn't her Tony anymore, and she dropped her gaze. "Being back, it is almost like a dream." She looked up. "But you know I love baseball."

He relaxed and let his hands hang loose between his legs. "Heck, that's not baseball. It's Little League."

She smiled then, without restraint or defense. *You always knew how to make me smile, Tony.*

He sat upright, his spine against the backrest of the bench. "You should have stayed and watched. We won."

"I had to run. I had to meet Miriam." She was quite sure he didn't believe a word she said. She never could fool Tony. "You have a nice-looking boy."

His face lit up. "His name's Ben. He's a great kid."

"How old is he?"

"Nine."

"Already? My goodness! Any more kids?"

"No. No, just the one."

"Ah." She rubbed her hands together and looked around, avoiding his eyes, fighting the piercing emptiness, the aching hurt, that threatened to over-whelm her. Somehow, she would get through this. Where was Cheryl? "You and your wife must be very proud of him."

He folded his hands again. He used to say he had "soft" hands, and that's what made him such a good fielder. She saw nothing soft about them.

"I'm divorced."

She raised her eyes, surprised, and yet half-ex-pecting something like that to explain Gene and Cheryl wanting the two of them to meet. "I'm sorry," she murmured.

"It happened a long time ago. How about you? Did you marry?"

She shook her head quickly, her gaze cap-turing the door, tables, the waitress, anything but him. "Never could fit it into my schedule, it seemed."

He rested an elbow on the back of the bench. "Must be hell being a rich, famous TV star."

His arm nearly touched her. She sat forward, putting her palms on the edge of the seat, her fingers curled under it. "Doing news is hardly stardom."

"Close enough. The way you're going, you'll end up owning the network if I know you, Lisa."

She felt his eyes measuring her. "Thank you."

"It's what you always wanted." He tried to force a harshness to his voice, but it sounded almost wistful to his ear.

She took a deep breath. Some emotion, long dormant and hidden deep within her, was responding to him in a way she recognized as dangerous. "So, what are you doing these days?" She tried to sound upbeat and casual, and failed miserably.

Over the years since she left him, he imagined himself telling her all he had done with his life, all he had accomplished. Now, though, it didn't seem so significant. "I own the Circle Z."

Her mouth dropped open. "You own it? You're kidding."

"No." He glanced at her wondering if he should say more, then dropped his gaze as he spoke. "I grew up thinking horse ranches were boring and dumb. A few years ago, my dad told me the owners were going to put the place up for sale and I realized it was home—more home than I'd ever known. I didn't want some stranger to buy it."

"You were able to buy that entire ranch? That's wonderful! Good for you."

Back in the days when he still thought about Lisa, he used to wonder why she broke off their relationship so suddenly, so hurtfully. He'd racked his brain for an answer, and finally decided it must have been because, while she was ambitious, talented and driven, he was a nobody, and she expected that was all he would ever be.

Her reaction at learning he had made something of himself was everything he ever dreamed of.

He spoke. "I made a few bucks while I played baseball."

She smiled, and he watched her pale blue eyes sparkle the way they used to do, the way he always loved. "So you *did* play."

He cleared his throat, suddenly aware that gloating over his success didn't give him the satisfaction he had imagined. Her pleasure at learning he had played ball seemed so genuine that to brag about it would have embarrassed him. "I played for a while. Now I raise Arabians on the ranch. Of course, my dad really runs the place. He's the expert. I just pay for it."

She didn't understand his sudden discomfort. "I'd imagine Vic's run every place he's ever worked," she said. "I remember going out to the ranch with you to help your dad exercise the horses. But he never found us much help."

"He'd blow his cork when we'd mess up his

schedule," Tony said, "or give the horses too much sugar." Tony laughed suddenly and, surprising them both, she joined him.

His laughter had a deeper tone than it used to, but still, she liked the sound of it. She always did. Abruptly, their laughter stopped, and they stared at each other. There was danger in laughing, in feeling comfortable, and it struck them both with sudden awareness, washing over them like waves hitting the shore.

"Would you care to be seated now?" a waitress asked.

Their gazes jerked apart, their attention directed toward the waitress, then back again, in silent recognition that Gene and Cheryl were probably both long gone. Tony shrugged. Lee smiled. Both stood and Lee began to follow the waitress.

Tony watched her, but he hung back. He should just leave. He managed to let her know how well he had done without her, so what more was there to say? He should go home, and on the way, stop off at Gino's house and kill him...

But instead of leaving, he followed Lisa. The waitress led them to a booth. Lisa sat on one side, he on the other. He opened the menu the waitress handed him, but Lisa left hers shut. "Just coffee for me," she said. "Black."

He ordered the same.

"Sure you're not hungry?" she asked, realizing he and Gene might have come here to eat.

"No. Gene was the one who was hungry."

Her lips curved in a slow smile that hit him like a Roger Clemens fast ball. The smile was so damned sexy, so provocative, it burned in his gut. "Cheryl was the one who told me she needed a shoulder to cry on about her marital woes," Lee said.

Tony's eyes widened. "You're kidding?"

"No." She grinned. "She even told me about the hot fudge sundae she planned to eat."

"She always did love chocolate."

"She wasn't the only one," Lee said, eyeing him knowingly, a dumb smile stuck on her face. She wasn't able to stop it. "Remember how we'd have a root beer float at my house almost every day after school?"

"Hey, that's right. When we used Mint Chocolate Chip, the green ice cream turned the root beer a sick gray." He grimaced.

"And all the chocolate chips sank to the bottom of the glass and clumped together."

They laughed. Tony's smile faded as he gazed at her, then he held up his water glass for a toast. "To old times."

As she clinked her glass against his, long-buried emotions leaped to the surface with a force she wasn't prepared for, and her words became a whisper. "Old times."

The waitress brought their coffee.

Both leaned toward the center of the small table as they slowly drank their coffee and talked. He was so close, she breathed in everything about him. Although he wore his hair much shorter now, and it had become a bit coarser, it was still shiny and meticulously groomed. She liked the style it was cut in, brushed to the side and back in a smooth, sleek line, the front lightly shadowing his forehead. His clothes were meticulous too. Even when they were kids and he wore blue jeans, they were always spotless and fit perfectly, so different from the usual teenage sloppiness.

Lee talked about how she had driven around Miwok, and how she had joined Cheryl and a bunch of the girls for dinner. Tony talked about the guys he kept in contact with in Miwok, as well as those who had moved away. Neither of them volunteered any further information about themselves, and neither asked any more questions.

Tony put his empty cup on the table and straightened. "I guess we've waited long enough. It seems we've been abandoned. Do you have a car?"

"No. Cheryl drove me."

Tony shook his head. "They thought of everything! I drove Gene in my Jeep. How would you like a ride home?"

"I'd appreciate that. Never was good at hitchhiking."

"With those legs?" He dropped a tip on the table. It was the first reference he made to her looks, and she rewarded him with a tentative glance and rosy cheeks. He hadn't intended to say it, but he had noticed those long shapely legs when he first saw her at the baseball field, when he saw her again only minutes earlier at the restaurant entry, and when he followed her to the booth. Hell, he noticed everything about her.

Lee walked with him to the cashier. She was a tall woman, but she looked up to him. He must have been about 6'1" or 6'2", taller than when she knew him. He kept growing after high school, she thought, suddenly realizing there was yet another change, another thing she had missed.

They climbed into his Jeep Cherokee. The ride to her house was short. Five minutes or less. It felt strange sitting in a car with Tony again. She remembered his big Bonneville far too well and being with him "making out" in it. It was so innocent, yet so sweet, just remembering made her throat seem to thicken.

She scarcely breathed until they reached her house. He walked her to the familiar front door.

Sometimes Tony used to feel more at home at Lisa's than in the cottage he shared with his father. Since her mother didn't get home from work until five-thirty or so, he would go to her house after school to eat, listen to music, talk, do homework, or just hang out.

Now, she unlocked the door and pushed it open, then glanced up at him to say goodnight.

But Tony looked past her shoulder to the doorway. Lee turned to find Miriam entering the foyer. She stepped inside, Tony following. Suddenly she found herself speaking words that were years overdue. "Aunt Miriam, this is Tony Santos. Tony, my aunt, Miriam Dailey."

Miriam's eyes never left his face as she walked up to him, her hand outstretched. "So you're Tony. It's about time you got here."

He stared in surprise, not knowing how to respond, as they shook hands.

Lee said, "What?"

Miriam's gaze seemed to drill through him, to his soul. "It wouldn't have been right for Lisa to finally return to Miwok and not see you."

"We have a couple of friends who agree with you," Tony said with a grin.

"Oh, I know all about that." Miriam chuckled.

Unflappable, cool Lee Reynolds actually looked sheepish. "You're kidding me."

"Not at all."

Tony shifted uncomfortably under her scrutiny. "I remember hearing about you," he said. "Lisa always told me how much she missed you after you moved away."

"Did she?" Miriam glanced at her niece. "I'm glad to hear it."

"It was no secret, Miriam," Lee protested.

Miriam continued to study Tony. "Would you like some tea? The water's still hot. Or perhaps a Coke, or beer?"

"No, thanks. I was just dropping Lisa off. We had coffee."

"Stay awhile, if you have time." She glanced pointedly at Lee. "I'm sure you two have a lot to talk about, and I was just heading upstairs to bed." As she again turned toward Tony, her face softened into a smile. "I'm so glad I finally got to meet you."

Tony felt her sincerity like a kick in the stomach. The last thing he wanted was to warm to "Lee" Reynolds's aunt. "I'm glad to have met you, too."

Miriam lightly touched his arm, then went upstairs. Lee couldn't stop staring at her aunt in surprise.

Tony, too, took a moment to regroup. "Your aunt is a very nice woman."

"She is," she said.

He stepped toward the front door, then turned

to face her. *Just go,* he told himself. "I heard you're leaving tomorrow."

The spicy scent of his Old Spice after-shave enveloped her—the same, simple scent he used to wear to school dances and parties. She had heard it said that smell was the sense that brought back the strongest memories, and with the scent of the after-shave, she remembered again being at dances with Tony, and at parties when the lights were turned low, and the night of the senior prom....

She never would have believed she could remember what Tony Santos *smelled* like, for God's sake. But she did.

She rubbed her forehead, doing all she could to avoid meeting his eyes. There was no reason she should feel so physically aware of him, not now, not after so many years. Obviously, it was simply a sentimental reaction to...other things. To all that had happened after she left Miwok.

They weren't kids anymore, there had been other men in her life, and now there was Bruce. She had no reason to let her feelings get out of control around Tony, and one very big reason not to.

"I'll be here until Monday," she said. "It's a bit more complicated than I imagined getting the house ready to sell."

"You are planning to sell it, then?"

"Yes."

He clamped his lips together as his gaze took in the entry hall, the stairs to the right, the family room straight ahead, the living room to the left. It was all so familiar. How had he spent so many years without thinking about those days, so many years allowing himself to forget?

He turned back to Lisa. He had expected to dislike the person she was now, or at least to be indifferent. But he found too much of the old Lisa existed inside the cool, sophisticated façade, and she made him remember too much that he'd rather forget. "I'm glad I saw you tonight," he admitted, then grinned. "Even if it was a set-up."

For a moment, he thought she wouldn't reply. But then she said softly, "Me, too."

Her cell phone rang. She pulled it from her purse, then looked from the phone to Tony. "I'll let myself out," he said.

"Wait." She picked it up. "Hello?...Bruce...Bru...excuse me, Bruce, I can't talk right now. I've got company. They're just leaving. I'll call you in a few minutes, okay?"

Tony's attention perked up at the "they" he had become, and that told him everything he cared to know about Lee's relationship with this Bruce. He pulled open the door.

She turned off the phone. "I'm sorry. A friend from New York."

"A good friend, I take it."

"Yes," she whispered.

"I see." He nodded. "Good, that's good. Well..."

All her caution and self-preservation seemed to have vanished along with her common sense. "Since I'll be in Miwok a few more days, will your team be playing anymore Little League games?"

His expression showed surprise, but then he smiled. Her heart skittered, and she moved closer to him. "We have one tomorrow at four-thirty," he said, his body straining toward her.

"Okay." Her voice was a whisper.

Their eyes met and held, his hand still resting on the doorknob as neither moved and both wondered what this strange feeling was between them. Was it simply nostalgia, two people rushing toward middle age and grabbing at the feelings of their youth, or—heaven help them—something more?

He wondered why she'd asked about a game.

She wondered why she'd said, "Okay."

He frowned as he stepped onto the front porch. What did it matter about the new Lee or the old Lisa? Once she left Miwok this time, she was never coming back. Once, he had tried to convince her to stay with him, and she refused in no uncertain terms.

He turned to face her, just to say goodnight, and the memory flashed before him of how he always used to turn around and kiss her as he left her house. The wide-eyed way she looked at him made him realize she remembered too.

But he held himself back.

"Take care of yourself, Lisa."

She soaked in his nearness, a sudden tightness in her throat. "You, too, Tony....And Tony?"

"Yes?"

"Thanks for the coffee."

"Goodbye, Lisa," he said, then turned and, hands in pockets, walked down the porch steps into the darkness.

"I want your body right here, right now." Bruce's voice purred over the phone. "I want to touch every beautiful part of it—and I want you to touch me. I can almost feel your hands, your mouth...I want to make love to you so bad, Lee..."

"Bruce, listen—"

"I can hardly wait until tomorrow night—"

"Bruce, I'm staying a few more days."

Silence. "Staying? You're kidding. You promised you'd be at my side for Baldwin's dinner party next week. I can't show up alone, and I sure don't want to find someone else to take."

She was stunned by his petulant complaint. He

hadn't asked why she was staying, how she felt, or even if the house was ready to be turned over to a realtor. "I'm sorry, but this is a bit more important than a dinner with Baldwin."

He sighed loudly. "You're right, Lee. I'm just upset that this is taking you so long, that's all."

"I refuse to tell my aunt I won't set things up properly because my ambitious boyfriend wants to show me off in New York."

"Relax, Lee. I'm doing this for both of us, remember?"

The shock in his voice was evident to her, but she couldn't stop herself from saying, "Maybe I should catch the red-eye right now."

"Don't get worked up. It's just that I miss you so much. I need you. I'm sorry, Lee." His voice was hurt and a little boyish, and the combination pulled her up short, making her feel even worse about the ugly way she was treating him.

She took a deep breath. "Bruce, I didn't mean to be sarcastic. I'll be leaving here Monday, so the dinner party isn't a problem."

"Thank goodness! I should have known you wouldn't let me down. I also know you wouldn't put up with that small hick town any longer than absolutely necessary. Too bad you aren't in L.A. I'd probably be with you if you were. But a small town in the north? I hear it's all cows and horses. Not even wineries where you are, right?"

"That's right, Bruce. Just me and the chickens."

"Good God! And I'll bet the people there make the cows and horses seem interesting. I mean, what can you possibly talk to them about? They probably don't know Hesse from Dinesen, Miro from Matisse, Schoenberg from Stockhausen."

"You'd hate it here," she said. "It's good you refused to come with me." The words were out of her mouth before she remembered she was trying to soothe his ruffled feathers.

"I didn't really refuse." His tone was icy. "It's just that the timing was particularly bad for me."

"I know. Poor choice of words."

"From you, Lee?"

She sighed. "I'm tired. This has all been more upsetting than I ever imagined. Coming back here has stirred up a lot of memories and some...well, some are difficult to deal with. I'll be home just as soon as I'm able."

"I can't imagine anything being difficult for you."

"I'm not Wonder Woman."

"Close enough. But it is boring there, right? No old high school boyfriends or muscular tow-headed surfers to sweep you off your feet?"

"I always told you I hated high school! Anyway,

this is *northern* California, Bruce. The Pacific is cold up here."

"Well, okay, then. I trust you, you know. Good night, Lee."

"Good night."

She stared at the phone a long time after hanging up.

NINE

Miriam was up early, made coffee, then mixed together muffin batter, just as she used to do when Lisa stayed with her in her little house in San Diego after leaving Miwok. Miriam knew she was going overboard with the nostalgia and poor ol' aunt routine, but she couldn't think of a better way to get Lisa to stay in Miwok long enough to face up to all that had happened seventeen summers ago and finally, one way or the other, put it behind her.

Lisa had fled Miwok to live with Miriam the summer after graduating from high school. Although Lisa had received a scholarship to UCLA, she switched to the University of California at San Diego to stay with Miriam. The girl threw herself into her schoolwork, making it her shelter and haven from the world.

The four years Lisa spent with Miriam were among the most wonderful and heartbreaking of her life. Early on, the girl needed her, leaning on her for support and at times asking for more than Miriam thought she had in her to give. Somehow, they made it through those days, and as the years went by, Lisa blossomed, and Miriam's heart swelled with pride.

In college, Lisa's interest in journalism developed. She had brought a passion and intellect to her reporting that brought her quick success with her instructors. She soon learned to present herself as a poised, self-assured woman no matter how inwardly nervous she might have been.

After graduation, Miriam saw that Lisa no longer had the time to spend long summer vacations and holidays with her. Although intellectually, she accepted it, it hurt her to watch Lisa grow apart from her. Miriam felt she did nothing but say goodbye to people she loved—her husband, her brother, and then her niece.

At least now, here in Miwok, they had a week together once more. Most people who lived alone reached a point where they disliked spending time around other people. Miriam wasn't that way. Nothing would have made her happier than to have Lisa settle down, raise children, and live near her.

But it looked like such a close-knit life was only for other families. Not for her. Not for Lisa.

Miriam filled muffin tins with batter and when she heard Lisa turn off the upstairs shower, she put the tins into a hot oven.

"Those muffins smell delicious, just like when I was in San Diego with you," Lee said a while later as she stepped into the kitchen in her bathrobe. "What a great way to wake up."

The oven bell dinged. "Perfect timing." Miriam took the muffins out of the oven and put them on the table.

Lee poured them each a cup of coffee then broke a hot muffin in half and smeared it with butter. Miriam did the same.

"I've missed these," Lee murmured between bites.

"I've missed having you around to make them for."

"If I were nearby, I'd grow so fat no one would want me on TV anymore." Lee touched her aunt's hand with affection. "I'd better stay in New York."

"I understand I don't have the allure New York does for you—national television and a handsome young man. I suppose you two will be marrying soon?"

Lee smiled. "That wasn't very subtle, Miriam."

"I'm not subtle where your happiness is concerned."

Lee's eyes met her aunt's a moment, then she took the coffeepot and refilled their cups.

I love you, Lisa.

She could still remember the exact timbre of his voice, surprisingly soft, yet rich, with a slight huskiness. His eyes had simmered as he spoke those words, and his arms, holding her, had trembled.

They had been so young...too young...but still....

She shook her head and concentrated on the job before her. The garage was stacked with boxes filled with junk—old tools, unused appliances, Christmas ornaments, lights...

I don't want to see you with that boy anymore, Lisa. He's wrong for you in every way—background, class, religion... race.... Wild boys like him only want one thing from a girl.

Don't you talk back to me, Lisa Marie! I know what I'm saying. You're too innocent. I protected you too much. I'm trying to raise you in a way that would have made your daddy proud. But this disappoints me. If only you knew how it tears at my heart when you're with him! If only you'd stop seeing him, Lisa,

I'd feel so much better. I could be proud of you again...

Lee's hand shook as she ran it over her brow. She picked up used paintbrushes and rollers and threw them in the trash bag. Why had Judith kept so much junk? She tried to think about what she was doing, only about what she was doing....

I can't see you anymore, Tony.

She remembered forcing out those words to him very early in their relationship, when they were still juniors, and she thought she could turn love on and off like a spigot. Judith had ordered her to stop seeing him, and she was young enough, then, that she foolishly had tried to comply.

I can't see you anymore, Tony.

Why? Is there someone else?

No! My mother doesn't want me to...to see any-one. I have to think about college, to prepare myself—

College is a long way off. Anyway, we're none of her damn business!

But we are. At least, I am. I'm all she's got left. Ever since the accident when my father was killed, and her leg...

Don't cry, Lisa.

I'm sorry, Tony.

She rubbed her eyes, not wanting to remember. He had been so young then...and she had been so willing to hurt him because Judith had demanded it.

Do you want to stop seeing me, Lisa?

No! God, no!

Then we'll just make sure your mother doesn't know.

She remembered staring at him in shocked silence. She'd never gone against her mother's wishes.

We'll be careful. She'll never know. Anyway, what can she do about it?

I don't—

Someday, we'll get away from this crummy town, like we both want. We'll make it big, have money, everything we've hoped for. And you know what else, we'll always be together, Lisa.

Tell me again, Tony. Make me believe you.

Always, Lisa.

Always...

Lee cleared the garage and den, throwing away everything but a few old photos of her father. She gave most of them to her aunt.

Cheryl called late the next morning, full of apologies and curiosity about the meeting with Tony. Lee told her all was forgiven, that she and Tony had a nice talk, then said goodbye and that was that. She decided it would be best not to ever mention they had talked about her going to a Little League game. That, she knew, had been spur-of-the-moment inspired folly.

"Well," Cheryl said, "you can't blame me for wanting you two to meet again. You guys had something special together. I don't know what caused the break-up, but I just thought if—as adults—you two talked, you could at least be friends again."

Later that day, Lee made the long delayed journey to the mall stores that sold carpeting and drapery, and selected neutral colors in standard draw drapery and wall-to-wall carpeting that would warm the heart of any realtor.

Miriam had been invited to dinner at a friend's house. "Would you like to come to Rachel's house with me tonight?" she asked.

"I don't think so. I'll just take it easy."

"In that case, why don't you call the Little League office and find out if Tony's team has a game today? And if they do, then go to it." With that, she breezed out the door.

Lee gawked at her. Had it been purely a coincidence that she ended up at Settlers Park on Sunday when Tony's game was being played? Miriam hadn't planned that, had she?

Actually, Lee was ahead of Miriam. She'd already called the League office and learned Tony's team had a four-thirty game. She wanted to go it. Why not do it? She'd seen Tony, talked to him, and her heart, mind and spirit survived quite nicely, thank you very much. Seeing him again made her realize she would always have a lingering fondness for him, a girl's romantic first love feelings, not those of a mature woman. And yet...

In the past, there had been such magic between them. What if it was still there, ready to erupt?

No. She wouldn't go. She walked into the kitchen and opened the refrigerator, then promptly shut it. Eating was not the answer. She walked to the family room and turned on the TV. Two rounds through the channels with the remote told her that wasn't the answer either. She went into the living room and picked up a book, but sat with it unopened. Outside, the grass was green, the sun warm. What was she doing in the house? This was California—nobody stayed indoors here.

Was she afraid to see Tony again? Had he taken on some mystical, mythical force within her psyche that made her see him as much more than he was? He was just a man, an old boyfriend, nothing special. If she couldn't see that now, maybe she'd better get to that game and look at Tony until she *did* realize it.

Placing him on some kind of pedestal was not a healthy thing to do.

She pinned her hair up casually, changed into a natural linen Jil Sander pants suit, a rust-colored silk shell, and ivory colored Ferragamo sandals.

Her spirit buoyed as she walked toward the ballpark. There was a timelessness to baseball, even Little League, that she loved. The games were interesting, and she honestly liked seeing how very much the kids enjoyed themselves.

She searched for Tony as soon as she reached the baseball field and found him pitching batting practice to the boys. He wore jeans and a loose gray sweatshirt with the sleeves cut off above the elbows. As she stepped nearer the field, he turned. The brim of his baseball cap shaded his eyes, but still she could see the quizzical look on his face. This time he lifted his arm high and waved at her. She waved back, smiling.

What the hell are you doing here, Reynolds? Her pulse began to beat a little too fast, and her smile spread a little too wide. *It's not because it's Tony. It's just that there's something about a man in a baseball cap, a devilish, carefree mischievousness that, mixed with athletic male sexiness, is disarmingly appealing.*

She bought a diet Coke then settled in the stands to wait for the game to begin. She noticed people eyeing her. Used to that, she ignored them.

Game time came and went. The coaches and

umpires were huddled together for a long time, and all of them keep looking toward the entrances to the park.

The players and their parents shifted restlessly.

Tony jogged over to the stands and looked up at her. "Lisa, we need you."

Everyone's attention turned to her. Her gaze danced from side to side, hoping against hope that he was addressing some other Lisa. No such luck.

"Please." He held out his hand to her. There wasn't much she could do but go to him.

He took her hand and walked with her to the other coach and umpires as easily as if they had walked hand in hand only yesterday instead of seventeen years ago. "Here she is," he said. "Lisa can do the announcing, if she's willing."

"What?" She gawked at him.

"Our announcer didn't show, and most of the parents get really nervous in front of a mike. But you can handle it easily. Okay?"

"Me?" So much for all her television-trained smoothness and eloquence.

The coach from the other team was an older man, tall, paunchy, with flyaway red hair and small eyes. He squinted as he grimaced at her. "She might know how to use a mike, but does she know baseball?"

"I taught her myself," Tony said.

"Yeah, but do you know it, Santos?" he said with a smirk.

Lee wasn't about to be discussed like some mannequin. "I know baseball." Her firm voice invited no-nonsense.

He put up his hands. "All right, I won't argue, lady." He jabbed a thumb in Tony's direction. "We're gonna cream Santos's team. I just want to make sure you get all our great plays right."

"Stuff it, Snyder," Tony said. "The only reason your team's gonna have a fighting chance is that you're too old to play."

Snyder laughed, and so did Tony. Lee looked from one to the other. She had thought they were on the verge of blows, and now they were laughing. Men! "So give me your line-up cards," she said, "and let's play ball."

She had to admit, announcing the game was fun. Not easy, though. She had to do some very creative thinking not to call almost every play an error on someone. She wondered if the pitchers realized they both pitched no hitters, even though the final score was Panthers 15, Bruins 9? Those walks will kill you every time.

She stepped out of the announcer's booth to

find Ben Santos waiting for her. Her mind whirled and for a moment, she stared at him before she realized what she was doing. She made herself stop and smile. Looking at player stats between innings, she learned he was nine years old and in the fourth grade. He was small for his age, and slender, though his face still had the roundness of a young child. His hair was black like Tony's, but it had a lot of waves to it. His eyes were big and brown, his skin, though olive, was fairer than his father's. He was of an age where his front teeth looked way too big for his mouth, but still, he was a very good-looking boy, so much so that she noticed a group of little fourth-grade girls watching and giggling over him. Oh, those Santos men.

His uniform was smudged and stained, but his face wore a big, proud grin. "I know you," he said.

That surprised her. "Do you watch Evening Newscene?"

Her question seemed to confuse him. "No. My dad's got a picture of you in his den."

Her breath caught, then she smiled at him, cool and polished, as if his words didn't mean a thing to her. "Well, I know you, too. You're Ben Santos, a very good baseball player."

"That's right." His face lit up just the same as she'd seen his father's do time and again. "My dad said I shouldn't let you go home until you go over and see him."

How arrogant of him! "Is that so?"

"Yeah. But he said I shouldn't make you mad. That didn't make you mad, did it?"

Her mouth tightened. "No, Ben. Not at all." She walked with Ben until Tony came into view, then Ben ran to join his father. Tony had gathered the team together and was giving them a talk about the game, praising good plays, instructing how to remedy bad ones, and making the kids feel good about themselves and their team. Her irritation vanished.

Shoulders square, back stiff, she waited. Before long, the boys were released. With whoops and hollers they charged off to their awaiting parents.

Tony turned around, as if searching, and stopped when he saw her standing by the fence. He grinned as he approached. "I was afraid you'd hurry off," he said, stopping in front of her, hands on hips. "I wanted to thank you for announcing. I figured Miwok ought to get some benefit from all that talent."

"Actually, I enjoyed it."

One eyebrow lifted skeptically.

"Hey, you two," Snyder called. "Pizza time. Come and join us, Lisa. You weren't half-bad. Maybe you'll do it again sometime?"

She nearly choked. "Unfortunately, I'm leaving town soon."

"Too bad." Snyder waved and hurried off with his team.

As Ben joined them, Tony lifted the duffel bag with bats and balls onto his back, then draped his free arm around Ben's narrow shoulders as they started walking off the field. She'd forgotten how easily Tony touched people.

Tony said, "We can understand if you don't want to join us. I doubt a 'pizza supreme' sounds like the kind of thing you'd want to eat."

"Tell her the place has video games, Dad," Ben said, then spun in front of Lee and started walking backwards. "They're great, Lisa."

"Oh?" she said, unable to contain a wide smile as she watched him."Do you play?" Tony asked. "Watch where you're going, Ben."

"I've never tried," she replied.

"Then you got to come," Ben shouted, jumping up and down in excitement. "I can show you a whole bunch of neat games, okay?"

She glanced at Tony, then her eyes lingered on Ben. "How can I refuse such an offer?"

"All right!" Ben threw both arms in the air like Joe Montana after a touchdown. God, where had that image come from, she wondered? Now she was even remembering old northern California sports scenes, and she didn't even like sports. Or, not anymore.

As they walked along, her gaze kept veering toward the man she used to know so well, and to his son, who greeted her with such openness and warmth. Ben was very much the way Tony used to be, open, curious, warm and friendly. Inexplicably, her heart felt heavy.

Ben must have felt her staring at him because he suddenly turned her way. "Are you really on TV?"

"Yes, I am."

"Wow, neat!" He ran ahead to the parking lot.

The Pizza Palace was the place to go if you were a Little Leaguer. It crawled with little boys in uniforms. Tony led Lee to the side of the Palace that had three enormous television monitors, each broadcasting a different game—the Giants on one, the A's on another, and a tennis championship on the third.

The video games were on the other side of the Palace, and Tony gave Ben two dollars to play them while their pizza was being prepared. Ben left, but immediately came back.

"I promised Lisa, Dad."

Tony looked at her. "She might want to eat first."

The thought of sitting alone with Tony was disquieting. "Now is fine. Let's go, Ben."

"Wait, son." Tony exchanged the two dollar bills for a fiver. "You'll need a few tokens—and Lisa will need a whole lot of them."

"Yeah, she probably will."

Lee gave them both a "That's what you think" look and followed Ben to the token machine.

Tony sat with his elbows on the tabletop, watching the two of them make their way through the crowd. She was as puzzling to him as ever. Lee Reynolds had the reputation of being one of the sharpest interviewers on TV. She did her homework well, went for the political jugular and her interviews had made a shambles of more than one career. He wasn't surprised. Even in high school she had drive, sharpness, an edge to her that made people take notice...and be wary. Yet, she showed up at two Little League games and came to a pizza parlor. He was afraid to speculate on why, but the attraction that had glued him to her side when they were teens still sparked between them, like kindling ready to ignite. It was still there...amazingly, wonderfully, frighteningly.

There was a cool control about her now, an odd formality that spoke of experience and poise, yet was provocatively seductive. Once she had been all

freshness and promise, but now she was changed—
much more a challenge, much more a woman. He
recognized her defenses because they mirrored his
own, and the hell of it was, they only made him
want to be with her that much more.

Christ, but he must have been an arrogant cuss
when he was young to think an intelligent, sophisticated woman like that would want to stay with him.
Even his wife had left him, and compared to Lisa,
she was nothing. He snorted. That was the problem
with their marriage. He had always compared her to
Lisa, and she had always come up short. His failed
marriage to Catherine had been as much his fault as
hers. Probably more.

He had been a fool about Lisa once. And she
had stripped him of everything—his pride, his self-
esteem, his very manhood. He had given her his
heart and soul, and she had turned her back on him.
He would never forgive her for that, as much as she
might charm him now. He was older, wiser. And he
wouldn't make the same mistake about her twice.

Still, she was the most beautiful thing on two
legs. And her baby blues, he feared, could still tie
him up in knots faster than a Cy Young winner
could pitch one over the plate.

He hated the confused way she made him feel.

A good half-hour after ordering the pizza, Tony
heard his name called over the loudspeaker to pick

up his order. The Palace liked its customers to have plenty of time to lose money on video games before they ate. He went in search of Ben and Lisa.

Lee was a study in concentration as she tried to get a little plumber to make his way through some sewers without getting killed by the monsters lurking within them.

"She's pretty good, Dad," Ben said.

At the words, she looked up, and flashed Tony a warm, radiant smile that snagged his breath. Suddenly it was as if the clang and cling and buzz of the electronic games were being played right in his head. "I don't have a clue what I'm doing," she said, facing the video screen again. "But Ben knows all about it."

"Jump!" Ben yelled.

Lee pushed the jump button and the little plumber leaped safely over a hole in the earth.

"All right!" Tony and Ben cheered.

She was so pleased, she eased up on the controls, immediately allowing a whirling dervish to plow into the plumber and blow him to smithereens.

"Oh, no!" Ben cried.

Lee stepped back from the controls. "Silly game," she muttered, her lips pursed as she glared at the screen. "One more try." She dropped another token into the slot.

Tony and Ben's eyes met, and they laughed.

Tony drove Lee back to the parking lot at Settler's Park. Ben had crawled onto the backseat. Lee sat at Tony's side, cocooned in the warmth of his big SUV. It was filled with sports gear, tack, and ranch tools, and smelled of earth, sweat and sunshine. When Tony pulled into the lot and stopped beside her Cadillac, she turned, peering between the bucket seats, to say goodnight to Ben. He was stretched out on the back seat, fast asleep, his baseball cap still on his head. He looked little, and completely angelic. She had spent enough time with him that evening to know he was no angel. He kept Tony hopping, not because he was bad—he wasn't—but he was all boy, full of energy, curiosity and fun. She cocked her head and kept looking at him, feeling a deep, wrenching tug at her heart as she did so.

"He had a busy day," Tony said softly. Turning like Lee, he, too, peered between the front bucket seats rather than trying to look over the headrests. His head moved close to hers, so close her skin tingled.

"He's a fine boy, Tony," she whispered.

"He is." Her gaze shift from Ben to him, and she

could see the pride in his eyes. Quickly, awkwardly, as if realizing they were too close, he straightened, sitting back away from her. Her chest tightened.

Tony got out of the Jeep and walked around it to open the door for her. He'd left his own door ajar and closed hers softly so that Ben wouldn't awaken. All the other cars but her rental were gone from the lot and the park had been given over to the night creatures of Miwok. She could hear an owl hoot, and she was sure skunks and raccoons and possums were scampering about, with only the stars to watch their play.

He walked with her the few steps to her car. She found her key in her purse and unlocked the door. When she glanced up, his features were highlighted by the moonlight. Seconds passed, and silence fell around them. The collar of his black jacket was turned up, and the jacket puffed out a bit from the breeze, "Thank you for inviting me this evening," she said, breaking the quiet.

Once he would have reached out for her now, touched her face, or at least a lock of her hair. He slid his fingertips into the back pockets of his jeans. "I hope it wasn't too dull, compared to what you're used to."

She gazed up at the moon peeking through the oak branches. "What I'm used to is sitting in an apartment with four locks on the door, reading summaries of news events and special features we'd be showing on the air." She faced him squarely. "Tonight was fun for me, not dull at all."

The silence built again as dark brown eyes pulled hers into their dizzying depths. They were close enough to touch, but didn't. He placed his hand on the roof of the car. "I'm glad," he said softly.

She looked at his hand, familiar yet different, and it was all she could do not to reach out and touch it with her own. How could she feel this way, this strongly, about him? And if she felt this strongly, what did that say about her? About Bruce and her? She stared hard at the back of his hand, the long fingers, the square, clipped nails. It was just a hand, she told herself, just a hand. "I guess I had better get home."

He gave the roof a light rap, then stepped back. "Right." She looked down, grasped the door handle and pulled it open. Quickly, before she made a fool of herself, she slid into her car. She reached for the door, but Tony held it. Their eyes met, then she drew her arm inside, eyes ahead, and waited. She heard the door shut, the lock catch. She gave him a little wave as she started the engine and backed out of the parking space.

Tony stood and watched as she turned out of the lot toward home.

TEN

The next day, Lee vowed to stop humoring her aunt and to empty as much as possible from the house. She couldn't believe how much work there still was to be done. What had she been doing all these days besides wasting time? She obviously left her brains along with her common sense back in New York. She needed to go home. Seeing Tony was madness—fun, she had to admit, and her pulse hadn't raced like that in more years than she could remember—but it was insanity, nonetheless. And getting to know Ben...

She had to leave Miwok soon.

She put on chinos and a tee shirt, and let her hair fall loose just past her shoulders. Dishes, linens, cleaning products, cosmetics, photo albums, not to mention all of Judith's clothing, still had to be sorted and bundled for discard or contribution to charity.

No sooner had she vowed no more distractions than Miriam announced that a lovely way for them to celebrate, so to speak, their last weekend together would be to go to the annual Miwok Indian Festival picnic and barbecue at Settlers Park on Sunday.

"Don't expect me to go with you, Miriam. I was never one for picnics," Lee had announced, looked up from the stacks of tax papers, receipts and home repair and maintenance records she was sorting on the kitchen table. The various utilities would probably have to be stopped—she needed to check with the realtor. At least the phone service could be disconnected.

"But you're special to this town, Lisa." Miriam filled a teakettle with water and put it on the stove. "You're one of the few people who made it big. People here proudly tell their friends that you're one of their own, and now you have a chance to say hello to a lot of people who remember you and have followed your career. You should do it."

She tucked a lock of hair behind her ear. "I scarcely know them anymore. I've been away too long."

"Yes, that's true, and that's all the more reason to let them know you haven't forgotten about them, and that you still care about your hometown." She placed tea bags in cups and put them on the counter.

"Do I?" Thoughtfully, she rubber-banded a batch of receipts and labeled them, adding them to other neatly ordered piles, then turned to face her aunt. "Most of the time, I feel like a stranger."

"There have been changes on the surface. But go below them, and you'll see that people are the same. That you're the same."

"I'm not, though. I've changed. What's strange, the longer I'm here, the more I realize how much and how complete that change has been."

Miriam took a seat at the table. "How can that be, when I see so much of the little girl I knew so well? And I'm sorry to say I still see too much of the unhappy young woman who came to me, too. But all that happened, it's all part of you, Lisa, it makes you who you are—just like Miwok does."

"That unhappy woman is completely gone now."

"Is she?" Miriam asked. "Or are you still hiding from yourself?"

"I don't know what you mean."

"It isn't anything I can explain. Someday, I hope, you'll understand." At the kettle's whistle, Miriam filled the cups with water and placed them on the table along with cream and brown sugar cubes, then sat again. "Let's just say I'd very much like to go to the picnic, and I'd feel awkward going alone. You wouldn't disappoint your poor old aunt, would you?"

At the guileless tone, Lee shook her head, pausing from her work in order to remove the tea bag from her cup. She remembered, from her time with Miriam how delicious milk and brown sugar tasted in tea. These days, she drank hers black. "Miriam, you still have so many friends in this town it isn't even funny. You won't be alone for ten seconds."

"Sure I will! And there's my knee, you know. What if it locks up on me? But then, if you won't go, I understand." She gave a heavy, hangdog sigh. "I'll just sit here all day Sunday, knowing my friends—and yours—are at the picnic, in the sunshine, enjoying themselves. Maybe somewhere along the line, they'll toss a fond thought my way, and raise a barbecued chicken leg in a toast—"

"No, Miriam, if they raise anything, it'll be a ham." At Miriam's expression, Lee smirked. Then they both began to chuckle. "Why do I let you talk me into these things?"

"Because you want me to. You just don't know it yet." Miriam sipped her creamy, sweet tea. "I wonder what I should wear? My but people will be happy to see you, Lisa. You know, since you'll be at the picnic all day Sunday, you probably will have lots of little things to do your last day here that might get overlooked. I think you need to put off going home until Tuesday, don't you?"

That night as Lee drifted off to sleep, in that half-awake, half-asleep nether world, her mind wandered back to the last time she went to the Miwok picnic, back to the early hours, just before dawn....

The door to her bedroom banged against the wall. She jumped, waking just as the light in her room was switched on. Blinded, she put her arm in front of her eyes. "Mother?"

"I won't have it!"

Lisa sat up, blinking hard, instinctively recoiling against the headboard even as she tried to wake. "Have what?" she asked.

"Don't play dumb with me!"

Judith leaned against the bedposts. Lisa smelled the beer on her breath and turned her head away. Judith put her hand under Lisa's jaw and yanked her head around so that they faced each other, their noses nearly touching.

"You're not going to a family picnic with that little beaner and his father. What would people think of you? Of me, for letting you go?"

Lisa jerked herself free and scooted toward the edge of the bed, tucking her legs under her. "I'm just going with Tony and some other kids. No one will think anything of it, Mother."

Judith grabbed her wrist, twisting it as she pulled her close. "Just Tony, she says! Just Tony! He's a dirty little Mexican. Don't you have any common sense? Didn't I raise you with any decency? Good girls don't go out with that kind of boy."

"We're just friends."

"You're acting like a slut!"

"Please mother!"

"He'll drag you down to his level. You could have been something. You could have made me proud— made the memory of your father proud!"

"I didn't do anything wrong!"

"You make me ashamed!"

Lee's memories hurled backwards to other times she'd been awakened by Judith screaming about something real or imaginary. She hated remembering those days, hated herself for the stupid things she did trying to appease her mother. She didn't want to think about it, but the memories wouldn't stop.

She turned over and over, peeling off the covers, tossing them aside. No one would have ever believed that the once beautiful, heartbreakingly tragic widow, Judith Reynolds, turned into Mr. Hyde when midnight came.

And Lisa never told anyone about it, not Cheryl, not Miriam, not even Tony. She had tried to act as if nothing was wrong. Not until years later, when she was away and able to look back on her life in Miwok and some distance and clarity, did she realize how transparent her brave little front must have been.

It was only some nights, like before that picnic, when Judith screamed and cried and acted as if she wanted to strike out, that Lisa thought perhaps she should ask for help or advice from someone. But she never did and instead helped Judith hide her drinking.

With the wisdom that came from experience, she realized that that had been the greatest mistake of all.

———

Miriam had said the town wanted to meet Lee Reynolds, so Lee decided to do it up right. She drove twenty miles to Nordstrom's in Corte Madera, and found an off-white DKNY dress, matching sling-back heels, and a flattering wide-brimmed straw hat. She wouldn't be caught dead wearing anything like that in New York City, but it was perfect for the Miwok picnic. She looked like she was going to a garden party on the White House lawn.

She brushed her hair into a loose knot at the crown, then used a hatpin to hold the hat in place.

The park was hot and crowded. She had perfected remaining unflappable and cool in the headiest of situations, and so her expression bore a constant, elegant smile as one person after another introduced themselves. She was surprised at how many people she didn't remember seemed to know her, and also by the number of stories they told her about her childhood. "Do you remember me, Miss Reynolds?" was a typical beginning for many such reminiscences. "I'm Mrs. So-and-so. I run the bakeshop and whenever your mother would come in to buy a cake I'd give you one of the red cupcakes with a clown-head on top. You always wanted a red one, remember?" Of course, Lee would nod and tell Mrs. So-and-so she'd always remembered how delicious her baked goods were, sending the woman off beaming.

Some people, though, she really did remember. She was touched to see Mrs. Campbell, her first grade teacher; Miss Gleason, the piano instructor she tortured with bad playing for over six years until Judith finally acquiesced that Lee would never become a female Horowitz; and even her high school journalism teacher, Mr. Roberts, gave her a stuttering hello. He was the one who started her off on the road to fame and fortune, he told her. "So you're to blame," she teased. He blushed and strutted away with as wide a smile as she'd ever seen on a man.

After a while, she took off her hat and held it in her right hand, which throbbed from having been crushed by overly friendly greetings. Even her well-practiced smile felt strained.

To everyone else, though, she continued to portray a picture of unruffled coolness and sophistication. Heads turn to follow the tall, slim, golden woman, who seemed unbothered by the picnic's swarms of people waiting to meet her.

One of the people who came by was Gene Cantelli.

"Well," she said, "weren't you the little prankster!"

He looked so sheepish she quickly let him off the hook. "It's all right. I was glad to get a chance to talk to Tony again after all these years."

He gave her a smile that showed white teeth under a thick mustache.

Miriam sauntered over to them. She was wearing a pale blue print sheath with spaghetti straps that showed off her tan, plus intricate silver and turquoise Navajo jewelry. "Gene, let me intro-

duce my aunt," Lee said. "Miriam Dailey, Gene
Cantelli. He's a good friend of Vic and Tony
Santos."

His gaze quickly flickered over her from her red
spiked hair to her white wedgies, then back to her
face as he stuck out his hand. "You're Lisa's aunt? I
thought you were supposed to be old. But you look
even younger than me."

Lee noticed that Miriam, taken aback, stood a
little straighter. "And how young is that, Mr.
Cantelli?"

"Call me Gene. I'm fifty-nine."

"Well, I'm a teensy bit older. But not much." She
peered down her nose at him, but Lee noticed that
her eyes sparkled.

He put his hand on the back of his neck, his
gaze catching Lee's then back to Miriam. "I'm sorry.
That was pretty rude of me. It's just...you're just...a
surprise."

The two eyed each other, then Miriam began to
smile, and Gene grinned broadly. Lee was surprised
to see a blush touch her aunt's cheeks, and to feel a
sudden crackle in the air. "I can imagine what Lisa
and Tony told you about Lisa's *old* aunt," Miriam
said, slanting a quick glance at Lee. "These kids
think of the Kennedy assassination as the Dark
Ages. Anyone remembering it has to be older than
dirt."

"That's nothing," Gene said, his arms folded. "I remember watching the Howdy-Doody on a big, boxy black-and-white TV with a tiny screen."

Miriam arched an eyebrow. "Is that so? Well, I used to get teary-eyed listening to 'When the Moon Comes Over the Mountain.'"

His amber eyes danced. "Ah, yes. *The Kate Smith Show*! What a gal. What a *lot* of gal. Remember Milton Berle?"

"Of course! How about *What's My Line?*"

He snapped his fingers. "With Arlene Francis!"

"And Dorothy Kilgallen."

"She was the smart one, along with Bennett Cerf." Head cocked, Gene eyed Miriam a long moment. "I'll bet you don't know Clayton Moore."

"How could I not know the Lone Ranger?" Hands on hips, she said, "I even know the name of Roy Rogers's dog?"

He stepped closer, a goofy smile plastered on his face. "Bullet! Garry Moore's show?"

Grinning, too, she met him practically nose to nose. "*I've Got A Secret*. Lonesome George?"

"Gobel! A knight without armor in a savage land?"

Eyes locked, they both suddenly sang out, "Pa-a-a-a-ladin!" Then erupted into laughter.

"Have you two gone nuts?" Lee said, looking from one to the other. "What are you talking about?"

Gene glanced at Miriam and shook his head. "I'll bet she doesn't even know who Mrs. Calabash is."

"Or Topo Gigio. Poor kid."

"How about some <u>adult</u> beverage?" Gene suggested. "They're serving white wine at the grandstand."

"Oh...that sounds lovely." Miriam beamed. "Lisa?"

"No thanks," Lee said. "You children run along. I'll take my poor ignorant self over to Cheryl and see how she's doing." She stepped away and then watched in wonder as Miriam and Gene walked off chatting and laughing like old friends. Miriam seemed to shed about ten years, and Lee noticed that her aunt's so-called bad knee had just made a miraculous recovery.

She walked over to Cheryl. Her friend surrounded Lee with her husband and children as well as her parents, Mark's parents, plus his two brothers and their families.

It was good to see Cheryl, but as time passed and the initial hellos with her family dwindled, Lee felt increasingly uncomfortable sitting there with nothing to do but try to follow the huge family's multiple conversations about people she didn't know. She fanned her face with her hat before putting it on again. Her nylons were hot and sticky and her slip had developed a severe case of static cling. She looked at the tee shirts and cut-offs the people around her wore with no small degree of wistfulness. And self-amusement. It was hard not to laugh out loud at her own vanity. Strangely, this flash of honesty banished the sense of obligation she had felt, and she soon found herself withdrawing into herself and relaxing, savoring the feel of the sun on her face, the smell of the many barbecues, the cool crispness of the heavily watered lawn under her feet.

As families settled down to the serious business of eating, Lee began to feel once more out of place despite everyone's best efforts to make her comfortable. Perhaps it was because of the special efforts that she felt so much in the way—as if the family could not sufficiently relax with her nearby. The constant watchfulness and even eavesdropping of people at nearby tables didn't help the situation any. Unfortunately, this sort of thing happened to her anymore with increasing regularity. She noticed that she took the attention much more in her stride than the others were able to do.

"Look who's here, Lisa." Lee was pretending to be fascinated by hamburgers browning on the grill when Cheryl spoke to her. She turned. "You remember Vic Santos, don't you? Tony's father."

Of course she remembered him. He was the

one person in Miwok she felt truly disliked her. "Hello, Mr. Santos," she said, holding out her hand.

Black eyes skimmed over her with barely concealed distaste. He was not a tall man, and he was built like a cannon ball—round, hard and explosive, "Lisa." He grasped her hand. His brown skin, worn from work and weather, felt like sandpaper against hers. "My grandson talks about you a lot. Another Santos on your side."

Her face grew warm. "Ben is a very charming boy."

"Too much like his father."

"That's a blessing, not a fault."

He tucked in his chin, almost belligerently. "A blessin', yeah, in most things."

She caught his eyes, but found them unreadable. "As you wish."

Cheryl tried to ease the tension. "Is Tony here, Vic?"

"I doubt it. You know Tony. He hates anything that don't have a baseball and bat."

"That's too bad."

Vic gazed hard at Lee. "Maybe. Maybe not."

Lee stepped back. "Please excuse me. I think I'll get something to eat."

"Good idea, Lisa," Cheryl said. "Will you join us, Vic?"

"No, thanks. So long, Cheryl. Lisa."

"I don't understand," Lee said to Cheryl when they were alone, "what I ever did to that man. He's always so unfriendly."

"I doubt you did anything to him, Lisa. You never can tell about people."

Lee wouldn't give in to the desire to look back over her shoulder in the direction Vic had headed. Vic was certainly one Santos she didn't have on her 'side' as he so nastily put it. She told herself she was glad to hear Tony was most likely not going to show up here today.

She sat at a table eating a barbecued hamburger when Ben ran up to her. She quickly glanced around, but his father wasn't near.

"Hi, Lisa!"

"Hello, Ben. How are you today?"

"Fine. Look." He held out a small metal car. "It's a Porsche 911, turbo-charged cabriolet, with a slope nose and front and rear spoilers."

"My goodness! You do know a lot about cars." It was hard not to respond to his contagious enthusiasm.

"I know all about Porsches. I'm going to own a bunch when I get big—maybe when I'm sixteen. My dad said I can't drive until then. There are some neat fish in that pond over there. Do you want to see them?"

"Fish? Oh, okay."

She was glad for an excuse to leave Cheryl's family and happily walked to the pond with Ben. Or, more correctly, followed him. He ran ahead, and it was only because he looked back to be sure she was coming that she knew he expected her company.

When she caught up to him, he was standing on a flat stone, bending forward and peering into the pond. She put her hand on his shoulder, fearful he might tumble head first into the water.

"Do you know what those are?" Ben pointed.

She bent forward almost as far as the boy. "Oh, God, we had to learn their names in the sixth grade, I think. Let's see. They're mostly varieties of gold-fish, as I recall."

"Except for the sturgeon and the blue whale," a familiar voice added.

She straightened and turned, a smile on her lips at the sound of Tony's voice, a smile that grew broader at the sight of him in a turquoise tank top that showed off well-tanned, muscular shoulders and gave a blue shininess to the rich black of his hair. But her smile fell away quickly when she noticed a young woman beside him, a woman who now reached over and clutched his arm. She was short, with auburn hair and brown eyes, and had the kind of body that men got whiplash following. Her white stretch halter-top and the jeans she must have been poured into only enhanced the effect. She had a soft, cuddly look, with plenty to cuddle.

"Hi, Dad. Hi, Trish," Ben called. "Lisa's gonna tell me all about the fish."

"You must be Lee Reynolds," Trish said, with a breathy catch to her voice. "The whole town is talking about you. I've heard about your fame since I was a little girl, and to think you're here now!"

Lee smiled at the young woman while contemplating tossing her into the pond.

"Let me introduce you two," Tony said. "Lee Reynolds, Trish Hollingsworth." There was an odd expression on his face, then it vanished so quickly that it could have been her imagination.

Lee cast a puzzled glance at Tony, so foreign was it to hear him refer to her as Lee.

"So nice to meet you," Trish said. "My goodness, you're not nearly as old as I imagined." Lee was stunned. At least when Miriam was told almost the same thing, it was a compliment. The young woman smiled sweetly while leaning against Tony as if she were in danger of swooning in awe.

Lee's teeth ached. She regarded Trish with unflappable coolness. "It's always a pleasure to meet a fan," she said placidly. "How fortunate you came along. Ben and I were just discussing slimy things...in the pond."

While Trish was still trying to decide whether

she'd just been insulted, Lee gave her and Tony a dismissive smile and turned back toward the water.

Tony choked back a cough and walked to Lee's side. She glanced again at his turquoise tank top and jeans, and grew acutely aware of the amount of bare flesh close to her, and of how well formed and muscular his upper torso had grown. She looked at his dusky, mysterious eyes, at his mouth. The mouth that had taught her how to kiss.

He seemed to stare at the pond with singular intensity, hands on back pockets of his cut-offs, feet spread so his weight was evenly balanced. She tried not to glance at him, tried to concentrate on the fish, but inside she was a tumult of emotions, not the least of which was chagrin that she had stooped to exchanging jabs with the woman he was obviously involved with. She had no right.

"The big black one is a carp." Tony pointed at it, his bare arm disturbingly close to hers.

"That's right. I remember now." She sidestepped away from him.

Tony drew back, irritated with himself for feeling upset at her coldness toward him, her obvious withdrawal. Christ, but he was a fool. He'd spent the whole week thinking about her, first with curiosity after seeing her at Ben's game, then with much more after talking at Big Bob's and the Pizza Palace. A few moments of clarity hit and he knew he was setting himself up for a big letdown when she left. But that hadn't been enough to keep him from standing too close to her in a darkened parking lot, or from dreaming about her at night in his empty bed.

He gazed at her calm, disinterested profile a moment. She'd surprised him again when he joined the picnic and saw her surrounded by admirers. His vow to stay clear of her lasted pretty long, too...until he saw Ben standing with her, talking with her, right where he wanted to be.

"When I heard Ben was over this way, I was worried because of the pond," he said, trying to offer some reason for his presence, any excuse but the real one. *I miss you, Lisa.* "I see he's in good hands. I guess I'll get going. Don't be a pest, Ben."

"It was good to see you today, Tony. And Trish." She gave each a nod. They said their goodbyes. Lee faced at the pond, as the couple walked away, but not too many seconds passed before she peeked in the direction they had gone. His arm was casually draped around Trish's shoulders, her arm around Tony's hips, her thumb hooked onto the belt of his jeans, and her fingers splayed almost to his hip joint.

How could he allow that ridiculously young...

Tony glanced back over his shoulder and caught Lee's eye. She snapped her head toward the pond once more, but not before she felt her face turn a fiery red.

Soon, she and Ben returned to the picnic area. Cheryl and company were engrossed in conversation, and Lee decided not to disturb them. She spread out one of the blankets Miriam had brought. She sat and Ben joined her.

He told her about school, about his friends, about baseball, and a whole lot about Porsches. After a while, he raced off to play with other kids. A couple of minutes later, though, he was back. "I thought you might not want to be alone," he said, joining her on the blanket once more. "I think a lot of people here are kind of scared of you 'cause you're on TV."

His perception astonished her, and warmth spread through her at his thoughtfulness. "I'd love your company, Ben. But I don't want to stop you from playing with your friends if you'd like."

He wrapped his arms around his knees. "No. I can play with those kids any time. Anyway, you're okay to talk to."

A dozen locks couldn't have stopped her heart from opening to him at that moment.

"If you wait here, Lisa, I'll get a surprise for you."

"A surprise?"

He scampered off again, and in a little while he

returned, carrying tiny lavender and pink wild flowers.

He held them toward her. "Here."

"Oh, Ben." She felt a tightening in her throat and held the few scrawny flowers as gently as if they were precious jewels. "They're beautiful."

His chest puffed up. "I'd have picked some of the big flowers, but the people at the park would get mad. I scraped my arm."

"You what?" she said, not used to his sudden jumps from one subject to another.

"See?" He lifted his arm. Right below the elbow was a scrape.

"Oh, dear!"

"I fell."

She carefully lay the flowers on the ground, then rocked herself up and onto her knees so she could look at the scrape more closely. It was very small, and there was no blood. She kissed the first two fingers of her own hand, then lightly pressed her fingers just to the side of his wound.

"What are you doing?" Ben asked.

She sat back on her heels. "That was a kiss to make it better. I'll bet it already doesn't hurt nearly as much."

He stared hard at the scrape, then sat facing her on the blanket. He crossed his legs Indian style. "Hey, you're right."

"I guess your dad doesn't do that."

"Heck, no." He laughed.

"What about your mother?"

His eyes wavered, then dropped to his lap. "I never see her. I don't think she likes me much."

Her gaze snapped to Ben's face, not believing what she had heard. But the stubborn set of his chin told her she had heard exactly right. She had so little experience with children she didn't know what to say or do. All she knew was if she had a child this fine, he never would doubt her love.

Awkwardly, she reached her hand out and ran her fingers through his black, wavy hair. It was thick, soft and shiny, and felt warm beneath her fingers. "I'm sure she loves you, Ben. I hardly know you and already, I think you're just about the best boy I've ever met."

He lifted his eyes to her. "Really?"

"Cross my heart and hope to die."

Ben laughed. "Grown-ups don't say that!"

She grinned. "But it's true."

He studied her face. "Could you come to another one of my games?"

Once again, he surprised her. "Well, I would like to, but I've got to go back to New York on Tuesday."

"Hey, cool! My next game is Monday after school. You can come! It's kind of nice to have someone I know in the stands. Some kids have whole bunches of people."

"I see," she murmured.

Lee noticed his gaze hungrily following a boy carrying a soccer ball.

"Looks like a game's going to start," she said. "How would you like to see what's happening down there for me, Ben?"

"Sure!" He jumped up and ran off again. Lee's smile slowly faded as she watched him go, the words he had spoken settling into her heart. Alone again, she sighed and looked over the crowd. Her aunt was still with Gene Cantelli, laughing and having a good time. Cheryl was in the middle of her family, holding one of her nieces in her arm while seeming to be watching all the other children at the same time. Ben talked with a group of boys in a nearby meadow.

Rarely was she around children in Manhattan, and it was even rarer for her to talk with one. But she enjoyed Ben's company. A child like that could be wonderful. Someone to love with no reservations, no hesitancy or fear. Someone to open her heart to and let pour out all the feelings she kept so carefully locked inside.

She leaned forward, her elbow on her knee and her chin resting on her hand as she watched Ben's soccer game slowly form.

Bruce didn't much like kids. It was one of the many things that attracted her to him. Their plans had centered around career and travel, and left little time for anything else. They would have each other, and that was enough. She had no desire to have his —or any man's—child.

She took off her hat and tucked Ben's flowers neatly into the band, folded the blanket, then, carrying both, walked back to the pond. She soon found herself on the far side of it, far from where people might pass, and where she wouldn't feel so conspicuous being alone at a picnic filled with families. She plopped down on some dry grass under an oak tree, kicked off her shoes, and making sure no one was looking, tugged off her stockings. It felt almost wicked to run her bare feet over the slightly damped soil. She leaned back against the trunk, her chin tilted upward, and enjoyed the bright blue of the sky and the rich, lush green around her.

Seeing Tony with a girl earlier today by the pond shouldn't have surprised her. He was an attractive man. He always had been. She wondered how serious he was about this Trish Hollingsworth.

Tony being serious about another woman, despite his marriage, even despite Ben, was foolishly hard for her to handle. In high school, she had been the one with other dates, largely to keep Judith happy, but also, it helped her to know that other boys found her attractive. Back then, anything that built up her ego was welcomed and sought after, particularly because she wasn't close to being the beauty her mother had been. As Judith had constantly reminded her, she was too tall, too angular, and too flat-chested.

Tony went out with a few other girls. But even when he did, she knew with absolute certainty, that she was the one he liked best, and most wanted to be with. But then high school was a long, long time ago.

Although she thought she had no memory at all of this area of the park, as she looked around she realized that, in fact, she did. Was that why she had come here?

The thought was jarring—as so many thoughts had been since she returned to Miwok. For seventeen years she had purposefully put Miwok and its people out of her mind, but now the memories wouldn't stop. Her forehead ached with remembrances she wouldn't let escape.

The first time she and Tony met they had just stared at each other. The second time they shared Twizzlers as he walked with her to class, and after that, it was as if a dam had burst. She met him in the school library, in line at the cafeteria, at the gym. And somehow they began talking after school, between classes, at lunch. She had liked his sensitivity and compassion, and admired his dreams to become a pro-baseball player. In him, she recognized a kindred spirit with hopes for a brighter, bigger, more meaningful future than could be found in little Miwok, California. They would spend hours discussing their plans and ambitions. She liked the way he laughed and the way he made her laugh. But most of all, she liked the way he accepted her without condition—her faults as well as her accomplishments. He made no demands, set no expectations to be fulfilled before love was granted. Who she was, what she was, had been fine with him. She'd never been loved that way before.

Or since.

As her gaze swept over the landscape surrounding the clear waters of the pond, she found the spot she sought. But the bench was gone now, and she couldn't pick out the exact spot where it had been.

Not that it mattered....

By April of their sophomore year, Lisa and Tony had been friends for six months, which was an eternity back then, when every minute was so full time lasted forever. They sat on a bench in Settlers Park, having walked there after one of Tony's baseball games. Since he was young, a sophomore, he was only in junior varsity, not the big team, but the coaches were letting him do a lot more than warm the bench. He played third base, shortstop, and on occasion, pitched.

A chilling breeze was in the air. Lisa wore a quilted jacket, and Tony, a blue zip-up with the words Miwok Mustangs in white letters across the back. In back, his hair fell in thick waves to the collar of his jacket.

New leaves glistened on the oaks and the pastel flowers of spring painted the area. Lisa turned to Tony to give him her news.

Stompin' Steve Peters had asked her to go with him to a movie on Saturday night, and all day she had floated somewhere between seventh heaven and cloud nine. Stompin' Steve was the star running back on the football team and he was a junior. Everyone just knew he was going to be student body president in his senior year, and even more of a football star. Yet, he'd asked her out, and she was only a sophomore. Everyone thought he was crazy about Amy Dunkirk. They were sure wrong.

"You're going out with that fat-ass jellyfish?" Tony jumped to his feet, waving his arms around. "That pile of muscular manure who shoves other people around and calls himself an athlete!"

Lisa sat sideways on the park bench facing him,

one leg curled on the bench, her elbow on the back-rest. "You sound jealous. It's not as if you and I are going together, or anything."

"Jealous? Me? Of the creature that ate Oakland? Fat chance!" He flopped down beside her, hands on his thighs, legs outstretched.

"You can go on dates, too, you know." She leaned toward him, her eyes teasing. "Maybe sometime Steve and I will even double with you."

He grimaced. "I don't think the Stomper would approve. It might interfere with his action."

That gave her pause. "His what?"

"Action, Lisa." He pulled himself up straight, his gaze intense. "You should hear him talk in the gym on Mondays. He's got more moves than an octopus, and old Amy Dunkirk was dumb enough to fall for every one of them."

"Oh?" In spite of herself, the corners of her lips turned down.

He gripped the arm she had on the backrest. "You don't want to be the center of gossip, do you?"

She yanked her arm free. "He wouldn't dare!"

On his feet again, he paraded back and forth in front of her, hands on hips. "What makes you so sure? He'll be all over you!"

She folded her arms petulantly. "What's wrong with a kiss? If I like him..."

He stopped pacing, his thumb slowly rubbing

his chin a moment as he looked at her. Again, he sat beside her, closer this time. Looking toward the horizon, he said in a very knowing voice, "I think I can guess what I'll be hearing about next Monday."

Her head whipped toward him. "What?"

"That Lisa Marie Reynolds can't kiss." A chortle erupted, and he bent forward as it grew to a full belly laugh.

She punched his arm. "What do you mean? Of course, I can!"

"Yeah? I never heard that you went out with any guy who took you off to be alone."

She gawked at him. "Why should you have? It's not your business! Anyway, I've been kissed before, Tony Santos!"

"Spin the bottle doesn't count."

She grimaced. "You are *so* funny."

"Remember, Stompin' Steve is an eleventh grader."

Her chin lifted. "So?"

"So? So, there's a technique to it."

Her brow crossed. "And I suppose you know all about it?"

"Sure."

She gave him a sidelong glance. "How did you learn?"

Now it was his turn to ease casually against the bench, his arms flung over the backrest, his face smug. "At my old school, I had an older girlfriend. She was seventeen."

She rolled her eyes. "No way! An older girl looking at you? She must have been totally desperate!"

He shrugged. "Maybe, but she sure could kiss."

She pursed her lips together, wanting to knock that smirk right off his face. She rocked her shoulders in a quick, small motion from side to side while thinking over his words. "Well, smarty, since you know so much about it, why don't you tell me?"

"Sure."

She froze, her breathing stopped, even as she forced herself to appear cool and calm. She peeked at him. "Okay," she said.

"Well, first, you, um... Well, you... Hell, I don't know how to describe it!"

Relief flowed through her. "Some help you are!" she said haughtily.

He folded his arms, his legs stretched out before him. "Well, I guess I can show you. But don't get any ideas! It's just to help you out, nothing more."

Her mouth dropped open. "Get ideas? Don't you wish!" Her heart thrummed. "Well, I'm sure I don't need help, but...I guess it won't hurt to find out what that seventeen-year-old taught you."

He took her hand and led her deeper into the park, to a secluded bench that faced the pond and was hidden from the walkway by large bushes. She sat, and he sat beside her. He turned her shoulders toward him, lifted her hands to his neck, then slid his arms around her waist. "Comfortable?" he asked.

Her heart beat so fast she was growing light-headed. She gave one quick nod.

His gaze held her captive. "Now, someone who knows what he's doing, when he kisses a girl, does it slowly and gently. Got it?"

She nodded.

"Like this." He pulled her waist closer, causing her head to drop back and her lips to part slightly as she gasped with surprise. He cocked his head, lightly kissed her mouth, and drew back. He lightly kissed her again, then tilted his head so that his nose was on the other side of hers while meeting her with light, feathery kisses that sent tingles through her body. She was ready to move a lot closer to him when he lifted his head.

"Only if the girl likes that and wants more, does the guy who knows how to kiss involve his tongue at all."

"I see." He pulled her closer. Her arms tightened around his neck as he lowered his mouth to hers. His tongue brushed over her lips, playing and teasing at the entrance to her mouth, until she lifted her tongue to touch his. As his lips slid sideways over hers, her breath caught, and, again he stopped.

"That's right. The girl invites when she's ready, then they can kiss well. Got it?"

She nodded vigorously.

"The guy who doesn't know how to kiss will simply go up to a girl, slap his mouth across her face like a slab of raw liver then cram his tongue down her throat as far as it can go. I'm surprised the girls don't gag."

Lisa put her hand to her throat and swallowed hard.

Tony smiled. "I guess some girls just don't know any better."

Her voice was tiny. "I guess not."

"Are you ready to put it all together?"

"I think so."

He reached for the top button of her jacket and, to her surprise, unfastened it. As each button fell open, she felt her stomach tighten and her breathing grow more shallow. Then he slipped his arms under her jacket, circling her back. She waited. He nodded. Slowly, she lifted her hands to his broad shoulders.

As their lips, she shut her eyes and leaned closer. His lips passed gently, lovingly over hers and she drew him closer, wanting more of his kiss. The moment his tongue touched her lips, she met it with hers and felt a tremor pass through him. His arms tightened as his tongue found its way into her mouth. She took it between her teeth, biting down lightly. Surprised he lifted his head and looked at her. She laughed and lifted her hands to his hair, stroking the soft locks with her fingers. She watched a grin steal across his face, his eyes crinkling in delight, and she pulled his head down to hers again. His soft groan of pleasure was a triumph to her, and she abandoned herself to his kiss, unzipping his jacket and sliding her arms within it, letting her hands travel along his back, upward, trying to reach his shoulders, until the fabric of his jacket stopped her. For the first time she became acutely aware of the difference in their bodies—he was hard, sinewy, smooth but steely to the touch. And she liked to touch him.

At the same time, he caressed her, but never higher than her rib cage, and never lower than her hips. Still, her body tingled with a new awareness, and every sense seemed heightened, and each moment, magical.

She discovered boys had a particular taste, and she liked the way Tony tasted. His scent, up close, was different, too, and she could feel the pulse on his neck, and his rapid heartbeat when his chest pressed against hers. With one finger, she traced the outline of his ears, she touched his nose, his cheeks, his eyebrows. Everything about him seemed unique to her, despite how well she thought she knew him.

Every new thing she learned, she liked. That day, she learned all about kissing Tony.

She did have her date with Stompin' Steve Peters that Saturday night so long ago. They went to the movies. Afterward, he drove out to a country lane, parked the car, took her in his arms and kissed her. She promptly gagged, and he, just as promptly, brought her home.

Lee giggled at the memory, then giggled harder, and finally, laughed until tears came to her eyes. She had spent years getting all but nauseated by nearly half the men who tried to kiss her and never, until just this moment, figured out why.

"What's so funny?"

She looked up. "Tony!" Her face was still shiny with mirth.

Dark brown eyes swept over her discarded stockings and bare toes wriggling luxuriously in the grass. The sight of those ten perfectly manicured red-tipped toenails rocked him without warning. He tore his gaze from her feet to meet her bemused eyes. "I don't know about this, Lisa. You're sitting here laughing all by yourself. It's good it was just old Ton' who found you. People have been locked away for less."

"Where's your friend Trish?"

"Gone home, I think. I haven't seen her for a good hour."

"Oh. That's too bad."

"Not really." He looked uncomfortable, as if he shouldn't be here talking to her like this, shouldn't be seeking out her company. "Ben told me he saw you heading this way, but you hadn't come back..."

Is that so, Mr. Santos? She suddenly felt good. "It was nice of you to check up on me. I'd hate for a blue whale to carry me off."

He smiled. "Is that what you were laughing about?"

Her gaze shifted to a white oleander bush, and she rubbed a fingertip over the smooth skin between her eyebrows. "Actually, I was just remembering Steve Peters. It made me laugh."

"Ah, yes." He put his hands on his hips. "The original liver lips."

That drew her back. "The *what?*"

He looked sheepish. "Nothing."

"You knew!"

His eyebrows rose in innocence. "Knew? Knew what? What are you talking about?"

She cocked her head. "Nothing. But if I ever find out you knew..."

He held out his hands, palms up toward her and

backed up a couple of steps. "I swear I'm innocent— whatever it is!"

"Oh well, it was probably for the best." She gazed up at him, his dark eyes, his mouth...and the memory of how good it felt to kiss him washed over her again, memories of nights in Tony's Bonneville where those "practice kissing" sessions continued. Good God! Where had that memory come from? Where had *all* these memories come from? Unnerved, she put her shoes on and stood.

He was sorry she put them on. He liked seeing her barefoot and relaxed, all warm and sunny and laughing. He liked it a lot. To his consternation he also liked the way she'd been looking at him before she turned away. He could feel heat throughout his body from her gaze.

"I wonder if my aunt is ready to go home yet," she said as she started walking back toward the picnic area.

He walked beside her. "I saw her talking to Gene Cantelli about ten minutes ago."

"Really?" She wondered if Miriam had been with Gene all this time. If so, she was glad.

As they reached the barbecue area, he began to chuckle. "God, Lisa—Stompin' Steve!" He shook his head. "He became a lawyer, you know."

She snorted, then held her hand to her nose, horrified at the unladylike sound.

He glanced at her, then both of them burst out laughing.

"Hey, don't laugh," Tony said. "I owe that man a debt of gratitude I can never repay. I'm sure you don't remember, but it was because of him we first—"

"I remember...right back there by the pond. They took away our bench, though."

Our bench. He seemed to notice the slip as soon as she said it.

"You do remember!" His voice dropped. "I'll be damned!"

"I seem to remember a lot more than I realized."

"Hey, that isn't why you were laughing, is it?"

She looked at the toes of her shoes as she walked along. "Not at you, Tony. Never at you. At me."

He stepped in front of her, stopping her progress and forcing her to look up at him, his expression suddenly serious. Then he slid his hands into his back pockets. "Why?"

She saw the way the setting sun's rays shone on the blackness of his hair, bringing out wine red highlights, the way his shoulders jutted straight and broad under the pale gray sweatshirt he now wore over his tank top, the way his dark eyes still mesmerized her and made her want to immerse herself in them and never walk away.

Then she lowered her gaze and shrugged. "No reason, Tony. Nothing I could even begin to explain."

"Try me."

"No, but thanks."

"You're sure?"

"Sure." She smiled, secretive and sensual. He was fascinated by these facets of Lee Reynolds, as enthralled as he'd been seventeen years ago.

She slipped her hands in her pockets and they walked along in silence. Now and then, their arms brushed, but neither moved far enough away to end the contact.

ELEVEN

One of the Circle Z Ranch's wild oak and brush-covered hills stood higher than the others. When Tony wanted to be alone, it was the perfect place to go.

He sat with his back against a tree trunk, one leg stretched out straight, the other bent at the knee. Before him lay rolling pasture land. A group of his horses ran free over an open field under the watchful eye of two ranch hands. Sometimes he came up here just to look at the scene below, as if to convince himself that the land before him was really his own.

At other times, like now, he came to think through problems. His father had warned him against seeing Lisa again, and he had to admit Vic was right.

Tony side-armed a stone high into the air and watched as it sailed down the hill to land far below his perch. Years ago, after Lisa left him, he often wondered what his life would have been if he and Vic had never come to Miwok. If he had never met her. He never would have known what it felt like to be completely in tune with another person, what it felt like to be with someone and know that only with them were you whole, and that without them you were no more than a shell of yourself. He would never have known the torture of losing the person he felt that close to, and would never have known a loneliness so complete and so black he had wished he could die from it.

He flung another stone, harder this time.

It had been his fault that he and Vic had moved here. He had caused Vic to leave the best paying job he had ever held. In the end, the move had been a good one for Vic, but at the time, it had seemed catastrophic.

Although born in Texas, he traveled with his father all over the west as Vic worked on different ranches. Out of the blue, an old friend offered Vic a job at a wealthy riding academy in Malibu. Vic quit his job in Albuquerque for California and checked them into a motel while he tried to find an apartment near the riding academy. Whenever the two of them showed up to look at a vacancy, though, they were told the apartment had been rented only hours before. Vic's search widened until, eventually, he ended up in the San Fernando Valley, the agricultural fringe just north of Los Angeles.

Tony had just turned fifteen, halfway through his freshman year, and found himself in a new high school. It was a nightmare. The kids saw him as a hick, and "Tex-Mex" was the nicest of the names he was called. The Mexican kids thought he was strange because he wasn't from a *barrio*, could speak almost no Spanish and didn't do anything they considered cool. To the whites, though, he was Mexican, one of "them," and ostracized from the white kids' world.

He fought his way through the first few weeks, then gradually changed his style of dress and speech. He was tired of being an outsider, tired of being lonely. When he was younger, he'd had baseball, the one thing he did better than any of the other kids. Baseball was what had helped him become accepted in new schools time after time. But as he got older, baseball wasn't enough. A part of him hated Vic for taking him away from the horse and cattle ranches where Vic had worked, from the nomadic life they both loved. Yet another part found him poking fun at the country-bumpkin image of the ranches he had grown up on. He wanted to belong. Other kids did.

Finally, he found a crowd willing to accept him. They were a tough group, one that Tony saw as the neatest, most savvy and most fearsome in the school.

Vic railed against the gang of boys Tony hung around with. When Tony took an interest in girls, Vic found them even worse. He called them nothing but *putas*. Tony defended his friends until he could scarcely say a word to his father without an argument.

Four weeks into Tony's sophomore year, he came home at three o'clock in the morning. The low-riding car's souped-up engine jerked to a stop in front of the apartment building where he lived. He rolled out of the car, too drunk to stand. The quiet street erupted with hoots and loud laughter by boys still in the car, and with lusty, raucous jokes by the girls.

Tony opened the door to the apartment to find Vic standing by the window waiting for him. He stumbled into the bathroom and threw up.

The next day, Vic quit his job, pulled Tony out of school, and left Los Angeles, heading north. Two weeks later, Vic found a low-paying job at a small horse ranch, the Circle Z, in an unknown northern California town called Miwok.

Miwok. The first time Tony saw it, he laughed at the place. It wasn't rugged like ranch land, or exciting like L.A. It was pretty. Pretty! How embarrassing for a kid who'd just learned how to be a big-city tough guy.

Tony grinned as he remembered meeting Lisa. She had a Social Studies class in the morning, and he had the same class in the afternoon. In both classes the students had to do a massive report on one state. Lisa had chosen New Mexico, which was the state Tony wanted, since he had lived there just before coming to California and he knew a lot about it.

All he had heard about her was that she was brainy, serious and nice. Compared to the girls he used to hang out with, she was plain, dowdy and prejudiced. He remembered how, his first week at Miwok High, she gawked at him as if he were from outer space. But he was desperate to get New Mexico for his state report. Hell, if he could have New Mexico, he'd hardly have to do any research or anything. He hated research. He'd approached her.

First she got all huffy about him talking to her, but then she gave him a look of understanding that bowled him over. No other girl had ever looked at him with such trust and compassion. To his amazement, he even told her about his mom dying when he was born. Was he nuts, or what?

But they began to talk, and he remembered thinking that the way her eyes sparkled, she wasn't very plain, and with hair the color of whipped butter, she certainly wasn't dowdy. The way she slowed her step, hung on his every word and acted as if she like being with him, made him think she wasn't prejudiced either.

He liked her so well, he didn't even ask for New Mexico. Instead, he did his report on Delaware. It was small, he reasoned. How hard could it be? Unfortunately, he found out. Right from the start their relationship had to have been pretty serious for a Mexican-American, southwestern kid like him to be willing to tackle one of the original thirteen English colonies for a state report.

He remembered the first time Vic saw them together. Vic had said, "She's trouble." How could she be, Tony had wondered.

But as he got to know her, he realized that she was quite different from the way she appeared on the surface. It was as if she were a river that seemed placid, but had treacherous rapids just out of sight. She wouldn't admit it, much less talk about it, but he could see it, and knew it involved her mother. Lisa's demeanor would change when she talked about Judith Reynolds. She was always trying to please the woman, but no matter how hard she worked, no matter how many achievements or awards or successes she attained, they were never enough. For Tony, who had never been given anything but unwavering support and love from Vic, the way her mother treated Lisa was unimaginable.

The worst part was that Lisa wouldn't talk about it, and would scarcely acknowledge that anything was wrong.

On several occasions, he almost told her that he knew—heck, the whole town knew—that Judith Reynolds drank a lot more than was healthy. She made the rounds of different stores to buy her beer, but that didn't stop people from noticing either the volume or the regularity of her purchases. But since Lisa never brought the problem up, he kept his mouth shut. He wondered if that wasn't the biggest mistake of his life.

He had thought being there for her would be enough, and she would talk to him if she needed to. After all, she told him how she felt about him. And later, when they were seniors, she told him that she loved him. He believed her. But then she left. He still didn't know why. The boy that he was believed she had rejected him, that she had been shamed by their love. The man he had since become questioned that belief.

He could see, to his amazement, that she still cared about him, and that she was still fighting those feelings. He wondered how long it would be before she left again.

———————

That same morning, Lee's agent called to say they had just received an offer from Nighttime News, run by one of the competing networks, for her to be the anchor on the weekend news broadcast. This wasn't another second-rung anchor position, like she had on Evening Newscene, but the actual lead. No more would she have to hear the announcer bellow, "Here is Evening Newscene with Rick Archer!!"—then wait a beat—"and Lee Reynolds." To no longer be the "and" following a long pause after Rick Archer's name was the kind of deal she'd long dreamed of.

Her Evening Newscene contract was nearly up. Her agent had been about to enter negotiations to renew when the Nighttime News offer came in. The agent said the offer was most generous and recommended careful consideration since, after all, she wasn't getting any younger. She knew what he meant. Television cameras were cruel to anyone overweight or aging. She could control her weight, but...

Soon after, her business manager called to say he'd spoken with her agent, and if the new contract materialized as suggested, he was working up some outstanding investment strategies that he'd need to talk over with her so she wouldn't have to pay a penny extra in taxes. That call was followed by her personal publicist who was already planning a campaign to further promote her name and career based on this latest move and promotion.

Hearing from her these people, considering the terrific opportunity presented, thinking about her career, caused her stomach to become so tense that, for the first time in days, she had to take some of her ulcer medicine. Oddly, the business-related nervousness, the tension, even the renewed stomach pain, reminded her of Miriam's comments about putting on an old shoe again. Granted, it pinched, but it was a familiar pinch. She had spent a lifetime working to get ahead. Push, pull, two steps forward, one back, but always, ultimately, her position and status improved. She knew how to make it improve even further. Jumping networks and shows was one of the means to her ultimate goal: to be the lead weeknight news anchor at one of the big network stations.

She didn't see how she could refuse the Nighttime News offer. To do so would be unlucky. Over the years she'd learned that building a career didn't take half as much talent as it did hard work and luck.

Ever since the seventh grade when she began to write short news bulletins and long columns about school events and happenings for the school newspaper, Lee wanted to become a journalist. She had always thought in terms of the print media, with her goal being the *New York Times*. Those plans were shelved when, shortly after graduation, one of her journalism professors, Paul Hastings, lined up a job for her with a television station in Los Angeles. Hastings' offer was too good an opportunity to pass up, even though her "production assistant" position was really no more than a glorified secretary.

After Lisa's first day on the job, Hastings showed up at her apartment with a bottle of Dom Perignon to celebrate. When he made it clear just how grateful she was supposed to be, she showed him the door. He was persistent, she was lonely, and eventually his persistence paid off. They had an affair that lasted over a year despite her not ever feeling entirely comfortable with him. Even in bed she had the disquieting tendency to think of him as "Mr. Hastings."

After four months of behind-the-scenes work, the six o'clock news show producer, who'd recognized Lisa's photogenic features from day one, began to send her out on news assignments with a cameraman. She was sharp, aggressive and ambitious. She covered shopping mall openings and community board meetings. Then, one day, the station sent her and a cameraman out to cover the mayor making an address to a civic action group. The address would have absolutely no news-worthiness unless it was an exceedingly dull day everywhere else in the greater Los Angeles area. On that particular day, however, three gunmen broke into the meeting, took everyone hostage, and demanded that the mayor free all political prisoners as well as give the gunmen three million dollars. Lisa and her cameraman got the whole thing on film. The gunmen decided to let the television people leave in order to bring their film to the studio and to air their demands in living color on the six o'clock news. They failed to realize that the same cameras that gave the public information would also help the police tactical squad plan a hostage rescue. By six o'clock, the hostage threat was over and Lisa had the whole episode on camera. She not only reported the story, she was a participant in it and documented the crisis with clarity, in the no-nonsense, nerves of steel manner that remained her style. Because of its drama, the national networks picked up the story.

After that, she was regularly sent out on assignment. Her all-American blond looks and poised, intelligent manner quickly made her a favorite with the public, and a year later, she was offered a job as a local news anchor on weekends. She threw herself into the job with fervor. Weekends led to prime time, and eventually, to New York, where she began using the name Lee.

In New York, Lee perfected what she had only been a novice at in Los Angeles—backstabbing, game-playing and newsroom politics. She thrived on them. The only way to get ahead, she quickly learned, was to be faster, smarter and dirtier than the competition. To her surprise, it wasn't very hard to do. She seemed to fit right into that world.

It was Miwok that was alien now. Seeing old friends confused her—especially Tony, and in a new, disturbing way, Ben did as well, She didn't understand herself around either of them, and that bothered her. They made her think about things she didn't want to think about. They made her ponder "if only's" that she didn't want to ponder. It was best to stay away from them both.

No matter how much she wanted to see them.

That afternoon, after sorting and discarding more of her mother's possessions, she sat in the garden with Miriam.

"Do you think I'm doing the right thing, Miriam?" she asked. They sat on the patio in the morning sun, tea, muffins and a tub of Clover sweet butter in front of them. Clover dairies dotted the Marin and Sonoma county headlands. She hadn't seen the brand for years.

"Are you talking about the cholesterol in the butter or selling your house?"

"Neither. Of course I'll sell. I meant choosing Janet Lettice as my realtor. Do I trust her?"

Miriam gave a slight shrug. "I trust her to sell the house as much as anyone. Of course, Lisa, once you sell you'll be cut off from Miwok forever."

"You did it."

"Because I thought the town had too many bad memories. You weren't the only one who couldn't get along with Judith, and a part of me always held her responsible for my brother's death. If it weren't for you, after Jack died, I would never have spoken to Judith again."

"I never realize that." Lee was startled by Miriam's words.

"I shouldn't have said anything to you. But you know what? My brother lived in this house. He loved puttering in this garden. The big rhododendron by the fence, he planted. The painting that hangs over the mantle in the family room was one he picked out. When I ran away from what hurt, I also ran from all I'd loved."

"Aren't you happy in San Diego?"

"Oh, I am. But now, I realize how much Miwok means to me as well."

"No regrets, then?" Lee asked.

"Only that I wasn't here while you were growing up."

"I didn't turn out that bad, did I?"

"You're lovely. Everything Judith ever wanted you to be."

Everything...successful, well known, wealthy. Lee could measure "everything" by the number of fan letters she received, the number of phone calls from politicians and the "in" people, even how many floors above Park Avenue her apartment was located. "I don't know what she wanted me to be," Lee said. "Half the time she said I could do whatever I set my mind to, and the other half I was called a complete failure." She chuckled sardonically. "Can that be a reason we never got along?"

"She could be very cruel." Miriam words were low.

Since they were being honest, Lee said what had been in her heart for a long time. It was difficult for her to do. She had kept her feeling about her mother locked up forever it seemed, and she wasn't sure if she could find the words. "A part of me still feels sorry for her. She was hurt, in constant pain. There were times, I admit, that I forgot that myself. There were times I hated her. As I grew older, I've come to understand her disappointments in life—how my father died at such a young age, and how her own career never even began, *me*. It wasn't really her fault, and yet, she could never forgive. And I could never forget."

"As far as I'm concerned, she was a bitter, self-centered, hateful woman," Miriam said. "Probably the poorest combination of all in a mother."

"It's a funny thing," Lee said. "I'll never forgive her for what she did, and yet a part of me is sorry we never got along. I spent years hating her. Then, the hatred disappeared and all that's left is disappointment."

"Has being back helped any?" Miriam's gaze was sad. "Has it helped the open wound that was you and Judith to heal at least a little?"

"I hope so." Lee grabbed her wallet and car keys from her purse. "I think I'll take a drive," she said, then hurried from the house.

She drove to the public library and parked. Soon she'd be back on television where she belonged. She'd scarcely paid any attention to world events this past week. Several days worth of the *New York Times* and the *Washington Post* would have to be devoured quickly. She hadn't even brought her iPad, thinking she would finish her task in Miwok more quickly if not distracted. She never expected to be away this long, or so cut-off from the real world.

She glanced at the bulletin board as she walked in. A large flyer caught her attention. The Miwok Schools' Athletic Association was putting on a benefit dance at Miwok High School on Friday night for parents and any adults who wanted to support school sports.

She read further. It would be an 'Oldies but Goodies' night with music from the 'fifties and 'sixties, plus a 'live' disc jockey.

A dance at Miwok High! What fun they had been.

With a sigh for all that used to be, she picked up the last three days' worth of the *New York Times*— the library didn't receive copies of the *Washington Post*—then found a cubicle with a desk and chair. There, she could sit, read, and take notes if necessary, undisturbed.

She found a detailed news report about the Middle East and began to read. Iran and Iraq, even the North Korea, seemed so far away...

Her mind wandered back to the flyer about the dance. She was in the ninth grade when she went to her first dance at Miwok High. She had defined the term "wallflower."

In the tenth grade, though, boys began to notice her. And, of course, in the tenth grade she met

Tony. He was a terrific dancer and could dance the socks off anyone else she had ever known.

She smiled as she slowly turned the pages of the *Times* without even seeing them. Although each had plans for their future, they never dwelled on the fact it would mean parting. Like most kids, they only saw the big picture, the ideal, and not how to achieve it.

Lee sighed. It'd been years since she was naïve about anything.

TWELVE

As much as Lee had enjoyed Ben's Little League games, she had to admit to uneasiness about going another game. It would be the last one she'd be attending, though, so why not go and enjoy it?

She wanted to see Ben one last time, and to say goodbye to Tony after a game would be fitting. Baseball fields were where she remembered him best and were where she would always want to remember him. Although she might always carry some bad memories—of Judith, of high school, even of Miwok, she was glad that Tony would never be one of them.

She would tell him how wonderful it had been to see him again, and to have met Ben. She would wish them both well and then leave. She had already spent far too much time thinking about them.

She arrived just as the game was starting. Tony waved to her, then Ben spotted her and yelled, "Yo, Lisa!" He smiled. "You came! Thanks!"

"I wouldn't miss it," she called back. "Good luck, Ben."

Ben played shortstop, and the game kept him busy since few players could hit past the infield. More than most games, this one was turning into a real duel, with both teams playing their hearts out. Ben's friend, Zachary, the Bruin's best pitcher, was on the mound. Lee found herself paying close attention to the game, agonizing over every pitch.

Try as they might, though, the Bruins were losing to the Firebirds, 4 to 3.

It was the bottom of the fifth inning—Little League "minor" league games only played six innings rather than nine. One parent explained to Lee, while getting an autograph, that it was more as a kindness to the parents than to conserve the strength of the children.

Lee bent forward to watch as suspense built.

The Bruins first batter walked. The second struck out. Zachary singled, but the following batter flied out. Runners were now on second and third, two outs, the game on the line. Lee's heart jumped into her throat when she saw Ben walking up to the plate. She remembered Tony in situations like this when they were in high school. She remembered how he felt the weight of the whole team rested on his shoulders. A hit, and he was a hero. An out, and he was the goat.

She glanced at Tony and saw him pacing back and forth in front of the dug-out. Ben stepped into the batter's box. Tony stopped walking, his concentration fully on the boy.

She held her breath as the pitcher threw. The ball sailed over the plate high. Ball one. She breathed again.

The throw. Ben swung and missed.

Lee chewed her bottom lip, feeling his disappointment.

"Good swing, Ben," Tony called. "You'll get it."

Ball two and ball three were low and outside. Only one more ball and Ben could walk, then all this pressure would be off him.

Lee's heart pounded at the next pitch.

"Strike two," the umpire called. Full count. Ben had stood there, the bat on his shoulder, watching the ball travel straight down the middle of the plate.

Lee squeezed her eyes shut. Poor child, she thought. This is too much pressure, simply too much for a nine-year-old!

"Step out of the box, Ben. Take a practice swing," Tony said.

Against her will, Lee opened her eyes again. Much as she didn't want to watch, she had to. She saw Tony rubbing his hands against his jeans and imagined he was remembering his times in such a predicament. As he had to learn to face it alone, so must Ben.

"Protect the plate, Ben," Tony counseled, hands on knees as Ben, again, stepped back into the batter's box. "Anything close."

Ben nodded at Tony, then raised the bat over his shoulder.

The pitcher went into his motion. Lee held her breath. The ball sailed toward the plate, straight and true. She froze as she saw Ben go into his swing.

The ball soared toward the outfield. Lee jumped up and down, cheering with the parents as the center fielder ran toward the ball, glove outstretched. The ball dropped, bounced, and went rolling toward the fence as all three outfielders chased after it.

Ben sped past first and second and was on his way to third as the throw came in to the third baseman. "Slide, Ben," Lee screamed.

The ball zoomed past the third baseman into foul territory when Ben took off toward home. "No!" She threw her arms up as if she could stop him, then, "Yes! Run, Ben, come on! Run!"

The ball got to the catcher just before Ben

reached home plate. He slid right under the tag.

Lee clapped, stamped and cheered as the Bruins emptied the dugout to give Ben high-fives for his "inside the park home run." Ben smiled from ear to ear when his teammates surround him.

Tony gave him a high-five, then patted his back over and over. Lee could see his inclination to give Ben a big hug at war with not wanting to do anything that would make Ben feel in the least bit babyish. Ben, though, settled the quandary by throwing his arms around Tony's waist. That simple gesture showed the easy affection and love between the two. Watching them, Lee's eyes filled with tears of happiness and a little awe at this special moment when Ben could feel pure, uncomplicated joy at what he had achieved.

The Bruins held their lead in the top of the sixth and won the game, 6 to 4.

Tony and some of the other parents decided to take the boys out for a pizza to celebrate. Lee had approached Tony, planning to say her goodbye as soon as they were alone.

"Can Lisa come with us, Dad?" Ben asked.

Tony's gaze met hers. "Of course, if she'd like."

Other parents were still nearby. In fact, one of

the coaches was watching Lee with bated breath. Suddenly, she realized she wanted to go, wanted to be with them both a little while longer. What difference would a couple hours make? There'd surely be a better time later this evening to say her goodbyes.

Despite the noise and bustle of the pizza parlor, Tony found a quiet booth in a corner. Tony bought beers for himself and Lee, and Ben went off to play video games with his friends while the pizza was being baked.

"Some game, huh?" Tony asked, barely able to sit still after the excitement. "Watch out, Lisa, you might turn into a Little League junkie."

"I can't tell you how exciting it was—or how nerve-wracking!"

"Even more than the big leagues," Tony added.

"And Ben was so thrilled. It was fun being there. I'm so glad he asked me to come. I really liked his company at the picnic, too."

Tony flashed one of his brilliant smiles. "Yeah? That's great. I was hoping you'd tell him to get lost if he was bothering you."

"He was no bother."

"He told me about you making him feel better when he got hurt. That was nice, Lisa. Thanks."

She smiled, then dropped her gaze back to her beer. Ever since the picnic, the conversation she had with Ben about his mother had been preying on her mind. She didn't know if Tony realized that Ben felt that way. If he didn't, he needed to.

"At the picnic..." She hesitated. This wasn't really her business, but she was making it hers.

"Yes?"

"Ben said something that got me wondering..."

"Oh?"

"Does he see much of his mother?"

"His mother?" Tony put down his fork, his eyes narrowed. "Why?"

"Well...he seems to think,"—she folded her hands—"he told me he thinks his mother doesn't love him because she never sees him."

Dark brown eyes widened, then his mouth tightened until grooves of anger etched on either side of his lips. He turned his head toward the wall. "God, that woman makes me sick!"

Lee blanched. "I thought you should know in case there's anything you could do about it."

"Do?" His gaze bored into her. "Hell, there's plenty I could do. But ask me if I want to?"

She shook her head. "No, that's between you, your ex, and Ben."

His eyes softened. "I'm sorry. It's just that for years his mother didn't want to have anything to do with him, and especially not with me. She saw him once or twice a year, and that was it. I should have talked to him about it, instead of just hoping he

wouldn't notice, or whatever in the hell I was thinking. Lately, though, she's asking to see him a lot
more. I'll be damned if I'll let her." He put his elbows on the table and ran his fingers over his eyes
and temples. "Poor kid!"

"I don't understand," she said. "How could she
not have wanted to be with such a wonderful little
boy?"

Tony clasped his hands on the table. "Maybe
because he's my kid." He stared at his hands. "You'd
have to understand the whole thing. It's not simple."

She placed her hand over his and warmth
surged through her. It was the first time she'd
touched him in years. She wasn't a person who
touched easily, yet something in Tony's anguish
reached out to her and made her want to offer comfort. She struggled to ignore the familiarity and
longing that coursed through her. "Do I look like I'm
in a hurry to rush out of here?" she asked. "How
many times have I told you my long stories, and you
listened to every silly word? There's nothing silly
where Ben's concerned."

He gazed at her, then at her hand. She pulled it
away. He picked up a book of matches and tapped
it against the tabletop as he spoke, first on one side
then on the other. "I met her in Phoenix when I was
on a Triple A team. She thought a ballplayer was
her ticket to high living and excitement. We got

married, but it was a mistake from day one. By the time she realized minor leaguers got low pay and spent hours either traveling to games or practicing for them, with only a slight chance of ever getting into the majors, she was pregnant. That extended the marriage longer than it ever would have lasted otherwise."

Lee felt as if all the blood had drained from her. "I see," she whispered.

"She left me when Ben was a year old. It wasn't much of a marriage and taking care of a baby wasn't her idea of a great life." He smiled wryly. "I don't blame her, Lisa. It was a tough life for anyone, and we were so young. She wanted glamour and fame. I was totally focused on the game, on winning. Marriage was the last thing on my mind, and I can't say I tried to make it work. I didn't much care. All I thought about was baseball. She was a lonely young wife. I'd say marriage to me must have been some kind of Hell."

Lee studied his face, solemn with silent agony for his son. The matchbook lightly rapped against the tabletop. Marriages had fallen apart for a lot less, she thought, and it sounded like this one wasn't strong enough to handle the kind of stress, hardship and traveling that made up minor league life. She had seen it in her own profession. "Is she still in Phoenix?"

"No. She went to L.A. Married a rich doctor." He lifted a steady gaze to her. "She contacted me a few months ago. Said they can't have any kids." His name came over the loudspeaker. "Our pizza's ready. I'll get Ben and pick it up."

As Lee watched Tony's back disappear into the crowd, pressure tightened around her heart. Ten years ago, when she'd briefly returned to Miwok, she had learned of his marriage. She had been offered a job in New York and had to decide what to do: to take the job and throw herself completely into her career, or try some middle course. She hadn't seen Tony since the summer after leaving high school, and more than anything she needed to see him. There was so much she needed to resolve, to explain, and to have explained by him in turn. She drove out to the Circle Z. Vic was traveling on a horse show circuit, and one of the ranch hands told her that Vic's son had moved away a few years earlier, was playing baseball with some minor league team, and had just gotten married. She didn't even know the ranch hand's name, yet his words changed the course of her life.

It was funny, but over the years she lived at Miriam's, attended college, and worked on local TV in Los Angeles, she always imagined Miwok and the people in it as remaining static. Rationally, she knew they would be living their lives just as she was hers. But deep down, she hadn't wanted to believe it.

Over her years of growing up, maturing, and observing people, she slowly began to understand herself, her mother, and the way she was raised. As she came to accept her upbringing, she wanted to see Tony again—if nothing else to bring to some closure to their relationship.

She still remembered standing there gaping as that stranger told her Tony was married. He must have thought she was a drooling idiot. She should have known Tony wouldn't spend his life pining for her. She should have expected he would marry. Still, it hurt like hell to think of him wed to someone else. Subconsciously, she always expected Tony would wait for her, just as she, at some level, had waited for him. She had left Miwok because of him and Judith, and because she was young and foolish and burning with ambition. Her life had spun out of control, taking turns she had never imagined. And because of that, she had lost him.

She rubbed her temples, tried to rub away the sudden ache that threatened to cleave her head in two.

Finding out about Tony's marriage and then trying to patch things up with Judith only to realize her mother was unwilling to meet her halfway—not even a quarter-way—she left Miwok and accepted the job in New York. The six a.m. to seven a.m. time slot was all hers.

She'd thrown herself into her work with a fire she hadn't known she possessed.

Work wasn't all she threw herself into during those early years, she remembered. She became a woman with a mission: to find a husband. She must have looked like a crazy woman on the prowl, discarding any man interested in her on the flimsiest excuse while at the same time scaring others off in equal or greater numbers by the manic way she'd question them about their outlook on love, life and children. She, who had always been so choosy and ascetic about relationships, suddenly freely offered herself and her bed in her search. But no one eased her hurt. No one took away the aching loneliness deep within her.

Fortunately, she soon realized the futility and waste of those relationships, and soon, Lee Reynolds began to grow her defenses, to erect that cool, pristine control and iron will she became known for.

How strange to hear what Tony's marriage was really like after the blissfully romantic way she had imagined it being. So much of it sounded ugly, but at least it had given him Ben.

She took a sip of her beer and soon, Tony and Ben were back carrying a pizza supreme. Tony lifted a slice overflowing with mozzarella onto her plate, then served Ben and himself. As they bit into the pizza, a collective, "Mmm" emerged from all three.

Tony and Ben laughed. Lee looked from one to the other. It hit her like a bolt. She loved being here with them. The feeling scared the hell out of her.

They all concentrated on pizza and small talk for a while. Ben finished and ran off to play video games with his friends. Soon Lee, too, pushed aside her plate. Tony ate the last two pieces.

Lee had met him this evening for a reason. Now that the food was gone while they dawdled over beer, she needed to say goodbye, and then leave. Tomorrow she had an early flight back to New York. As she prepared herself to take her leave, Tony spoke.

"I've been debating about something all evening," he said.

That was a curious thing to say. "Oh? What is it?"

"There's a dance at the high school Friday night."

"Yes. I saw a flier about it."

He smiled. "It's to raise money for athletics in schools. I'm on the committee to publicize it."

She brushed aside some pizza crumbs. "It's a good cause."

His words came out in a rush. "Would you like to go with me?"

Her hand stilled and her eyes shot up to meet his. The way she felt, he might have suggested slashing her wrists. She was tempted—very tempted. *You've gone crazy, Reynolds.* She knew she should refuse his offer. She should tell him she had a plane to catch. Instead, she said, "Well, it is a good cause."

"Most definitely."

Her spine stiffened. "Then I accept."

His eyes sparkled as a slow grin spread over his face. "That's great. I was afraid you'd laugh!"

Her heart leaped. "Never."

He placed his hand on hers. "I'll pick you up at eight."

"Why don't I pick you up instead?" she said. "I'd love to see the Circle Z again, one last time."

He sucked in his breath. "You'd really like to see it, Lisa?"

Her boldness vanished for just a moment, then her voice turned clipped, businesslike. "Of course."

"No need to wait until Friday. Besides, you don't want to wear nice clothes to tramp around a ranch. Come now. It's not late."

"Well, I don't—"

"No problem, Lisa. I'll get Ben. Follow in your car. We'll be there in ten minutes."

THIRTEEN

They drove northwest from the center of town, into the valley that edged the coast range hills separating Miwok from the Pacific Ocean. A country lane brought them to the Circle Z Ranch. Tony turned onto a gravel road and Lee saw again, after so many years, the modest, two-story, clapboard house that belonged to the owner of the ranch. Only now, that owner was Tony.

Years ago, Lee had gone inside the barn and corrals, and even in the cottage where Tony and his father lived, but she had never set foot in the main house. Now, she parked beside Tony on the wide, circular driveway. She joined him as he gave last-minute instructions to Ben.

"'Night, Lisa," Ben said as he walked toward the house.

"Goodnight." She turned questioningly to Tony.

"Let's go down to the horses," he said. "Wait until you see Double Play. He's the Arabian I've built my line around."

Solar footlights lined the gravel path to the stables. Other than that, the night was dark, and early wisps of fog from the Pacific misted the oaks with haze. Tony took her arm so she wouldn't stumble in the darkness. His nearness, the feel of his hand, and the faint, lingering scent of beer, pizza, sunshine and baseball, captured her senses.

She studied the horses with awe and excitement. These sleek, beautiful animals, this gracious land, were Tony and Ben's future. She was struck by the rightness and the thrill of it.

Double Play was magnificent, as were Easy Out and Bunt Single, his prize mares. Evening Star, a two-year-old filly and Easy Out's first foal, was Ben's horse.

"Why wasn't Evening Star named for baseball?" she asked.

"Ben's a poet. Not like his old man at all."

They laughed, and the laughter eased their awareness of the quiet of the stables, of being alone together. They walked through the occupied stalls, and Lee saw that four of the horses were sired by Double Play.

"They're beautiful," she said, stroking the velvety nose of one of the mares. "I can see why you love it out here. I always suspected, even when we were kids, that you didn't dislike the Circle Z half as much as you said you did."

"Well...what do kids know?"

He led her back up the hillside to the house. He gripped her arm once more, and with each step, the mysterious effect he had over her increased.

They stepped onto the large, wooden front porch. The front door had an etched glass window with a rose design. Tony stepped aside as Lee entered the house. The interior had a turn of the century charm. The door opened to a hallway with oak-stained chair-rail molding and cream-colored wallpaper with delicate flowers. She lightly ran her fingers over the paper.

Tony scarcely took his eyes off her, studying her reaction as he showed her to a cozy living room off the hallway. A white, rose and green striped sofa faced a white stone fireplace. Overstuffed emerald-green armchairs were on each side of the sofa, and a beautiful antique secretary stood against a far wall. He discovered he had dreamed so often of having her here in this very room, that now that she was really here, it felt like deja vu. In his dream, he proudly showed her all he acquired, all he accomplished without her. She begged his forgiveness, but he turned his back to her and pointed to the door.

In the real world, he discovered, there was no way he would turn her out.

"This is lovely, Tony." Lee looked from the hallway to the beckoning warmth of the room. "It isn't what I expected at all."

"No?" He walked into the room and stood at one end of the sofa, watching her. "What did you expect?"

"Oh, leather, chrome, a small trampoline in the living room."

He laughed aloud. "What every good jock should have."

"Exactly." She paused at the cherry wood desk and found herself running her hand over its satin-like surface and hand-carved molding.

He stepped beside her and placed his fingers on the top rail of the desk chair. His hand was sizes larger than hers, his skin shades darker. She looked from his hand to hers and the old familiarity struck.

"This is the kind of home I always dreamed of when I was growing up," he said. "Old-fashioned, warm and big enough for Ben and me to fit in at the same time—not at all like a couple of the places Vic and I lived in. Sometimes, when Ben's not here, though," he paused a moment, then rushed on, "I feel like I rattle around in it. When he's home, it's perfect."

She thought she knew him so well, but she hadn't known that about him. The cottage he and his father had shared was small and stark, the antithesis of this.

She walked over to a group of old pictures hanging above a library table.

"Those are old pictures of relatives back in Mexico," Tony explained, welcoming the chance to pull his thoughts away from things so personal. "My grandparents and great-aunts and uncles. I never knew any of them, but I like the photos, and my dad's able to tell Ben stories about every one of those people."

The sepia pictures were set in intricately carved frames. The people in them, young and old, were lined up, either standing or sitting, and staring straight at the camera. She could see the Santos eyes in every one of them. "I like these," she said.

He smiled as he walked to her side, put his arm to her waist and led her to the hall. "Just so you won't think everything's old in this house, step this way."

Down the long hallway, he stopped to show her the family room where an assortment of Mattel cars and G.I. Joes and video games were scattered about. Sliding glass doors led to the back yard. Past the family room was the kitchen which drew a long 'ah' of approval from Lee. It was white except for one brick wall that held a huge fireplace with iron and brass pots and utensils hanging from hooks that had been worked into the mortar. Between the large sink and double ovens stood a granite-covered island with a massive cook top. The countertops and appliances gleamed from obvious loving care. A pine table and chairs were against floor to ceiling windows on the far side of the room.

"The kitchen was old—old appliances and everything. So I gutted it and had this built. I always wanted to have a big kitchen. You should see the mess when I cook."

The pride in his voice warmed her. "This is a great kitchen, Tony. You've made a wonderful home. I can see why you love it here." Their eyes caught, and the spark that always existed between them suddenly flared, bright and hot, consuming the very oxygen around them.

He took a step toward her, then another. His hands cupped her elbows. Her pulse race.

"I could show you the upstairs. My room."

He meant more; she saw it in his eyes, heard it in his voice, felt it in the center of her being.

She was too intensely aware of him, even more so now, with a woman's desire and knowledge, than she'd been as an innocent teenager. She wanted to

climb those stairs, but a last remaining fragment of
sanity warned her against it. Her heart was too vulnerable here, and there was too much in both their
lives to risk. She had never been a "one-night stand"
person. She couldn't become one. She owed Bruce
more loyalty, and Tony more honesty.

She broke his gaze and turned away. "The
downstairs is lovely, Tony."

Tense silence spread between them. She
couldn't hold back from looking at him. He waited
until their eyes joined, then he nodded. He walked
over to the counter, and in his ever-restless way,
reached for the salt and pepper shakers. He shifted
them one way and then another. That was Tony—
always moving, with more activity and energy than
any four other men she knew.

"That guy you're with in New York," he said,
moving the shakers, first the salt in front, then the
pepper. "I guess it's pretty serious between you?"

She knew she should say yes. That would be
the easiest way to avoid entanglements with Tony,
but as she stood there, she was struck with doubts—
doubts that had been struggling to surface from her
first day in Miwok. Doubts that, if truth be told,
were there even before she left New York. "I
thought it was. But I don't want to complicate
things. I could never treat you casually. I still can't."

He faced her again, his hands still. "I could

never treat you casually either. I guess that was the problem." He pushed the shakers back against the wall, then folded his arms. "Well...at least that's settled." His words were serious, but as their eyes met, his face slowly broke into a grin.

Despite herself, she smiled too, relieving the sexual tension that had filled the room. Maybe she couldn't stop her heart from beating faster or her blood from heating when he was nearby, but she was an adult, not a young girl with her first crush. Whatever happened in the past, and whatever the future might bring, Tony would always be her friend. The unhappiness of their parting, all that happened afterward, the different directions they had taken in their lives, all the years and silence in between had brought them here, to this point—two older, wiser people.

She turned quickly toward narrow built-in shelves near the stove and tried to study his collection of spices while waiting for her heartbeat to stop doing the crazy rhumba it had launched into. "It looks like you've become quite a cook."

"Not really, but I enjoy it." He ran his fingers through his hair, glad to change the subject. "I'll put on that coffee now."

Lee walked to the opposite side of the kitchen and sat at the table while she watched him grind up some coffee beans and fill the coffee pot with

French roast. He moved smoothly through his kitchen, obviously comfortable with it. Her eyes devoured his broad back, the deftness of his hands as he worked, the play of his muscles as he bent and stretched to get the things he needed.

When done, he turned to her. "Why don't we go into the living room while the coffee's brewing? I'll build a fire. The fog came in over the hills tonight. It's getting a little chilly."

"Fine." She jumped to her feet.

He made a fire, then put on a compact disc of the Modern Jazz Quartet.

They drank their coffee by the firelight. Tony pulled off the sweater he wore over his black turtleneck and sat on the hearth. Lee sat on a chair at his side watching the fire, enjoying the warmth of the coffee, the peacefulness of the room.

"So, tell me," Tony asked, "how does it feel to be home?"

"Strange. Everything's different, yet there's so much the same. I'm still baffled by it all."

He smiled. "But, aside from clearing out your mother's house, have you enjoyed being back while it's lasted?"

"Yes. There's no doubt. For the longest time, I felt awkward and thought I'd made a mistake. But Miriam was stubborn. She found reasons to keep me here, and as time passed, I think she was right. I needed to come home. I'm glad I got to see the town, to spend this time with my aunt, to see...old friends."

"It's good to see you, Lisa. Different. Better than I expected it would be."

Better than I expected, too, she wanted to say, but she didn't. "Tell me about yourself, Tony. What have you been up to all these years?"

"There's not much to tell."

"There's baseball."

"Baseball...yes. Two years with the Cubs, three with the Braves, and a few months in Montreal."

Lee's mouth dropped, and she leaned forward. "You spent all that time in the majors? *The majors?* Tony, that's wonderful! You did it!"

He smiled broadly at her excitement, then dropped his gaze to his coffee cup. "It was the best," he whispered.

She gazed at the wistful expression on his face. "What happened?" Her voice was soft.

"It was a combination of things. Lots of people think that once you make it to the majors, you're set for life. But it's not so. I started out as a utility in-fielder. When someone was hurt, I'd go in, but I never made the regulars—the starting nine."

"But at least you were there."

He nodded. "Yeah, that's true. Just to stay sharp and in shape meant I had routines of exercise and coaching and personal trainers. People thought that it wouldn't take much to get my playing up to a level that I could become a regular. If not with my team, through a trade. That meant a lot more coaching, a lot more exercise, winter ball, a lot more pressure to do more, watch the stats, never screw-up."

"I know what you mean," she said. "It's exactly that way in television."

"It worked. I was traded to Montreal. I was their starting shortstop."

"Tony, that's wonderful."

"Yeah, wonderful. I had everything I thought I wanted. Then I looked around me—not just at my teams, but at all of baseball at that level. At the egos, and the competition, and the salaries, and the pressure—the god-awful pressure—not only from owners and managers, but from fans, as well as myself."

"Tell me about it," Lee said. "The money and back-stabbing because of it, in broadcasting, is really ugly."

He nodded, then sipped his coffee and looked at the fire a moment before replying. "One day, I remember I was looking at a schedule my agent had sent me. More coaching, more practice, winter ball, lots of PR events—both personal and for the team. I said, wait a minute. I had a child I barely knew and my father was getting older. I had to make a decision: was it worth it? I'd made enough money to live comfortably the rest of my life. Not high on the hog, but okay. I got into baseball because I loved the game, and I'll always love it. But I realized there was more to life. I spent years playing ball in the minors and majors, and I'm glad I had that time." He stopped talking.

"What did you do?"

"Consciously, nothing. But subconsciously, I wonder. I started getting hurt—hamstring pull, broken finger. Nothing big, just enough to get in the way of being the best I could. When the team sent me down to the minors, I quit."

As his story concluded, his low, deep voice took her vividly back to the days and nights they had spent together, sharing their dreams of the future. The future he'd dreamed of had come and gone already, and she had missed it. Missed his joy, his excitement, and missed the bad times, the down side. The weight of those lost years was like a physical pain to her. The decision to leave baseball, the thing he loved so much, must have been agony for him. She lowered her gaze. "It must have been hard, Tony, so very hard."

He nodded, glad she understood. "Yeah, it sure was. I spent a lot of sleepless nights worrying. But then, I bought the ranch. I'm glad it worked out this way. I'm...content."

She noticed he didn't say happy. But as she'd grown older, she'd concluded that "happy" was a state only for the young. Maybe he felt that way, too.

He rose and walked to the built-in shelves on one side of the fireplace. Trophies and mementos filled it. "This baseball, Lisa, is from the first home run I hit when I was in Little League. I always wanted to be a baseball player, but it demanded more, in the end, than I was willing to give."

He ran his fingers over the baseball, then looked at the other trophies a moment. She could practically see his memories ticking by. Finally, he returned to the hearth and sat, his legs bent and his hands resting on his knees. "Now, I'm enjoying Ben's team. Eventually, I'd like to work with high school boys. That's where you get the ones who are really serious, and where a coach can make or break a talented boy. I want to be a good coach for them."

She touched his hand, the way his words touched her heart. He turned his hand over, palm up, and wrapped his fingers around hers.

She looked at their entwined fingers, and raised her eyes to his face to see that he, too, was studying their joined hands. And what had begun as a gesture of understanding, catapulted into something stronger, as a sharp awareness of him radiated from her fingers throughout her body. She took in the long, black lashes that fanned his cheeks, and the sensuousness of his lips. She wanted to trace the line of his lips, she wanted to feel his mouth against hers, his arms around her, just as she used to. But also, she wanted more. More than she had even known about as a young, high school girl.

"Why did you leave, Lisa?" he whispered, his face stark. "What went wrong? Was it because of me? Because of what started the night of the prom? Were you so ashamed of me—of us?"

She stared at him, horrified by his words, her heart breaking. "Oh God, Tony. Is that what you thought?" Her hand tightened on his, and with her free one she touched the side of his face, his hair— so much thicker and coarser than the soft locks she had loved to stroke when they were young. There were times she thought she knew Tony's face better than her own. "It wasn't you."

"What, then? Everything was fine, then I left for baseball camp and you turned completely cold. It was as if you'd flipped a switch. One day we were in love, and the next...You went to San Diego to go to school instead of Los Angeles, but you didn't say why. You wouldn't talk to me; wouldn't explain."

Memories washed over her. "You're wrong. I tried to explain."

"You said a lot of words. You never told me the truth."

She stared at him.

"I thought...so many terrible things," he admitted. "Why, Lisa? Won't you tell me?"

What could she say? The truth screamed in her head, but she couldn't do that to him, or to herself. It had been pushed far in the past and had to stay there.

"I was confused," she said finally, weaving the lie she'd learned to live with. "I was...I thought I was doing what was best—for you as well as for me. I thought I shouldn't see you—that you needed to concentrate on your baseball career."

He drew his hand away from hers. "Stop. It was more than that, whether you admit it or not. Tell me, was it that easy for you to forget me?"

"No." She felt pressure behind her eyes. "I never did."

"Then, I don't understand—"

"Please. It was so long ago. It was a mistake, one of many mistakes." Her body trembled, and she folded her arms, hugging them to her chest.

As if he, too, needed to put distance between the emotional bond that connected them still, he stood and went over to the window, resting his hands on his hips. "It's so foggy out you can't even see the trees in the front yard."

He did nothing she could see, but as always, he drew her to him. She stood at his side, also facing the window. "Perhaps they aren't there anymore. Perhaps nothing is." She took a shuddering breath. "It's so strange, Tony, being here...in Miwok...with you. I feel as if I've drifted away somewhere, that I'm not quite the same person, and it's not quite the same year as shown on the calendar."

"Things in some ways are the same," his words echoed hers, but his voice was hollow, "and in some ways altogether different."

"I don't know what to make of it. The Lee Reynolds I've been in New York seems to grow dimmer with each passing day, but Lisa Marie isn't here either. She's gone. She doesn't exist anymore. I know that. Yet, it's as if I'm drifting as aimlessly as that fog bank. And everywhere I look, it's the past I see."

"I know one thing," he said as he slipped his arm around her shoulders and drew her against his side. "The past might haunt you sometimes, but it's gone, no matter how much you might wish otherwise. And there's not a damn thing a person can do about it." His embrace was both a sanctuary and a prison, offering security and bliss, but asking for promises she could not keep.

She shut her eyes a moment, then glanced at him, her voice so soft he barely heard it. "I can't help but think, if things had turned out differently, of what might have been."

He heard a wistful longing in her voice that tugged at him. He couldn't let her do this to herself. Or to him.

He placed both his hands on her shoulders and held her straight out before him. "The funny thing about people, Lisa, is when they see life in a certain way, they make choices that fit what they see. As strange as people may seem, they're remarkably consistent creatures. Time after time, given the same circumstances, they'll make the very same choices."

Her shoulders sagged under the weight of his words. "So Lisa Marie will always choose to become a journalist, and Tony will always choose baseball."

"Was that how you saw it, Lisa?"

"Wasn't it?"

He pulled her into his arms in a hug, as brotherly as he could manage. He shut his eyes, as if not seeing her could protect him against the feel of her, the scent of her, but it didn't. He was rocked by her nearness, by the need that was always just below the surface when she was with him.

He wanted her as much as when he was a boy. No, he realized. Even more. Back then he didn't know an iota of what he knew now about loving a woman. But he still remembered the pain of losing her. Once was enough. Choose baseball? He had no choice. And in a way, a much worse way, neither did she.

Lisa left him once, and she had already told him she was leaving again. This time, he was not going to let it shatter him.

He set her from him and turned to tend the fire.

She folded her arms again, hugging them tight against her rib cage so as not to reach out for him. What was happening to her? Why? Why, suddenly, this longing? This ache?

"Would you like more coffee, Lisa?" he said, his back still to her as he struggled to maintain the composure he had nearly lost.

"It's very late. I should go."

A jazz saxophone played softly in the background and the fire logs snapped and popped. He straightened and brushed the ash from his fingers against the back of his jeans before he faced her, his expression carefully neutral, then picked up her jacket and held it open.

She slipped it on. The light from the fireplace cast a warm, orange glow over the soft lines of the living room furniture. She liked this room. It was a room that shouldn't know loneliness. Not his. Not hers.

He held open the front door, and she forced herself to walk toward it. But as she stepped in front of him, he reached out and placed his hand on her arm. Even through the jacket she could feel her skin burn where he touched her, she could feel her heart nearly stop, and her breath catch. Her eyes flashed to his, then drifted downward to his nose, his lips. She wanted him with a force that left her weak and trembling.

His fingertips rose to her cheek, then to a stray wisp of hair near her ear, brushing it back away from her face. He cupped the back of her neck.

"You know, don't you, that if I were to kiss you, I wouldn't want to stop?" The words were thick in his throat.

"If you were to kiss me," she whispered, "I wouldn't want you to stop."

His fingers trailed against her jaw line, his thumb slowly tracing the side of her face as his eyes softened and grew warmer. Blood pulsated hard through her body. It was all she could do not to wrap her arms around him, pull him against her, and kiss him hot and slow and sensuous. But she hesitated, and then it was too late.

She felt as if a wall separated them and she was suddenly scared to death of what would happen were she to step over to the other side of it. She thought of the words he had spoken earlier about the past being over. It was. Lisa Marie had grown up.

And so she turned away from him and walked out the door.

———

Her conversation with Bruce that night was very short. He was too angry to talk after learning she wouldn't be home for the dinner party at Baldwin's.

FOURTEEN

The next morning, Miriam was up early. She was packing lunches when Lee walked into the kitchen. "What's this?"

Miriam's face turned fiery red. "I'm going to a rodeo in Salinas with Gene. I think it's the biggest one held in California, and it's going on this week. I've never been to a rodeo before, so I said yes. I...um...had thought you'd be on your way to New York, so I didn't mention it. But now, you're staying, and I didn't want to leave you, but then Gene has been so excited about taking me, and...oh, God!" She pressed her hands to her hot cheeks.

Lee grinned. "I think it's great that you're going, Miriam. I didn't know you wanted to see a rodeo."

"I didn't either." She bustled about, her eyes

avoiding Lee's as she began building huge sand-
wiches of cold meats and cheeses. "Gino used to
ride in them—he rode the bulls. The goal is to hang
on for a certain amount of time. Can you believe it?
He made it sound so exciting!"

"You call him Gino?"

"I don't know where he found the nerve,"
Miriam mused, lost in thought about the man. "I'd
be afraid to touch a bull, let alone try to sit on one."

Lee laughed. "Well, you and *Gino*, have fun."

"Oh, I will. And...um...don't worry about me if
we don't get back tonight."

Lee's eyebrows shot up. "Oh?"

"It's three hours to Salinas and another three
back. Gino will be driving, and if he seems too tired
to drive all the way home..."

"Ah, of course, can't let that happen."

Miriam eyed her stiffly, daring her to say another word. "My feelings exactly!"

After Miriam and Gene left, Lee faced the job
she dreaded more than any other. In fact, she had
planned not to do it, but to throw everything in Judith's bedroom away after the house sold. Now,
though, in the big empty house, she decided to do
things the right way.

Memories flung themselves at her the moment
she stepped into the room. Struggling to keep her
thoughts focused only on what she was doing, she

unfurled a Goodwill bag, opened her mother's top bureau drawer, scooped up armfuls of underwear, nylons and nightclothes, and shoved them into the bag.

When she reached the bottom drawer, she sat on the floor to go through it. Under a layer of scarves and handkerchiefs, a metal-framed picture lay on its face. She turned it over.

It was her favorite portrait of her parents. She thought it was lost.

Judith Reynolds was beautiful in a sparkling rhinestone necklace and a low-cut, royal blue evening gown that showed off her full-breasted but otherwise petite figure to perfection. Her platinum blond hair was styled like Marilyn Monroe's.

Lee had never been as delicate or beautiful as her mother. "You're such a cow," Judith used to say to her as she was growing up. Even now, as Lee watched her diet carefully to stay thin enough for television cameras, Judith's condemnation rang in her ears.

In the photograph, standing behind and slightly to Judith's side, his hands on her waist, was Jack. He was much older than Judith, tall and breathtakingly handsome, with dark brown hair, and a sparkling glint in his brown eyes.

When Judith heard he had been a soldier during the Vietnam War and had been captured and tortured, she was overwhelmed. He was her hero, her own Burt Lancaster, just like in *From Here To Eternity*.

But what he had been through was no movie script, and his nerves had been shattered by his experience.

Lee set the picture upright on the dresser top and looked at it. Judith's ideas of marriage to her handsome war hero and the reality of it were apparently quite different.

Although Lee was only six at the time, she never forgot the last night of her father's life.

She had been asleep, and something woke her. The bedroom door had stood slightly ajar. Down the hall in her parents' room, she saw movement and heard loud voices. She crawled into the hall and knelt on the floor, her nightgown tucked under her knees, trying to make herself small so they wouldn't notice that she was there. It wasn't unusual for her parents' fighting to wake her, but something about that night's fight was different. That night, she was scared.

The hall was dim, but light blazed from their bedroom. Judith, young and healthy, was leaning over the dressing table, close to the mirror, applying a fresh layer of pink lipstick to her full mouth.

The crash of her father's fist slamming on the top of the vanity, shaking and rattling bottles of perfume and make-up caused Lisa to cringe and bite back a frightened cry. A canister of talc fell onto the floor with a dull thud.

Judith paid more attention to herself than to Jack's anger. She raised her arms up to fluff her whitish-blond hair, then gave her head a saucy shake so that a couple of strands fell over her forehead. She plucked at them, making them lay just so, then squirted her hair with her cologne atomizer.

Lisa hated Judith's dress. Bright pink, the front was cut in a deep heart shape so that it showed off her breasts. At one time, Lisa thought her mother looked like the movie star she had always wanted to be. But as she got older, she realized Judith's look was years behind the times—a Marilyn Monroe type in a world of Meryl Streeps and Jane Fondas. She wished her mother would wear the loose, casual dresses and slacks that other kids' mothers wore. Men never stared at other kids' mothers. Even at age six she perceived the uncomfortable undercurrents.

Her mother ran her hands over the hips of her dress, smoothing the polished cotton, then practiced her pout in the mirror in between words about going to Hollywood to become a star. She was sick of wasting her life on a crazy old man and a squalling brat. She'd had it. Judith tossed her coat over her arm and picked up her suitcase. Lisa backed away as her parents walked out of the bedroom.

Her mother was going away, but the most shattering, the most devastating, was when she heard her father say he was going, too.

She could understand Judith leaving. Judith spent most of the time bemoaning not being a star. But her father...he wouldn't leave her. He couldn't. He told her he loved her.

She remembered sitting all alone on the hall stairs, crying silently before her father came and got her. He picked her up in his strong arms and said he was taking her to Aunt Miriam's. She clutched his neck and cried and begged him not to go. He had promised her he'd be back. He had promised....

Lee twisted a lock of hair around her finger as she remembered her terror at being left that way. Why, she'd wondered? What had she done that made her mother want to leave her? Was she really so unlovable? Had she really been so bad? But she knew Daddy loved her. At least Daddy would come back.

Lee bent forward to ease the burning ache in the pit of her stomach. That night, on the road to San Francisco, a drunken driver crashed head on into the car Jack Reynolds was driving. He was killed instantly, and Judith returned to Miwok, her pelvis crushed, her dreams of glamour and fortune shattered as completely as her hip.

Miriam didn't return to Miwok until four o'clock Wednesday afternoon. She looked sheepish, yet floated about three feet in the air and bubbled with enthusiasm as she told her about the brave, dashing, handsome and exciting rodeo riders. When Lee asked about one particular handsome and exciting ex-rodeo rider, she was surprised to see Miriam grow flustered. Miriam soon went upstairs to lie down a moment—the ride back had been a long one. A half-hour later, Lee peeked in the guestroom and found her aunt sound asleep. Lee chuckled and pulled the door quietly shut.

She spent Wednesday and Thursday discarding, recycling, and boxing clothes, appliances, dishes and so on for charity. She worked with Janet Lettice on which furniture should be kept, which discarded, and when the painter, drapes and carpet would arrive. In between, she spent hours on the phone with New York. She decided to skip the special about Moscow. It would have taken her away from the action for too long, and if she made the jump to Nighttime News, it wouldn't be at all feasible to do a major report for the competition.

Friday morning, Tony called and asked Lee to dinner with him before the dance.

She thought she should check to see if her dress needed to be pressed. She had brought a Bill Blass original with her, having learned to always be ready to look her finest in case she was called on to attend a gala in San Francisco or some such event. It was a smooth dove gray silk dress with thin straps and a jet-beaded bodice. Taking it out of the closet, she studied it a long time. It was too elegant for a dance at the gym...but it looked terrific.

She sorted through the few clothes she'd packed, trying to decide if dressing one of them up, a scarf here, a new belt there, or a pin, or a corsage, or a jacket, would work. She remembered watching a rerun of *Gone With The Wind* and how Scarlett O'Hara made a gorgeous dress out of drapery. She eyed her bedroom curtains with mock desperation. Too flimsy.

She tossed the clothes aside.

She hadn't brought—and didn't own—anything befitting an oldies dance. Her clothes were too so-phisticated. Hell, she was too sophisticated. What was she thinking, going to such a thing?

Her angst grew. From a bureau drawer she took out the small jewelry box she'd brought with her and poured through it. Boring! Everything in the box was plain, practical—expensive—but boring. Now what?

Shoes! She dived onto the floor of the closet. She'd only brought a few pairs, and tossed them out to the middle of the floor, one by one. They were all pumps—stylish, business-like, but more for comfort than something one would wear to a dance—except for dark gray silk with four-inch heels that looked great with the Bill Blass dress.

She sat on the floor. Shoes, jewelry, and clothes covered the carpet, the bed, and the bureau top. She was definitely losing it.

Gene Cantelli helped Tony carry the baseball bats and helmets to his car after the team practice. Gene wasn't an assistant coach because the hours his shop was open usually conflicted with games and practice, but he had a good arm and batting eye, and Tony welcomed his help to work one-on-one with the boys whenever his schedule permitted. This Friday afternoon the sun was bright, the air crisp and clean, and Gene left his part-time assistant minding the store so he could join Tony's Bruins. He helped Ricky and Paul with batting, Jimmy and Bobby with throwing accuracy, and had a special fondness for Micah, a fatherless boy who needed help with every fundamental. If ever a kid might run the bases backwards, Micah was the one. But he had a big heart, guts, and a fantastic desire to learn. Gene gave the boy all the time he could.

"Hey, *paisan*," Gene said to Tony as the boys ran off to meet parents and carpools for their rides home, "I heard you're taking Lee Reynolds to a high school dance."

"Yeah. So?"

"What are you? Last of the big-time spenders?"

"It's not a date. It's a charity thing. That's the only reason I asked her."

"Ah...charity."

"Why don't you come see for yourself?"

"I would, but I'm taking Miriam to a play in San Francisco. Tom Stoppard. I want to show her that even us cowboys got some 'culcha'."

Tony eyed him. Gene and Vic had been friends a long time. Tony thought of him almost as a big brother. He'd never known Gene to care what any woman thought of his culture, or anything else. "You seem to like her quite a bit."

Gene walked in silence a long time. "I'll tell you a secret, Tony. For a long time I went out with girls a lot younger than me. I thought it would keep me young. Instead, they were a constant reminder that I'm getting old. Miriam, though, sees my age as just fine. Around her, I can be myself. I really like it. I really like *her*. She's smart, attractive, sexy as hell, and she's got a great sense of humor."

"Interesting," Tony said.

"Yeah...that it is. No one is more surprised than me, *paisan*, let me tell you. Say, why don't you come over to the saddle shop. I've got some new gear I'd like to show you."

"I'd better not. I'm taking Lisa to dinner first. I can't go smelling like horse gear. That stuff gets in your pores and there's no getting rid of it. Besides, I'll have to pick up some clothes at the cleaners. They won't be ready until four-thirty, then the place closes at five, and if I'm late—"

Gene gave a belly laugh. "I'm sure glad this date doesn't mean anything to you."

———

That evening, Lee's hands shook as she put on silk stockings held up with a black garter belt. She poked a fingernail right through one leg. Nervously, she tossed the stocking aside and got a new one. Next, as she dabbed on Joy de Jean Patou perfume, her fingers slipped and a bunch of it splashed onto her cleavage. She put the perfume vial down and took several deep breaths trying to relax, but all they accomplished was to make her head feel light.

This wasn't a date, she repeated. But who was she trying to convince? And why?

Tony couldn't find a decent tie in all fifty or so that he owned. Everyone he knew gave him ties for father's day, his birthday, Christmas. You'd think that at least one of all those people had good taste.

He settled on a gray, brown, and rose print tie. He thought it would go well with his casually cut, soft tannish-gray Armani suit, and a white shirt.

He shaved and nearly slit his throat. Wearing a piece of toilet paper to stop the bleeding—he sure hoped he remembered to take it off before he left the house—he began to dress. His tee-shirts were all wrinkled. As he set up the ironing board, he stopped and wondered what the hell he was doing.

He put on his socks and noticed that one was black and the other navy. At least his shoes matched. He switched to two black socks.

Luckily, the nick stopped bleeding before he put on his shirt. Then he tried to tie the damn necktie he'd picked out. His thumbs kept getting in the way. Maybe he should use a clip-on.

He could imagine Lisa's face if he showed up with some dorky clip-on tie. She'd cancel the date right then and there.

He sat on the bed. He hadn't even left the house, and he was already exhausted.

The last time Lee had stood in her bedroom getting ready to go on a big date was the night of the senior prom. She remembered doing everything she could to make Judith happy with her, as usual. And as usual, nothing seemed to work.

She was so upset over her difficulties with Judith, she had even fought with Tony. That made it easy, then, to say yes when Ken Walters asked her to the prom. She and Ken were like two peas in a pod. Their coloring was the same, their interests, their straight-A grades. Judith was ecstatic. Ken was every mother's dream. Good-looking, honor roll student and filthy rich. When Ken was accepted at Harvard, even Lisa was impressed.

The problem was, when Tony found out she was going to the prom with Ken, he started seeing another girl. Lisa was consumed with jealousy.

That situation lasted about a month, then Tony and Lisa got together again. Ken was furious.

In retrospect, Lee couldn't blame him. Ken thought she'd broken up with Tony to go with him, when all she was doing, she realized later, was using him to make Judith happy. It was not one of her finer moments. She should have expected the trouble such deception would cause.

Ken had gotten even, however. On prom night, he stood her up.

She would never forget her humiliation, standing at the window in her fancy prom dress, watching the empty street as the minutes ticked away. And Judith's outrage—at Lisa, not at Ken. Lisa had failed her again.

An hour and a half later, Tony showed up wearing a tuxedo, with prom tickets in his pocket and a gardenia corsage in his hand. Lisa had burst into tears.

Judith was beside herself with rage as Lisa walked out the door with him. It was the first time she had ever openly defied her mother. Always before Lisa had tried to please, to give in to Judith's wishes. Not this time, though. The end of her high school years had come, and she had almost...*almost*...missed celebrating it with the one person who was more important to her than anyone else in the world.

She paid for defying Judith, though. In a sense, the cost had been the life she'd known, because that was the beginning of the end.

Now, she applied her make-up with great care. Just a couple of minutes before six o'clock, she reached for her dress and slipped it over her head.

Standing in front of the mirror in her old bedroom, the smells of make-up and shampoo, perfume and bath oils mixed around her just as they had long ago.

Her stomach jumped and twisted like a demented acrobat as she looked at the clock and studied her image again.

Jewelry! She looked at the ugly holes in her earlobes with a shudder. Reaching for the box with her diamond stud earrings, she put them on.

A small diamond pendant on a platinum filigree chain was perfect with the dress.

She had just fastened the clasp when the doorbell rang. She froze, remembering prom night...hearing the bell and seeing Tony, standing in her doorway, looking more handsome in his black tuxedo than she'd ever seen him.

I won't let Ken do this to you, Lisa. You're going to your prom, and you're going with me.

Now, she slowly walked down the stairs. Taking deep breaths to compose herself, she waited a moment then pulled open the door.

He stood in front of her, his expression wary. Then, as he looked at her, his face slowly crinkled into that old, familiar smile. Warmth filled her. She noticed the casual Armani cut of his suit, his tie, the way every hair was in place, the scent of Polo. She was relieved that he'd gone to this trouble for her.

She'd have felt awfully foolish in her Blass original if he were in jeans. But then, Tony had always been a cool dresser.

His breath caught as she stood before him, her sophisticated beauty dazzling in the understated elegance of her gray dress. From the wives of highly paid major leaguers, he had learned to recognize designer originals. That was one.

"Hello, Tony," she said.

"Hi."

She realized she'd kept him standing in the doorway far too long. "Would you like to come in? Miriam already left for the city with Gene or she would have loved to see you."

"Well, if you're ready," he said, gesturing toward his car.

"Yes, I am." She grabbed her tiny purse, and shut and locked the door.

His hand barely skimmed her elbow as he walked her to the Jeep Cherokee parked in the driveway. "My only other car's a truck that smells to hay and horses."

"This is fine." She climbed in and suppressed a small smile. If only her fellow newsmen could see her now, Lee Reynolds, star anchor, dressed in a designer original worth a few thousand dollars, riding in an SUV on the way to a high school gym. Somehow, though, it felt right. It felt comfortable.

They drove to Miwok's finest restaurant, the Hillcrest Lodge, situated, appropriately, at the top of a small hill.

After the waiter prepared and served their Caesar salad. Tony asked Lee about living in New York, and she told him about her job. He asked her about her friends, and she told him about the offer she was given to switch to Nighttime News from her current situation.

"Your job means a lot to you, it seems," he said quietly.

"I love my work."

"That's great."

"That's also why I'm hesitant to change networks, even though it's the best way to reach the next level."

He put down his fork and waited until he had all her attention. "Lee Reynolds can work anywhere she wants," he said. "You're one classy lady. Take your time. You should be happy and proud of what you're doing."

His words warmed and filled all the empty corners of her heart. Tony had always offered unconditional support and understanding, and he just did again.

"I've been thinking about this a long time," she said. "The greatest pressure to change to what might seem to be a more prominent job comes from the outside—from other people's expectations. I'm not convinced it's what I want to do."

"Then don't move until you're sure."

"That's what Miriam said."

"And your, uh, friend in New York?"

She dropped her gaze to her salad and pushed the arugula around with her fork. "He said, 'Go for it'." She saw the surprise on Tony's face as he quickly averted his eyes and concentrated on his salad. She tried to explain. "He's very much in favor of doing all one can to get ahead. He's a very successful man."

Tony reached for the wine to top off their glasses. "Successful. I wouldn't expect you to be with anyone who wasn't. Sort of a grown-up Ken Walters."

She winced at the memory of the boy she'd promised to go to the prom with. So Tony, too, must have been thinking of the last time they went to a dance together. She had trouble finding her voice a moment. "Much nicer," she said finally.

"I should hope so."

They ate in silence, then the waiter took away the salad dishes and brought their prime rib.

She picked up her fork, then put it down again. "Let's forget about New York and business and all of that tonight. Let's just talk like friends—the way we used to do."

"That sounds like a good idea." His megawatt smile sent all topics of conversation flying from Lee's mind. She had the girlish notion she could sit there all night looking at his smile. But then Tony began talking to her. He had a knack for conversing she always admired. He could talk to anyone about anything at any time. He claimed it came from playing baseball—that he had to learn to spend long hours sitting in the dugout or at practices with a group of guys. They had nothing to do but talk and tell stories, and so they had to learn how to do it in a way that was interesting, passed the time and put each other at ease.

Tony had been a good conversationalist when he and Lee were young. Lee had to learn to become one, learn how to soften up the elusive politicians, publicity-seeking celebrities, and distrustful citizens involved in newsworthy events with idle patter and simple questions, and then delve deeper, move to tougher questions, hard-biting comments. When she was "on," in other words, working, she was always verbally quick, and because of that was often invited to be a guest on one of TV's numerous "talking-heads" political shows. With Tony she relaxed, without the edge caused by constantly being on her guard or trying to pierce through any subterfuge and double-talk. She let him carry the conversation, and he did, easily and entertainingly.

They discussed Tony's ranch and how much Vic taught him about making the ranch profitable, and he eventually got her to talk about her personal life in New York, about her friends and how she liked the big city.

They talked about politics, movies, and even the San Francisco Giants chances for winning a World Series again (nil, they decided). Before they realized it, it was past eight o'clock. Time to go to the dance.

The feelings that came over Lee as they rode along the familiar streets to the high school were so confusing and conflicting she could scarcely breathe. The last time she was at a dance at the gym with Tony had been prom night. Yesteryear seemed suddenly so close, as if all the time in between had vanished into nothing. She struggled to convince herself that it was already a new century, that she was rolling rapidly towards forty, and that the man beside her wasn't her boyfriend anymore, but practically a stranger.

He turned into the parking lot and found an open spot. Neither moved to get out of the vehicle, but instead sat, feeling the moment. In the soft light of the parking lot, she was sure that the wistful expression on Tony's face mirrored her own.

"This car is all wrong, Tony." Her voice was soft. "We should be in your big Bonneville."

He glanced at her, eyes dark and deep, then his

eyebrows rose and a saucy grin stole over his face. "We can pretend. I've got some fond memories because of that car."

Yes, many memories. She laughed. "Hmm, maybe we'd better go inside."

They got out of the car and he took her hand as they walked toward the gym. Her stomach grew increasingly tense as they neared it. Every step she took made the memory of the last time they were here that much stronger. That was the night she realized how much she loved him. Always before he'd been her "boyfriend" with all the light-hearted romantic notions that went along with a teenage girl's use of that term. But as they danced the prom away, she saw that the scraggly boy she'd known for three years had grown into a handsome young man. Her friend, her partner, her everything. Love—it seemed too small a word for the feelings that swept over her that night. She needed a word at least fifteen syllables long.

"Ready?" he asked, his hand on the door handle.

"Too late to back out now, Santos."

He laughed and pulled open the door.

The gym was decorated in metallic blue and silver, with big-hole "45" records dangling from the ceiling, and a cardboard cutout of a giant jukebox decorating one wall. A large crowd had already gathered, a lot of people who appeared to be in their forties or fifties, and a few who were scarcely out of their teens. Lee was relieved to see that most people were dressed to the nines.

The loud strains of "Do the Locomotion" nearly blasted them back into the parking lot.

A ticket-seller sat just inside the door. Tony reached into his back pocket for his wallet as Lee opened her purse. "No," he said to her, taking two twenty-dollar bills from his wallet and handed them to the ticket-seller.

She handed another two twenties to the curious ticket-seller. "It's for a good cause."

As "The Monster Mash" played, Tony looked for a table. "We'll sit this one out. God, I wonder if I know how to dance to any of these old songs? Where are Gino and Miriam when we need them?"

Her eyes caught Tony's, and they grinned.

They no sooner sat, though, when the DJ put "Runaround Sue" on the record player. Tony jumped to his feet. "That's more like it," he said. "Come on."

He held out his hand.

"Oh, Lord!" She was suddenly startlingly aware of what she'd set herself up for. She hadn't done "fast" dancing since college. Tony's feet tapped to the music. She could see he was aching to dance. It made sense. He was the best dancer she'd ever known.

She held her breath, feeling clumsy before she even stood, and followed him to the center of the floor. Walking across the dance floor helped. The floorboards reverberated with the heavy, steady beat, so that by the time Tony faced her and took her hands, she was at least ready to give it a try.

It took her most of the song, however, to get over her awkwardness and to get her body to remember the way she used to dance years ago. The pattern and the steps must have been engraved somewhere in her psyche, though, because once she let herself really listen to the music and watch Tony, she was able to follow his lead.

Tony was as limber as ever. He moved easily, as if his whole body was attuned to the beat. She loved watching the rhythm in motion of his body. She always had.

The disc jockey was merciless. Immediately, he put on "Please Mr. Postman", a Motown favorite.

"Remember the calypso, Lisa? Let's try it!"

As soon as the song ended, Tony took off his jacket and rolled up the sleeves of his shirt, but returned to Lee's side in time to twist and calypso their way through some rock classics—the Isley Brothers' "Twist and Shout," Buddy Holly's "That'll Be the Day," and Bobby Darin's "Dream Lover." Lee was exhausted, but laughed and somehow managed to keep up with him. Being with him was like trying to follow a comet. Neither of them knew the steps to "The Stroll," and tried to follow some of the older couples on the floor. As they nearly tumbled over with laughter as their feet kept getting tangled up, Tony suggested a breather.

They no sooner finished their iced punch when they heard the slow, dreamy strains of Sam Cooke's "You Send Me."

Tony glanced at her, and the look in his eyes rocked her. There was no need for him to ask. All night she'd wondered what it would be like when the first slow song played, how it would feel to be in his arms again. All night he'd wondered if it would be as good as the first time they had slow-danced, how it would feel to hold her close to him once again.

She put down her glass and stood. He took her hand, lightly at first, then his fingers tightened and he led her onto the dance floor. He turned and held out his arms.

She walked slowly into them, then placed one hand in his, her other on his shoulder. His shoulder was thicker, more muscular than she remembered.

He touched her waist, then eased her nearer. She swayed closer. His arms tightened until his cheek rested against her temple. The feel of his head, the way his body curved around hers in the dance position, being in his arms, was wonderfully familiar to her.

Taut and sensitive, her body fairly crackled with awareness of him.

He took one tentative step, and she followed, then another and another until in some magical way, as they moved to the music, they melted into one. She shut her eyes, swaying to the seductive strains of the music. She felt the heat of his body from their fast dancing and felt the dampness of perspiration on his skin. The scent of his soap and after-shave surrounded her, and she remembered so many times being with him like this. It was like coming home again, but this home wasn't the cold, forbidding place where Judith lived, this one was welcoming and filled with love.

He tucked the hand he held to his chest, and she could feel his heartbeat. She relaxed against him, her eyes shut to everything but him.

His hand lowered to her hip, pressing closer to her and the fast, erratic beat of his heart pounded through her as if it were her own. "You smell good," he said, his voice husky and low.

"You, too," she murmured.

He pulled his head back, looked at her. His eyes spoke reckless volumes, while his words tried to be light and joking. "You're crazy."

"Yes," she whispered. But it was his eyes she answered. Her gaze drifted over his face, different yet so familiar, so...with a jolt she realized she loved the shape of his nose. It was smooth and shiny, thin, with arched nostrils. She never before thought she could love the way a nose looked, but suddenly, she did. "I am crazy," she agreed as her arms tightened around him.

For the briefest moment a look more of agony than pleasure flitted over him. Then he nodded as if to say, "Me, too." Crazy to be here, like this, wanting her, loving her, all over again.

She pressed her face against his cheek, lost in a medley of emotions. When the music stopped, it hurt to pull away.

"Where Did Our Love Go?" began and the question in the title resounded through her. It was like a knife wound. Stricken, she turned and walked back to their table, trying not to listen to the words.

He followed her and stood while she sat, still not able to look at him. "Lisa," he said. "Let's go outside."

FIFTEEN

They stood on the landing at the top of the stairs that led down to the parking lot. She ran her hand over her hair, trying to push loose tendrils back into her chignon. "It was quite warm in there."

"The breeze feels good."

"Excuse me." A middle-aged couple stood before them. "Aren't you Lee Reynolds?" the man asked.

"My name's Lisa," she said.

The man looked skeptical. "But—"

"Give her a break," Tony said, taking Lee's arm and leading her away from the two. "Don't you know all blondes look alike?"

Embarrassed, the couple backed away, muttering an apology.

Lee did all she could not to laugh aloud.

"I'm sorry," Tony said. "I couldn't help myself."

"It's all right. You did just fine."

He smiled at her. "Are you enjoying this, Lisa?"

"I can't begin to tell you—" She began enthusiastically, then stopped. "Are you?"

"It...it's good. It's..."

"Yes?"

He shook his head. "Nothing. Is it too cold for you out here? Evenings in Miwok—cold wind and fog, just like always."

She folded her arms. "It's scarcely chilly at all."

He wrapped an arm over her shoulders and pulled her against his side. Someone swung the door to the gym open all the way so that it caught and didn't close again—apparently others were also feeling the heat inside.

She glanced back at the door, then at the man beside her, and let herself lean against him, enjoying his nearness.

"It's strange to be here again with you, Tony. It's as if seventeen years of my life didn't really happen, and I'm here, and this is what's real..."

"Don't, Lisa!"

Startled, she hid her hurt. "It's not that I want to have such thoughts. I can't help it. I spent so many years not letting myself think of those days. And then I came back."

He touched her jaw, his thumb under her chin as he lifted her face toward his own. Her pulse raced at his touch. The distant sound of "Since I Fell For You" reached them.

His arms circled her, and he slowly drew her closer to him. She didn't draw back as their eyes met.

"Dance with me?" he whispered.

She nodded.

His fingers started at her shoulders then traveled the length of her back, to her waist, her hips, molding her to him as they danced.

She could feel the raw desire that had teased them all evening, making her hot, cold, and wound tighter than a top, suddenly let loose and gnaw at her insides.

Still holding her close as he swayed to the music, he said, "Come home with me, Lisa."

She stopped and drew back.

"Not for old times." His gaze was penetrating. "For now."

"But..." She could think of a thousand reasons not to go, and only one reason that she should. She wanted him, wanted to be with him, wanted to love him. And with this feeling so strong, what did they tell her about all the reasons that kept her away? Reasons like Bruce, like the life she now lived? But then, didn't she know right from the beginning where this night would lead? And wasn't that why she agreed to come here with him? Why she *wanted* to come here with him?

"Our lives have gone their separate ways," he said. "And they're both filled with other people, other obligations. But for some reason, hard as it is to believe, you're here, and we have this one night to live a lifetime on. Come with me."

Still, she hesitated.

"We're a man and a woman, not kids anymore. I want to make love to you, and I want to do it right. No kisses on a gym floor or a school yard, no park benches or car seats. My house, my bed. Is that so wrong?"

"No, but..."

"But?"

She never could win with him. Especially when she didn't want to. He waited.

"All right," she whispered.

Silence, then surprise, relief, anticipation, and yes, even anxiety, all flitted over Tony's face. He took her hand and led her to the parking lot. His eyes were dark, sultry, but with the same mischievous twinkle that always made her want to go along with him. Just like the night of the prom.

When the dance had ended those seventeen years ago, they had started out for Big Bob's restaurant with friends. But, like now, she wanted to be alone with him. He parked in a secluded area and kissed her.

Kisses weren't enough that night. She wanted him. She wanted to be sure he'd never forget her.

I love you, Lisa...I always have. That's what he'd said when the fumbling and awkwardness were over. But it wasn't clumsy to her back then. It was nothing short of miraculous that he could become a part of her, physically join with her, like that. That he, and only he, could make her feel whole.

A wistfulness, poignant and bittersweet, touched her heart at the memory of that evening. Youthful and precocious, their feelings were so full they could have burst from the sheer pleasure of being together. They never would have believed that the moment loomed so close when she would have to let him go.

On this night, Tony drove the Jeep through the foggy streets of Miwok, and in no time turned down the country lane to his house. The front porch was lit, and Lee saw that he left a lamp on in the living room. It cast a warm, yellow glow in the window.

They walked in silence from the car to the front door, then into the house, into the now familiar hallway with its oak-stained chair rails and floral wallpaper.

He showed her to the living room, then

stopped. "Well..." He cleared his throat. "Here we are."

On leaden legs she walked into the room, then quickly went to the sofa and sat, her hands folded on her lap. "It's nice and warm in here." *How obvious!* she groaned inwardly.

"You're comfortable, then?" He asked. "I shouldn't light the fireplace."

"No need. I'm fine. Thanks." She was about as comfortable as she'd be sitting on a powder keg.

He took off his jacket, and laid it on a chair, then patted his hands together, as if he, too, wasn't quite sure what else to do with them. "Thirsty?" His voice sounded a little choked. He cleared his throat. "Would you like cognac, perhaps? Or coffee? A beer?"

"No, I — On second thought, cognac sounds good." A quick cognac, then home. This was a colossal mistake.

"Cognac, great. Be right back." He hurried off toward the kitchen, and before long, returned with two brandy snifters.

She took a sip and felt it warm her down to her toes.

He hunkered down in front of his stereo and flipped through some CDs and tapes a moment, then stopped and reached for some old record albums. "I just remembered an old song I've got here someplace," he murmured. "Perfect for tonight. Ah!"

He stood and put the album on the turntable. "It'll be scratchy, but you'll get the message.

She waited through a slow, melancholy big-band introduction she didn't recognize, then a silky-smooth Bing Crosby type voice began to wistfully croon, "*Seems like old times...,*"

Tears sprang to her eyes. The song captured her joy, but her madness, too, for as much as it seemed like old times, it wasn't. And no amount of regrets could ever undo the past.

Lee glanced at Tony, then quickly away as the refrain ended, *Seems like old times here with you.*

He noticed. "What is it?" he asked, easing himself beside her on the sofa. "I'm sorry. I didn't think you'd find it sad."

She blinked away the tears. "This isn't like me. I'm making such a fool of myself."

With his thumb, he brushed away a tear that fell to her cheek. "The only time you're a fool is when you criticize yourself for opening your heart."

She raised the glass in her hand and gave a wry chuckle. "Maybe it's just the cognac."

He took it from her and put it on the table. "Two sips?"

"I'm easy," she said with a watery chuckle.

"No." He tilted her chin upward. "That's the last

thing you are." He leaned forward. She looked into his face, then lifted hers, her hands to his chest as his head lowered. His lips met hers, softly, tentatively.

Finally.

A starburst of feelings erupted in her so powerfully, she pulled back, afraid. Their eyes met. *My Tony.* The way she used to think of him in high school came back to her. *He's always been my Tony.*

His hands gripped her upper arms as if to steady himself; to steady her.

She lightly ran her fingers over his face, the straight brows, strong cheekbones, finely shaped mouth. He turned his face into her hand, his eyelids fluttering shut as he placed a kiss against her palm.

Her body trembled, and she felt a similar quiver in Tony's. His hands slid along her back. Hers rested on his shoulders for a moment, then touched his neck, the back of his head. She moved closer and their lips met a second time.

He lightly kissed each lip, the top, the bottom. She cocked her head slightly, and her lips parted as his met hers.

Finally.

The wonder of times past, old recollections, familiar tastes, stirring them along with something new. Something mature, adult, and blatantly sexual. The hunger and longing of half a lifetime captured them, and their kiss exploded into a mouth open, tongue-touching, head twisting kind of kiss. The fervor built, carrying them on a swell of feelings. Lust, yes, but more, much more.

He pressed close to her, she pulled him closer. He captured her against the back of the sofa. She gathered him to her, clutching the material on the back of his shirt in tight fists.

He touched her hair, back, shoulders, face.

She touched his ears, neck, arms. As much as she had tried to deny the feelings he aroused in her, her heart was involved, much more than she'd allowed herself to imagine. But deep down she knew; she'd always known.

"I can't tell you how long I've wanted to do this," he whispered.

"So have I," she said.

He stood, pulling her to her feet with him, then walked to the stairs. "You're sure?"

"Yes." She smiled, and her smile was smothered by a hard, fiery kiss he pressed on her mouth.

He took her hand as they climbed the stairs. He opened the door, pulled her into the room, then pushed the door shut behind him. Only then did he stop moving long enough to look at her.

"Finally," he whispered, echoing her thoughts, as he cupped her face with his hands and kissed her reverently, almost like a benediction. "Your taste, your scent, the way you feel in my hands...it's familiar, but strange. I feel as if you're going to disappear on me. That this is all a dream."

"That's how I feel, too," she said. "Promise me you won't vanish and I'll do the same."

"I promise," he whispered.

She smiled, then noticed he was frowning at her. "What is it?"

"Your dress." He put a hand to his chin, studying it. "I've never helped someone out of anything so expensive. I don't want to hurt it."

She spun around feeling like she was floating. "It's got a zipper—just like normal dresses."

"Is that so, m'lady?" In one quick motion, he unzipped the dress.

"Yes, James," she said in her best upper-crust accent. "You may remove my gown now."

He helped her slide it off, then kissed her bare shoulder. "I believe I already have, m'lady."

As she placed the dress on a chair, he removed his shirt and tie, shoes and socks. She had to smile. As teenagers, they hadn't worried about her prom dress or his rented tuxedo. She guessed this was another sign that they'd matured.

In the bedroom fireplace, logs and kindling had been stacked. He touched a match to the papers under the kindling, then shut the bedroom lights. She watched as he crouched, coaxing the fire to burn stronger. She wondered if he felt the same nervousness she did, if that was why he suddenly found other things to do. As he turned toward her, the silver crucifix around his neck glistened in the firelight. He looked disheveled, sexy, and completely irresistible.

She stepped toward him, covered by a black slip of satin and lace. She no longer had the eighteen-year-old body he had known. Her breasts were heavier, her hips wider, her bones were more pronounced, and she sagged here and there. She came to him a mature, experienced woman now, at ease with her body and every nuance of her needs, far more than she ever had been as a teenager.

As she looked at him, she saw the changes to his body as well—the thickening of his chest, and the black hair that spanned it where he'd been naked as a jaybird in his teens. The arms that used to be long and lanky, were hard with muscles, as were his thighs. His stomach was a washboard of powerful sinew. Even his voice was deeper, gruffer. Everything about him seemed bigger, sleeker, stronger...more masculine and sexier than ever.

"Lisa," he stood and walked toward her. As he put his arms around her, he seemed to sense her uneasiness. "Come and sit by the fire."

A rug was in front of the hearth and she sat on it, her legs curled under her, facing the fire. Tony knelt behind her and removed the pins from her hair, one by one. When they were out, her hair fell thick and lush past her shoulders. He raked his fingers through it like a comb. She tilted her head back, her eyes shut, enjoying the sweet sensuousness of the feeling.

He moved closer, settling her hips between his knees. His hands went from her hair to her neck, surrounding it, then slid forward. She arched back against his solid chest. Her eyes shut as his kisses ranged along her neck and ear, his hands and fingers stroking and caressing her.

She turned in his arms, seeking his mouth. The jolt that hit her each time they kissed came again, stronger still now.

He slid the straps of her slip off her shoulders and arms, then unhooked her bra and removed it. She swayed pliantly, a moan sounding deep in her throat from the teasing, aching pleasure of his kisses. Her hands went to his head and her fingers gripped his hair.

"Want me, Lisa," he whispered. "The way I've want you since I first saw you last week."

She stood and let the slip fall to the floor. She removed her shoes and stood before him wearing nothing but gray silk stockings and the belt. She took his hand, and he stood, then she unbuckled the leather belt at his waist.

He felt her touch like an electric jolt. His arms went around her tight, his mouth pressed hard to hers as he backed her onto his bed, then quickly shed the rest of his clothes. As she reached down to unfasten a garter, he stopped her, doing it himself. Slowly, he lowered one silk stocking, then the next.

She ached for him, wanting him, sure that his merest touch would be enough to drive her over the edge.

He kneeled on the bed beside her. "You are more beautiful than ever," he said.

"So are you," she replied. "Handsome, that is."

He grinned at that and she lifted her arms to him. She reveled in the feel of his smooth, muscular body hot against hers. She ached to touch him everywhere, but hesitated.

"Don't he shy with me," he said, stroking her ribs, her waist, her hipbone. "Who knows you better? Who thinks you're more beautiful?"

Hearing those words, if she'd ever had any defenses against Tony, they were gone now.

She twisted toward him, pulling him closer. He ran his hands over her sensitive skin and her body throbbed, aching for him.

Her fingers slowly traced along his chest downward. *You feel like velvet,* she'd exclaimed years ago in her innocence.

Only Santos are velvet, he'd answered. *Other men are scaly, with stickers.*

Yes, she thought. Maybe so. She lifted her mouth to his, beckoning, demanding, pleading. It seemed she had waited her life for this moment, for this man.

She moaned with pleasure at his touch, at the building pressure within her. He scarcely lost a beat as he put on a condom, his hands, his mouth, seemed everywhere on her, and each place they found was more sensitive than the last. He played her body until she thought she might die from the sheer ecstasy of his caress. Until finally, no more teasing, no more soft caresses, she wanted him, all of him, body and soul, to be hers.

Their reunion was all fire and energy. Tony had exploded into her world, broke down her barriers, her defenses, leaving her to deal with him with honesty and with an overwhelming sense of trust. His lovemaking was the same—open and honest. Holding him was like holding lightning in her arms. He was more thrilling, more stirring, more loving, than any man she had ever known. A lost part of herself was found, old memories captured, new ones created. *Her Tony.*

She felt like a fool when her eyes filled with tears, but the rightness of the moment, more than the ecstasy, and more than the passion, had touched her heart.

He lay beside her, his head propped in his hand, elbow on the mattress, with the firelight flickering over his features. "How can I let you go again?" he whispered, brushing a stray lock of soft blonde hair back from her face.

"I wish I could stay," she admitted. "But..."

"I know." He stopped her with a kiss. "I understand."

She didn't go home that night. One night to build a lifetime of dreams on, he had said, and she didn't want it to end.

At two in the morning, they shared a huge bowl of strawberry ripple ice cream. At two-thirty they each drank a beer, and by three, each suffered a horrible stomachache. Soon after, they found a new cure for stomach troubles. At four, they splashed in a bubble bath, laughing and loving, and by five, they were sound asleep in each other's arms.

SIXTEEN

Lee awoke to a room filled with sunshine. She twisted around to look at the clock on the nightstand—9:30 a.m.—then back at Tony. His arm around her was warm, tucking her against him as if to be sure she wouldn't run off during the night. As if she'd want to.

Others probably saw him as merely handsome, but his features were, to her eye, as close to perfect as any she'd ever seen. The shadow of his beard showed on his chin and cheeks, and even that added to his attractiveness.

The arm he had flung over her lay across her midriff, just below her breasts, his leg crossed her thighs. As her awareness grew of his body, she could feel changes taking place in hers. She edged closer to him, part of her not wanting to awaken him, but another, stronger part, needed to feel him inside her again. As she moved closer, causing his arm to ease higher on her body, she could desire for him swelling within her.

Voices in the distance, growing ever louder, caught her attention.

"Tony," she whispered. "Tony, wake up!"

"What?" he mumbled.

The front door opened. "Dad?" Ben called.

She touched his shoulder. "Tony! It's Ben, wake up!"

He opened his eyes, heavy with sleep, looked at her, then heard Ben's footsteps running up the stairs.

"Dad, are you awake?" Ben was closer.

"Holy sh—!" Tony leaped from the bed and twisted the lock on his bedroom door just a second before Ben ran into the door, hitting against it with a thud when it didn't open for him.

"Dad, what the hell's going on around here?"

"Watch your language, Benjamin!" Tony called as he grabbed a pair of jeans from his closet and struggled to get them on fast.

Lee sat up, clutching the sheet to her neck.

"Why's your door locked? Open up, Dad! What're you doing?"

"I'll be right out."

Grabbing a shirt, he leaned over the bed, kissed Lee hard then unlocked the door and slipped out of it, blocking the room from Ben's view.

"Hey, there, Benito, good to see you. How was it at Grandpa's last night?"

"Fine. How come your door's locked?"

"Is Grandpa down stairs?"

"Yep."

Lee breathed again when she heard their footsteps on the stairs. A fine fix, she thought. He didn't want Ben to know she was there—that made sense —but how could she leave without being noticed? Would Ben believe she was an extremely early morning visitor? She got out of bed and picked her underwear up off the floor.

"I guess I shoulda phoned first, Tony." She heard Vic's gruff tones. She tiptoed closer to the door and quietly opened it a crack. "I thought you had more sense!"

"Look, Pa, I need you to spare a little more time this morning, okay? Ben needs a new batting glove, and if you could take him for just a half hour—"

"Oh, please, Grandpa!" Ben said.

"Yeah, yeah. Go wait in the car, Ben." Lee heard the boy's running footsteps, then the front door opened and slammed shut. "What the hell's goin' on here?" Vic demanded.

"It's all right, Pa!"

"Yeah? When's she goin' back to her fancy job? When's she gonna get tired of you this time?"

Tired of him? Was that how Vic thought she felt about Tony?

"Keep your voice down, she's not that way," Tony said.

"Like hell, she's not!"

The tension between the two permeated the house. Lee scarcely breathed. "Here," Tony said, his voice gentle. "Take this money and get Ben whatever he wants."

"She's leaving, isn't she?"

"Tomorrow. I'm all right, Pa. Don't worry."

Lee's fingers pressed against her mouth.

"I'll be back in an hour, son." Vic's gruff voice had also turned surprisingly soft. This time, perhaps for the first time, Lee heard beyond Vic's words. She heard his concern, his love, for Tony. She felt her eyes sting.

After the front door opened then shut, she closed the bedroom door and hurried into the bathroom. She took a quick shower then dressed, the whole time struggling against tears, not even knowing why they wanted to fall, except that she felt so damned bad. Her hands shook so much she could barely manage the zipper, but eventually she was dressed. Another few seconds were lost in agonizing indecision, then she took a few deep breaths, gathered her dignity and composure, and went in search of Tony.

In the kitchen, coffee was brewing, and he was putting mugs and cream on the table for them. She stood in the doorway, watching him. He was everything she'd remembered all these years—and more.

He turned quickly, as if sensing her presence, then straightened, the creamer still in his hand. "I'm sorry about the way things were around here this morning. I should have realized Ben would show up."

She feigned indifference. "No need for apology. Neither one of us was particularly thoughtful last night."

He put the creamer down, and was in front of her in two steps, her hands in his. "Look, I don't feel bad about last night, and I wouldn't hide the fact that you were here except that kids his age don't realize what it means, and they can go around blurting things out to others. I wouldn't want anything said that could embarrass you, or hurt you."

What did it mean to you, Tony? She nodded, forcing her mind back to Ben. "I didn't realize..."

He smiled. "You don't know much about nine-year-olds, I guess."

"I'm afraid not."

He put his hands on her shoulders. "I was glad for last night."

She met his eyes. "Me, too."

His fingers tightened just a moment, and she thought he was going to take her in his arms once more, but the moment passed, and he let go of her, his expression carefully placid. "Coffee's ready."

She squeezed her eyes shut. She knew what he was doing and why. She had to do the same. Control. Lee Reynolds was a master at it. She needed that mastery today more than ever.

"I could use some," she said, hoping her attempt at lightness sounded less feeble to his ear than it did to hers.

As he turned to get the pot, she stared at his broad back, unaware that he was gazing at her reflection off the glass cabinet. She looked incongruous, yet more desirable than any woman had a right to as, wearing a designer dress, her hair loose against her shoulders, sleepy-eyed, and with lips still puffy from his kisses, she sat at an oak table, surrounded by hanging pots, glass covered shelves of dishes and countertops filled with kitchen appliances.

He placed their coffee on the table and sat across from her. Over and over he'd told himself that what he felt for her was nothing but horniness —a purely masculine reaction to a hell of a beautiful woman who had once been in love with him. But he'd learned last night that it was more than that.

He wished he could tell her what was on his mind, but he didn't have the right.

"What do you think about me calling you when you're back there in the Big Apple, Lisa?"

"I...I honestly don't know." She knew he'd turned her life upside down, but that was nothing she should admit. "I think it would be best if you didn't."

His eyes were solemn. He held up his coffee cup, his face, his body intense. "Here's to no regrets."

She clinked her cup to his. "No regrets."

The room became somber with their parting. They drank their coffee quickly, then left the house.

Tony was holding the Jeep's door open for her when a car turned onto his driveway. The driver, a thin man with straight, straw-colored hair, got out of the car and walked quickly toward him.

"Mr. Santos?" he asked.

"Yes."

"Anthony Santos?"

Tony put his hands on his hips. "That's right."

The man stood right in front of him now, then reached into the inside pocket of his jacket and pulled out a folded piece of paper. "I have a summons for you."

He thrust the paper into Tony's hands, then

turned and ran back to his car, jumped in and sped away.

Stunned, Tony looked from the man to the envelope. He ripped it open and scanned the document inside. A black scowl darkened his face as he read.

"What is it?" Lee asked.

A tirade of expletives, both Spanish and English, erupted from him. He waded up the paper, threw it on the ground, then strode back and forth.

"What's wrong, Tony?"

"My ex-wife! That bitch, that selfish, rotten bitch!" He kicked a tire and slammed his fists against the roof of the 4x4. His hands still clenched as he struggled to control his temper.

Lee bit her bottom lip, not sure if she should interfere. "What does she want?"

"Ben."

She gasped. "What?"

He ran his hands through his hair then leaned heavily against the roof of his car. After a movement, he lifted a furious gaze to her. "Remember I told you she married a doctor in Los Angeles—a real big-shot, lots of money, lots of friends? And they can't have kids?"

"I remember."

"So now she wants 'her' son back. She gave up all rights to him when she walked out. He was a just a baby, and she left him. Now, she's changed her mind."

Lee felt her stomach tighten. "Oh, Tony, no!" Tony couldn't lose Ben, he simply could not. "She just wants to have him visit, right? She wouldn't try to take him from you."

"Wouldn't she? She's his mother. She's got a beautiful home, a rich husband. All I've got is a small ranch that barely shows a profit. It's coming down to a court fight."

"A custody battle, after all these years?"

Tony gave a bitter laugh. "Belated maternalism, I guess. But I can just see her standing in front of a judge, crying for her little boy. What mere father could compete against that?"

Lee's heart sank. She had seen many cases in courts take bizarre turns. Logic and fair play often had nothing to do with the outcome. "What terms is she requesting?"

"Full custody."

"My God!"

"She calls it joint custody, but she expects him to live with her and go to school there. I'd see him only on holidays and two weeks in summer." Tony sucked in his breath and held it a moment before continuing, his voice heart-wrenching. "Hell, when he finds out his step-father could buy him a Porsche when he's sixteen, he'll probably want to go live with them!"

"Don't you believe that for one second!"

Despair clouded his eyes. "No, I don't. I'll fight her right to the Supreme Court. Even if she wins, Ben will be thirty before all the levels of appeals are gone through."

"That's right!" She wanted so much to hold him and comfort him.

"Damn right."

He looked so miserable she couldn't stop herself from touching his arm—just his arm. "It's so wrong, Tony. So awful that you have to go through this!"

He slid his thumbs in his belt loops and turned away from her. "I'm sorry," he whispered.

"Sorry?" She stepped closer. "For what?"

"I didn't want to tell you about this!" He looked at her with a wry, rueful grin, and something in his dark, bright eyes lit a warmth in her that reminded her of the kisses he had given her, of the caresses they had shared. "I wanted you to think of Miwok as a place where only good things happen. I wanted everything—you, me, how it used to be between us —untouched by any ugliness. I couldn't do it. Everything's different now...even us. Last night was special. I'm sorry the real world intruded today."

She could have cried. "You always tried to protect me, Tony, but I'm a big girl. And I'm glad you told me. If there's anything I can do..."

"I don't think so."

"You're probably right. But if you need anything, if you need me, or...or anything, call me. Promise?"

He took one of her hands. "You always did want to set the world right, you know."

"And now I report all that's wrong with it." She shook her head at the irony of it all. "Do you have a good attorney?" she asked, ever practical.

"Yes." His voice was monotone. "We've been talking to Catherine and her husband's lawyer all along, but things broke down. I expected this might be the outcome. Even expecting it, though, to actually see it..."

"Maybe you can get an extension?"

"Right. He might be nine and a half instead of just nine before she takes him from me!" He let go of her and walked toward the car, out of her reach, leaving her hand, her arms, feeling empty. He swung the car door open. "We'd better get going. This doesn't have to concern you."

She got into the passenger side. When he was in the driver's seat, beside her, she said, "I can make some phone calls to people I know. I can ask if they have any advice on cases like this."

He started the ignition. "Sure," he replied, but she thought he barely heard her.

The ride to her house seemed too short. They were there before they had a chance to talk. Lee opened the door and got out at the same time as Tony. He walked with her to the front door, then tucked his fingers in the back pockets of his jeans, waiting for her goodbye.

Lee stared at him. How could she leave him when they still had so much to say, when he had just been hit with the news about a custody battle?

She turned and opened the front door, stepping into the living room with a silent invitation for Tony to follow. He did.

She put her purse on a chair, her head bowed.

"I know you'll be finishing up here," he said, "spending your last evening with your aunt, then going back to New York in the morning. I guess this is it, then."

"I...I don't know what to say."

"Will you need a ride to the airport?"

She shook her head, then finally turned and looked at him. Her eyes filled with tears.

"If you've got time, now and then,"—his voice was hollow—"even if you don't want me to call you, I'd like to hear from you. Tell me how you're doing, if you'd like. I imagine you'll be real busy, but we don't have to wait seventeen years again."

Her heart was breaking. "I used to ask about you, years ago, whenever I talked to someone from home. Once when I came home to visit, I went out to the Circle Z. A man was there, a stranger. He told me you were married."

"I never knew." His voice was a whisper. "I always thought as soon as you left, you'd forgotten."

"Not forgotten. I just stopped letting myself remember. It hurt too much."

He stepped closer, letting her words seep through him. "God, Lisa—"

"No." She placed her fingertips against his lips, then cradled his head to hers. His arms circled her. "I'm glad for my memories. Old and new. You're a fine man, Tony the best." Her words caught in her throat.

A part of her wanted, more than anything, to stay with him. If he asked, what would she do? If he told her he needed her, loved her for who she was today and not for the girl she used to be, what would she do?

Her arms tightened on his neck, but as she waited, she knew he would never ask such a thing of her again. It was too late for them. They'd both changed too much and their lives had moved too far apart from each other. As much as she knew a part of her loved him and would always love him, she had worked too long and too hard to get where she was. Lee Reynolds couldn't exist in Miwok, as she well learned. The young, ambitious girl Tony knew had matured, a woman now, with a career she'd worked hard for, and its ensuing responsibilities. As much as her mother had pushed her to succeed, so, too, had she pushed herself. Lee was all the potential in Lisa, fulfilling its promise.

So if Lee couldn't live in Miwok, could Tony exist in New York? A country estate, not terribly far from the city, somewhere that she could see him on weekends or, at least, those weekends when she didn't have to attend special functions or dinners, or cover a story out of town, or do a news special report because of a crisis somewhere in the world.

Could she ask that of Tony?

She knew the answer.

He lifted his head and looked at her, studying her features as if trying to commit them to memory. "I should get going."

"I wish I could be two places at once," she murmured.

He smiled, understanding exactly what she meant. "You always were an over-achiever."

"Oh, bull!" She fought off tears.

"I'm going to miss you, Lisa Marie Reynolds."

"And I'll miss you too, Tony Santos."

He looked at her mouth and bent closer, then hesitated. She looked at him, and leaned toward him, then stopped. She could feel his breath against her face, could feel his muscles grow taut. "Tony," she whispered.

Then he kissed her, his fingers twisting in her hair, holding her head near as he captured her mouth, then delved and explored it with his tongue in a way that shot rapture through her, taking her breath away. The force of the wild yearning she felt for him, the aching surge throughout her body for this man rocked her.

He took his mouth from hers and pulled her to him in a crushing hug as they realized this was goodbye.

He stepped back and lay his hand along the side of her face. "Knock 'em dead out there in the big world, Lisa."

"I'll try, Tony," she whispered. "You, too."

He let go of her and walked to the door, glancing at her one last time as he pulled it open, then he turned and was gone.

SEVENTEEN

Lee stood at the window. Nearly a half-hour passed before she went in search of Miriam and found her seated on the deck in the back yard looking out at the oaks that covered the hillside. A bleakness lingered in Miriam's eyes that Lee hadn't seen before. "What's wrong?" she asked.

"Oh, nothing. Was that Tony I heard?"

"Yes."

"Has he gone?"

"We said goodbye," she whispered.

Miriam dropped her gaze. "I see. You didn't tell him?"

Lee knew what Miriam referred to. "No. Never."

"Don't you think he's owed an explanation?"

"Why open up old wounds, Miriam, or create new ones? What we had together is gone now. Life goes on."

Miriam nodded and sat in silence a long moment. "I guess some things aren't meant to be."

No matter how much it hurts, Lee thought. She tried to push away the feeling. "You look troubled, Miriam."

Miriam studied a yellow rose a long while before answering. "I'm just feeling a bit sentimental. That's all."

"You don't want to leave."

Miriam shot her a glance as if ready to protest and then realized the futility of lying. "I'm telling myself it's foolish to want to stay in Miwok. I've made a home elsewhere. A lovely home. But I enjoyed it here so much these past two weeks. I was so comfortable, and my dear old friends..." A soft sigh escaped from her aunt.

"And Gene."

Miriam harrumphed. "Don't be silly. What do I want with a broken-down, has-been rodeo star?"

"A star? I didn't know he'd been a star."

"That's because the man's modest." Her voice turned wistful. "You should see the trophies he's got, and a big championship silver belt, and—"

Lee was laughing.

"What's so funny, Ms. Reynolds?"

"You are, Mrs. Dailey. You'll miss Gene Cantelli whether you admit it or not."

She nodded. "I'm afraid you're right."

"Reconnaissance pilots, rodeo stars—you like wild men, Miriam."

"That's me," she said with a sad sigh. "One hot momma."

Lee covered her hand. "If you want to move back here, do it. Why not?"

A little brightness and a little hope sparkled in Miriam's eyes, but then they dulled again. She pulled her hand away. "Moving so far is a big step for a woman my age. What if I move and decide I don't like it here? What if I can't sell my house in San Diego? Or, what if I can't find a house here that I like or can afford? Or, what if Gene Cantelli decides he's making a mistake spending time with a woman like me when he's handsome enough that women half his age throw themselves at him?" She shook her head. "I'm past the age to take risks, Lisa. In anything."

Lee watched Miriam look up again at the tall, spreading oak before her, its limbs wide, like arms in welcome. "Stay here. In this house." The words were out of her mouth before she even thought about them.

Miriam glanced at her. "What?"

Lee stared back as the rightness of the idea

warmed her, banishing any confusion, and leaving a certain peace. "It's perfect, Miriam." Lee slid forward in her chair. "I don't need to sell the house right away. Actually, I don't need to sell it at all. The only reason I was going to, was to get it off my hands. But if you lived here, I wouldn't have to worry about it."

"I don't know."

"Think about it. You could live in Miwok long enough to decide if you really do like it here enough to move—Gene Cantelli or not. If you do, you could put your home up for sale. Even once it sells, this will give you a place to stay until you find a house you like well enough to buy."

"You make it sound too easy."

Lee took Miriam's hand. "Nothing's easy. But it's possible—if you'd like to try it."

"I'd have to go back to pack some personal things—and get more clothes. I'll pay you rent."

"You will not! How many ways can I say I don't need the money? If you take care of the utilities, that'll be plenty—if that's all right."

Miriam stared at her a moment, not quite believing, then pleasure lit up her whole face. "Of course it's all right. It'd be lovely, Lisa. What a wonderful, generous idea."

"I'm glad I can help. It's so little after all you've done for me."

The next morning, Lee left early for the drive to the airport. Soon after, Miriam would lock up the house and drive back to San Diego.

As Lee pulled out of the driveway, she concentrated on the road in front of her, not wanting to look at the familiar sights around her again, the homes of people she had known, the school, the shops. She felt as if there'd been a vacuum in her life, and that vacuum now formed a hole in the pit of her stomach that was aching and empty. She felt surprisingly envious of Miriam for being able to come back here.

It'll be better when I'm in New York, she told herself. *That's my life now. I'll feel better once I'm working again. I feel content there, content at having achieved many of the goals I set for myself, knowing I'm on the right path to achieve even more of them.*

Miwok confused her. It made her question her life in New York, and she didn't want to question it. Questions were painful, they left her restless, even longing—but for what? That was the problem—restless and longing for what?

She lifted her gaze then and took in every detail of the town until she turned onto the highway and it disappeared from view.

EIGHTEEN

Manhattan put on its best face as Lee rode the taxi from Kennedy to her apartment. She was anxious to get on with her life as she had known it. The life she had struggle to succeed at and was comfortable with. A nagging uncertainty about that life when she was in Miwok, when she was with Tony, had to be set aside. After all, she was proud of her achievements, and she loved New York.

She looked out the window as the cab crawled along Fifth Avenue. It would inch forward a while, make a sudden, terrifying spurt around cars turning or double-parked, then inch forward again. People filled the streets, eyes ahead, walking in a straight line in singled-minded briskness the way people in truly big cities learn to do. Neon lights flashed, restaurant and exhaust smells blended, the ever-present sound of a jack-hammer slammed somewhere in the distance, along with honking horns, and rumbling trucks. But throughout it all was the familiar pulse of the city, the almost primitive beat that soared through her veins with vitality and life.

It was familiar. Home. And good to be back.

She walked into her sleek, stylized apartment. Everything was exactly as she'd left it: perfect. A flash of Tony's warm home hit her—toys scattered over the family room, old family photos on the walls of the living room, overstuffed chairs and comfort. She couldn't let herself think of that now.

She quickly unpacked, showered, and changed. After going through her mail and messages on her answering machines both at home and work, plugging in her laptop, taking one look at the overflowing e-mail system, and shutting it off again, she left for Bruce's place. Earlier, she had phoned him from the airport and told him she would see him this evening.

The evening air was sultry, but not uncomfortable. A smoky gray sky, electric with life, brought the kind of evening that, back in Miwok, would have neighbors standing outdoors, talking and joking with each other. But a friendly hello was as

SEEMS LIKE OLD TIMES

far as Lee's conversation went with the strangers who lived nearby.

Especially on a night like this, the streets were filled with people. So many of them, so busily going somewhere. Lee glanced at the happy couples among them.

With a polite smile and friendly nod, the doorman to Bruce's condo apartments waved her through. As she fished around in her handbag for Bruce's keys she stepped into the elevator. Her fingers tightened on the keys as she watched the floor lights go by in the elevator, bringing her closer and closer to fifteen. With a 'bong' the elevator stopped and the doors opened.

Her steps slowed as she walked across the small alcove to the front door. Drawing in her breath, she put the key in the lock, turned and pushed the door open. "Bruce? Bruce, it's me."

The lights were on, but the apartment was silent, Bruce must be working. He didn't like any sound, not even music when he worked. She dropped her jacket and purse on a black teak bench beside a brightly painted three-foot tall ceramic Thai dancer on a chartreuse pedestal table, then walked across the white marble foyer to the living room.

It was empty. Bruce usually sat in the wine-red, high-backed easy chair, his feet on the antique jacquard footstool, while she sat more stiffly on the Victorian tufted silk chesterfield with the high mahogany crest rail that stabbed into her back whenever she tried to relax against it. Victorian furniture, Bruce said, best showed off his collection of Southeast Asian and Hindu artifacts reminiscent of the Orientalia of the British Raj. Guests always complimented Bruce on his fine pieces. The Panchantantra collection frowned at Lee now, as if aware that her thoughts about the room were less than favorable.

She went down the hall to the den. The door was shut. She knocked. "Bruce?" There was no sound. "Are you in there? It's me, Lis...I mean, Lee."

She heard the rustling of papers, then the door swung open. Bruce was just under six feet tall and rail thin. He had blond, blue-eyed good looks that reminded her of a young Peter O'Toole.

"Lee, I didn't expect you so soon. I'm sorry, darling." He placed his hands on her arms and gave her a quick kiss then held her from him. "Let me look at how beautiful you are."

In her high heels, they stood nearly nose to nose. She could see the red-rimmed fatigue of his blue eyes even with his glasses on. His fine blond hair was usually immaculate, but tonight he'd been running his fingers through it as he worked, making it spiked and awry.

"You look tired, Bruce."

"I need you here to take care of me, darling. Haven't I told you that more than once?"

"You have."

"Well, thank God you're back." His arms went around her waist and he pulled her close into a long, tongue-involved kiss. She tried hard to feel some response, some quickening of her pulse, a tightness in her stomach, but she felt flat. Even the joy of seeing the man who professed to want to marry her, simply wasn't there, wasn't right.

She didn't want to be disappointed with Bruce, with their relationship, but she knew herself well enough to know she couldn't have felt the way she did about Tony, or allowed herself to have sex with him, if she truly loved the man before her. She wanted to be fair to him. She had come here, kissed him, to see if she had simply been dazzled by Tony and by the past and all she had loved—and lost. But she felt no magic now, causing her to question if there'd ever been magic between them, or if she'd been fooling herself because she was so very tired of being unattached and, as such, "fair game" to too many advances, including those of married men.

Now she knew. She was going to have to tell him.

He stepped back and looked at her quizzically.

"I'm exhausted, Bruce," she said with a forced

smile, then turned away from him. "This whole experience has left me an emotional and physical wreck."

He placed his hands on her shoulders and began to knead them as he stepped closer behind her. "My poor little star."

She stepped away. "I don't know why I came over tonight. I'm tired. The time change, you know. Why don't we just have a cocktail...talk....and then I'll head back home."

"You're joking, aren't you?"

"I'm afraid not."

His face fell. "All right. Give me a minute to finish up here."

Instead of going straight to the living room, she continued down the hall to the master bedroom. Everything in the bedroom was black lacquer, and so low to the ground Lee felt ten feet tall. The bed was nothing but a legless headboard and a king-size mattress resting on the floor. Bruce said sleeping on the floor was much better for the back than were box-springs, as well as reminiscent of a Japanese *futon*. Why she'd want to be reminded of futons—or *futon* as Bruce corrected her, noting that there was no plural form in Japanese—while trying to sleep, was something she hadn't bothered to ask.

She had slept with Bruce in this room, made love with him, told him she loved him and wanted to spend her life with him. How could she change so quickly? She never considered herself a shallow person, or a frivolous one, yet she was acting that way. Right now, she didn't like herself very well. She wasn't being fair. Yet, even as she turned away, she couldn't help but compare Bruce's bedroom to the one where she'd spent Friday night. Once again she found herself trying not to think of the world she left behind. The more she tried, though, the more she remembered the little things—the sound of a child's laughter, the pride in a man's eyes as he looked at his son, the sparkle in those same eyes as he looked at her. They had, as Tony had said, one evening to live a lifetime on. Now, it was over. She couldn't upset the life she had carefully built because of one wild, passionate fling for old times. She was more practical and logical than that.

And yet, as she settled into Bruce's living room, neither could she live a lie.

She had hoped that coming to see him would help her set aside the past. It hadn't. Her feelings about Tony and all that had happened between them ran too deep. Eventually, she knew she would be able to place all the feeling he had stirred up back behind the steel wall she erected around her heart and go back to her life. She had to. She had the control, the drive, and the ambition to take care of herself and get ahead, and she would do so again.

At this moment, she was being a foolishly sentimental twit. She despised twits. *Time to get over it,
Reynolds.*

"Sorry it's taken me so long." Bruce entered the
room. "How about those cocktails?"

"All of a sudden I don't feel well. Maybe it's jet
lag," she said, standing. She couldn't deal with all
this now. "But I had better head back home."

"Are you sure? You can stay here. I promise to
be a good boy and let you sleep, hard though that
will be, darling."

"I'm sorry. I really must go." She gave him a
quick kiss and walked toward the door.

"I love you, Lee," he called.

She could do no more than force a smile as she
walked out the door.

Lee entered the CABN-TV complex and was
walking down the main corridor to her office when
she saw Rick Archer, Evening Newscene's star anchor, approaching. "Welcome back," he cried, taking
her hands and scarcely touching his make-up covered cheek to hers in an air kiss while keeping his
eye on the approaching news director.

"Thank you, Rick. Good to see you."

"Wonderful, wonderful. Take care." He spun off

toward his dressing room. His hair was a pouf of blue-white magnificence, his back ramrod straight in his $2500 suit, but his feet pointed outward, giving him a disconcertingly duck-like waddle. It was good that news anchors never had to walk around while TV cameras were on them.

The news director, Max Hobbs, tossed her a "Welcome back. It's about time!" then hurried on his way.

Lee continued down the hall. She opened the door to the newsroom and waved at the staff. Reporters, film editors, cameramen and production assistants greeted her with some warmth, to her surprise. Well did she know that every person here coveted the anchor position, and each felt he or she could handle it better than any anchor alive. That kind of envy and jealousy went with the territory. She'd been the same while she was working her way up the ladder—although when one is on the lower rung, it's seen as having "drive and ambition."

She stopped in the studio to wave at the noontime news producer, cameramen, light and sound people. The noon news was on the air and the studio pulsated with frenzied activity. She loved it here. It wasn't work; it was an aphrodisiac.

She smiled as she again continued toward her office. This was her milieu. This was where she had made her mark, Lee Reynolds, anchor with ice

water instead of blood. She of the unflappable presence, able to go anywhere, interview anyone, and
not blink an eye.

Lee entered her office and shut the door. The
room was filled with papers, books, atlases, newspapers, a computer—all neatly hidden behind a variety of built-in white shelving with doors so that,
when they were shut the office looked very smart,
very elegant. It was practically a full-time job for
her personal secretary, Xantha, to keep papers
neatly filed and labeled for Lee.

The walls were papered in white texture and
on them hung bright Georgia O'Keefe originals. No
personal photos or frivolous-but-loved items were
displayed. She had never noticed their absence before, only noticed the calming peace of the office.
Now, it seemed cold.

In the bottom drawer of a file cabinet was a
folder marked "Christmas cards—Non-Business."
She took it out, then went to the high-backed, ivory
leather chair behind her desk and sat. It was a
rather slim folder. The "Business" related cards took
up an entire box. Opening the folder, she flipped
through the envelopes, looking at the return ad-
dresses until she found Cheryl's card. Inside, as she
remembered, was a picture of Cheryl's three children. Lee plopped the picture up on her desk, then
leaned back in the chair to look at it.

She liked it. She'd get a frame for it as soon as she had a chance. Or, maybe Xantha could—

"Miss Reynolds?" Her secretary knocked on the door.

"Hello, Xantha. How good to see you. How have you been?"

Short and round, with graying-blond hair in a fringe of curls around her head, Xantha stepped into the office with an armload of folders. Her eyebrows rose up at the question and she appeared a little flustered. "Why, I've been fine, Miss Reynolds. Quite fine."

She put a stack of folders on Lee's desk. "I brought you the briefs on the big stories this week. I thought you might like to do some studying."

"Studying? You mean not go on television and read my script for the first time in front of my audience the way Rick Archer does? Why shouldn't I be surprised every night on TV? He seems to enjoy working that way."

Xantha chuckled. "That's why you're so much better than he is."

"Ah, if only the boss knew that."

"But he does! Oh, Miss Reynolds, it isn't my place to say, but the rumors about you going to Nighttime News are hot. Mr. Hobbs is furious that he might lose you. He sees how much Rick Archer needs you to smooth over his tongue-twists and bloopers. Why, one night, he reported that the IRS bombed a bus station in Northern Ireland, and another night he said an AIDS rally was held to raise money for Ethiopia."

Lee winced. "He didn't really, Xantha."

"It's on tape." Her expression was so solemn, Lee couldn't help but smile. "Mr. Hobbs chewed the carpet." Xantha winked and left the office.

Lee was about half-way through them when her telephone buzzed. She picked it up.

"Lee, glad to have you back on board." Jake Metcalf, the general manager of the Cable American Broadcasting Network news department, assumed anyone he personally telephoned had to be important enough to recognize his voice. Lee recognized it immediately.

"Thank you. It's good to be back."

"I'd like to talk to you about a few things. Could you come to my office in, shall we say, a half hour?"

Lee's smile was smug. She knew exactly what he wanted to talk about. "We say, that'll be just fine, Jake."

"What do you mean you're going to turn down Nighttime News?" Bruce dropped the fork that held a morsel of poached salmon onto his plate. The other diners in The Russian Tearoom glanced at their table. "That was the perfect opportunity for you."

"Metcalf made me a better offer. And I'm happy at Evening Newscene."

"That job goes nowhere. It's nothing but a simple news show. We need better than that."

"It's on a national network."

"Tawdry," he said with a sneer.

She couldn't believe him. "Tawdry? You think my job is tawdry? As if Nighttime News isn't?"

His face was nearly against hers. "I'm thinking of your future, Lee. Of *our* future." He was all but scolding her as if she were a child. "How could you make such a decision without consulting me first?"

"Bruce, we're talking about *my* job, *my* career."

He sat back, his cheeks streaked with red. "Well, pardon me. I see I'm put in my place. I was simply saying that if I were you, I'd jump at the chance to do NN. It beats EN in the ratings. You know everyone talks about it. You'd have it made."

"I won't argue about it, Bruce. I like my job. I'm happy there."

His mouth wrinkled in disgust. "What's all this happiness business? It sounds like touchy-feely California claptrap if you ask me. Maybe you should"— he wriggled his fingers—"channel with your aura to get a holistic reading on your future life?"

"Very funny." She took another bite of scallops. Bruce had been nagging her since she first learned about the Nighttime News offer to make the switch. Her heart simply wasn't in it.

He placed his hand on hers, lightly stroking it with his fingers. "Lee, darling, where's your sense? You've always been the practical one, the one who could look at all sides and then coolly—some might say coldly—make the right assessment to get ahead. It was always one of the things I admired about you. My God, Lee, I've used you as a model. I just don't understand what's going on. Talk to me, darling. Have I done something to offend you?"

She pushed away the plate, her appetite gone. "You haven't done anything, Bruce. It's not you—it's me." She studied him for some acceptance, some understanding. Nothing but confusion showed in his face. What did she expect? He was so much like her—ambitious, driven and ultimately self-serving. They saw themselves as a team. But she had suddenly changed the rules. "I need time. Time to sort out everything—including us."

He was stricken. "Us? I don't—"

"I'm sorry, I truly am. I know it doesn't look that way, but I am trying to be fair to you, and to me."

"You're damned right it doesn't look that way! Are you saying you don't love me anymore? Is that why I haven't been able to even touch you since you've been back? What happened in Miwok, Lee?"

She felt terrible. He'd always been good to her— exactly what she thought she wanted. She looked at his movie-star perfect face and hair, his expensive clothes and watch, the manicured nails, the fashion- ably reed-slim body, and the politically savvy wheeling-and-dealing nature that used to intrigue and interest her. In a sense, she and Bruce had been made in each other's image, and had been perfect together. Just like she'd been perfectly matched to Ken Walters and even—God help her—Stompin' Steve Peters.

Was it love she had felt for Bruce, or was he the type of man she'd been taught she should have to move ahead in life, to fulfill her ambition? Good God! Was she really so callus?

"Something did happen in Miwok, Bruce. I came face-to-face with a part of myself I hadn't known was still there. And I don't know what to do about it."

He lightly traced his finger along her jaw. "Can I help?"

"The only one who can help me in this, is me. Give me time. Give me distance."

He nodded. Big blue eyes searched hers, and the hurt in them went straight to her heart.

NINETEEN

On Saturday night, Lee agreed to accompany Bruce to a party. He said it wouldn't be fair for him to go alone, and that she needed to be seen there. It was just a little get together for some dear friends, given by Sissy Springfield. Bruce rented a limousine to bring them the seven blocks to the Springfield townhouse. Lee spent a king's ransom on a new Donna Karan outfit, a black sheathe with a see-through, black lace, long-sleeved over blouse from her neck to the top of her bust line where the black voile began.

"All your friends will be so happy to see you," Bruce commented as they sat in the limo, sipping champagne. It was given as an amenity to compensate for the exorbitant cost for a seven-block ride.

Lee didn't respond. She couldn't exactly picture the other guests falling over themselves with joy. She had been too busy working to spend time cultivating friendships. Her so-called friends tended to be business associates and colleagues, scarcely bosom-buddies. She rarely socialized with women, preferring the company of men. Women, she discovered, considered her too cold and aloof. With men, though, she donned an unapproachable demeanor, making sure it was clear to them she wasn't one to sleep around.

He took her hand and raised it to kiss her fingers. She allowed it to remain. She had been in a malaise ever since returning from Miwok. Nothing seemed to matter much to her anymore.

She floated into the party as if watching her body from afar. Sissy swooped down on her, gave her a hug and an air-kiss, then pulled her into the crowd of at least two hundred people. But then Sissy was renowned for her parties, so when Sissy said it would be a little intimate thing, everyone knew it would be the largest, most formal "little intimate" party anyone had ever been to before. Sissy made a big splash with everything she did. She deposited Lee in front of the assistant to the deputy ambassador from Gambia, then flew away again, cawing at the newest guests to step into the doorway.

Lee and the tall African man stared at each other. She smiled. He smiled back. "I watch you on TV every night," he said.

"Thank you. I don't believe we've ever done a story on Gambia yet."

"Good. That means we're keeping out of trouble." His accent was vaguely British, and he smiled broadly.

"Except for the weapons deal with China," she murmured, then sipped her champagne. "Our government will be most unhappy when they hear about it."

He gawked at her, shifting from foot to foot, then cleared his throat. "I have no idea about that."

"Oh really?" she asked sweetly.

His face darkened and a small bead of perspiration appeared on his upper lip. "Would you like more champagne, Miss Reynolds?"

"Why not? If you don't make it back here in this crowd, I'll understand."

She watched him disappear. The poor fellow must be new to this game; that was far too easy. But now she knew the rumors she had heard were all true. Very interesting. She turned and walked toward the windows with their breath-taking view of Manhattan.

"How beautiful."

She glanced over her shoulder at the stranger staring intently at her. His eyes were as gray as his hair, and he had the Shake'n'Bake skin tone of someone who spends too much time in a tanning salon, rotating like a too-white chicken on a spit. "Is it?" she asked.

"Not it, you."

Disappointed, she turned again to the view. "Clichés are so boring."

"Even clichés can be true."

She didn't answer.

"I'm Chandler Hastings." His back was so straight he appeared skewered, and he had to tuck in his chin to avoid staring at the ceiling. "I know you're Lee Reynolds. I'd recognize you anywhere."

"Perhaps I merely resemble her."

"That's possible." He turned shoulder to shoulder with her and also looked out the window, making her mind flip to a recent time when she stood just this way with another man. "Lee Reynolds probably doesn't bother to look at the scenery anymore," he said. "She must be a very busy lady. So what do you see, lovely stranger, when you gaze out these windows?"

She moved forward, resting her palms on the sill and she studied the Manhattan scene so long he must have imagined she had forgotten him. "I feel like I'm sitting inside a cloud," she said, "and far below, is a place teeming with life that I can't quite reach."

"Aren't we part of that life?" he asked.

"Oh, no. We're up here. Observers. Down there,"—she placed her finger on the cold glass, running it through the mist her breath created—"people are living, dying, loving. But not us. We're above it all, untouched."

He placed his hand on her shoulder, and ran his fingers down her arm to her elbow, then back again. "You can be touched, Lee."

She drew back and gave him a sad, wistful smile. "No, Chandler, I'm afraid not." She walked away.

"Lee?"

She heard him call, but she kept going.

Three women surrounded Bruce, all oohing and aahing over his words. It would have been déclassé for her to approach him at this point. He was, after all, one of the city's most eligible bachelors. Maybe that was why they had never set a wedding date despite their protests of undying love. That, or a more profound, destructive reason.

"Lee, are you all right?"

Pulled out of her reverie, she saw that she'd wandered into Sissy's library. She spun around to find Melanie standing in the doorway. She smiled, glad to see her best friend again. Melanie's big green eyes were owlish and her black hair too curly, as if she just stepped out of the shower and couldn't control it. "Melanie, I didn't know you were coming to this. How good to see you."

Her friend's gaze shifted furtively as she walked into the room. "I'm glad we're alone."

"Alone? Why? What's up?"

Melanie glanced from Lee to the floor. "I feel bad about what happened between Bruce and me. That's what I wanted to say to you."

A myriad of suspicion rushed through Lee's mind at Melanie's "Bruce and me," but she dismissed them as fast as they struck. Melanie was her friend, Bruce her fiancé...although the engagement hadn't stopped her and Tony. But her situation was different... or was it? She raised an eyebrow, waiting for an explanation. "What do you mean?" she asked emotionlessly.

Melanie looked shocked. "He didn't tell you?"

Lee's back stiffened. "Tell me what?"

"Oh, God, Lee. I was sure he would." Melanie twisted her fingers. "I wished I'd kept my big mouth shut! He was lonely. He missed you terribly and was upset that you weren't here to go to a party given by some guy named Baldwin. I met him at CoCo's and got him to take me home. I tried hard to get him to come inside with me—but he wouldn't.

He was true to you. He was angry, too, and I was sure he'd told you."

"I see." Lee was quiet, her thoughts only that Bruce had a chance to do what she did, but he had been true to her. She felt worse than ever.

"I was pretty blasted, Lee. That's my only excuse," Melanie said. "I want you to know what a great guy you've got there. I'm so ashamed. I hope you can forgive me."

Lee just looked at her. "Thank you for telling me about Bruce. As for forgiveness...it seems a lot is going to have to be given out around here."

Lee got her jacket from the maid and quietly left the apartment after telling Sissy she had a headache. The doorman found her a taxi and in a little while she was back in her apartment.

"What in the hell is wrong with you? How could you walk out on me tonight? Do you know how it looked to our friends? Do you? What will they think?" A blue vein stood out on Bruce's forehead, bisecting it at an odd angle as he stormed back and forth in front of her sofa.

"I was upset. I wasn't thinking."

"You *always* think. Image is everything to you, and you know it."

"I'm sorry. I'd been talking to Melanie."

He flushed. "Did Melanie say something to you about me?"

"She said you took her home after an evening at CoCo's and—"

"Christ! Lee, listen to me. I was lonely and...and, damn it, I was scared."

That threw her. "Scared? You?"

"Yes, damn you! Don't you think I could tell there was something going on with you? That you met someone...an old friend, or a new one. I don't know who or what, but I could tell. I could feel you slipping away from me. I love you, Lee. And that means I know when you're falling out of love with me."

Lee closed her eyes, feeling the dull, throbbing behind her temples, and suddenly she was tired and sad. And lonely. As easy as it would have been to lie, she couldn't do it. "You're right. I did meet someone." She laughed bitterly. "Melanie told me you were a perfect gentleman with her. That you refused her invitation. That you were true to me, and I'm lucky to have found you."

A slow smile spread over his face. "She told you that?"

"Yes, and it made me feel even worse than I did already because...because when faced with a similar situation, I didn't walk away."

"No, Lee, you can't mean..."

"Yes." She averted her eyes, unable to look at him.

He collapsed in a chair, deflated and looked at her a moment. Then he lifted his chin. "How many times?"

"What?" She was shocked by his question.

"How many nights were you with this bastard, damn it! I have a right to know."

"One night."

He stood and began to pace. "That's...that's more or less understandable. It was probably a stupid mistake on your part, that's all. Maybe it was simply a last fling for you, before our marriage. We've been true to each other for eighteen months, after all." He faced her. "I forgive you. We can make this work."

"What if it wasn't a mistake? What if it meant a lot to me?"

"Darling, you don't know what you're saying." He knelt in front of her, grabbing her hands. So many times in the part he'd done this when she was upset, and it gave her a sense of love and security— that this proud man would do anything for her. "I think this is all...a delayed trauma from your mother's death."

His word confused her. "A trauma?"

"I was worried when you never cried after her

death. Now I see I had good reason to worry. I know you still love me, and I love you."

She rubbed her hands over her eyes, her forehead, trying to push away the hazy gray lethargy she felt, the strange numbness. He was right that she hadn't cried over her mother's death, but she had shed all her tears over Judith years earlier. "I'm tired, Bruce."

He got off the floor to sit at her side, his arms around her. "Let me stay." As she tried to stand, he pulled her close and kissed her hard, caressing her breast, his tongue jammed into her mouth. She wrestled herself free. "Please. I said I'm tired."

"Lee, don't do this!" He pulled her close again.

She shoved hard to get him away from her. "I'm sorry."

He stood. "I'll give you time to get over it. Going home, remembering your youth, I can see the appeal in that, even the appeal of old friends and lovers. The thing is, Lee, you aren't that young girl anymore. She's gone, changed. No matter how many affairs you have, you can't bring her back. You're my companion. We have each other. This is our world, our lives. When you come to your senses —and you will—I'll be waiting."

She dreamed she was flying, and below her the lights of Miwok glowed. Lee saw a Porsche, a 911 cabriolet, winding up the street to her mother's house, but instead of her driving, it was Melanie. Cheryl opened the door to Judith's house when Melanie reached it. "How nice to see you!"

— *She's not me, Mother. She's Melanie. You don't even know her!*

But no one could hear her, and Melanie stepped inside. Sissy was there, throwing a party in the family room, and Judith sat on the wing-tipped chair, a can of Budweiser in her hand.

Melanie walked up to Judith and kissed her cheek. "How do you feel, Mother, dear?"

"Fine, darling. How good of my beautiful child to come and see me."

— *Mother! She's not me. I'm your daughter. Me!*

"I love having you here. I love you, child."

— *What about me, Mother? Don't you love me, too?*

Sissy walked by. "Oh, Sissy," Melanie called. "You did invite Tony, didn't you? I can hardly wait to take him home with me." Her smile was broad and knowing.

— *No! Leave him alone!*

"Of course! He's waiting for you by the windows."

— *No! Stop, please stop! Not Tony! Don't take Tony from me...please, don't take Tony...*

Lee awoke with tears running down her face, her heart pounding. She rolled onto her back and stared at the ceiling, knowing sleep wouldn't come again that night.

TWENTY

Each evening, after the news broadcast, Lee telephoned Miriam. She loved hearing the happy, gentle lilt in Miriam's voice.

Bruce refused to accept that her feelings about him had changed. For days he brought her presents and sweet-talked her. He liked to say that things would soon be as blissful as they had been in the past. Was he right? she wondered. Were things ever 'blissful' between them, or simply comfortable and secure? She wasn't sure.

But then, she wasn't very sure about anything anymore. Always before things were either black or they were white. Now, they could have been chartreuse for all she knew.

One day, Bruce's exasperation boiled over. "I've

got better things to do with my time than to watch you burn up the phone lines with a small town that's not even a dot on a Triple-A map!"

"Then don't let me stop you."

"Considering that you don't want to let me do anything else around here that just might be a good idea."

"I've never stopped you from doing anything."

"Oh? That's not what you say whenever I try to get close to you."

"I've been under a strain."

"You're always under a strain, or tired, or that ulcer you finally decided to tell me about is acting up, or any other damn thing to keep me away. We haven't made love since you returned. You aren't still carrying a torch for some country-bumpkin from Muckwuck are you? Some rube? Some hayseed who would embarrass you around all your friends the minute he opened his mouth. Tell me, does he raise cows or is it chickens?"

"Horses."

He gawked at her. "Tell me you're joking."

Her voice was small. "No."

He frowned. "You don't need me to tell you how wrong he is for you. You know it. That's why you're here and he's there."

"Please, Bruce, don't do this."

He stood. "I should do what you want—leave

and not come back. You'll find out how lonely it is around here without me. Who exists in your life except the people you work with, and me? And as much as you get invited to parties and hot-shot social functions, it's not because of who you are, Lee, it's because of *what* you are—a national TV news anchor."

"That's enough, Bruce."

"I'm the only one who cares about the real you. And where is this new lover of yours? I don't see him visiting you, or calling, or even sending flowers. I think he used you. I think he's going all over that pig-shit town telling all the other yokels how he got some glamorous New York news-babe into his bed."

"Do you feel better now, Bruce?" Her tone was as calm and cold as she could make it.

Exasperated, he turned and stormed out of her apartment, slamming the door so hard the walls rattled.

Friday night, four weeks after returning to New York, Lee sat alone in her apartment.

She had told Bruce earlier that she wanted to move her belongings out of his place, but he asked her not to, saying that he understood that she was upset right now, and it wasn't the time to take any rash actions. He wouldn't push her, if she would simply give them both more time to work things out. She agreed, only because she didn't want any more ugly confrontations.

It was one a.m., but she wasn't in the least bit tired. She glanced at her cell phone. Burning up the phone lines to Miwok, Bruce had said. Perhaps. She could do more calling, if she wanted to. She scooted to the opposite side of the sofa, closer to the phone. But she didn't want to, did she? She was getting over Miwok. It was an aberration, childhood regression, nothing more.

She felt like one of those crazy old women that sit around and telephone people all night long. They especially love to latch onto radio talk shows where they can be heard any evening, usually whining about UFO's or ESP. She put her elbow on the arm of the sofa and pressed her knuckles to her mouth. He isn't asleep yet, she thought. It's only ten o'clock there. What could she say if she called him? *Hi, it's Friday night and I'm lonely.* Lonely...Bruce had often said she would be lonely without him, but actually she wasn't. Not until now. Not until she began thinking about the one person she missed.

To be alone had always been fine with her. She'd prided herself on her self-containment, never hungered for another person's company, and surely, she didn't now. Maybe she should phone him just to prove to herself that he didn't mean a thing to her? That she didn't need anyone. After high school, she had learned that lesson well. She had walked out on her own mother and never looked back. Her aloofness was part of her persona—the core, the heart, the black hole that was Lee Reynolds.

She picked up the phone and punched in his number, determined to prove to herself how unimportant he was.

"Hello," Tony said, and the sound of his voice told her she'd been wrong. The memory of him came with startling sharpness into her mind: thick black hair, sultry eyes, sexy, sensitive mouth, strong hands and arms. And with that memory came also thoughts of the night she tasted his kisses, felt the warmth of his broad muscled chest, felt his fire.

"This is Lisa." She used her full name without realizing it.

"Lisa..." His voice was soft as if he scarcely believed it was her. She could picture him standing, probably a half smile playing on his lips, maybe his free hand running his fingers through his hair. "You called. I kept hoping...then I gave up."

His voice was beautifully smooth, musical, with a hushed delight in the tone and cadence that made her feelings soar. "I've thought about calling. A lot," she said. She wanted to tell him she missed him, but she was finding her emotions so strong it was hard to speak. It was all she could do not to blubber and feel more foolish than she did now.

"I can't believe you're so far away when I see you on TV every night."

She felt as if the floor dropped out from under her and her fingers tightened on the phone. "I can't either...not when you sound so close...." *Close enough I should be able to touch you.* She remembered the warmth of his silky skin under her fingers, the heat yet gentleness of his kisses on her lips. She swallowed hard. "How's Ben?"

"He watches you, too. He's learning a lot about world news."

"Glad I'm doing something right, then."

"I've run into Miriam a couple of times. She tells me she still loves being here. She and Gene are getting pretty serious."

"Yes, I think you're right." She smiled at the thought of Tony and Miriam running into each other, talking and probably laughing together. "I'm glad you've seen Miriam. She never mentioned it."

"I kind of asked her not to. I wasn't sure you'd even want to remember knowing me now that you're back in New York."

She shut her eyes, drawing in her breath. When she spoke, her voice was soft. "I could never forget you."

There was a long pause before he said softly, "Miriam told me I was wrong."

She fought the sudden tightness in her throat. "Yes."

"Work's all right, then?" He forced a chipper tone.

"Yes."

"I guess you're still with your boyfriend, old what's his name?"

"It's not important."

"Don't want to say, huh? He must be some big shot, I guess."

"Not really."

"Like a Kennedy or something."

"He's no one famous, Tony. I see him on occasion, that's all."

"Is he still telling you how to succeed in business without really trying?"

"Yes."

"Ignore him."

She laughed. "I am. That's just the problem."

"That's the best news I've heard all month." There was a long pause during which neither said anything, as the impact of her words and his reaction settled over them.

"God, I've missed you," he whispered.

That did it. Her stomach twisted and the longing she felt was almost more than she could bear. "Well, I'd better go....I just wanted to say hello."

"Hello, Lisa."

Her eyes filled with tears. "Hello, Tony."

"Will you call again sometime?"

"I...I'm not sure."

"You asked me not to phone you, and I'll honor that until you say otherwise," he said. "But I'll be here anytime you want to pick up that phone, okay?"

"I'm glad, Tony."

"Goodbye, Lisa."

"Goodbye."

Lee didn't let herself dwell on the reasons why, but she phoned again the following Friday night. The shyness of their phone conversation vanished after their simultaneous "hellos." It was as if they had never parted, as if three thousand miles didn't stand between them. Tony was ecstatic that his attorney had succeeded in getting Ben's custody hearing postponed a month. Now, it was six weeks away. Tony decided he and Ben should celebrate. It was June, the time school year ends in northern California, and the two of them were going to Yosemite for a few days so Ben could see its high waterfalls.

The thought of Tony and Ben going off to the park, a place of such incredible beauty it scarcely seemed real, made her feel wistful, and more than a little lonesome for their company and even for California.

When Tony said he wished she could be with them, she almost replied, "Just ask me." But she didn't, and had he asked, she wouldn't. Still, it was nice to dream.

The following Friday, Tony was full of happy tales of his vacation, and Lee had lots to say about the nasty 'politics' going on at the news station, so they both talked and laughed until they were quite worn out.

Lee had to go out of town the Friday after that night to handle a special assignment for the weekend. She tried to reach Tony a couple of times on Saturday when she was free, but there was no answer. She left no message. Each time her cell phone rang, she looked at it with anticipation, but none of the calls were from Tony.

He'd asked twice if he could call her, and both times she'd said no. Had that been wrong of her? She couldn't help but wonder how it made him feel. Did he think she didn't want him interrupting her life, or did he realize it was purely self-defense on her part? Or, was there something more going on here, more than she dared admit?

The following Friday night, the same time as she usually phoned Tony, she sat staring at her phone. All week long she had agonized over what to do this evening. To carry on a long distance whatever-this-was with him didn't make sense. He might have even thought she was chasing him, which she didn't think she was doing because she didn't know what she'd do if she caught him. She had a full life; she had friends, even if her best friend, Melanie, had disappointed her. It was just that her life seemed a little fuller, a little richer, with Tony in it again. Was that so wrong?

On the other hand, a part of her argued that it might not even be healthy to make these calls. It set up the semblance of a long-distance relationship that, in truth, didn't exist. And shouldn't exist. And had no hope for existence given their differences.

Her apartment was ungodly silent. Beyond silent. Empty. Finally, she couldn't stand it any longer and picked up the phone.

"Hello?" His voice sounded tentative.

"Hi, Tony."

She could hear his breath come out in a rush.
"Lisa..."

She had planned on sounding calm and indifferent, but instead the words poured out of her. "I
was out of town last weekend."

"Ah. Well, sure, I expected it. I mean, I never
expected you to sit alone in your apartment every
weekend, especially with your important
boyfriend—"

"I was working."

She could hear his smile as he exclaimed,
"Working?"

Relief filled her like helium, lifting her ten feet
high. "It was actually an interesting assignment..."

The next week, Tony told her how surprised and
pleased Gene Cantelli was to get a big order for his
top English saddles from a ranch near a small town
in Pennsylvania. Lee said she, too, was surprised.
Tony told her he looked up the town on a map. It
was right near the New York border.

Tony was lower than Lee had ever heard him the
following Friday. The court hearing was postponed

again, but this would be the last postponement. He would have gladly kept postponing the hearing as long as he could because, until the hearing, Ben was his. After it, anything could happen. He didn't trust the courts or judges. He didn't trust anyone to do right by his son except himself. In eight more weeks, he would be meeting his ex-wife, and Ben's fate would be decided. Lee did her best to cheer him up. They talked for almost two hours, and he thanked her for listening to him, for just being there when he needed her.

Gene Cantelli got more orders for saddles from Pennsylvania, as well as some from New York and Connecticut. Lee confessed to Tony, as she had earlier to Miriam, that a few weeks earlier she had visited some friends at their estate in Pennsylvania. The friends owned four beautiful horses. Through them, she met other horse lovers. Could she help it if the saddles they were using weren't half as interesting or distinctive as the ones Gene made? She was doing them a favor by telling them about the exclusive shop in a small, northern California village.

Tony laughed at her description of Miwok, but she pointed out she had bent the truth only a little, and that to Easterners, everything in northern California seemed either weird or quaint — San Francisco and its jaunty little cable cars being prime examples. He believed it.

Tony's phone rang without answer when she called the following Friday. She phoned again, then once more.

There was no reason she should have grown to expect him to sit home every Friday night. He was young and handsome. She shouldn't be surprised to find he had gone out on a Friday night and didn't want to answer her calls.

Could he be with Trish Hollingsworth? He had never mentioned her after the Miwok picnic. Judging from the way she acted around him, though, they had been quite close.

Feeling jealousy three thousand miles away was terrible. Even worse was the detailed way her mind imagined the two of them passing their time this evening. Trish's hand, low on Tony's hips as they walked away from her at the Settler's Park picnic, gave her a clear picture of the kind of relationship those two had. She remembered her own hand on his hips the night she spent with him. He had solid, sexy hips, tight buns. The kind of body that looked great in jeans...or out of them.

The thought of Trish Hollingsworth touching him that way made her wild.

The hypocrisy of being jealous of Tony when she had scarcely raised an eyebrow at the possibility of her own fiancé's infidelity with her supposed best friend wasn't lost on her. But it made sharper the fact that she and Bruce had no relationship worth saving.

She went to bed, facing a restless sleep when the phone rang. It was almost three o'clock in the morning.

"Hello," she murmured, half-groggy, as she struggled to sit up.

"I know I promised you I'd never call, but—"

"Tony?"

"Oh, hell, I'm sorry. Christ, it's not even midnight here, but I just realized you must have been sound asleep. I shouldn't have disturbed you. Go back to sleep—"

"No! Wait, I'm glad you called." She swallowed hard, trying to get her tongue to function, her head to clear. "I was worried."

"It was my father's birthday. Vic turned 65 today—ready for Social Security and everything. We went out with some of his old friends."

"Really?" She settled back against the pillow.

His voice was so sexy it made her toes curl. "How great."

"I missed talking to you, though." He sounded suddenly hushed. "I saw that you called...I guessed you had hoped to talk awhile..."

"Of course I did." A couple of beats passed in the silence of her dark bedroom, then she spoke softly. "I missed you, too. I still do miss you, in fact. I miss seeing you, going to games...being with you."

"God, Lisa, don't," he whispered. "Please. Hell, I hate being so far from you!"

"Me, too."

"Hey," he tried to make himself sound playful. "You got too much special stuff to do to waste time missing old Tony. You know that."

Tears welled in her eyes, and when she spoke, her voice quivered slightly. "The 'stuff' I do is my job. After a while, it doesn't seem all that special. For sure, I'm not special."

He didn't say anything for a long moment. "Tell me what's wrong, Lisa."

"Nothing."

"Your job?"

"No. It's fine."

"Friends? That jerk you hang around with giving you trouble?"

"Oh, Tony..."

"Well?"

"Nothing."

"If only you were here, Lisa, if only I could see you...it's so hard on the phone sometimes...."

She wondered what was wrong with her. She couldn't love this man; she had no business being in love with him. Nonetheless, somehow, lying here on her back in the dark, silent tears flowing into her hair, her ears, and her pillow, she realized she just might be. And that worried her. She wiped the tears, coughed, pretending her hoarseness was a cold, nothing more. Certainly nothing involving her heart.

She was making a mess out of everything. Why was she saying these things to him, upsetting him, herself, when she knew she couldn't act on her words? She rubbed her eyes. "Maybe I'm just tired. Maybe I need to try to get to sleep now."

Silence stretched for an eternity. "Are you crying, Lisa?"

"No. I...I'm fine. I'm glad you called."

He gave a half-laugh. "Oh? You could have fooled me." She thought she could hear tears in his voice as well.

She laughed as best she was able, wanting to tell him what was in her heart, but instead saying, "Oh, you."

"And Lisa?"

"Yes?"

"No one ever said you had to *stay* in New York, you know."

They had twice as much to say the following Friday, since they had missed their usual marathon conversation the week before. How had she managed to live so many years without Tony in her life? Without feeling the way she felt when they spoke together? Strangely, everything else throughout the week seemed to take on a warmer, happier glow as well. She felt better about the job she was doing than ever before.

For a little over an hour, once a week, she knew what it meant to live with her heart and not simply with her intellect, to act and speak on a gut level, and not for any logical or practical reason. Was this love?

In October, Tony's ex-wife, Catherine, had detectives combing the town for any unsavory piece of gossip they could find about him. Luckily, he did little that anyone could look askance at. Living in a small town with his father and his young son, he was so squeaky clean he should have gotten a medal.

The knowledge that someone was purposefully prying into his life, however, made him mad. If those detectives got too nosy, they would at least learn something about his temper.

Despite his blustering, Lee could hear the worry in his voice. Using news sources, it was easy to check out Catherine's new husband, Dr. Graham Durelle, a Beverly Hills plastic surgeon. The man was everything Tony had claimed—well respected and very wealthy. His only weakness had been an eye for younger women, but since he married the young, vivacious Catherine Santos, his roving eye had wandered no more. He was said to be passionately in love with his wife, and heartbroken that he couldn't give her children. He would do all he could, therefore, to get back her child.

Lee tried to find out if there was anything more Tony could do to fight Catherine. There wasn't. He had a good attorney, and all that was left was to state his case and hope.

"We go to court next Thursday," he said on the telephone on Friday night, "so, I guess when we talk on Friday, I'll tell you what happened."

"Call me as soon as there's a decision," she said. "Please."

"I will...if I can." His voice broke. "I don't...I don't know what I'll do if I lose him, Lisa. I just don't know."

TWENTY-ONE

Tony's words, his voice, his heartache filled Lee's thoughts throughout the weekend, pushing aside everything else she tried to concentrate on. On Monday, a thought struck her that was so impulsive and irresponsible she doubted her own sanity. By six a.m. Wednesday, she was en route to JFK airport.

On the plane somewhere over the Rocky Mountains, the possibility she'd taken leave of her senses hovered around ninety to one. She should take the next plane east and return to her job.

A family crisis, she had said when requesting time off. In a sense, it was. *Her* crisis.

Max Hobbs had given her the leave while making it clear he didn't like it one bit and demanded she return to New York as soon as she could. She knew one person, at least, would be ecstatic by her absence—Edie Canham, her Newscene temporary replacement.

For the first time in her adult life she was acting against her career's best interest, and it scared her to death. And yet, her instinct told her Tony needed her now.

Her spirits leaped as she gazed upon the sparkling whiteness of San Francisco's skyline against the deep blue of the bay. Driving her rented Lincoln Towne Car over the orange-hued Golden Gate Bridge, her excitement grew, settling finally into a deep, clutching warmth as she turned off the highway and headed westward toward the rolling hills of Miwok.

A couple of weeks earlier Miriam had called to say she had decided to move back to Miwok permanently. She would have to return to San Diego for a while to get her house ready to be put up for sale—a new paint job, inside and out, perhaps some new carpeting or other cosmetic touches that could mean the difference between a fast sale and a slow one. Surprisingly Gene Cantelli was going with her to help. Most of Miriam's belongings would be placed in storage, but all the things that were truly precious to her would be taken back to Judith's house. Then, after her current house sold, she would begin to look for a small, easy-to-care-for house in Miwok. She had made up her mind that she would buy only if the house was exactly what she wanted. Once settled this time, she said she would leave only to go to the cemetery.

Lee knew that Gene Cantelli had played a big part in Miriam's decision on where she would live. Lee still couldn't get over the way her aunt had fallen hard for Gene. She could scarcely imagine two people more different, or whose tastes were less similar. There was no logic behind a confirmed bachelor and a longtime widow becoming devoted to each other. But perhaps the whole point was that such things defied logic?

When she reached home, the front door wasn't even locked — ah, Miwok!—and she walked right in. Miriam came out of the kitchen, a dish cloth in her hands. Her eyes grew wide with astonishment when she saw Lee and her suitcase, "What's this?"

"I missed you."

Miriam opened her arms, and in a moment Lee was getting a tremendous hug. It did feel good to be home.

Miriam put her hands on Lee's shoulders. "Is anything wrong?"

"Everything's fine. I just have some unfinished business I need to take care of."

"I could have taken care of any business for you."

"Not this kind."

"Tony's case?" Miriam asked.

Lee nodded.

Miriam patted Lee's arm. "Your room's waiting for you. I'll make a pot of tea while you get settled."

"Thank you, Auntie." Lee gave her a quick kiss on the cheek. As she stepped back, she was surprised to see tears in Miriam's eyes. "What's wrong?"

"You haven't called me 'auntie' since you were a little girl. I'd thought you'd forgotten. It touched me, that's all. Good God, I must be getting old!" In her usual no-nonsense way, she brushed the tears away and briskly walked toward the kitchen.

After tea, Lee changed into casual slacks and a blouse. As much as she wanted to visit with her aunt, that wasn't why she had traveled three thousand miles. She found, however, that it was a lot easier to decide what to do while sitting in her apartment in New York than it was to actually do it here in Miwok.

Before long, she told Miriam she was going to Tony's house, and left.

As she neared the Circle Z ranch, her nerve

failed her. She slowed the car to a crawl. *What if he's not home? What if he is home but has Trish or some other woman with him? What if he doesn't want to see me? What if, what if...*

Reaching the gate, she took a deep breath and swung the wheel to the left, nosing the car onto the oak-lined driveway that led to his house.

His 4x4 and old Chevy pickup were in the driveway, and no other cars were there. So he was home, and probably alone.

As she got out of the car and walked to the front door her heart pounded so hard she could scarcely breathe.

She rang the doorbell, then waited a long while before ringing it again. Where was he?

She knocked. Still no answer.

He was probably working somewhere on the ranch in the company of his father or the foreman, or some of the hired hands. She dreaded the thought of running into Vic Santos.

She hadn't traveled across the country to give up now.

Tony might be in the back of the house. At the pool, perhaps, unable to hear the bell or her knocks.

As she walked along the side of the house, she heard the faint sound of a radio in the distance.

On the patio between the pool and the house were an umbrella table, a couple of lounge chairs and a barbecue. Past the pool was a field with apricot, plum and peach trees, and to one side, a small building that looked like a workshop. The sounds of the radio were coming from that building.

As she got nearer, she could hear the broadcasters speculating on the World Series. Her spirit leaped—baseball. What else?

She stopped at the open doorway and looked inside. He stood at a table, his back to her, bent over what looked like a small engine. Pieces of it were spread over the table and onto the floor. The back of his white tee-shirt was damp from perspiration as he wrestled to loosen some bolts. His hair flopped forward and his hands were black with grease. She watched the muscles on his back and arms strain. Dark grease stains smeared the jeans that rode low on his hips, hugging his legs, outlining the firm muscles that braced him as he worked.

Bruce was right—he didn't fit in with her New York City crowd at all. Thank goodness.

Lee watched, waiting until a commercial came on the radio. The broadcast ended with the statement that the San Francisco Giants would finish in fourth place. She smiled at the choice language Tony muttered. It could have been directed at the team or the stubborn bolts on the engine.

"Hello, Tony," she said as casually as if her heart wasn't racing a mile a minute.

His head jerked up and snapped toward her. Dark, tension-filled eyes met hers. They softened, and he slowly straightened, putting down the wrench he had been holding. But almost immediately, his expression changed and his brow furrowed with worry. He shut off the radio. "Has something happened? Why are you here?"

She smiled. "I like it here, you may recall."

As he studied her expression, the truth struck him like a fastball between the eyes. No, it couldn't be. He had to be wrong.

She folded her arms, still grinning. "I've never seen you tongue-tied, Santos."

His heart began to pound, and he stood motionless in the shed, grease smearing his hands and perspiration dripping from his brow. He scraped a hand over his forehead, changing sweat for an oil smear. He had spent weeks telling himself he had been a sentimental fool over her when she was here, that he couldn't still be in love with her, not after so many years. He told himself he scarcely knew her anymore. Then, when they began to talk over the phone and he would spend each week waiting for Friday night, when he would chase Vic out of the house on those nights and saw that Ben was with friends or playing a game or watching TV or somehow amused, when he would go into his bedroom and wait for the phone to ring—all that time he told himself he didn't love her. It was liking, or lust, or nostalgia. Now, facing her, who had he been trying to fool?

"Lisa." He moved toward her in long, purposeful strides, feeling his pulse in his chest, against his temples. He glanced down at his hands. "Christ, let me wash this stuff off. Then we can get out of here."

There was a basin in the workshop, and he took a bar of Lava and work at the grease on his hands and arms, building suds up his forearms to the elbows before he washed his face and neck. As he bent over, his silver crucifix slipped out from under his tee-shirt and swung freely, rocking back and forth against his chest. He splashed water like a five-year-old as he rinsed the suds off, wetting the back and front of his hair in the process. With his eyes shut, he groped for the towel lying beside the wash basin. He held it to his face a moment, his hands still as he wondered—feeling as he did, admitting it —what he should do now?

He came out of the brisk rubdown with the towel looking like one reborn, a shiny glow on his chin, cheeks and forehead. As he ran the towel over the back of his neck, his eye caught hers. She could scarcely breathe, his gaze was that strong, that filled with need, and more.

Their eyes held for several beats while she felt

her color heighten and she smoothed a stray hair back to her chignon.

Abruptly, he turned, tossed the towel aside and reached for the blue and white striped shirt that hung on a hook next to a hacksaw. Shrugging the shirt on, he folded back the sleeves to just below the elbow and left it unbuttoned, the whole time taking care not to catch her eye. His sudden discomfort spread over the workshop.

"Want to go in the house?" he asked. "How about a soft drink?"

"Sounds fine."

They crossed the yard to the patio and entered the kitchen. Taking two cans of Diet Pepsi from the refrigerator, he put them on the counter, as if needing to avoid chance of contact if he handed her the can. Then he opened the cabinet for glasses.

"Don't bother." She popped open a can.

He did the same.

They took the sodas outside and sat at the patio table. "So tell me, Miss Reynolds, what brings you out to these hick parts so soon? I thought it'd be at least another twenty years before I saw you again."

She heard the sarcasm in his voice, but she also saw the cautious hope in his eyes. He had learned over the years, as she had, how to protect himself. She debated her answer. Tell him straight? Make jokes? Or simply lie like hell? This was no joking matter, and she never was any good at lying.

She took a deep breath. "I thought you could use some moral support tomorrow."

Carefully, he placed the soda can on the table. Without looking at her, he walked to the pool and stared down at the water.

She sat forward, her hands clasped. "I'm sorry. I didn't mean to upset you. I just thought, perhaps, you'd like...I mean, I wanted to do more than talk to you on the phone. I wanted to be here. To help, if I could, in any way."

He kept his head bowed.

She stood. "I'm sorry, Tony," she whispered. "Perhaps I shouldn't have intruded. I just wanted..." *I wanted to be with you.* Didn't he want her there? Had she misread him so completely? She watched him, hoping. When he didn't speak, didn't face her, with a shake of her head she turned and hurried toward her car.

"Wait," he called, running after her. She stopped, and he spun her around, his hands on her shoulders. His eyes were soft then, loving, yet his face was pinched and filled with worry. His strong, blunt, man's fingers gently touched her jaw as if not quite believing she was real, and that she had come here to be with him. He brushed back a strand of hair caught by a slight breeze and blowing toward her mouth. "It'll be ugly, Lisa. You don't know her. Her tongue's sharp, and she'll use it on me. If you're there, you might get caught in the cross-fire."

She held his waist. "I've been attacked by experts. I'm not worried. If you'd like me there, I want to be with you."

"Are you sure?" He seemed to hold his breath awaiting her reply.

"Listen, Santos, I just flew three thousand miles to be with you and you ask me if—"

She couldn't say any more because his mouth pressed hungrily against hers. His arms slipped around her back, pulling her closer, as hers went around his ribcage, holding him tight.

His hands traveled along her spine, over her hips, then to her breasts, as if they were trying to remember all they had learned those months ago, as if trying to convince himself that she really had returned.

"Tony," she murmured, "Tony," and raised a hand to his neck, feeling the damp strands of hair. He smelled like strong soap and sunshine and engine oil, and where she touched him, his body held the heat of the day and of his labors. He spanned her ribs with his large, warm hands, then higher. He kissed her ears, her neck, as she ran both hands into his hair, clutched it with her fingers, messing it even more than it already was. He drew back and straightened, looking down at her, trying to regain some control. Slowly, she moved closer, her eyes never leaving his, giving no doubt what she wanted.

He led her back to the house, up the stairs and in a moment he was lying beside her on his bed wearing nothing but his crucifix, and she wore even less. The half-shut blinds in his bedroom allowed in slats of golden sunshine that cast an amber glow over the room. She didn't shut her eyes. All she wanted to do was to look at him and see that they were together once more.

They made love quickly, desperately, their bodies aching and ready, as if sharing a mutual fear that if they didn't seize the moment, it would be gone and they would have to part again.

Even when their love-making was over, and their breathing drifted back to normal, they continued to keep their arms around each other, to hold, to touch.

It was the first time they'd made love in daylight, and she marveled at the beauty of his body, the tawny color of his skin, the firm, muscular strength of him. She ran her fingers over his face, the face she knew as well as her own, bringing back memories of the fifteen-year-old's face she'd touched so long ago. He was even handsomer now, his face more interesting in its maturity—the lines, the toughening, the wisdom and the sadness that came with living, feeling, loving.

Her hands lingered over his shoulders, his chest, his hips. "You've grown so handsome, Tony," she said. "And I've only grown more bony."

He trailed kisses down her neck to her breast. "You're a bony old hag, all right. But I wouldn't throw you out of bed for eating crackers."

"Tony, I'm serious!"

"I know. You're also beautiful. And too thin. Don't they feed you in New York?"

"Nothing worth eating. There's not a Big Bob's in the whole city," she said with a weighty sigh.

He lifted himself onto his elbow and stroked her hair back from her face, his eyes drinking in every feature. "God, I'm glad you're here. Thank you."

She shut her eyes a moment and swallowed until she was sure her voice wouldn't quiver. "Good," she whispered, then lifted her hand to his neck and pulled him down to her once more.

TWENTY-TWO

The next morning, Lee was up at six. She puttered around the house, looking at the homey touches Miriam had added indoors and the beautiful garden she was creating in the yard. Miriam joined her soon after, and they sat and talked, mainly about Tony, but also more than a little about Gene, until it was time for Lee to get ready to go.

She pinned her hair into a loose chignon and wore a navy blue double-breasted suit with a red trim, conservative yet smart. Navy blue shoes with three-tiny red buttons, a small navy clutch bag, and gold earrings completed the outfit.

Lee drove alone to the county courthouse. At eight o'clock the night before, she'd gone home to give Tony time to collect his thoughts and try to get a good night's sleep. Since he'd be driving Vic, she suggested it would be best for her to meet them there. Ben would be sent to school and afterward, if Tony weren't back from court when school let out, the ranch hands would watch him. Tony didn't want Ben anywhere near the courtroom proceedings.

As Lee pulled into the parking space, she saw Vic and Tony walking toward the entrance to the courthouse. Vic wore a suit that was a little too snug. He looked like a raging bull itching for a fight. Tony, in a dark gray pinstripe suit, looked handsome despite his deep, worried frown. His skin was sallow, dark circles cut deep under his eyes, and she wondered if he had been able to sleep at all last night.

She sat a moment watching him, her hands clasped tight. "Don't let him lose his son, God," she thought. "Please, don't let him lose his son." For a woman who never had time to pray, she was doing a lot of it these days.

After a while she picked up her purse, tucked it under her arm and went inside.

She found the two men in the waiting area outside the courtroom. Vic nodded at her and went back to his pacing. She caught Tony's eye. He stood as she approached, then clasped her hand. He con-

tinued to hold it tightly as they sat down on the
bench to wait.

Tony's attorney walked up to him. "It's time," he
said.

She squeezed Tony's hand a moment before letting it go. His gaze held hers, no words spoken, then
he went forward with the attorney. She followed
Vic to a seat in the back of the courtroom.

The courtroom door opened again, and one of
the most beautiful women Lee had ever seen entered the room.

Vic nudged her arm. "Catherine," he murmured, nodding toward the newcomer.

Lee blanched. Catherine Durelle was about
thirty, but looked younger. Tall and statuesque, she
had silky blond hair, combed back from her face to
fall sleek and shiny to her waist. Her skin was the
golden tan of the southern California beaches, and
her eyes a blazing, brilliant blue. She wore little
make-up. Her white dress hung in a simple, straight
line from her shoulders to her knees, caught at her
waist by a woven belt. Everything about her cried
out purity and the American dream. Lee died a
little inside.

But at the same time, she could see how much
Catherine might have resembled her back in the
days when she was younger, when she was Lisa
Marie—the same coloring, the same body type, the

healthy California looks she had before she learned how to enhance and accentuate her best features for television.

A few steps behind Catherine walked a short, heavy-set man, with brown hair that had been permed and knitted to cover a thinning top. He wore thick, black-rimmed glasses and a black suit. Lee assumed he was Catherine's attorney until she saw the man take a seat behind her in the visitors' area and pat her shoulder. The infamously impotent Dr. Durelle, she thought.

A stylish, middle-aged woman approached the Durelles—Catherine's attorney. After a few whispered words with the doctor, she joined her client.

Lee's stomach knotted. She had fantasized that Catherine would come storming in looking like a low-class Hollywood tart, wearing a striped tee shirt, a red miniskirt and black lace nylons. The judge would take one look at her and throw her and her case out the door.

Inside, she knew Tony wouldn't have married someone like that. She also knew Catherine couldn't be half as sweet as the role she played. Sweet, pure people don't hire private eyes to dig up dirt on ex-spouses. But then, custody battles were often the nastiest and cruelest of court cases, and even normally gentle people turned cunning and crafty over them.

A female lawyer was inspired. Who could argue with more feeling for a mother's rights than another woman? Lee could see why Tony had been so fearful of this confrontation.

The plaintiff, Catherine, was the first one called to the stand.

After the routine questions to establish who she was, her attorney went straight to the heart of the matter. "Please explain to the court why you're here, today, requesting joint custody of your son."

She took a deep breath. When she spoke, her voice was throaty and quivering with emotion. "I'm here because I miss my child. When he was born I was young, too young, to understand or appreciate the gift of life that he was. Now, I'm older, more mature. I love him. Without him, there's a terrible void in my life...in my heart." She glanced at the judge then dabbed her eyes with her handkerchief.

Lee knew the woman was playing up her act for the judge, yet she couldn't help but suspect that some of Catherine's words were true. She *had* been too young. Tony wasn't an innocent in this, but Catherine had walked out on her son, and Tony had given the boy a home.

"Why do you believe you can care for your child at this time?"

Catherine cleared her throat. "Because I have a wonderful husband and a large home in Beverly

Hills. It has five bedrooms and I've already prepared one for Benjamin. My husband makes a good living as a surgeon and I don't work, so I could be home with my son whenever he needs me."

"Thank you, Mrs. Durelle. Please describe to the court your attempts to have your son visit you."

"I asked Tony, that is, my ex, Mr. Santos, to let Ben come and visit me for a while but he said no. I knew I had to get Ben because Tony's an unfit father."

"Objection!" Tony's attorney stood. "That's a conclusion of the witness."

"Sustained."

"You've used the word 'unfit.' Do you wish to prove to the court that Mr. Santos is an unfit father?"

"I didn't want to hurt Tony's reputation. I'm not after vengeance against him for keeping me away from my son. All I want is my little boy back." She began to cry silently. "I'm only asking for what's fair. For joint custody so that my little Benjamin can come and live with me sometimes, too. So I'll have some say in the upbringing of my son. I'm his mother, and I love him and miss him so much." She turned to the judge. "I'm his mother," she pleaded.

Lee felt her stomach churn sickly at Catherine's words—they sounded sincere, even fair.

"Are you concerned about Ben's upbringing

now?" The attorney continued."Well, I hired an investigator to check up on Tony. I found out he has lots of women going through his house. He doesn't work. He made a lot of money as a ball player and blew it buying a fancy house and some fancy horses, but he didn't save anything for our son. I've heard of Ben going to school with holes in his jeans and holes in his Nikes. Tony drinks too much, too—and so does his father! There are a bunch of other men living there too, and they throw wild parties—I hate to imagine what that boy has seen at those parties!"

"Your honor," Tony's lawyer protested. "Your honor, I am shocked and dismayed by my colleague, leading this witness to make unfounded allegations and wild conjecture against my client. She wasn't there, she hasn't been in my client's house, and she certainly hasn't attended a party with him. And I ask the court, what healthy nine-year-old *doesn't* wear holes in his jeans and his tennis shoes?"

Catherine's attorney stepped toward the bench. "Would your Honor please ask my learned colleague to wait until it's his turn to question the witness before he launches into his argument?"

The judge harrumphed and turned to Catherine. She smiled up at him. He smiled back. "Was any of what you just said learned from your own observation?"

"No, your honor, from the investigator's report. But I remember when we were married, that Tony used to drink, and swear, and women were always hanging around him."

Her attorney spoke. "Are you saying he was unfaithful while you were married?"

Catherine raised her eyebrows and looked at her lawyer as if she had to be joking, "To *me*? No, I couldn't say that."

The attorney turned to the judge. "I believe, Your Honor, we have some proof here, today, of the kind of high living Mr. Santos has been doing. Would you care to elaborate, Mrs. Durelle?"

"Yes. We all know about movie stars and TV stars, and how they always use drugs and alcohol and bad language. Well, my investigator learned that Lee Reynolds, the news anchor on CABN-TV was having an affair with Tony a few months ago, and now I see that she's back. I recognize her from TV—she's in the back of the courtroom."

"I object most vehemently, Your Honor!" Tony's attorney shouted over the buzz of voices that filled the courtroom as all eyes but those of Tony and his attorney turned toward Lee. "These are inadmissible generalizations and this witness's comments border on slander."

Lee's body went rigid. Her fingers gripping the

edge of the bench on which she sat. Her head felt light, swimming from Catherine's vitriol.

"Objection sustained," the judge bellowed.

"No further questions, Your Honor."

Lee let out the breath she had been holding.

Tony's attorney rose to cross-examine Catherine.

"Is it true, Mrs. Durelle, that you abandoned your son when he was only one year's old?"

"I didn't abandon him. I left Tony, but I wanted my son. Instead of letting me have him, Tony gave Ben to his father to raise."

"You left a year-old baby with a man who was playing baseball and traveling for six months out of every year and you're surprised that he asked his father to help care for the child?"

"I told him I wanted Ben!"

"Why didn't you take your son with you to begin with?"

"I didn't know where I was going or how I'd get along."

"Does the name Dwayne Davis mean anything to you?"

"No!"

"How about Lefty Davis, then? Does that re-fresh your memory?"

"Oh. He might be someone I've heard of on some baseball team."

"You should have. He was a big star in the miners, on your ex-husband's team in fact."

"Objection!" Catherine's attorney snapped. "This has no relevance to this case."

"I'll show that it does, Your Honor," Tony's attorney replied.

"Overruled."

Tony's attorney tugged at the cuffs of his shirt-sleeves as he turned his attention back to Catherine. "Is it not true that you couldn't take your child with you because you left Phoenix to follow Lefty Davis when he was sent to the major leagues?"

"No, it isn't."

"Do you know what perjury is, Mrs. Durelle?"

"Well, I didn't follow him! I left Tony, and I heard Lefty was in the town I was going to, so I asked if I could stay with him until I got settled, that's all. It was no more than that. We were just friends."

"And once you got settled, why didn't you send for your son?"

"I tried. But Tony wouldn't let me have him."

"Are you saying Lefty Davis had such a large place he was willing to let you and your baby stay with him?"

"No. It was later."

"What was later?"

"Later. When I was on my own again. That's when I asked to take Ben."

"How much later?"

"I don't remember."

"A month? A year? Nine years?"

"Objection! She already stated she doesn't remember."

"Sustained."

Tony's attorney stroked his chin. "Well, given this unspecified amount of time, how did you expect Mr. Santos to care for his child at the same time as he was trying to build a baseball career—a career that requires travel and mobility?"

"I hadn't really thought about it."

"You hadn't thought!" Sarcasm dripped from his voice. Catherine bristled.

"What do I care? Tony wasn't my problem."

"What was your problem, then?"

"Nothing."

"Nothing? You leave your infant child and you have no problem? Now, that's a loving mother!"

"Objection! Conclusion of council and improper line of questioning."

"Sustained."

"As I understand it, Mrs. Durelle, since you and Mr. Durelle cannot have children of your own, you've decided to take back the child you abandoned. In other words, he means nothing to you except as a substitute for other children you cannot have. Is that correct?"

"Not at all! He's my son and I have every right to have him live with me."

"Didn't you give up that right when you walked out on him?"

"No!"

"Objection! Conclusion of council!"

"Sustained. Strike the witness's answer."

"You abandoned your son," Tony's attorney said.

"I left Tony. It's his fault." The judge pounded his gavel, but Catherine wouldn't stop. "He was no good. A lousy husband. Lousy in everything!"

"Your Honor!" Catherine's attorney was on her feet.

"Mrs. Durelle," the judge roared, "please limit your response to the questions posed. And I direct counsel to keep refrain from inflammatory remarks and keep to the semblance, at least, of questions in this courtroom."

"Yes, your honor." Tony's attorney faced Catherine again and took a deep breath. "So, Mrs. Durelle, let me get this straight. Will you explain to the court why you left your baby with this supposedly terrible man?"

"I didn't want to do it!"

"But you did abandon your child and went to

live with another man. Is that not correct, Mrs.
Durelle?"

She burst into tears.

"No more questions, Your Honor."

Tony was called to the stand next. Under his attorney's guidance, he explained about the Circle Z and
that his father also lived there.

"When did you buy this ranch?"

"Two and a half years ago," Tony answered.

"Why?"

"I used to live there, my dad still worked there.
When I heard it was for sale, I knew it would be a
good place to raise my son."

"When did you leave baseball?"

"Two and a half years ago."

"Why?"

"My son was nearly seven, and I thought that,
particularly as he got older, he'd need a father to
watch over and guide him, especially since his
mother wasn't interested in raising him."

"Do you throw lots of parties?"

"No."

"Have lots of women at your place?"

"Hardly!"

"My learned colleague brought up the fact

that Lee Reynolds is in court today, and that somehow means you're involved in fast living. What can you tell the court about her presence here today?"

"Her real name is Lisa Marie. We went to school together. We're old friends, that's all. Her aunt is moving to Miwok and staying at Lisa's place. When Lisa heard this trial would be today, she offered to come along for moral support. That's all there is to it."

"Do you expect to continue to see her?"

"She's engaged to someone in New York. I have no idea when or if she'll visit Miwok again."

"Thank you, Mr. Santos. Now, about your ranch, does your father still live on your ranch property with you and Ben?"

"He does."

"Does he help take care of his grandson?"

"He sees Ben every day. The two of them are quite close."

"As are you and your son."

"Yes, we are."

The attorney glanced at Catherine, then the judge. "No more questions, Your Honor."

Catherine's attorney stood. "Isn't it true that you, Mr. Santos, grew up without a mother?"

"She died."

"Did you ever wish she hadn't died?"

Tony stared at the woman, then shrugged. "Sure."

"So, even though you had a father, you'd say that there was something different, something special, about a mother that you missed, right?"

Tony glanced toward his attorney, then back to Catherine's attorney. "I don't know."

"You do know that there's a difference between a mother and a father, right?"

"I guess."

"And yet, you wish to deny your son the right to know his own mother, when you yourself admit that you missed having a mother of your own. How can you be so selfish, so heartless—"

"Objection!"

"—to both of them, Mr. Santos. How can you keep this woman and her child apart?"

"I object to this line of questioning!" his attorney bellowed.

"Sustained."

"No more questions, Your Honor."

Following the closing arguments, the judge announced that he would issue his decision in a day or two.

Lee and Vic walked out of the room. Tony

stayed behind with his attorney, looking shaken. Lee waited near the door to join him when he came out.

Before he appeared Catherine stepped through the doorway. Her eyebrows rose when she noticed Lee. She squared her shoulders and approached her. "So, you're Lee Reynolds, in the flesh."

"Catherine." Lee nodded curtly.

"I never expected to see you here. Do you slum for kicks these days, or is this how you always have fun?"

Lee gave the woman a cold stare, wondering what was behind this attack. "I wasn't slumming until a moment ago."

"She speaks! And without a teleprompter yet!"

Lee wasn't about to waste her time trading barbs. "Why are you doing this, Catherine?"

Catherine's eyes narrows. She folded her arms. "Is it so hard for you to believe that I want my son?"

"Your motherly instincts are a little belated, aren't they?"

"I can make it up to him."

"You're wrong. Ben may forgive you for walking out on him, but he'll never forget it. He'll never trust you."

Catherine's eyes turned hard. "I could use those exact words about you and Tony. I know all about you seeing him when you were here a few months ago—how you went after him to relive your youth. Well, it's gone, Lee Reynolds. Have you looked into a mirror lately?"

Was Catherine jealous? Is that what was behind her venom? "You know nothing about Tony and me."

"I know a lot more than you think! I know you hurt him. But as the years went by, he got over it. And now, he's one of the coldest, hardest bastards I know."

"I can't believe you were married to the man and be so wrong about him. There's nothing cold or hard about Tony," Lee stated.

"You'll find out. You don't know him as well as you think." Catherine's eyes were icy and flat. "At least I've got a son to fight for. You haven't got a damn thing, Lee Reynolds. You're no more useful than yesterday's news." Catherine spun on her heel and stormed down the hall. A clerk stepped out of a room in front of her and she pushed him aside and kept going.

Lee said nothing, holding herself still so she wouldn't shatter into a thousand pieces.

Dr. Durelle, looking and acting almost gnome-like, stepped out of the shadows and glanced up at Lee. "I...I'm sorry." He lifted his arms in a gesture of helplessness, then hurried off in the direction of his wife.

Lee stared after the woman. She shut her eyes a moment, trying to block out the ugliness and pain of Catherine's words. Tony had warned her.

After a short while, Catherine briskly strode back down the hallway, her husband following about three steps behind. Lee folded her arms and stood her ground. If Catherine wanted to play ugly, she was ready to accommodate her.

Just as Catherine neared, the courtroom door opened and Tony stepped out. They arrived at almost the same spot, face to face, and for the first time, they looked directly at each other. The air between them crackled with hatred—and something more.

Lee stood as if rooted to the spot as she watched Ben's parents together. Despite the bitterness, the two of them had a bond, a living, breathing wonderful little boy that they had created. She saw them both stiffen, then Tony stepped back and let Catherine pass. She abruptly turned and reentered the courtroom.

Lee had never felt as alone as she did at that moment. That other woman, that travesty of motherhood, had no right to be here. Or...was she the one who had no right?

She turned to the window and looked out, seeing in the reflected glass the elegant woman Lisa

Marie Reynolds had become. Who was the *real* person—Lee or Lisa?

Tony walked to her side. She faced him, cool and in control as always. "I'm so sorry, Tony. I never imagined my coming here could be used against you. I'll do anything possible to correct it."

He leaned both hands on the windowsill. "I don't think it'll matter much one way or the other."

"You did a good job deflecting criticism in the way you explained our relationship."

"I tried."

She waited for him to say something more, but he didn't. No words, it seemed, were left between them.

After a long pause he said, "There's nothing more we can do here. We may as well go home."

TWENTY-THREE

When Lee got back to the Circle Z, she went to look for Ben. Tony and Vic hadn't arrived yet. They had been delayed by Tony's attorney as they were leaving the courthouse.

Lee found Ben in the barn brushing his horse, Evening Star. The boy shot her a solemn, brown-eyed gaze, not at all surprised to see her, and with studious concentration returned to his chore.

"Hello, Ben."

"Hi." His tone was downcast, his voice soft.

Lee patted the filly's nose.

"Is Dad home?" he asked, still brushing.

"He's on his way."

There was a long pause, with only the sound of

the brush raking through the horse's coat being heard. "Is it over?" he asked.

She had the impression Tony had kept the proceedings from Ben. "Is what over?"

"I know what's going on. I've heard Dad and Grandpa talking when they thought I was busy in my room." His eyes were large and worried. "What happened?"

She wasn't surprised to learn that. "We just have to wait and see what the judge decides."

Ben's hand stilled a moment, the brush in mid-air. "Oh."

Lee picked up another brush and began working the other side of Star's coat.

"It'll be okay, Ben. You'll see."

"I guess I'm going to have to go live with her."

"Not necessarily. Your dad tried very hard to make the judge understand he wants you here."

"Maybe."

She was shocked. "Maybe? Of course he did."

Ben shrugged. "Maybe my dad's tired of me. My mom didn't want me, you know. I heard my dad say that. Sometimes I even hear him say it's a lot of work to raise a kid by himself. I got into a fight in school last year and broke Larry Larson's finger. Dad was really mad."

She put down the brush and walked around Star to Ben's side. "Ben, come here." She held out her hand to him. He put down his brush and took it. She led him to a bench. Sitting down, she looked gravely into his dark eyes. "Your dad would never grow tired of you. You mean everything to him, Ben. He's fought for you every way he knows how. The problem is that your mother loves you, too. Maybe she thought she didn't want you, but that was years ago. She was much younger then. You're a lucky boy to have two people who want you so much."

He stared at his shoes, his lower lip trembling. "I think it's bad luck."

"It's never bad luck to he loved, Ben."

She ran her hand along his soft, thick hair, brushing it back off his handsome face. She felt herself growing attached, too attached, to this child. She dropped her hand.

"Whatever happens," she said gently, "never doubt that your dad loves you and wants you with him very, very much."

He sat beside her and put his elbows on his knees then bent forward so that his chin rested on his hands. He looked so downcast, she wrapped an arm around his shoulders and pulled him to her side in a hug. His frame was surprisingly small. She couldn't remember having hugged a nine-year-old child before. Ben's shoulders were narrow, his arms delicate, and the smell of him reminded her of playgrounds on a sunny day. She kissed the top of his head, then squeezed her eyes tight as she lay her cheek against his hair. He eased against her with complete trust and acceptance.

"Well, that's my kid, all right," Tony said. "Already he's got the prettiest woman in the county kissing him."

Ben and Lee looked up to see Tony in the doorway, his hands on his hips, his feet slightly apart, and his eyes warm as he looked at the two of them together.

"Dad!" Ben broke from Lee and threw his arms around his father's waist. "Lisa said you fought hard for me."

At Tony's stricken look, Lee hurried to explain. "He overheard you and Vic. He knew what was going on today."

Tony shook his head, then lifted the boy off his feet in a big hug and kissed him on the cheek. They were silent for a long moment, Tony holding Ben, and the boy with all but a stranglehold on his father's neck. Lee could see Tony struggle to hide his worry from his son. Then he lowered him to the ground. "I told that judge if he tries to send you away from me he'd better be ready to put up his dukes."

Ben's eyebrows rose. "What're dukes?"

Tony and Lee laughed. "This." Tony lifted a big

fist, gently bopped Ben in the nose, then ruffled his hair. "Homework time. Tomorrow's a school day."

"Aw, Dad. You're too tired."

"I'm too tired? It's your homework. Go get started."

"But I need help with math."

"Try it first, then if you're still stuck, I'll help."

"Hell, I mean, heck." Ben slumped off toward the house.

Tony faced Lee. Awkwardness hung between them, created by Catherine's words, her ugly innuendoes. Lee didn't say anything as she approached him. She placed her hands on his chest. He held her waist, and they stared until they could bear it no longer. With a groan, they came together, holding each other tight. "I thought you'd hate me after that," he said. "I shouldn't have let you go there, shouldn't have put you in the line of her venom."

"I wanted to be there, to see."

He kissed her, then their arms went around each other once more in a long hug, as if hoping that holding each other could erase the ugliness of the day.

Finally, Tony held out his hand to Lee. She took it and they followed Ben, hand in hand, up the hill.

Lee warmed at the scene before her. A vermilion sunset glowed over the coast range mountains and cast the clapboard house in rose pastels.

Tony had made a loving home for himself and his son. But Ben was his driving force. If he lost Ben, it could destroy him.

They found Ben sitting at the kitchen table, his backpack with his books and binder unopened in front of him.

"Take your books out of there, Benjamin," Tony said. "I'll start dinner and then help you."

"But I don't understand it!"

"Ben! Read the book, study the examples—you can do that."

Lee stood back, her attention bouncing from one to the other. Tony removed a package of hamburger from the refrigerator and put it on the counter.

"What are you making?" she asked.

"Spaghetti."

"Oh, I'm a fine spaghetti cook." She took the skillet from his hand. "You see to Ben, I'll put on dinner."

"You sure?"

"Absolutely. You're lucky. It's one of the few meals I can cook."

He grinned, then placed parsley, onions, mushrooms, tomato paste, spices, plus a pound of spaghetti on the counter. Before joining Ben, he helped Lee with the chopping. By the time he finished, Ben had attempted to work a few of the math problems.

Tony rinsed off his hands. "Go ahead and cook all the spaghetti, Lisa. I like it cold for breakfast."

He has to be joking, she thought, but did as requested.

While she cooked, she watched Tony bend over the table, his head nearly touching Ben's as he tried to explain the mysteries of fractions to the boy.

They worked well together, and Tony showed more patience and ability to sit still than she ever dreamed he possessed. She was so intrigued watching the two of them in the warm kitchen, the savory smell of her sauce filling the air, that she nearly overcooked the spaghetti.

"Dinner's ready," she announced.

"That's enough homework tonight, Dad. You want to have time to talk to Lisa, don't you?"

"All that's left is English, and there's plenty of time for you to do it after dinner," Tony said. "Anyway, Lisa's a lot better at grammar than I am. She probably even understands diagramming sentences. I'm sure she'd love to help you. Right, Lisa?"

She froze in the middle of pouring Italian dressing over a simple lettuce and tomato salad. "Oh, it's been so long, I don't know if I remember."

"Sure you do! Let's set the table, Benito."

"Actually," Lee said as she put the bowl of

spaghetti on the table, "at one time, when I was growing up, I wanted to be a school teacher."

Tony glanced at her. "There you go, then."

They sat.

Tony and Ben made the sign of the cross. "Grace," Tony said.

"Grace," Ben repeated.

Tony glanced at Lee, his fork poised over his food, and shrugged. "It's better than saying nothing."

She held her breath as Tony and Ben took their first taste of the food she'd prepared. She couldn't remember the last time she cooked an entire dinner for anyone—she always went out to dine with friends and associates, or telephoned for home delivery. While with Miriam, she'd help, but Miriam was the one in charge of the kitchen.

"Great spaghetti," Ben said, then slurped a noodle.

"Nice," Tony added, digging in enthusiastically.

She sat back with a smile. Her cooking did taste good. She liked making this dinner for Tony and his son; she liked hearing them praise her efforts; and she liked watching them enjoy eating it. Maybe a sophisticated news anchor wasn't supposed to like such domestic, plebeian things, but she couldn't stop herself from smiling as she ate.

After dinner, Tony cleared the kitchen, Ben loaded the dishwasher, and both insisted that "the cook" sit and relax. They worked quickly and efficiently, joking and laughing. Once again, Lee was struck by the terrible injustice it would be if the two of them were separated.

Tony made coffee while Lee helped Ben distinguish subjects from predicates. The boy caught on quickly, and within minutes the day's English assignment was completed. Tony sent him out of the kitchen to play or read, issuing a "No TV" order.

"Not even the National League play-offs?" Ben asked.

"The Na—." Tony glanced at the clock. "Holy Christ! With everything else going on, I forgot!"

He all but leaped over the kitchen table in his hurry to get to the family room to turn on the television.

Lee chuckled as she poured coffee for herself and Tony, then carried it to him.

"Score's tied, Lisa. Pull up a chair."

"Dad knows every player," Ben announced.

"Not every player. It's been three years since I played."

"It would be great if you still did!" Ben said.

Tony's face paled. "Oh...well..."

Ben smiled at his father. "But I like having you home more."

Lee knew the exact moment when a pang of love, family, and possible loss speared Tony's heart because it struck hers as well. He glanced at her, and a closeness stole over them, binding them with unspoken prayers. Tony turned to Ben. "Thanks," he said, and probably only to her ear was his voice a little too husky, a little too soft.

They settled into the game. Lee hadn't imagined how entertaining it could be to watch baseball with Tony. He had insight and an insider's knowledge of the game, plus he was up and down like a jumping jack. He'd tell players what they should be doing and exactly what he thought of them if they failed to execute a play, or he'd be thrilled and shouting praises when someone succeeded at an especially tough maneuver. Ben copied everything his father did. The game was close, but the Braves pulled it out in the ninth.

By the time the game ended, it was past Ben's bedtime. Tony sent him upstairs to take a shower.

"He keeps your evenings busy," Lee said.

"Yeah. It's fairly typical, though, from what I've learned talking to other parents."

"It's nice."

He nodded, then his gaze became hollow and Lee knew he thought of how empty his evenings would be if Catherine won her custody fight.

After the shower stop running, Tony waited about ten minutes before he went upstairs to be sure Ben was getting ready for bed.

He stepped into Ben's room. "How are you doing, son?"

Ben sat on his bed, his pajamas on, playing with a fleet of tiny automobiles. A long moment passed. "Fine." He hadn't looked up when Tony entered, hadn't looked up when his father spoke.

Tony stood a moment watching him, then crossed the room and sat on his bed. "Lights out time."

Big tears well up in Ben's eyes and the boy suddenly lunged forward and wrapped his arms around Tony's neck, holding on tight. "Thanks for fighting for me today, Dad."

The words went straight to Tony's heart and unshed tears stung his eyes as he held his son. "Don't cry, Ben." He choked out the words. "Don't worry. It'll be all right."

"I love you, Dad."

Tony hugged his son hard, his eyes shut tight. "I love you, too, son. More than anything in the world."

He held Ben a long time. There were few things that smelled so good or felt so squeaky clean as a just-bathed little boy after a long, hard day of play. What would he do without Ben to hug? He sat beside him until Ben fell asleep, and for several minutes after that.

From the stairs, Tony saw Lisa below, kneeling on the floor of the living room, in front of his stereo system. His heart was heavy with worry over Ben, and having her here helped, probably more than she realized. He walked down a few steps. In a way, seeing her here, in this house, seemed so right it scared him. He descended more steps, hoping he would always remember how she looked there tonight, on the floor, flipping through his CD collection as if she belonged here. Her shoes were off, her skirt hiked up slightly baring long, shapely legs. She had removed her jacket and under it she wore a gossamer-thin little nothing of a blouse that showed the fancy lace bodice of her slip.

Throughout the summer months, he had replayed the night she spent in his home, his bed, until he thought he would go nuts. He hadn't known it was possible to miss a woman that much, or to want her so badly. He tortured himself with thoughts of her and her fancy boyfriend and what they were doing together. And then she had called.

Hearing her voice, he was surprised he hadn't dropped the phone, or yelled at her for having waited so damned long! As much as he rearranged his whole week to be sure that Friday evenings he would be home to get her call, he hated thinking about the other days of the week—especially Saturday night, when he would picture, in great detail, her going somewhere with Magnifico Man, the nameless jerk she was supposedly engaged to. Her going somewhere with the guy was bad enough to imagine, but their returning home was sheer torture.

He nearly leaped through the phone with joy when she started hinting that things were not as they should be with the guy. Having her here, now, was proof that her other relationship was over. He knew Lisa. She wouldn't be with two men at once.

Now, for a while at least, she had chosen him. And he fell in love with her all over again. It wasn't by choice. He had no choice about such things where Lisa was concerned. Never had. Not from the first time he laid eyes on her in a schoolyard by a bicycle stand.

That didn't mean he was unclear about the future. He knew it would end just like last time. He knew that one of these times, when she left, she wouldn't be back.

"Hi." She looked up when he entered the room. "I was hoping you had some old songs."

"You'll have to look at the records. They're in

that cabinet. They're probably pretty scratchy, though."

"Think we shouldn't play them? I wouldn't want to damage your phonograph needle."

"No problem. I never play records anymore, just CD's or MP3's."

"So high-tech, Mr. Santos." She saw the far-off look in his eyes, and she knew what had put it there. "How's Ben doing?"

He rubbed his forehead. "He's pretty upset, poor little guy. It's surprising how much kids pick up even when you tell them there's nothing to worry about."

"He knows you're trying your best to keep him," she said. "That's important."

He sat on the chair near the stereo system. "I remember how proud I felt when I learned how much my own father wanted me."

That surprised her. "I thought you were always with Vic."

"No. The first four years of my life I never even saw him."

"You never mentioned that."

"I didn't like to talk about it. I understand it now, as an adult, but I didn't always."

"Yes?"

He smiled at her curiosity. "I've mentioned that my mother died in childbirth. Well, it was really hard on Vic. He left me with his sister, that's my Tia Maria, and took off. Even Tia didn't know where he was for a long time. She used to tell me stories about my father, that he was a great *caballero*, working with strong, beautiful horses all over the west."

"And he didn't visit you?"

"Not until I was four. I remember the day he finally arrived at Tia's farm. I buried my face in the heavy, brown skirt my aunt always wore and wouldn't look at him. She insisted, though, and when I finally looked, he scared the hell out of me."

"I'm not surprised!" Lee's words came out a little more vehemently than she intended.

Tony laughed. "He was frowning like the Devil. And he had this huge, black mustache covering his top lip."

"And here I thought he only frowned at me," Lee said wryly.

Tony chuckled. "Vic had no idea what to say or do around a kid—at least not his own kid. So he just stared and scowled. He told me later that he saw my mother in my face and my eyes and it made him feel bad for leaving me. All I remember is that his eyes got all watery, then he asked Tia what he should say to me. She said, 'Tell him you love him, you big peasant.' I couldn't believe my Tia would talk to this fierce man that way. He didn't seem to mind, though."

"He probably knew she was right," Lee murmured. The thought of Vic Santos being intimidated had its appeal.

"I guess. He just lowered himself onto his knees and looked me in the eye. No words came. But as we looked at each other, it hit me that this big, ugly man was my father...my father...and I walked over to him. He lifted me up. His arms were like mallets. But I felt good and secure. Maybe for the first time in my life. I liked the feeling. I always wanted Ben to know it, too."

Lee's eyes grew misty as she listened to his story. She nodded. She had known that feeling once, long ago, but then it had died...her father had died. And she had forced herself to forget.

"He took me with him," Tony said. "I was only four, but I lived on the range with my father and the other ranch hands. When I started school, he had to take care about the jobs he took—to be sure there was a school nearby. But we were always together."

"Like you and Ben."

His eyes clouded. "Like me and Ben."

She covered his hand. "You'll continue to be. I know it. I believe it."

He shut his eyes, his shoulders slumped. He withdrew his hand and seemed to withdraw all of himself into a shell of fear of losing Ben.

She quickly flipped through the records again,

needing to take his mind off the ugliness of the day. "Say, look at this." She held up Johnny Mathis's *Chances Are* album. "Remember how, at parties, when it would get late, we would stop playing the Van Halen or Def Leopard and put on these old songs?"

He stood beside her, looking down, and took the record. His face was still haunted by the day's events. "There must be a couple of decades of teenagers who learned all about 'making out' to these songs."

"Let's listen."

His eyebrows went up slightly, then he removed the album jacket, blew on the record to remove any loose dust, and put it on the turntable. "I hope my heart can take it," he muttered.

A nasal, quavering voice, breathy and emotional, singing "Chances Are" came over the speakers. With her older, more sophisticated ear, she realized that the singer wasn't the Pavarotti she used to think he was, nonetheless she felt a thrill go right up her spine as the familiar music filled the room.

Tony turned off all the lights but one lamp, then he held out his hand to her, and drew her to her feet to dance with him.

Her breath caught as his arms went around her, and she nestled her head against his. She shut her eyes, drinking in the feel and scent of him, hoping her warmth, her touch, could help ease his pain. This was where she wanted to be, since the day she left Miwok, months ago. Maybe years ago. She didn't deny it, couldn't deny it anymore. Under her ear she could feel his pulse drum strongly through his body. Its cadence matched the own.

He slowly led her around the room and as they passed the lamp, he switched it off altogether.

"Just like high school," she said.

"Even better." He kissed her.

As "A Certain Smile" began, he lowered her to the sofa, then stretched out beside her.

His mouth sought hers then he unbuttoned her blouse and rolled on top of her. "You don't know how often I wanted to do this back then."

"Be careful of what you hope for," she warned, her voice a thick whisper, her skin tingling and alive where his fingers brushed. "It just might come true."

"If you're lucky enough." His mouth trailed along the curve of her jaw to her throat then back to her mouth as he took her heart, her mind, in a long, demanding kiss.

Her smile was wobbly when they both came back up for air. "Would you like to go upstairs? You'll be more comfortable," she said. Her hands pulled his shirt free of his slacks, then unbuttoned it and pushed it aside to stroke the hot, muscled skin.

"Uh uh." He kissed her eyelids, then her nose.

"Even after all these years—this music, and Lisa Marie Reynolds half-dressed beneath me on the sofa. God, it's everything I'd ever dreamed of as a teenager. Almost," he added rakishly.

Her eyes widened in surprise a moment, then she laughed huskily. His hands surrounded the sides of her face as his mouth lowered possessively, as if she were his girl again, as if she had always been his girl.

A hot, wild rush of desire swelled through her. She yanked his shirt off, tugging at his belt as he did the same to her blouse, her skirt.

He was lifting her slip to pull it over her head when he saw she was wearing that sexy garter belt again, and silk stockings. If he didn't have a strong heart, they'd be his undoing. He liked very much the fact that he alone knew the sexiness under Lisa's proper suit.

He drew back and removed the belt and stockings.

He took in every inch of her. She was willow thin and so fair he wouldn't have believed she was real except that he knew her so well. Knew every inch of her, committing her to memory for the lonely days and nights ahead.

He bent over her, tasting her, starting with her breasts then working his way lower, slowly, slowly, until he shattered her world.

After a while, her eyes opened, dazed with pleasure, to find him propped on an elbow looking down at her. "I've never seen you more beautiful," he whispered.

She held her arms open for him. He held himself above her, then slowly lowered himself. "Look at me, Lisa," he demanded. "Know it's me. It's always been me."

It's always been you, Tony, her heart answered. *Always.*

TWENTY-FOUR

Tony's lawyer called the next morning. The judge's decision was due in an hour which meant that the judge felt it was a clear-cut case. But whether it was clear-cut in favor of motherhood, apple pie—and money—or of a caring, loving father, they would have to wait to find out.

Lee stood beside Tony as he put the phone back in his pocket. "It's coming in."

"The decision?"

"I've got to meet my attorney in an hour."

"Would you like me to go with you?"

His dark eyes met hers. "No."

"Vic, at least, should be there. I'll stay here, in case you two are still out when Ben gets home from school."

He shook his head. "I'm not telling Vic. I'd like to be alone when I hear. Just in case." He walked to the stairs. "If the decision is bad, I don't really know what I'll do. Okay?"

Don't face this alone, Tony. Please. She was suddenly afraid—of the outcome, of his reaction if it went against him, of his temper, his despair. But she said nothing.

Minutes later he reappeared wearing a gray suit, white shirt, and yellow and gray striped tie. It seemed wrong to her that he had to dress up and look so handsome to go hear a verdict that could rip out his heart.

She hugged him as he stepped toward the door, and a shudder went through her. "Someone's walking on your grave," Miriam liked to say. She didn't know if it was a premonition or not. All she knew was that the gaze he cast on her was forlorn, and that when he left, her heart went with him,

She called Miriam to tell her where she was, and not to worry, then she sat down to wait for his return.

What would he do if the verdict went against him? It couldn't happen. No judge would take Ben from him. She ran her hand over the warm red floral upholstery of the sofa. This ranch, this house, were wonderful places to raise a boy. There was so much love here, the very walls throbbed with it.

Her love was here as well.

She had fought it, but from the time she first saw Tony, standing on a minuscule Little League baseball field, wearing a red Bruins and figuring out "who's in the hole," her heart was his. It was as if she never stopped loving him. That must have been why no one else ever really mattered. Her relationship with Bruce wasn't love. It was a business proposition. They had used each other to get ahead.

She could admit that now. As he often said, he was one of the most eligible bachelors around—a power job, money, youth and knock-out good looks on top of it. People's heads turned when she walked into the room with Bruce on her arm. It felt good. But it wasn't love.

Love was what she felt around Tony. Just to look at him made her smile inside. They could talk or be silent with equal comfort. She wanted to tell him everything she did and thought, and wanted to hear the same from him. When he hurt, she hurt. When he bled, she bled. And when he felt joy, she felt joy.

The way Tony felt about her...her heart told her it was a lot more than lust, more than old times— that it was love or the next best thing.

Where it would lead, though, was beyond her ken. She didn't know and didn't want to think about it. Tony had a strange caution around her. He never talked about how he felt, or their future. Maybe it was because of Ben and the uncertainty in his life. Or, maybe it was something deeper. An uncertainty about her. About their past.

What did it matter? She had her life on one coast; he had his life on the other. She had worked too many years to become Lee Reynolds to give it up. She loved her work. Could he leave his? Come with her? Could he be happy doing that? Living in New York City? Going to Sissy Springfield's parties? She was filled with doubt, and very little hope.

Vic Santos opened the back door and walked in.

"Hello." Her tone was tentative.

He grunted in greeting. "Where's Tony?"

"The lawyer called. The decision is being issued. Tony went to meet him."

Vic nodded, then turned to go back outside.

"Mr. Santos, wait, please." She stepped closer.

He stopped and glanced back at her over his shoulder.

She lifted her chin. "I don't know what I did to make you dislike me so much, but whatever it was, I am sorry. I hope we can get along. For Tony's sake, if not our own."

He faced her squarely, "I've known a lot of people like you. Everything with you is your plans, your hope, your dreams. But you don't give nothing. I'm gonna be glad when you go back to your job. I just hope Tony can forget you like he did before. So, no, I don't want to 'get along' with you. I don't even like you."

He stalked out the door.

Hours passed before Tony's car pulled into the driveway. He remained seated a moment, not moving. After a while, he slowly opened the door and climbed out. Gone was the bounce in his step, the easy, carefree manner that was Tony. Lee pressed her hand to her heart. She knew.

He walked into the house without a word. She could smell the alcohol on his breath, see the glazed look in his eyes. She followed him into the living room, saying nothing as she watched him take off his jacket and tie and toss them onto a chair.

"Is it over?" she asked.

"Yes. Very straightforward." He stepped around her, not looking at her or touching her, and went down the hall to the kitchen. She followed.

He opened a kitchen cabinet and took out a bottle of bourbon, then got a small glass. "Would you like some?" he asked, his back to her.

She shook her head, then realized he wasn't watching. "No." Her voice was a dry croak.

His hand shook as he poured the drink. He took

a large swallow then waited, still facing the counter. She walked up to him and placed her hand on his shoulder. He flinched, and she pulled her hand away again.

"She won?" Lee asked and yet knowing.

He nodded.

"Tell me about it."

"What's to tell?" He finished his drink. "Ben can spend holidays with me. But throughout the school year, he's with her."

"You can appeal."

"Sure. And listen to some other judge tell me Ben's better off with his mother. The pompous bastard said he had to think of the boy's future—that with Catherine he could go to the best schools and have endless opportunities that I could never give him. He made it sound as if I should have stayed in baseball where there were money and connections." He faced her and the pain and anger in his face was terrible. "I willingly gave it up to make a home for Ben. That meant nothing. All that mattered was money, connections and the 'cultural mainstream of society.'"

She shut her eyes a moment, unable to look at the raw agony in his. "I see," she whispered.

He slammed his fist against the counter, his shoulders heaving with each breath. "I'm glad you do, 'cause I sure as hell don't." His control was on the edge. His voice shook with rage and frustration. "What more could I do? God damn all of them! What the hell does it take to be able to keep my own son?"

She took hold of his arm, trying to get him to calm down, but he yanked his arm away hard. Savagely, he paced back and forth across the kitchen floor. "Not a damn thing I do matters," he bellowed. "Has it ever? I thought it did, but I had it shoved in my face just how wrong I was."

"It does matter," she cried, trying hard to get through to him, past his outrage. "You've come a long way. You've achieved many great things. And you have a boy who loves you, who'll want you to fight for him."

"Don't preach at me!" In two steps he stood in front of her, his face contorted. "You, of all people, know my worth—or lack of it. You left, didn't you? I wasn't good enough for you."

She was astounded. "You were always good enough. Too good."

"Hell!"

"Believe me—"

"Believe you, Lisa? *You?* Give me one reason why I should?" His fury raged over her, intense in its scope and blind in its focus. "One reason why I should believe you, or trust you, or even care about you? You just flit in here for a while then take off again. When are you leaving this time?"

She pressed her hands against her stomach. She knew he was lashing out at her because she was there and the judge and Catherine weren't. Still, his words hurt. "I haven't decided—"

"You haven't decided!" He gave a mocking, bitter laugh, pacing around her like a prowling tiger. "No one else is involved, right? No one else matters, do they? How easy do you think this is for me, knowing one morning I'll wake up and you'll say, 'Time to be off, Tony. See you some decade.'"

Her heart breaking, she tried again to clutch his arm, to still his angry pacing. "I came back because I wanted to be with you."

"Why, damn it?" He wouldn't let her hold on to him. Instead he pulled free and grabbed her upper arms. He walked toward her as she stepped backwards until she backed hard against the wall. "Why? That's what I don't get. You came because you were lonely?"

She shook her head, her arms hurting. "No, Tony."

He leaned into her. "Because you were curious about the kind of hell people can put themselves through when they don't live the pristine life of Lee Reynolds? Maybe you wanted to see that first-hand?"

Her breath quickened. "No! Let go of me!"

"Maybe you just wanted a little stud service, then?" He shoved her from him.

She stumbled sideways, catching the counter-top, holding it to steady herself. "Tony!" Tears welled in her eyes.

His shoulders, his entire body seemed to sag, and he turned his back to her. "Get the hell out of here, Lisa. I don't want to see you again. Not ever."

"You don't mean that. Not any of it."

He glanced at her. "Don't I? Years ago you walked away, and you've never had the goddamned decency to tell me the truth about *why*. Not back then, and not now. I kept waiting for an honest ex-planation. I told myself not to ask, not to show you how you made me feel by leaving. Do you know the hell that put me through? Do you even care?"

She felt as if all the blood drained from her face. "I told you the truth."

"Like hell! I told you I loved you, damn it! That I wanted to marry you. Didn't that mean anything to you at all? I loved you so much I would have done anything for you. Anything! I thought you felt the same. What we had between us—Christ, I re-member being scared half to death by it—but it was Heaven. I should know, because after you shut me out, I learned all about Hell."

Her knees seemed to give out. She reached for a

chair and almost fell into it. She dropped her eyes, unable to look at the pain in his. "That was long ago."

He closed his eyes a moment, his head tilted back. Then he looked at her again, scowling fiercely. "I tried to forget about it, Lisa, I really did. Seeing you again, I tried to enjoy each moment with you and ignore the past. But it won't go away. It's with me whenever I look at you. I relive those last days and nights we spent together as kids, and wonder what happened."

"We grew up," she said softly.

"There's more to it than that. I've always wondered...were you really so ashamed, Lisa? Of what we started the night of the prom? Did I really make you feel so...soiled?"

The raw pain of his words slashed through her. "God, Tony, no! You couldn't have thought that."

"Couldn't I? You were Lisa Marie, everybody's golden girl, and I was just a Mexican kid with dreams of baseball."

He turned away.

She bowed her head against his pain; against her own.

They sat alone in his big Bonneville after the prom. Her hands ran up and down his back, knowing that tonight the kind of petting they used to do in this car wasn't going to be enough. They had done so much together, had grown up, and had fallen in love. But there was still one thing left, and she knew her first lover had to be Tony.

"I never lied about the way I felt about you," she whispered.

His flesh was like fire against hers, and she sought his lips as a remedy for the heat, only to find the fire that raged between them growing worse.

Her hand rubbed against the zipper of his trousers, feeling the swollen hardness beneath. "Don't, Lisa." *He took her hand away.* "It'll be too hard to stop. It may be too hard already."

"I don't want to stop. I want you to show me that you love me. Show me."

"I've always..." *He claimed her mouth again, sending shooting sensations stabbing through her. She would make him realize that there would never be anyone else for him. Not ever.*

"That summer...after I left for baseball camp," he said, "you decided to leave early for college, and then that was it. It was over."

Sudden lightheadedness rocked her, her breath coming in short gasps, as the agony of how he had felt, of how completely he had misunderstood all these years, hit her.

He sat in silence, his lips pressed firmly together, his face rigid.

Unshed tears pressed hard against her eyes.

The time had come to tell him, but she wondered how she could find the words. "I can't believe, thinking back, how very innocent we were," she began. "And, for supposedly bright kids, how very stupid. Remember how I took a bus into San Francisco and went to Planned Parenthood for birth control pills *afterward*? And how we even made love to celebrate my getting them?"

He stared at her, a dawning unease in his eyes as he slowly nodded.

She drew in her breath, held it, then let breath and words out in a mad rush. "After you left Miwok, I took a pregnancy test—one of those I bought at a drug store. It was positive. I was happy about it, Tony. I wanted the baby. I believed that somehow, even with us both having big plans and wanting careers, it would all work out. I was going to tell you when you returned from camp..."

Judith burst into Lisa's bedroom. "The test is positive, isn't it?"

"How did you know?" Lisa asked, shocked that her mother had been spying on her.

"Get rid of it, damn it!" Judith screamed. "I won't have you ruining your life. I've done all I can to make sure you make something of yourself."

"I will. With Tony—"

"You stupid little fool! That's what I once thought—that even with a kid I could get ahead, be-

come somebody. But I couldn't. You held me back. You! And now, that damn Mexican's brat will do the same thing to you. Get rid of it!"

"I won't!" Lisa tried to run from her bedroom. Judith grabbed her arm.

"Don't you run from me," Judith ordered. "I was talking to you."

"I don't want to hear it. Leave me alone!" Lisa tried to pull free, but Judith's grip was strong.

"What don't you want to hear? The truth? Isn't it about time I told you? I never wanted you! Not one little bit."

"Do you really think I didn't already know that?" Lisa cried, tears streaming. "Go away. Just go away from me. I'll keep my baby, I'll take care of it!"

"You've been nothing but one disappointment after the other. And this is the worst."

"Get out of here!" Lisa shrieked.

"You've never lived up to my expectations, not once. You're truly your father's daughter."

Lisa moved towards the stairs, practically dragging Judith with her in her struggle to get away from her. But Judith pressed her face so close Lisa could feel her breath, see the alcohol-crazed fury in her eyes. "You're just as worthless as he was. I've always known it. How long before your 'boyfriend' learns it, too? Before you disappoint him the way you've disap-

pointed everyone else in your life, with your cheap, disgusting—"

"Shut up!" Lisa shoved Judith hard, needing to get out of that house.

Judith let go of her cane and grabbed Lisa's hair. "Damn you! Don't you dare push your mother!"

"You're no mother! You never have been." Lisa tried to pull free, but Judith's fingers were like talons, gripping her. She twisted toward the stairs, toward freedom, half-dragging Judith with her.

"You ruined my life." Judith spat out the words. "You and your father both, and now you want to ruin my plans, my dreams."

They reached the top of the stairs.

"Why didn't you die instead of my father!" Lisa cried, still struggling. "I hate you."

"You evil child!" All of a sudden, either Judith let go, or Lisa somehow pulled herself free. She couldn't tell, but she saw Judith's look of triumph only moments before she felt herself falling, screaming as she banged against the parade of childhood pictures that hung along the staircase....

"Judith and I fought, " Lee said, trying to push aside the horrible memories of that night. "She said terrible things...words that made me doubt everything about who and what I thought I was." She paused, then and took a deep breath. "I fell down the stairs. All I remember is waking up lying on the sofa, a cold compress on my head, and Judith looking scared. I was in a lot of pain, but Judith insisted I didn't need a doctor. All I know is the next time I took a pregnancy test, it came up negative." She shut her eyes. "I don't know why—if the first test was wrong, or if I lost the baby. The next day, I left that house to go and live with Miriam. Miriam helped me through it, through all of it."

He sat across the table from her, shocked, scarcely able to believe what he was hearing. When he spoke, his voice was husky. "My God, Lisa. I never imagined."

"It was an accident, nothing more," she murmured, then shook her head, unable to tell him what she believed had truly happened.

"Why didn't you come to me? At least tell me?"

"And say what?" Her voice was too sharp, too curt. "I was young and hurting. I just wanted to forget all of it...Miwok, my mother...even you. I was just a few weeks along, Tony. It was as if none of it was real to me, that if I didn't talk about it, I could more easily forget how much it hurt, how much I grieved. I know now that I was wrong, but I felt...I felt like...everything Judith said to me was true."

He waited, as if knowing there was more she wasn't telling him, but she remained silent. "Whenever I called you from camp, Judith would only say you were out and hang up. Cheryl didn't know

what had happened either. It wasn't until I came
back that I found out you were in San Diego. Remember when I called you? You sounded like a
stranger."

"I was...even to myself." She slowly rubbed her
hands, trying to find a way to explain those days.
"I'd convinced myself there was no room in our ambitions and careers, at our age, for a baby. I didn't
want you to know what had happened. What
would that have solved? Besides, you were being
scouted, you had a future in baseball, and I had college....That was why I said we needed to go our own
ways, to think about our futures. I needed, at that
time, to forget the past."

He shook his head as if disgusted by her explanation. "It wouldn't have been a matter of 'solving'
anything. It had to do with feelings and caring
about each other."

Lee tightly clasped her hands. "A few months
afterward, when I had the distance and perspective
to cope with telling you, I did try to reach you, but I
learned you were in Florida playing ball, and that
your prospects were good. You'd gotten on with
your life. And so, I resolved to do the same with
mine. One of the last things Judith said to me was
that I would disappoint you, that I would ruin your
life just as...well, that I would hold you back. Drag
you down. I didn't want to do anything that might

disrupt your life, so I decided I'd wait, and one day, tell you face-to-face."

He felt as if she had stabbed him through the heart. "I just don't get it. We were in love, we shared everything..."

"And suddenly, my world went to hell, while yours was getting better. We were only eighteen, and I was angry and hurt and grieving. I convinced myself that a high school romance was immature, my memories colored and surreal. I wanted to forget."

He didn't respond, but averted his eyes to the wall as he shook his head, his jaw tight, his face cold and twisted.

"A few years after college," she continued, "I was offered the job in New York City. Before I went so far away, I returned to Miwok, to settle things here in my mind...and my heart. I knew I owed you an explanation, and I finally thought that since we were both older, wiser, I could somehow reconcile my past.

"The visit was a failure. My mother was even more hateful, and I learned that you had married. I finally put you out of my mind and went to New York. I kept going forward and never looked back...until four months ago when I came home."

He stared hard at her, as if seeing her, really seeing her, for the first time. "I'm sorry, Lisa," he said, his voice low and icier than she'd ever heard it. "Sorry about the past...sorry that you didn't see fit to tell me what was happening and let me try to help you through it. Sorry that you still haven't told me all of it, probably because you're trying to hide some ugliness involving your miserable drunk of a mother who wasn't worth your time of day...And more than anything else, I'm sorry that you're still fooling yourself."

She replayed his words, sure she had misheard. "Fooling myself?" she repeated, confused.

He got to his feet and poured himself another shot of bourbon, drinking it down in one gulp. He stared at a wall a moment, then ever so slowly turned and faced her. His eyes were flat, his shoulders sagged, and his expression was one of utter defeat. "You were raised well: to be ambitious, to do what was needed to get ahead. You seem to want to remember our relationship back then as all rosy and light, but it wasn't that way. Not one goddamned bit. You were determined to get ahead—I was a piker compared to you and I was the most ambitious guy I knew. You pushed and stepped on people like hell to be the best and brightest in high school, and I knew it."

"No—" she protested, but he cut her off.

"I watched you go after Steve Peters, I watched you go after Ken Walters, and a few guys in be-

tween. You always came back right away, and I was
so damned crazy about you I put up with it. You
said they were the type of guy your mother expected you to be with, but they were the type *you*
expected yourself to be with."

She stared at him, the shock of his words
crippling.

"You know what's funny, Lisa? When you
talked about your future, you never bothered to
factor me in. I assumed you meant I'd be with you,
and maybe on some level you did, but deep down,
can you see the elegant Lee Reynolds with some
Texas-born Mexican baseball player? I can't. It
doesn't fit her image—and she's got an image, Lisa.
One you've carefully created."

He leaned closer. "Each action you took,
starting with running away after your miscarriage
and not,"—his voice suddenly broke—"and not
telling me, or even your closest friend about your
pregnancy, all of it was a means to an end, to your
carefully conceived plans and ambition. You can
blame your mother for teaching you well, if you
want. But, Lisa, you were a star pupil."

She wanted to scream that he was wrong, but
she couldn't speak, couldn't do a thing but ache
from the pain of his accusation, from her fear of its
truth.

She said nothing, breaking inside for him, for

the foolish girl she once was, for all the might-have-beens between them. The woman she was now told her it was time to leave. Wobbly, she rose from the chair. Scarcely breathing, she somehow made it to the door. With her hand on the knob, she turned and faced him, her voice calm.

"You're a wonderful man, and a wonderful father. You'll get Ben back. It might take time, but you will." She pulled the door open. "I've made a lot of mistakes, Tony. But I love you. The hell of it is, I always have."

TWENTY-FIVE

She didn't hear from Tony on Saturday, and Sunday she returned to New York.

The day after, she went to Bruce's apartment. He opened the door immediately to her knock. Color drained from his face as he looked at her.

"I'm sorry, Bruce." She handed him his apartment key. "Someday, I hope we can once again be friends."

He stared at it lying in his palm, then closed his fist around it. "Would you come in so we can talk about this? You owe me an explanation."

"What can I say that hasn't already been said? I really am sorry. You deserve better." She turned to leave.

"I'm not through with you." He grabbed her arm.

She pressed her lips and stepped into his elegant Victorian and Oriental living room. "This isn't about you, Bruce," she said immediately. "It's me. I'm feeling very confused."

His next words only emphasized the rift between them. "Confused? Teenagers are confused. Thirty-five-year-old women are not confused. You were fine until you went back to that...that Mukluk-whatever place. You act like you're the one who died instead of your mother."

She rubbed her arms. "I know it doesn't make sense—"

He grabbed her wrist and pulled her toward him. "Get clear on one thing right now, Lee. I've tried to be understanding, but I'm through. I don't want you walking out on me."

"You can't stop me, Bruce." Controlling her anger, she freed her arm and took a step from him— one step that stretched like a chasm between them.

"Good God, Lee. Don't you get it? I want us to marry. Now. I want you here, with me as your husband. We make a good team. We would be America's sweethearts. You on Nighttime News—if they'll still have you after you've waffled all these months —and me as CEO for Atlas Insurance. I don't see how you can throw it all away."

"America's just going to have to find another couple, sweetheart." She turned to go.

"Will you wake up to what you're doing? This is important!"

That stopped her cold. Important? How odd. She once thought it was very important—just like Bruce did. "I guess I just don't care anymore."

Her indifference increased his animosity, and he spat out his words, pointing his finger at her accusingly. "You don't care, but I do. You need me—if nothing else to help guide your career. Those people you snub today are the ones who'll make or break you tomorrow. Don't forget it! You need their support. When wrinkles show on TV, don't think the producer's going to keep you around unless he has to. And another thing, that Edie Canham isn't half bad as your replacement. There were lots of people who noticed her. A hell of a lot!"

"Are you through?"

He got the door ahead of her, blocking her way. "I won't allow—"

"Bruce! Don't you get it? We used *each other* to get ahead." She was sorry that the friendship they once shared had vanished, but at the same time, she experienced a sense of relief. She could see how far apart they had grown. "What we had was good for both of us while it lasted. But no more."

His jaw tightened and she could see the mus-

cles twitching. Then he raised his quivering chin,
stepped aside and let her go. "You're a cold bitch,
Lee Reynolds. I don't think you have one honest
emotion in your whole body!"

"Lee, thank you for coming by." Jake Metcalf, general manager of CABN-TV, held out his hand to
her as she entered his office. It was mid-November,
a little more than a month after the play-offs, the
World Series, and the last time she saw Tony.

"Hello, Jake, how have you been?"

"Not bad, Lee. Especially the way our ratings
are going through the roof. I want you to know that
I know it's you, not Rick Archer, who's the glue that
holds that fabric together, the...the...thread in the
stitches of that station, the...the..."

"Pin on the donkey's tail?" she suggested. Much
of the credit of Newscene's success was due in part
to Jake, whose award-winning astuteness managed
of every aspect of a news show.

"Exactly!" he said. "And now we all know what
part of the donkey Rick Archer is, don't we?"

She smiled. It was her first smile in weeks and it
felt surprisingly good. "I won't argue."

"Now," Jake leaned forward on his desk, his
hands clasped. "The bottom line, as you know, is

that Rick Archer has been here for decades. The public sees whatever comes out of his mouth as the next best thing to the word of God. He's an institution, and I wouldn't want to change that. However, we're starting a new weekly news show. We call it One Hour Report. I'll personally oversee its production, at least the first month or two. It'll run for an hour and be made up of short segments of topical interest—interviews and investigations involving politicians, actors and actresses, crooks. You name it."

"It's a familiar format," she said, not even trying to force cheerfulness. She learned this past month that such feelings dropped like rocks into some hollow place within her. Blessedly, the numbness that came from her parting with Tony overlaid everything else. She tried to deny his parting words to her, then raged against them, then cried as the devastating realization of their truth hit her. He was right—she had learned well from Judith. Too well. She became everything she was taught she should want to be. Judith had called her worthless, and she devoted fifteen years of her life to prove her mother wrong. That was what Tony was really saying, and he was right.

The irony of it was, Judith had won. She drove Lisa away from Tony, even from her friend Cheryl, and caused Lisa to push herself harder than she would have otherwise. Without Judith, Lee Reynolds never would have existed.

"It's familiar, but the public eats it up," Jake said. "Anyway, we want you on our team. We want you on a couple of five to ten minute segments a week—your choice, for the most part. We'll have a list for you to choose from if you don't have a burning desire to work on a particular topic of your own on any given week."

"You want me as a reporter?"

"Not just as a reporter. We want you as co-host with Aaron Josephs. He's one of our best. Good-looking and smart. Together, you two will be dynamite! And...your name would get top billing."

She was shocked. Her agent indicated a terrific offer was in the works, but this was far more than she dreamed. This was exactly the type of news show she had always wanted to work on. "What about Evening Newscene?"

"I like that about you, Lee. You're loyal. You don't want to leave anyone in the lurch. Look, we'll have all week to put the new show together, then air it on Tuesdays. I can get you out of your anchor job for the Tuesday evening broadcast. That way you'll have an entire week, plus the weekend to develop and film your own segments."

Such a schedule would be nothing less than

grueling, but she liked it. She wanted it. "You've thought of everything."

"I hope so, Lee."

"Give me some time to consider it, Jake. My agent will call you."

"The show will start in three weeks. We're yanking a turkey off the air as fast as we can. We need your decision right away."

"You'll get it."

Lee threw herself into the excitement and hard work of beginning a new show. She got along terrifically with Aaron Josephs, whose dry wit appealed to her. On the air, their chemistry made them instant media darlings. On a personal level, the new show kept her so busy that she had little time to think about the past, or Tony, or Ben.

She was a demanding taskmaster, intolerant of sloppiness and expecting no less than perfection from her crew. Her energy and brains intimidated the younger employees on the set, and yet, they loved being there. The studio had a hunger and energy in the air when she was near that kept everyone invigorated.

At night, she fell into bed exhausted, and went straight to sleep. She lost weight, which brought out the dramatic contours of her face even more strongly.

Gradually, the numbness wore off around her heart, leaving behind regrets and a lingering sadness. She could do no more than to accept the past —its joy and its grief, its good fortune and its terrible mistakes. Her love for Tony would always be a part of her. She knew that. If, at times, a seemingly familiar dark head in a crowd, or a sultry pair of brown eyes would cause her heart to race, she could accept that, too. And with that acceptance, she found herself beginning to enjoy life again and to shake the cool detachment that had sheltered her emotions from pain for so many years—and had blunted her from life.

As the first hectic weeks of starting a new show winded down to a dull roar, her schedule eased up a bit, and she found time to socialize. As the news of her break-up with Bruce made the rounds, she discreetly fielded questions about the cause of their separation. Invitations from all the other eligible bachelors, including some who were hardly eligible or bachelors, filled her answering machine and e-mail. She went out with a few, but was never moved to give more than a goodnight kiss.

Only on occasion did she have a sleepless night wondering what was happening with Tony and Ben. Ironically, although she tried to explain everything to him that day after the hearing, he ended up explaining even more to her. As time eased the harshness of their words, she hoped understanding would come, and he would call. But he didn't.

That phase of her life was truly over. Time to move on.

Slowly, but steadily, the weeks went by. Day by day, the New York weather turned colder. In the excitement of starting up the "One Hour Report" show, she missed Halloween, but there was no ignoring the major holidays.

Lots of parties and festivities were going on. Lee went to a couple of them and enjoyed the company of friends and associates. Bruce showed up at one with Melanie. Lee greeted them, but they were clearly uncomfortable seeing her.

One of the women she worked with invited her to a quiet Thanksgiving dinner at her apartment. The woman, Rhonda, had no family in New York. Despite Lee's invitation to dine at the home of the state senate's majority leader, she decided to join her co-worker. Rhonda served something called "turkey a la king" over boiled noodles. They ate, joked, laughed and got drunk together. Riding home in the cab, Lee knew she had made the right choice.

Soon, snow was falling, turning everything a beautiful white. Miriam complained about the cold in Miwok—fifty to fifty-five during the day, dropping to the low forties at night—but got no sympathy from Lee who faced wind-chill factors of zero degrees in New York City.

She bought a sad little Christmas tree that stole her heart. It was far too scrawny, which was probably why it was still in the small corner lot when she passed by. Only three feet tall, she stood it on a lamp table, and decorated it with old fashioned, colorful glass ornaments. Lee had never bothered to buy a tree before, but something made her want to have one this year. She hoped she wasn't turning sentimental. Lee had bragged for years that she had all the sentimentality of a commodities broker.

She liked the tree a lot.

Christmas approached. Since she had taken off so much time earlier in the year, she offered to work extra shifts and let the other anchors spend the day with their families. There were several requests for dates, and invitations to parties, but she turned them down, half-truthfully pleading a busy workload. Even her new friend Rhonda flew home to Wisconsin to be with her family for Christmas. Lee talked to Miriam, who was going to spend the holiday with Gene. Right after New Year, the two of them would join her for two days in New York City, and then fly to Rome for a week before picking up a cruise ship in Venice that would head for Greece.

Miriam said if she could stand two weeks on a ship with "that man," in one little cabin, the two of them might give serious thought to getting married. Lee was sure Miriam was going to love every minute of the trip.

On Christmas Day she was exhausted by the time she got home after the eleven o'clock broadcast. She had pre-ordered an elegant ready cooked meal from Balducci's, including dessert, and ate until she thought she'd be sick. It was a heavenly— and heavy—indulgence.

She put on the radio to listen to some carols, lit the lights on her Christmas tree, got out the Osterizer, and made herself a delicious, giant-sized Brandy Alexander. She'd forgotten how delicious they were.

January 18 was Tony's thirty-sixth birthday. She thought about it all day, and as much as she tried to force it out of her mind, it obstinately stayed with her.

When she went home, her telephone beckoned. But she wouldn't call him. It was up to him now. She had hurt him more than she had known, and he turned her out of his life because of it. She needed to accept that.

She tried to eat dinner—a salad with some canned shrimp—but she couldn't seem to swallow. Her gaze kept drifting toward the phone. She wondered if he was having a party, who was with him. Gene was still on the cruise with Miriam. The two had been like a couple of kids when Lee saw them over New Year's, Gene looking handsome and her aunt more stylish and vivacious than ever. She had never seen Miriam so happy, or so much in love. They bickered constantly, and Lee knew they wouldn't have had it any other way.

She put down the fork and walked to the sofa to sit beside the phone. Maybe if she were beside it, she wouldn't look at it so often. She folded her hands, then peeked out of the corner of her eye. He would call her when, and if, he was ready.

Suddenly, her phone began to ring. She stared at it, scarcely believing what she was hearing. By the second ring, she lunged for it. The caller ID showed only "California."

"Hello?" Her voice was breathless, excited, hopeful.

"Hello. This is Vic Santos."

Vic! Her stomach knotted. "Is everything all right?"

"Not so hot. That's why I call you."

"Tony and Ben are all right, aren't they?"

"Yeah, they're okay. Except Tony...sometimes he don't listen to me. He's stubborn."

"What's wrong, Vic?" Lee asked, knowing something had to be terribly wrong for him to contact her.

"He's gone. I'm stayin' at his house. Keepin' it up for him."

She felt as if her heart stopped. "Gone? What do you mean? Where is he?"

"I tried to talk to him."

Her voice was hushed as she asked firmly, "What happened?"

She could all but hear Vic's struggle over talking to her, and bit her tongue, forcing herself to be patient. "He wants to get a job as a coach on some major league team. He thinks he might be able to get Ben back if he does. He thinks he'll have more money, more prestige. And that might help him win his custody appeal."

A coach? Her mind raced with the possibilities —and there were few. "He's been away from baseball so long. I suspect lots of players want to coach, especially in the majors. The competition has to be horrible."

"I know, but he won't listen. He's playin' winter ball, tryin' to get back his skill, hopin' the scouts will see him. Then he'll go out and try to find a coachin' job."

A chill touched her. "But what if he can't do it? What if he's not good enough?"

"That's why I called you, Lisa. I worry. It's his birthday today."

"I know."

"Yeah, I shoulda guessed you would. So, maybe you can talk some sense into him?"

"Me?"

"There's only three things my boy ever really loved—baseball, his son...and you. And now, he don't have none of them."

Her throat tightened. "You, too, Vic. He loves you very much."

"That's not enough for a man."

She took a deep breath. "Where is he?"

"The Dominican Republic."

"The Dominican—"

"That's where winter ball is."

She shut her eyes. "You know, don't you, that he told me he never wanted to see me again?"

"Tony's got a temper. He usually keeps it under tight control, 'specially around you. But when he loses it, he says things he don't really mean. He's stubborn, too, so sometimes he don't back off."

She held the phone with both hands, like a lifeline. "I'll do what I can, but I can't force him or even push him to a decision that he's not happy with."

"That might be enough."

"Thank you for telling me."

"It's okay, girl. I'm glad, too. I think you changed some. For the better."

She smiled. She guessed she would always be some troublesome "girl" to Vic. "How's Ben?"

He sighed. "He's got nice clothes. Goes to a school costs a few thousand dollars each month. Got lotsa toys."

"Is he getting used to being there?"

"His mother treats him well. He's strong. He didn't want to go, though. Tony had to push him away when that Catherine came to get him. It was hard for Tony...hard for both of them."

Her heart lurched. She couldn't imagine...she shook her head, trying to dispel the wretched scene Vic's words brought to mind.

"Did Ben spend Christmas with you?"

"He stayed with Tony in the Dominican for a few days."

She nodded, her throat tight. "I'm glad they could be together."

After hanging up the phone, she sat on the sofa, vacantly staring at the wall. How worried Vic must have been to open his heart to her, of all people.

She walked to the windows, rubbing the chill from her arms. The moon was full over Manhattan tonight. Vic had said that Tony had to push away the small child who loved him. Her eyes filled with tears for him. She didn't know where he found the strength.

TWENTY-SIX

Lee sat in her office, sipping her second cup of coffee. She was groggy from having stayed awake so late last night trying to figure out what to do about Vic's call. She wasn't sure why she told him she would try to talk to Tony. It wasn't her place to call him and have a heart-to-heart about his future. Vic had made it sound as if Tony wasn't himself, and hadn't been, since he lost Ben. There had to be some way to help.

Max Hobbs, the news director, opened her office door and then knocked on it, his head already peering at her. "Lee, thank God you're here!" Hobbs was a one-time campus radical who had now become part of the establishment and spent his time trying to show how concerned and caring he still was. Right now he looked concerned and panicked.

"Good morning, Max. I was just finishing my coffee, then I'm off to interview Senator Lofton."

"It can wait."

"Not hardly. It's taken me two weeks to line it up. I need the senator for One Hour Report."

"And I can't put Archer on the show tonight! He said something unkind about the President and now half the country is in an uproar! I need you to handle Archer's slot as well as your own. I'll get someone on with you, but you'll be carrying the ball."

"You've got other anchors, Max."

He put his hands on her desk and stared at her with puppy-dog eyes. "But none as good as you are. I need you to bail me out of this one. I'll owe you, Lee."

"You already owe me. My own show needs the senator's interview."

Max lifted his glasses and pinched the bridge of his nose a few times. "Okay. After the interview, rush back here as fast as you can and I'll have the staff ready to brief you on the news pieces we're lining up.

Xantha, Lee's secretary, put her head in the doorway. "It's time to go, Miss Reynolds, so you won't be late."

"Be right there, Xantha." Lee picked up her purse and soft leather briefcase.

"Can I count on you, then?" Max asked, stepping to her side, his pudgy hands clasped together, a woe-is-me expression and a sly twinkle in his eyes.

"This will cost big-time, Max." Lee left him standing in her office.

She wasn't late, but the senator was by over forty-five minutes. She rushed from that interview back to the station, was briefed on the day's news, got made up, and went on the air.

When the show was over, she went into the engineers' room where Max was finishing up instructions for the late night broadcast.

"Sissy Springfield is having a big party tonight," Max said. "I know you're invited. We can't be late."

Lee collapsed into a chair. "We can't be late?" She had run around all day and the man had a party on his mind?

"The show was terrific with you anchoring! Don't worry about anything else," Max dashed about, writing notes and barking orders to his staff. "I'm really looking forward to Sissy's spread. She serves the best of everything. I even skipped lunch."

"I suppose everyone's going to be there," Lee said.

"Everyone who's anyone, as they say. Oh, before I forget, try to make it here early tomorrow. The

Egyptian ambassador will be giving a talk at the Plaza, and he's agreed to let us interview him afterward. Because of the stink with Archer, I don't want to send anyone but our best interviewer to see him. That's you. Okay?"

Mentally juggling her schedule, Lee stood. "And what's Archer doing?"

"He's miffed about the way he's being treated. He'll be back next week."

"So I run around and fill in for him while he sulks?"

"You're the greatest, Lee."

"Since I'll be doing that, you can do something for me."

"Anything."

"Take the Lofton interview I did today and set it up for my show tomorrow night."

"Tomorrow? There isn't time."

"Sure there is. You've got all night. Also, you know how fussy the senator is. Make sure you don't let anything go on the air that will upset him—but at the same time, Jake wants controversy. You get to please them both. Heaven forbid either complain. I would have done it myself, but no time now." She breezed out the door. "I'll give my best to Sissy for you."

The following week, Lee watched Rick Archer come back to work like the prodigal son.

"I saw your interview with the Egyptian ambassador," Archer told her as they passed in the hallway.

"Oh?"

"You really shouldn't let them have you do grunt work like that, Lee. It lessens the value of the anchor position. I'd never allow myself to be used that way."

The world flashed red before her, but she kept her poised reserve. "Thank you for that observation, Rick. I'll be sure to let my friends, Katie Couric, for example, know that Rick Archer advises them to stop their interviews. I'm sure they'll appreciate it."

His face turned a bright purple, then he turned and duck-waddled away.

She returned to her office, sat at her desk and looked at the pile of papers around her. Turning toward the window, she spent a moment just looking outside, even though her main view was of the fifth, sixth and seventh floor offices of the high rise next door. Just then her phone buzzed. She jumped at the sound.

"Yes?"

"It's a Mr. Abdullah Ibn Akbar," Xantha said.

"You're kidding. Thanks."

Xantha clicked the phone to the caller. "Hello, Mr. Ambassador," Lee said. "How's Egypt?"

The man chuckled. "Much better than I, Miss Reynolds. I'm sitting here with an extra ticket to the New York Philharmonic program tomorrow night, an all Stravinsky program. I was wondering if you would do me the honor of accompanying me?"

Lee hesitated. He was a handsome, wealthy, powerful man, intelligent, sophisticated and single. She had no romantic feelings toward the man, but why not go with him? She loved Stravinsky. An evening out would be fun—and she deserved some fun.

"'That sounds quite lovely."

TWENTY-SEVEN

It snowed on her birthday, February 9. Miriam called before Lee left for work to wish her a happy birthday. They had a cake for her at work, and after the news show, she went out to dinner with the weatherman. They had dated three times now. He was a gentle, kind, intelligent man, and she liked him. Everyone said he was a wonderful weatherman, attractive in a meteorological sort of way. Unfortunately, his precipitation didn't supply the chemical reaction she wanted in a lover, so they were friends and nothing more.

After dinner, he brought her home. She gave him a friendly kiss and didn't invite him into her apartment.

Alone, she showered and put on a warm, fluffy

robe, and made herself a cup of coffee. The thick slice of birthday cake she hadn't eaten earlier now sat on a plate, and she planned to enjoy it.

Three weeks had gone by since Vic told her Tony needed her help, but she still hadn't come up with a way to approach him. Maybe she never would. Tony wouldn't want her to interfere anyway, she was sure.

It was probably safest to do nothing, because if she did get involved with Tony again, she didn't want any holding back or reservations between them although, in truth, she didn't know what that meant with her here and him there.

Damn, but she wished Vic hadn't called her. She wanted Tony out of her mind, but instead, Vic's words made her dwell on him, and worry, and wonder how he was doing.

The telephone rang. She saw the caller I.D. and her heart nearly stopped. "Hello."

There was a pause, then, "Happy birthday, Lisa."

She was breathless. "Tony." Silence hung a moment before she said, "A belated happy birthday to you, too."

"Thanks for remembering! Listen, I want to apologize for what I said the last time—"

"No need, Tony. Please, don't! Don't..." She couldn't go on.

He hesitated, then asked, "How are you doing? I've watched your new show. You're terrific on it. Better than ever." His words came quickly, nervously, as if he half-expected her to hang up on him.

"Thank you. I enjoy it a lot. I really do."

"That's great." A pause, again.

"Where are you?" she asked.

"Tucson. I, uh, I was offered a job as a scout for a Double A team."

"You were? Congratulations. Tell me all about it. Did you accept the job?"

"I'm thinking about it! Baseball is my life. You know that."

"I know it once was." Her voice dropped. "I thought ranching was your life now."

His voice, too, grew softer, his words more from the heart. "Yeah, well...it got kind of quiet after Ben left. What can I say? Anyway, this job has potential for big money. It's not as much as a player makes, but if I do okay, and can move up to Triple A, or particularly if I can scout or coach in the majors I...I might even be able to get Ben back sometime."

"All of this...it must be so hard for you."

"An appeal is coming up soon. If I get a Triple A job, even a nibble, it could help big-time." The quiver in his voice was slight, and those that didn't know him well probably wouldn't even have noticed. But she did.

The many hours she'd spent thinking about Tony's predicament and ways to help suddenly gelled, and without analyzing it any further she said, "I've been thinking of doing a segment about Little League on my show. I'd like to feature Ben in it. He's a great little guy and epitomizes a lot of what sports and children are all about. I wouldn't do anything to hurt him, trust me. But would you be willing to give me a release to talk with him and film him?"

"I guess it's okay with me. I don't know if Catherine will agree, though."

"I'm sure she wouldn't even listen to anything I have to say. I'll get the network to work with her. We've got people who can talk Santa Claus into coming out against Christmas."

"I don't know..."

"I need you, too."

"Me?"

"You had a career in baseball, and now you've gone back to it as a means to get your son once more."

"No way, Lisa. I'd be a laughingstock!"

The concept quickly grew clearer in her mind. "People will see this, Tony. Our ratings are good. People will see how much you care. They'll talk— they'll apply their own kind of pressure on the case, maybe even on the judge. I've seen it happen before."

"You want to put my custody fight on TV? No way!" His decision was firm.

"I thought you said you'd do anything to get Ben back? Was that true, or is your pride more important?"

"No, of course not, but still..."

Excitement over the idea bubbled up within her. "Listen to me, Tony. My perception of what I can do to help you is a valid one. I've been in this industry for over thirteen years, I do have some insight on public opinion. You've got to understand, though, that this won't be a hit piece against Catherine either. It can't be. It'll be about Ben and Little League, but the audience will learn about you, too, and that Catherine also wants her son. But this way, everyone will know how much you want him and how hard you're trying. Trust me, Tony, please. Trust me...in this at least."

His breath seemed to catch. "I do trust you."

"I can give it a try, then?" she asked, her voice filled with hope.

"Yeah. Give it a try." He gave her information on how to contact him, Catherine and Ben.

When he was finished, she expelled a breath of relief. "Thank you. After"—she hesitated to bring it up but left unspoken made it even worse—"after the way we parted, I'm surprised you phoned."

"The way I talked to you was uncalled for," he said. "I was expecting you to hang up soon as you heard my voice. You've got every right to hate me, but I was upset and—"

"It's okay. You don't have to explain to me, Tony. I'm the one who owed you an explanation. And...and there was truth in what you said, as much as it hurts to admit it."

"I shouldn't have been so hard, so critical of you. You were still a kid. After you left, I thought a lot about what you said. I'm sorry, Lisa. I never wanted to hurt you."

"I know. Memories of you were the only bright spot for me during that time. It's hard to imagine we were ever so young," she said with a lilt, needing to lighten their emotions. She had had years of grieving, but for Tony this was all new and shocking and, she realized, also painful. "At least you had your time in baseball just like you wanted, and I've got the career I wanted." Her voice sounded a little too bright.

There was a long silence. She clutched the phone tight.

"You're right," he said finally. "It all turned out." His voice rang hollow and empty. "No regrets," he added.

"No regrets," she whispered.

There was more silence. The awkwardness of unspoken emotions, of words they dared not say, stretched out between them.

He spoke first. "Well...like I said, I called to wish you a happy birthday."

"Thank you."

"Take care, Lisa."

"You too, Tony."

With that, they said goodbyes and hung up. She sat a long while. They hurt, these feelings about him, and there wasn't a thing she could do about it.

She stood and paced. At least she could do her damnedest to help him with Ben. She had no idea where her concept of a TV special on Ben and Little League had come from, but the more she thought about it, the more she knew it was perfect. Her gut reaction, honed by years of TV reporting and observing public opinion, told her it was good.

Painted against a background of a small, all-American town, she'd show a cameo of Little League, zeroing in on one boy. She needed to bring Tony and Catherine into the story as well—her producers would earn their pay to get the two of them to agree, or at least to make sure lawyers went over the piece so that, without agreements, the show didn't get sued.

She needed to be fair. Catherine wouldn't be all

evil and Tony wouldn't be all good, but they would
be two people who both had faults and positive
qualities, and who both loved and wanted their
child. At the same time, she wanted a tribute to the
love of a divorced father for his son, to show that it's
wrong to automatically dismiss fathers as custo-
dians of their children in divorces, and that the
mother—or the parent with the most money—isn't
automatically the best custodian.

She would show a custody fight's effect on that
child and on his team and friends, but also, she
would be giving a message of love.

She envisioned the entire segment, including
the ending. Maybe it was a little corny, but she
wanted an uplifting ending that would show Ben's
strength of character, and that he would do fine. As
in baseball, there was always a new season, and
with it comes new beginnings, a chance to right
wrongs, or simply to learn from mistakes of the past,
and to go forward as a better, stronger person.
Springtime, baseball, a clean slate, and hope. That
was Ben's story. That was what she wanted to show.

She kicked her shoes off and stretched out on
the sofa, lost in thought. She remembered that some
parents had video camcorders at the games. If any
of the films were halfway decent, she would borrow
or buy them, clean them up and use them to show
actual footage of Ben playing.

The piece should be heavy on nostalgia—field of dreams and all that. Something to tug at the heart. She hadn't done a segment like that yet for the show. It would make a nice contrast to the celebrity paeans or gory murder-related stories they usually presented.

Yes, nostalgia. That was good. She shut her eyes to try to visualize how she wanted the Little League piece to begin.

TWENTY-EIGHT

She called Vic Santos the next morning for two bits of information. The first was about Miwok's Little League organization—the coaches, the main office, all the people whose permission would be needed before a project such as the one she proposed could happen.

The second was the date of Tony's appeal on the custody decision. It was February 28, only eighteen days away.

"I want to do a piece on Little League," she told One Hour Report's honcho, Jake Metcalf, a half-hour later.

"It's been done." He didn't even look up from his desk.

"Not the way I want to approach it. Kids are big

business, and team sports are becoming more and more important in their lives. Even girls play on organized teams, and Little League's the biggest of them all."

"No way. All that fresh air and sunshine crap. Nobody cares anymore."

"I care. You people owe me, if you recall. This will be a great piece, and I want it. I've already talked to people about it. I want it on the February 26th broadcast."

He straightened and caught her eye. "The 26th? Impossible."

"No, it isn't. It'll be a small piece. I need the legal team to get all the clearances and a production crew to get out there and do some filming! I'll help edit it myself. I've got a good idea of what I want it to look like."

Jake looked at her shrewdly. "Why does this piece mean so much to you?"

"Spring's coming. A time for renewal. Didn't you ever hear that 'life begins with spring-training'?"

"I was a Tiddly Winks man, myself. Forget it."

"I won't forget it. I want this segment."

"It's a bad idea."

"I don't care!"

"I do! I'm not showing any crap on this program!"

"Then you're not showing me either! You told

me I could go with my own ideas. Well, this is my idea. I want it."

He stared at her hard, his jaw muscle twitching. "If it bombs, it's your neck in the noose, you hear?"

"Fine."

"And it's the last story of the night. We don't want people switching channels until the show is almost over."

She folded her arms. "My, but it's nice to have your confidence, Jake."

"You got my okay. My confidence is my business."

With her busy schedule, Lee had no time to travel to Tucson to see Tony, or to Miwok to pick up Little League tapes of Ben's games, or to Los Angeles to film Ben or Catherine. Catherine refused any contact, and refused to allow the reporters to speak to Ben. Lee sent her crews to film and interview Tony, and to Miwok to talk to coaches and parents. She got Gene and Miriam to talk to parents who had videotaped Little League games into lending their tapes to the TV crews to be copied for TV viewing. Lee couldn't actually pay for the tapes, but she sent new, top-of-the-line digital camcorders as gifts to everyone who helped.

Finally, since shots of Catherine, Ben, and the Durelle estate in Beverly Hills were taken, Lee had the network's attorneys go over every camera shot and scripted word to be sure no one was liable for a lawsuit. She was going to do this right—for everyone else, if not herself.

It was ironic that she built a career on the image of cool, classy intellect and geo-political sophistication. If Metcalf was right, she was going to nosedive it with all-American nostalgia. Knives were out for any new show, and this one was on the receiving end of constant proctological examination. Strangely, that didn't bother her half as much as did her fear that her concept for the show might backfire on Tony, or that he would hate her for the realism with which she would be forced to portray his attempt at getting back into baseball.

Although Tony was looking for a job coaching, the film crew made tapes of him playing ball with the team as well as giving the players direction. Watching Tony playing baseball with men who were, for the most part, between nineteen and twenty-five, was hard for her. Watching it over and over in the studio, analyzing his plays and emotional ups and downs as the game progressed, hurt even more.

Through most of the game he played first base. The remarkable agility and speed that made Tony

Santos special before, when he played shortstop and second base, were gone now. As Lee watched a ball get past him "through the gap" between first and second base and into the outfield, she knew that, in days past, Tony would have fielded it. In the fifth inning he moved to right field. A ball was hit deep, over his head, and although he ran back, gloved hand outstretched to catch the ball, he couldn't quite reach it, and it landed at the foot of the fence for a double. Lee's heart sank. She couldn't remember ever seeing a ball get past him that way.

At the plate, he wasn't much better. He was seventh in the line-up. Lee could tell, by his stance and swing, that he was one of the few players never surprised by the pitch thrown. He could anticipate a curve, a slider, a fastball; inside, outside, or straight down the middle—which would make him an excellent coach. The one thing he couldn't do, though, was catch up to a good fast ball. The opposing pitchers soon realized it was foolish to try to finesse a pitch. They could simply blow a fast one down the middle of the plate, and Tony Santos didn't have the bat speed anymore to get it out of foul territory.

How much of this could she, or should she, show? To show him playing the way she saw it, to show the misses and the slowness—even if they helped get Ben back—might be devastating. She would never strip Tony of his pride.

She began the film again, steepled her fingers and watched again. She could all but hear him railing against himself, disgusted over what he would surely call a pathetic performance.

But it wasn't pathetic. It was noble. He was like a Roman gladiator who had aged and slowed and had fought and won too many great fights, but wouldn't give up, even though he knew he wouldn't survive this last challenge. His pride wouldn't let him give up, nor his beliefs, nor his courage.

Courage...determination...spirit...in the face of overwhelming odds. Heroic. That was Tony. Yes! That was the man she'd portray in her film.

She leaned back in the chair, weary, but feeling a little better, a bit more hopeful. She knew the tack she wanted to take. She only hoped she had the ability, the pure talent, to weave the story and the emotion together so that the viewer would understand and sympathize. With Tony, with Ben, and yes, even with Catherine, the woman who decided, perhaps a bit too late, that she wanted to be a "mom."

Night after night, she stayed at the studio, working with the tapes of Tony, as well as home videos of Little League games that parents in Miwok had given her, and the footage that had been shot of Ben in Beverly Hills. She edited the sound on tape, the B-roll of background scenery and noise, then wrote a script and made a track of it.

Slowly, as Lee put the pieces together into one final tape, the package was complete. She was pleased by it. Her fear that it would backfire with the public had been put aside. True, the public was fickle, but thirteen years as a newscaster had taught her how to slant the news anyway she wanted and have the public think it was getting the unvarnished truth. Journalism, especially TV journalism, was a lot more about propaganda than anyone wanted to admit to.

Late Monday night, Tony phoned her. He was no longer in Arizona, but back in Miwok. His 'hello' was so subdued she barely recognized his voice. "How are you doing?" she asked.

"I've been better."

"Coaching?"

"Hell, I stunk up the place. My only hope is some near-sighted major league manager who's really desperate."

"I'm sorry," she murmured.

"I called about the show you were working on, the one about Ben," he said quickly. "My custody hearing is Thursday. You aren't still going through with Ben's story, are you?"

She drew in her breath. "Of course I am. It will air on One Hour Report tomorrow night."

"Shit. Can you pull it?"

"Pull it? Why?"

"It's a bad idea. Catherine's furious. Her lawyers are howling. I don't want to deal with it."

"I've seen these things work before. My own reaction is that the piece came out really well. It doesn't show you doing everything perfectly. Trying to get back into baseball at age thirty-six isn't easy, and the camera shows just how hard it is for you."

"So on top of everything else, I get to look like a jerk on national TV."

"You look...wonderful."

His shock at her words came through the phone lines, even though he didn't reply. She guessed he didn't know what to say to that, and neither did she. But she'd told him the truth.

"Don't show it, Lisa."

She bit her bottom lip a moment. "It's a good story."

"I've changed my mind about it."

"Don't worry. It'll be fine."

"Lisa..."

"It's too late, Tony."

"I don't want to chance it!"

"I'm sorry."

"Damn it! Will you listen to me? I don't want the goddamned thing on the air. We're talking about my son."

"I know what I'm doing, Tony."

A long pause ensued, and then his voice more low and deadly than she had ever heard it. "You damned well better!"

He hung up.

Her heart pounded. She would show it, no matter what Tony or anyone else said. She was proud of the segment. She felt as if she had devoted her life, her dreams, her youth, everything, to her career. In this segment, though, she felt as if she got back, a little at least, of her soul.

Tuesday, she nearly collapsed from nervousness. What if she was wrong and Tony was right? What if the segment made it even harder for him to get Ben back? Who was she to interfere? Or to open herself up this way?

She had never done anything so nostalgic or emotional before. She was letting people see a whole new side of her. Would they laugh? She had lectured Tony on not being afraid to show himself openly. She needed to take her own advice—to let Lee Reynolds's heart show, for a single ten minute segment.

For the first time since One Hour Report began, her legs felt wooden as she walked to the staged TV set. To viewers, it looked like a large, expensive chamber. In fact, it was about eight feet across and plywood. Cameras aimed at her, lights blared white hot. Aaron Josephs kept giving her odd looks as if pleading with her to loosen up. She couldn't. When the show began, her hands shook so badly she had to fold them and keep them on her lap or anyone would have known that there was something terribly wrong. Somehow, she got through the first forty-five minutes of the show. Jake Metcalf leaned back in his chair, smiling broadly as he conversed with his two assistants.

Although the segment break seemed endless, when she finally heard the producer's voice in her earpiece giving the ten-second countdown to show time, she jumped with nervousness. Coming up was her segment. Hers alone. Josephs sat back and watched along with hundreds of thousands of viewers.

The commercial ended. The camera light came on.

Looking into the lens, Lee Reynolds sat poised and self-assured. She smiled and took a deep breath as she read the teleprompter.

"Hot dogs, peanuts, and baseball. What could be more American? Today, the popularity of baseball has reached new heights. From sandlots to major league diamonds, more people than ever before are playing and watching the sport. For many, organized baseball begins with Little League. And for some, it's more than just a game..."

The tape rolled.

[Wide-angle shot of California coast hills, small town nestled in a valley, camera zooms in for a close-up.]

This is Miwok California.

[Street scenes of Old Town using rose-tinted filters. Quiet streets, kids on bikes, casual, slow-paced.]

Located just thirty miles north of San Francisco, Miwok has been spared most of the hubbub, turmoil and strife of the city and its surrounding Bay Area communities like Oakland and Berkeley. Instead, the residents of Miwok live a quiet, safe existence, much as they did many years ago.

[Park scenes, kids playing baseball.]

In this town, Little League flourishes. Ben Santos is the shortstop on a team called the Bruins....

[Camera zooms in on Ben standing between second and third base, staring hard at the batter.]

Against the background of a Little League game, Lee's voice-over quickly described Ben's family situation—the custody trial and the decision that Ben would live with his mother, and visit his father, former major-league player Tony Santos, four weeks each year. The large, white-pillared, formal house of Ben's mother and new step-father, Dr. Graham Durelle, was shown. The house stood in stark contrast to shots presenting the casual ambiance of the Circle Z and the Little League game.

[Cut to video of Tony and Ben together at Little League game.]

Tony Santos gave up his career to raise his child in the best way he knew how. He isn't sure what caused the judge to take his son away from him. He doesn't know if it's because he's a single father who never remarried, or because his small ranch doesn't bring as much profit in a year as Dr. Graham Durelle makes in a month performing plastic surgery for the rich and famous, or—and he personally doubts this—if it was simply a case of ugly, old-fashioned prejudice against the son of a Mexican ranch hand.

[Scenes of Tony diving for balls, colliding with the catcher at home plate, standing in the batter's box, clearly determined and not giving up.]

He believes that if he can again become involved in baseball, perhaps as a coach this time, instead of just a small horse rancher from a tiny town called Miwok, he might have a chance of winning Ben back. So he practices long hours, and hopes for a miracle.

But baseball is a game in which miracles do happen.

[Scenes of happy Little League players, some humorous, some touching, camera quickly shows the laughter and the tears of the game, and ends with shot of Ben hitting a home run and running the bases.]

Spring training is a time for growth. A time for change. And a time for hope.

[Scene of Ben sitting alone on front steps of the enormous Durelle mansion holding a baseball. He wistfully tosses the baseball into the air and catches it, over and over. The camera pulls back and the image of Ben becomes smaller and smaller as the scene fades.]

The tape ended. The light on the camera aimed at Lee flashed on. She blinked, then released her clenched fingers, and, unsmiling, faced the camera. "This is Lee Reynolds in New York," she said, her voice throaty. "Good night."

As the camera switched off, the released tension of the live show broke loose. People laughed and shouted at each other and the dismantling of the set began.

Her co-host, Aaron Josephs, shook her hand heartily for the Little League piece, while several women who worked the Kyron and other equipment came over and told her how moved they were by Ben's story.

Jake stopped her as she was going to take off her make-up. "You better watch out, Lee."

"What?" She was shocked. Had the complaints begun already? "What do you mean?"

"Any more schlocky pieces like that and you're going to have to turn in your Ms. Hard-ass badge. Good work!"

He strode off down the hall, leaving Lee gaping at him in astonishment.

That night, when she got home, her answering machine was filled with messages from friends and colleagues, as well as Miriam, Cheryl and others in Miwok congratulating her on the beautiful and touching piece about Ben, Tony, and the lessons of Little League.

The accolades continued the next day. Scenes from the film kept playing over and over again in her mind. Miwok had put on its best face for the film crew. It looked beautiful—green, filled with flowers, broad oaks, bays, weeping willows, and colorful gardens.

Only one thing marred her happiness. Despite all the praise, the one reaction she most wanted didn't come. She received no word from Tony.

TWENTY-NINE

Tony Santos appeared at the courthouse Thursday morning. Vic was with him. The day after the airing of the One Hour Report segment, Tony had received an offer from a minor league team to be a coach. He had three days to give them his decision. He was thankful the offer gave him something definite to tell the judge. If it meant keeping Ben, he would coach the Devil himself.

Tony had brought some evidence regarding Ben's wishes to offer the judge. He had a stack of letters from his son. One, in particular, he hoped the judge would read. It was the reason Tony had gone back to baseball.

He ran his fingers over the small packet of pencil-smeared envelopes. He lifted a letter out, the one post-marked November 10th, opened it, and skimmed it once more. Ben wrote that his mother was being quite nice to him, and Dr. Durelle was as well. He had lots of games and toys, and he got to ride in a Mercedes Benz to school and back each day. But then he asked about his horse, Evening Star, and about the ranch, and his best friend, Zach, and his room, and his old toys...."She's nice to me, Dad," Tony's gaze slowed as he neared the end of the letter, "and I think she's trying real hard to make me happy. But this isn't home. She says it is, but it isn't, and you're not here. I miss you. Sometimes I even cry. I know nine-year-olds aren't supposed to cry, but I can't help it. I hope you don't think I'm a baby. I just want to come home. Can't you do something? Please, Dad, I don't like it here. Tell Star not to forget me, okay? I love you. —Ben."

Tony stared at the letter a long moment, then, his lips in a grim line, he carefully refolded it and tucked it back into its envelope.

Ben had also sent a couple of letters to Vic, and Tony had those with him as well. Ben asked Vic to be sure to take care of Tony, much to Tony's amusement and heartache. He never realized his son worried about him; he had thought only fathers did that.

He had received a number of calls about Lisa's show, telling him how much the callers admired what he was trying to do, and expressing how bad they felt about the custody fight. One aspect of the show, though, embarrassed him. He wasn't being half so noble in going back to baseball again as the show made him out to be. He loved baseball. It had been his life as far back as he could remember. To be out there again, to smell the clean air and pine tar, to feel the smooth, warm leather of the glove, the springy grass under his feet, to have the camaraderie of the other players, were things he loved. He was grateful to realize that some teams still wanted his help, even if it was as a scout or a coach and no longer as a position player. And yet, to realize he couldn't play well any longer, to come face to face with his own aging and mortality, that part was painful.

Etched forever in his memory, too, was that last scene of Ben, tossing his baseball and looking so alone as he sat on the stone steps in front of that enormous house. That image of his son bolstered Tony's determination to do all he could to get Ben back, and for that he applauded Lisa's program even more.

His attorney rushed down the corridor toward him, a big smile on the man's face. "Sorry I'm late, Mr. Santos," Manning said, "but I was on the phone with Mrs. Durelle's lawyer. Good news. Mrs. Durelle is dropping her case."

Tony slowly rose to his feet. "What did you say?"

"You've won. All they're asking is that the joint custody stand so that Catherine will continue to have some say in her son's upbringing, and that you let Ben spend some time each summer with her. Other than that, he'll live, full-time, with you."

"I don't get it. Is this a trick?"

"Apparently not. It seems a number of Dr. Durelle's associates, friends, and patients were not pleased with his wife's behavior, both the way she abandoned her son when he was an infant, and the fact that she took him from his father now. I guess all that targeted publicity in Beverly Hills for the TV story about Ben paid off. Lots of Durelle's friends watched it. As much as they sympathized with his wife's position, they seemed to think it wasn't 'fair.'

"Dr. Durelle has always prided himself on being absolutely upstanding and fair in everything he ever did. Having received so many critical calls from people he thought well of has greatly disturbed him. In addition, it seems Catherine's perception of how much fun it would be to raise a son was at great variance with how difficult it, in fact, is. She decided motherhood isn't for everyone and, in particular, not for her. Does all of this sound plausible to you, Mr. Santos?"

Tony looked at Vic, then smiled broadly, slapping his attorney on the back. "It sounds very plausible, Mr. Manning."

"Excellent."

"Does this mean I don't have to get a job in baseball? I can go back to my ranch?"

"You can do anything you'd like. But I thought you loved baseball."

"I do. And it was a great part of my life. But it's time to move on. It's time to go home again."

Manning nodded. "Good. I'll inform Judge Powell of what's happened here, then we'll go to my office to work out the details of the settlement. Shall we meet in, say, a half hour?"

Tony agreed, shook hands with Manning, then gave Vic a big hug. "Excuse me. I've got to make a phone call."

He took out his phone and called Lisa's number. Her answering machine picked up, and he hung up. Damn, why didn't she pick up? Actually, why should she? She was close to the top of her profession and still moving up.

He stared his phone. He wanted to tell her his news, listen to her reaction. She knew exactly what she was doing when she put that piece together on Ben. And the irony of it was she had done it fairly—that was what Dr. Durelle's colleagues saw and reacted to.

That piece of film more clearly than anything showed her talent, and her heart.

When he watched her in the past, night after night on TV, telling news stories and, at times, commenting on them, he had seen a beautiful, ambitious, self-confident woman. What he failed to see, or hadn't allowed himself see, was a woman with intelligence, passion and talent for her work. She could do anything she set for herself. His own Lisa Marie could hold her own with the best of them.

An all-encompassing pride swept over him.

He loved her and he knew he always would. But Miwok would have stifled her. If they had married at age eighteen or nineteen like he had wanted, he would have taken her to every pit stop through the minor leagues. How long would such a life have satisfied a woman like her? How long before she would have resented being tied to him that way? How long before that resentment turned to hate?

Or, if they had married that young and pursued separate high-pressure careers, would their marriage have survived it? Youthful marriages were the shakiest under the best circumstances.

He could see all that now, years later...years wiser.

When he did marry, he made a botch of things with Catherine. She, too, had been beautiful and ambitious, and still was. She wanted to get ahead, but instead of doing it on her own, she tried to use others.

Strangely, the bitterness he had carried for so long against both women was gone now. Catherine shared a son with him, and she did love Ben. Lisa shared his past, his present, and maybe, someday, they would meet again. If she ever came back home, he would be here for her if she wanted him.

He glanced at the phone, then picked it up and punched in her number.

"This is Tony. I wish I could talk to you in person right now, but I recognize how busy you are so I better give my news to this machine if I want you to hear it, right? Anyway, Lisa...I got Ben back. You did it. The Durelles and their friends learned some things about themselves they didn't like. And Catherine's decided kids are too much work, anyway. So Ben's coming home. I don't know how to thank you, Lisa, except to say, thanks.

"I can see why you love your work, Lis'—you're a pro. I admire what you're doing. Hell, I admire you...

"Well, that's all I wanted to say. Just, thank you, and...and if you ever get tired of the rarified air up there and want a little oxygen remember your friend Tony okay? Shoot, I'm making a botch of this. What I'm trying to say is, I'm always here, okay? If you ever need me. Not that I imagine you ever will.

I guess you've only got one way to go, and that's up. So...good luck, and lots of happiness to you...I love you...Knock 'em dead, Lis—, I mean, Lee. Knock 'em dead, Lee."

He hung up the phone and shut his eyes a moment. Then he went in search of his father to make the happy trip home.

———

It was late when Lee returned to her apartment. She could scarcely believe the continuing praise she received about the baseball segment. People were saying it had more emotion and more heart than anything they had seen on One Hour Report in the four months it had been on the air—and, they liked it. They liked it a lot.

She took out her cell phone and turned it on. She turned it off to do some interviews for her next show. It kept beeping and interrupting her.

She went through her messages one by one. When she heard Tony's message, she played it again.

She sat on the sofa in her living room, still holding her phone. Right before she left the studio that evening, her agent had shown up, in person. Although he'd been irritated that he couldn't get through by phone, he was also so ecstatic he couldn't maintain his serious, cautious, legalistic self as he told her he'd received an inquiry from *60 Minutes*. A major milestone in her goal toward becoming a lead network news anchor was to get a reporter's position on a network news show. Now, one of the Big Three news organizations had actually inquired about her.

It was everything she'd always wanted. She should be proud. She was proud, in fact.

She walked to the windows and looked out on Central Park. It was a beautiful slice of nature in the middle of one of the most dynamic, exciting cities in the entire world. To live overlooking Central Park, and to work on a major network news program were her goals, her dream. And it was within reach, finally within reach.

If Judith could see her now, what would she say?

Would Judith finally say, "Good job, daughter"? Or would she find something else to criticize?

She felt as if she spent a lifetime scaling an enormous tree. Out on a narrow bough was an apple of solid gold. After much climbing and backsliding and scraping of knees, she had finally reached that apple. She had her fingers around it, and all she had to do was pluck it and it would be hers. Everyone constantly told her she should want that golden apple, and eventually, she even convinced herself. But far below her, at the tree's trunk, she saw a man, and a loving little boy...

She raised her eyes to the Manhattan skyline, as thrilling to her today as it was the first time she saw it. These past months since Judith's death had forced her to look back on her life, to remember her years of trying to make up for her mother's disappointment in her, and to face things about herself that she had been unwilling to face before. Finally, she came to understand, and with understanding, to forgive or at least accept, the way she had lived her life.

She had achieved a lot. She could be proud of the national prominence and wealth she acquired by strength of will, hard work, and a bit of dumb luck.

And yet, one thing about the past stood out with crystal clarity. As she pondered it, it told her everything she needed to know. It was simply that, despite all her success, she had never been quite so happy, or her days quite so filled with the joy of simply being alive, as she was many years ago in a small town called Miwok, as she was when Tony loved her.

THIRTY

Spring training came to Miwok in the pale green and pink pastels of lawns and flowers, and the white pants and colorful jersey tops of Little League teams. Watching his team, Tony felt as if he, too, had been reborn. He slid the outfielder's mitt onto his hand, pounded his fist into the pocket a couple of times, and then ran onto the sweet-smelling grass. Time for fielding practice, teaching the best way to scoop up a grounder and use two hands on a fly ball. No Willie Mays' style "basket" catches allowed. The coaches started with the fundamentals, getting the ball from second base to first, or third to first, throwing, batting, base running. Nobody had to teach base stealing—the boys did that naturally. The ability to hit a small sphere with a thin, cylindrical club has been said to be one of the most difficult feats in all sports. Tony didn't know about difficult. To him, it was heaven.

This day, everything learned at the team's earlier practice sessions would be tested. It was their first spring training game. The season opener was only three weeks away.

The Tigers, Ben's new "major league" team, was warming up in the infield. Suddenly, Ben left short stop and ran over to his father.

"What're you doing?" Tony yelled, waving his arms in exasperation. "You belong out there. The game's going to start in a just a little while."

"Dad, look." Ben pointed to the stands.

High in the bleachers, a woman sat, a hot dog in one hand, a coke in the other, and a Tigers baseball cap on her head.

"Holy Christ," Tony said, staring at her, unbelieving. He peeled off his glove, tossed it into the dugout with his cap and started to walk toward her, then he started to run. She put down her coke and hotdog and scrambled over the bench seats down to him.

Just seeing him again was enough to make her head spin and her face break into a broad smile. She stood on the second step from the bottom as he reached the stands.

He stopped running and looked up. "Hi, there."

She stopped there and looked down as she lifted her cap off, nearly crushing the bill in her fingers. Her hair was in a French braid, and she wore a light blue blouse and white slacks. "Hello, Tony."

"This is sure a surprise. I guess you're here to see how Miriam's doing, right? I run into her now and then. She's sure proud of you."

"She's part of the reason." Her breath was short and shallow. "Isn't today the start of the spring training games?"

He looked over his shoulder at the kids on the field as if having to check that they were still there. "Yeah, as a matter of fact."

Her heart thrummed so loudly she was sure he could hear it. "Well, then."

"Then...?" He waited.

She tried her best to act nonchalant. "I can't remember when I enjoyed anything as much as I enjoyed baseball with you and Ben last spring." Her blue eyes searched his face for understanding. "I didn't want to miss a second of it this year."

His heart leaped, but then he frowned, refusing to let himself believe the words he was hearing her say. "But baseball goes on for months."

"I know." Her gaze didn't leave his. "That's the best part about it."

His throat felt dry. "You can't mean you'll be staying all that time."

Somewhere she found the strength to step down one more stair so she was only one step up from him. She dropped her cap onto a bench and lifted her hands to his shoulders. "I'm not working in New York City anymore. I asked for a transfer to San Francisco, to be a West Coast correspondent, and they gave it to me. So, you see, I'll have plenty of time."

He placed his hands on her waist. "You transferred out here?"

"Yes."

Disbelief and more than a little confusion filled the dark brown eyes she loved. "You've left it? Your dream?"

Understand, her mind pleaded. "There are other things, I've learned, that mean more to me."

His hands gripped her tighter at the look in her eyes. "Are you sure?"

"Yes. I'm sure," she whispered. "I just hope I'm not too late."

He moved closer to her, his hands spread wide against her back. She swayed closer at his touch. "I watched you walk away from me three times in my life," he said. "If you're here with me, it's for keeps."

"I know."

His eyes narrowed. "I mean, year 'round. Even in winter when there's nothing but," he shuddered, "basketball."

She laughed. Her eyes grew moist as she slowly ran her fingers against his thick, straight hair, watching the way it shimmered in the sunlight. "I like basketball."

He jerked his head away, studying her hard, his expression solemn. "I need all of it, Lisa. Marriage, kids, Miwok. I'm too old for half-way deals. I'd rather have no deal."

"I know."

He frowned, still not able to believe her. "There are times I can scarcely breathe I get so full of feelings for you, but I've had to learn to live without you."

She knew this side of him, the caution, the fear of trusting. Teaching him to trust again had to start with her. "I love you, Tony Santos. I've spent a lifetime growing up without you, and I think it's time to change that."

She could see the hope growing in his eyes.

He shook his head as if he were afraid to believe her, afraid to trust. "I'm a has-been ball-player, I run a postage-stamp size ranch, I've got a kid who's almost a teenager, an old car, no frills and lots and lots of baseball. That's it. No fame, no fortune."

Her eyes slowly took in every inch of his face, the face that had haunted her memory for so many years. Then she smiled. "You've also got my heart, and I can't live without it any longer."

His brow furrowed, as if he were still not quite daring to believe her.

"It's been a long journey finding my way back to you, Tony. But I'm here, and if you'll have me, I want to stay."

His expression was solemn. Her Tony, who had always been the one to laugh so easily, to smile, to touch, stared at her as if afraid to hope. "I think I've loved you from the first day we talked, so many years ago," he said. "The hell of it, Lisa, is that I still do."

"Like old times?" she asked.

"No." Slowly, his face crinkled into the smile she knew, and he said, "Much, much better."

His arms tightened around her, lifting her off the step as their lips met. Slowly, he let her slide against him as her toes touched the ground, their kiss never breaking.

The sun was high in the sky as the Red Sox players gave a shout and ran onto the field. The first batter for the Tigers walked up to the plate, tapped it with his bat, wriggled his butt as he dug his cleats into the dirt, and then lifted the bat high over his head.

The umpire shouted, "Play ball," and a new season began.

PLUS ...

Dear Reader,

If you've enjoyed Seems Like Old Times, you might also be interested in finding out what happens when three half-sisters (each has a different father) inherit an old cabin in a remote location in Idaho. There's only one problem ... the cabin is haunted.

The trilogy starts with the middle sister, Carly Fullerton, going to the cabin in hopes of being alone to decide what to do about her nearly bankrupt business. She doesn't know that her sister has rented it out to a thriller writer who needs to be alone to deal with his own problems, including a major case of writer's block.

Both hope the other will leave ... but the ghosts have a different idea.

Here's a brief opening from If I Loved You: The Cabin of Love & Magic, Book 1:

Carly Fullerton unlocked the cabin's front door. As she stepped into the entry hall, everything seemed smaller and older than she remembered. Sixteen years had passed since she was last there.

As a child, she'd been convinced that the cabin was haunted and maybe even held a touch of magic. Of course, there was nothing magical or scary about the old place. It was simply a cabin built in the 1890s in a remote Idaho valley and handed down through her family from generation to generation. The original building had been no more than a square built of logs. Over the years, relatives had remodeled and added to it so that it now stood two stories tall.

The knotty pine walls had darkened with age, but shimmered in the light that shone through the window beside the door. An elk-horn lantern hung overhead. The rough-hewn wooden staircase to the far right of the entry hall led up to three bedrooms and one bathroom. Carly stood a moment remembering how, as a child, she often wished she could live there year round.

Of course, it never happened. Not only did her parents develop "irreconcilable differences" when Carly was only five years old, but her mother would never have agreed to live in a place where it snowed in winter.

Carly pushed aside such memories and continued straight ahead to what was once called the parlor.

Her jaw dropped. Was this really the cabin she'd visited all those years before? The change was remarkable.

Last year, her mother, Roxanne Donnelly, had died from a sudden heart attack, leaving the cabin to her three daughters, Carly Fullerton, Julia Perrin, and Mallory Conway. The women had different fathers, all were unmarried, and didn't resemble each other at all. Julia, the eldest, was small and blond; Mallory, the youngest, had black hair and a sleek, model's figure; while middle-child Carly was tall, with red hair, and a comfortably curvaceous build.

Carly's immediate thought had been that the three should sell the cabin and each take their share of the money—money Carly desperately needed. But her sisters didn't agree. Julia was adamant that the cabin was part of their family history, and Mallory apparently didn't want to argue with her oldest sister. Carly "in the middle" went along with them, as usual.

At the time she never expected she'd turn to the

cabin as a refuge. But that was exactly what she was now doing.

But before the sisters could do anything with the cabin, they needed to be practical. Because their mother had neglected it for years, they had to use the little money they'd inherited from her to make it habitable again. Julia had volunteered to oversee the project. Now, seeing the finished renovation, Carly couldn't help but admire all she'd accomplished.

The walls between the kitchen, dining room, and parlor had been removed to make a great room that was open, airy, and bright. A large granite-covered island now divided the kitchen from the rest of the space, and its new stainless steel appliances glistened.

French doors led to the cabin's wooden back porch, and a new sofa and cushy easy chairs surrounded the stone fireplace. The original wooden tables and cabinets, many of them antiques, remained to give the room a rustic charm.

"Julia, you astound me!" Carly said with a laugh, parroting a line often said in the Sherlock Holmes mysteries she loved.

The way the cabin now looked, Carly understood why Julia had mentioned the possibility of someday turning it into a vacation rental. People might actually want to spend time here, as long as they didn't mind being so isolated.

And didn't hear stories of the ghosts that haunted it.

The many ghost stories Carly had heard about the cabin and the creepy things she and her sisters had sworn went bump in the night came back to her now. She couldn't help but shiver.

She didn't believe in ghosts or enchantment or magic. But still...

Her gaze shot to the portrait over the fireplace of Elijah Donnelly, who was was her mother's great-great uncle. The story was that Elijah had built the cabin for his bride, but they both died at a young age. The son, Lucas, was said to have painted his father's portrait. It showed a handsome young man with blond hair parted just off center and slicked down. His white shirt collar stood high against his neck, and a gray and white striped tie formed a full Windsor knot. His charcoal gray jacket had narrow, notched lapels with a white carnation pinned to one of them. The jacket lay unbuttoned to show a light gray vest.

But how, the people in the area wondered, did Lucas know what his father looked like? After all, he had been an infant when Elijah died—Lucas was raised by his aunt—and no other portraits or photographs of Elijah existed. Did Lucas make-up his father's appearance, or did he—in some mysterious way—actually know how he'd looked? And, most of all, were Elijah's eyes really the strange violet shade Lucas had painted them?

Those eyes. Even now, they filled Carly with the same uneasiness they had given her as a child. They intrigued and mystified her, and she couldn't shake the eerie sensation that Elijah was staring at her, trying to tell her something just beyond her ability to grasp.

Continue with If I Loved You wherever fine books or ebooks are sold.

ABOUT THE AUTHOR

Joanne Pence was born and raised in northern California. She has been an award-winning, *USA Today* best-selling author of mysteries for many years, but she has also written historical fiction, contemporary romance, romantic suspense, a fantasy, and supernatural suspense. All of her books are now available as ebooks and in print, and most are also offered in special large print editions. Joanne hopes you'll enjoy her books, which present a variety of times, places, and reading experiences, from mysterious to thrilling, emotional to lightly humorous, as well as powerful tales of times long past.

Visit her at www.joannepence.com and be sure to sign up for Joanne's mailing list to hear about new books.